THE MALTA ASSIGNMENT

John Granito
THE MALTA ASSIGNMENT

HRM Publishing

Copyright © 2021 by John Granito with all rights reserved
Cover Design by Alexis Conners
Cover Copyright © by HRM Publishing

HRM Publishing supports the value of copyright. The purpose of copyright is to encourage writers to produce creative works that contribute to our culture and education.

The scanning, uploading, and distribution of this book without permission is a theft of the author's intellectual property. If you would like permission to use material from the book (other than for review purposes), please contact

HRMPublishing@gmail.com Thank you for your support of the author's rights.

HRM Publishing
2614 Croyden Rd.
Charlotte, NC 28209-1622
HRMPublishing@gmail.com

First published paperback edition: October 2021
First published ebook edition: October 2021

The publisher is not responsible for websites (or their content) that are not owned by the publisher.

The HRM Publishing speakers bureau provides its authors for speaking events. To find out more email:

HRMPublishing@gmail.com

Library of Congress Control Number:
ISBN 978-1-66780-931-1 (paperback edition)
ISBN 978-1-66780-932-8 (eBook)

HRM Publishing
Printed in the United States of America

With thanks,

Most of all to Dolores, who strengthened everything from the very beginning to the very end,

Ruthann, who made the trip to Malta, read it all, advised, and steered the book through printing,

Michele, who challenged the twists and turns of each character, and read it all again to be sure, and

Harry, who soloed before he had a driver's license and could now 'check ride' all Rudy's flying.

HONORS PRESENTED TO MALTA
DURING WORLD WAR II

This is the only time in history the English *George Cross* medal for bravery, equivalent to the military Victoria Cross, has been awarded to an entire population. A replica of medal still appears as part of the national flag of Malta. The name of the country may be followed by the award's letters: Malta GC.

United States President Franklin Roosevelt visited Malta in 1943, and presented a letter to the people of Malta. The words of that letter, dated December 7, 1943, were engraved on the facade of the Grand Master's Palace in Valletta, Malta. The first two paragraphs of his letter follow:

"In the name of the people of the United States of America, I salute the Island of Malta, its people and defenders, who, in the cause of freedom and justice and decency throughout the world, have rendered valorous service far above and beyond the call of duty.

"Under repeated fire from the skies, Malta stood alone, but unafraid in the center of the sea, one tiny bright flame in the darkness—a beacon of hope for the clearer days which have come."

MALTA ARCHIPELAGO

VICTORIA

GOZO

LAF. FARM

FERRY ROUTE
3 miles

COMINO

MEDITERRANEAN SEA

MEDITERRANEAN SEA

SLIEMA

MALTA

TA'QALI

VALLETTA
FORT
ST. ELMO

GRAND
HARBOR
PORT

LUGA

HOTEL

RAF HAL FAR
KALAFRANA
SHOPS

MARSAXLOKK
BAY

LEGEND
- ● CITY
- ○ DESTINATION
- □ AIRFIELD
  BODY OF WATER

SEARCHING FOR A GLADIATOR

Valletta, Malta
June 1965

ON Saturday afternoon, June 24, 1965, had you been sight-seeing in the World War II exhibit room at Malta's National War Museum in Valletta, up at Fort St Elmo, you might have noticed a young couple approach the flush-faced man unsteadily bent over one of the many exhibit signs alongside what appeared to be part of an airplane. Shoulders noticeably trembling, he was pressing a handkerchief to his face and wiping his eyes. The couple judged him to be quite upset, or perhaps even ill.

"Sir, are you feeling unwell? May we get you a chair, perhaps?", the woman asked, as her husband scanned the narrow room, unsuccessfully searching for one he could drag nearer.

"No, no. Thank you," came the muffled reply. "I'm O.K. Must be an allergy, I think. Thanks, anyway. I'm OK now." This last was accompanied by his rising, assisted by the younger man's hand at his elbow. He straightened up and, putting away his handkerchief, he now did appear well enough, the red in his face and his tearing eyes becoming more normal as he spoke. At least six feet in height, sandy brown hair and slightly balding, he was fashionably dressed in a blue open collar shirt, darker linen jacket, gray pressed trousers, and well-shined shoes. He had the appearance, the younger man thought, of a vacationing, recently retired executive, perhaps approaching sixty years. Obviously a bit embarrassed, the man continued. "Thank you both for your concern, didn't mean to trouble you. I must admit, I was quite perturbed, seeing that very partial plane and trying to find out what it was from the sign."

"Ah," the woman exclaimed, "By accent, you're an American!"

"Yes, an American. I was first here on Malta for a time just before the war, about twenty-five years ago, although I've revisited once or twice since my first trip. But I'm revisiting again, this time to attend some meetings, along with my wife. She's at the Barrakka Gardens right now, since she wanted to see the firing of the cannon at noontime and the little military show. So she's missing this interesting museum. Speaking of accents, I'd guess Britain is home for you two. London?" He spoke more strongly now, his self-diagnosed allergy no longer evident.

"We *are* English," the husband replied, "but not London. A little village down near the coast in Somerset. I'm with Westland Aircraft Company at our Yeovil plant. We're Patrick and Fay White. My father was a soldier in the British army, an anti-aircraft gun unit, and was here on the island during the bombing. We diverted here on holiday because it was time we saw the place he told all those wild war stories of, how terrible the bombings were and all. So two days touring here in Valletta and then we're off to Sicily tomorrow. We flew down here directly from Rome. Didn't want to miss it, we were so close, and it seemed like a break from the sights of Italy. Have you toured Sicily as yet?"

"Sicily?" The older man, now standing straight, chuckled. "No, and I barely made it there on my original visit to Malta! By-the-way, I'm Rudy Worth, Miami, or near Miami, in a place called Hialeah. Just did a little work back then in Malta, as I said. Going up to Sicily never even crossed my mind when I was in Malta. I really got up there just by accident. Don't suppose I would have made a sale in Sicily! Anyway, I appreciate your concern when we met. Really, when you came over to help I guess I was a little upset. I was trying to read about this plane's fuselage, standing on its wheels but missing the wings and other vital parts, and almost hanging from the ceiling. But the words on this card are a bit faded. Apparently it's supposed to be a rebuilt Gloster Gladiator."

"Gladiator you say? Well, I don't know about gladiators, but allow me to demonstrate my fashionable new glasses," the woman exclaimed, as she bent over the table at the front of the exhibit and read aloud:

"Gloster Gladiator Aircraft N. 5520

This is "Faith" the sole survivor of the three Gloster Gladiator Aircraft, known as FAITH, HOPE and CHARITY which fought alone against the Italian "Regia Aeronautica" between June and October 1940. She survived all her combats, finally to be put out of commission by an enemy bomb in a hangar at Hal Far Airstation.

Presented to the people of Malta by Air Vice-Marshal Sir Keith Park KBE CB MC DFC on behalf of the Royal Air Force on September 3rd 1943."

"Well, thank you, Fay", her husband Patrick observed, "at least it's got a bright and shiny engine, and it does have the word *Faith* painted on it. I take it you're interested in airplanes, Mr. Worth?"

"I am" was the reply, "but I came here this morning thinking I was going to see a complete famous Gladiator that flew against the Italian Air Force back in 1940 when Malta was attacked. Being able to see only this fuselage is quite disappointing, but perhaps I'll see what I'm looking for at one of the other museums or the old airfield. Or perhaps up at Gozo island.

"You'd think that Malta, saved as it was by Gladiators and the Hawk, and then, of course, the Hurricanes and Spitfires, would have a real aviation museum! By the way, and to change the subject, you said you're with the Westland Company. That's a great aircraft manufacturer. As I recall, they designed the Lysander, made famous during the war. I actually had the opportunity to fly as a passenger in one. Are you with the engineering group?"

"No," Patrick grinned, "not an engineer. I'm with the finance department and usually trying to convince our engineering design people that the new model doesn't really need whatever they're pushing for. But now, I see my wife signaling that she's ready to go, so I'll say good-bye and wish you better luck in finding that Gladiator. Perhaps as you tour Gozo? My Dad always said Gozo was a really interesting little island."

Still early that afternoon, Patrick White, sitting on a bar stool in his hotel's pub and finishing a pint of Malta's Cisk lager, turned a quick glance at the man slipping onto the next stool. "Well, Mr. Worth, isn't it? Feeling OK, I hope? Over your allergy? Good! Well, I'm happy to see you again. Fay and I leave very early in the morning and she's upstairs packing our bags so we can have dinner off the hotel tonight at some fancy restaurant she's heard about. I'm here having my last afternoon pint on Malta. And you've been here all along with us, at this same fine hotel?"

"Looks as though we are, and yes, I recovered quickly. Allergies are tricky, I guess. I noticed you sitting here as I walked to the elevator...I mean lift. I want to wish you both a safe journey to Sicily." He motioned to the barkeeper, and with his own pint soon in hand they raised their mugs.

"Yes, and we're excited. Do I recollect you said something about never making a sales there? I take it you were in sales before the war, but not in Sicily?"

"A little bit in sales, just a little. And as it turned out," Rudy observed, "sales here in Malta didn't do well at all, but my stay certainly was interesting. Now I don't want you to miss the last of your wife's packing, so I'll end my tale by saying that I was told this afternoon that I won't see any other Gladiators here on Malta. But I'll keep looking. My wife is upstairs getting ready for our evening conference event and I'd better go up myself and prepare for her inspection of my clothing selection for this evening. I hardly need this excellent lager anyway; I'm sure they'll be drinks at our event. I do wish you both a safe and interesting visit to Sicily, and please tell Fay I'm glad she was wearing her new eyeglasses at the museum.

"Although, you know, I had expected to see an entire Gloster Gladiator, not just a fuselage squeezed against a ceiling, minus its wings. Was it really the one called *Faith*, do you suppose? How would they know, and who rebuilt the fuselage, and where's the rest of it? Well, at least King George gave their country that prestigious George Cross award near the end of it. That's why the older locals often call it 'Malta GC' instead of just plain Malta. It's the only GC country in the world, but they really earned it. Too bad they didn't get the additional anti-aircraft guns they were promised before the shooting started!

As Rudy waited for the lift to his hotel floor, he thought back to his days as the youngest engineer at Curtiss-Wright Aircraft Company in Buffalo, and then his abrupt switch in 1939 to HRM Aviation, London. Assigned to Malta, a place he'd never heard of. Controlled by the British and lying between Italy's Sicily and the strategic north coast of Africa, it would be his first assignment, and later known as *the most bombed place on earth*". But as more information unfolded, he learned that more was expected of him than simply talking up some additional fighter planes to the Royal Air Force. It never occurred to him that the assignment would change his life!

As he walked from the lift to his room, he realized that here he was, back in Malta again, hoping to reconnect with his life of twenty-five years ago. "And never mind the mysterious Hawk," he said out loud, " I can't even find a real Gladiator!"

CHAPTER 1

A MEDITERRANEAN VACATION

Buffalo, New York - Curtiss Aircraft Company
April 1939

RUDY Worth spent almost all workdays on Curtiss-Wright engine design, looking to switch from radials to inline liquid cooled engines for the upcoming P-40 fighters. His position, listed as "aeronautical power plant engineer," described his job perfectly. But the call telling him to report to the Site General Manager's office came from the administration building and not Hal Greene, his boss in the Engine Design Division. He had never met the Site General Manager, but Rudy, 29 years old and the youngest engineer at the Curtiss-Wright plant, immediately sensed trouble. He could hardly believe they had waited this long to either chew him out or fire him. He calculated that the cost of repairing that plane's damaged wing tip would be taken from his final paycheck, if the paycheck were large enough to cover the bill. Rudy's fondness for weekend racing other small planes around a haystack course at a country airstrip was strong, but not strong enough to think that losing the job he loved was worth it.

Of course, he reasoned, the little red plane he raced, the engine of which he had vastly improved on his own time, was not even owned by Curtiss, but by Mercury Aviation down at Hammondsport, New York, a sometimes sub-contractor. And that race was last October, months ago. Rudy's friends at Mercury had repaired it, recorded it in the plane's log-book, and told Rudy he owed them the next round when the next racing season started up at Penn Yan airport. As he walked quickly toward the Administration Building, at times almost half-jogging, Rudy pondered justice to himself. For Pete's sake! The big boss's office for a lousy wingtip!

Rudy's anxiety increased when, after running up the stairs to the third floor of the Admin Building, he saw Hal waiting for him down the hallway leading to the General Manager's office complex. Oh Boy, he thought, here it comes!

"Rudy," Hal almost shouted, "It's a good thing you came over right away. The big guys are waiting inside for you. I can't wait to see your face when they tell you the news!"

"Good news?" Rudy hoped.

"Just wait," Hal said, and Rudy realized his anxious sounding supervisor was sweating. Hal was dressed in a long sleeve white shirt, blue tie emblazoned with the Curtiss logo, suit jacket, and well pressed trousers. This was quite unlike the informal short sleeved shirt and work pants he wore daily in the Engine Design shop. It meant that Hal had known about Rudy's summons yesterday, before dressing so formally at his home this morning. Not a good sign at all. As Rudy, pushed along by Hal, moved into a large and well furnished conference room, he judged that this session was either going to be very interesting, or very bad for him.

He had laughed when another engineer had once observed that when the crap hits the fan, it is not evenly distributed around the room, but he now unconsciously glanced around for the proverbial fan. Here comes my extra share, he thought. The walls, he saw, were the backdrop for more than twenty paintings of Curtiss airplanes, going way back to the original *June Bug*, designed and flown in 1908 by Glen Curtiss himself. They ended with the very plane and engine Rudy had spent so much time with as part of the design team, the P-36 Mohawk, introduced in 1937.

"Rudy," said the short, thin man in the dark blue suit headed toward Rudy with outstretched hand, "I'm delighted to meet you finally and to thank you for coming over on short notice. I'm Phil Juddson, and I'm sorry it's taken me so long to get to know you personally. We've simply gotten too big for me to know everyone. We're the largest aviation company in the country, as you know.

"But let me introduce you to Pete Murray, Curtiss-Wright's Vice President for our Airplane Division, and Harold Byers, Vice President of our Engine Division." Both of the Vice Presidents leaned across what had become a welcoming semi-circle to shake hands with a smiling Rudy, who suspected now that maybe he wasn't going to be fired. "Our Propeller Division isn't involved in this get together," said the man Rudy assumed was the Site Manager, "but this trim man in the grey suit who's waiting to shake you hand is very important to our purpose today. Bob McDonald runs the Curtiss-Wright Export Sales operation. The gentleman and lady already seated over by the windows are visitors today, and I invited them to sit in on our meeting, just to get a good sense of the level of our great engineering staff. I didn't think you would mind.

Well, folks, why don't we sit while my assistant brings in some coffee, and we'll get going. And Mr. Greene, special thanks for getting Rudy over here this morning and for your understanding in the staffing matter Mr. Byers discussed with you. I know your shop is a busy one, and Harold won't forget his promise to you. We understand that you need to get back to your engineers. That due date for the XP-40 prototype engine is almost upon us, as you well know! Thank you again for getting Rudy here this morning."

Hal Greene, clearly understanding that he was being dismissed, but with thanks, said a good-bye to all, winked at Rudy, and departed. He still wondered what this was all about, but wisely considered it to be a question above his pay grade. Once outside the Admin Building he spoke softly aloud to himself: "Shit, if Rudy is let go, and my Vice President doesn't send me an experienced engineer as his replacement, we'll never make the prototype's due date!" His thinking, now conducted silently as he took the stairs to ground level and headed for his engine shop, raised two puzzling questions. The first wondered how management could even consider getting rid of or 'laying off' from Curtiss such an excellent engineer, if that's what this was all about. The second was an even greater mystery. Who in hell were the two visitors? He certainly had never seen them before anywhere on the Curtiss Buffalo plant.

The real business part of the meeting began, as Rudy judged it, when Mr. Juddson asked him to tell the group first about himself and then his assignments at Curtiss. Rudy quickly listed his vital statistics, as he called them, saying that he came from Watkins Glen in New York State, where his father was the local Ford dealer and also owner of a car and truck service and repair center. Rudy had hung around the shop whenever he could, learning about engines but much more interested in the world of airplanes by the time he entered high school.

After all, Watkins Glen was close to the original home of Glen Hammond Curtiss, and Hammondsport was home to the first Curtiss factory, and now Mercury Aviation, the Curtiss sub-contractor. Hammondsport village was at the southern end of Keuka Lake – where Glen Curtiss designed and flew the first seaplanes – and farther up the lake was Penn Yan village, the home of Penn Yan Aero Company's engine rebuilding plant. Even after Rudy's father threatened to eventually retire and turn over the business to Rudy's sister unless he gave up this flying idea, Rudy continued to bike to the local airstrip to wash planes, cut grass, and run errands for the couple of aircraft and engine mechanics, and especially the pilots.

To make a long story short, as Rudy told the group, he had earned a private pilot's license by the time he turned nineteen and was enrolled in Buffalo University as a freshman. As a sophomore he was admitted to the University's new aeronautical engineering program. The year after that he had a summer internship in the engine design shop at Curtiss plant in Buffalo, and was hired there right after graduation. His Curtiss work assignments had bounced him between the Engine and the Airframe Divisions, and he had "engineered" on both engine and related aircraft design, but most especially on the P-36 and, recently, on the upcoming P-40 prototype.

Rudy added, "My father footed the college bill, hoping the engineering degree would apply to cars and trucks as well as planes, I guess. He still hasn't fully retired from the business, but my sister, with a degree in accounting, is vice-president of the company back in Watkins Glen, and waiting to take over. So I've been very happy here at Curtiss doing what I really like to do."

Rudy felt like a school teacher as the Export Sales manager, Mr. McDonald, raised his hand, prompting Rudy to say "Yes, sir?"

"Rudy, you mentioned Penn Yan village earlier. Isn't there a fairly well developed airport there, maybe a bit larger and busier than you might expect for a Finger Lakes Village?"

"Yes, there is," Rudy responded. "The Penn Yan Flying Club is located there; it may be the oldest continuously running flying club in the country, so the airport is pretty busy."

"Well, I understand that you occasionally participate in a club activity on weekends. That little red low wing racer that Mercury built?"

Oh Boy, Rudy thought. Here it comes! "Yes, I love to fly, so I do sometimes race others around a few flagged haystacks out in the fields. But I've been able to increase the output of that engine quite a bit, so I feel there's a direct carryover to my work at Curtiss." At that point, an embarrassed Rudy realized that his audience was chuckling out loud, and he was the hook.

"Rudy," Mr. Juddson questioned to quiet the others down, "You mentioned your father and sister back home, but are you married? Do you have your own family? I think someone said you were single, but I thought I'd ask."

"No, I'm not married. A couple of girlfriends during college, but nothing serious enough to think about tying the knot. Although I am seeing one or two young women here in Buffalo. Kind of juggling dates, I guess. Besides, both the P-36 and its upgrades, and now the XP whatever we're going to call it, have kept me pretty busy."

"Rudy, your performance reviews are excellent. They say you're bright, innovative, and dedicated to the future of aviation. We'd like you to stay with Curtiss as we move into the future, because that's where your engine performance research will be very crucial. But right now something important has come up, a very important and somewhat more complex type of project which will mostly take place abroad, and we want to make you aware of it, in case you're interested. But more of that in a minute. Right now I'm going to turn to Mr. McDonald to raise a couple of points with you."

"What I'd like you to do, Rudy," Mr. McDonald said, "is tell me what you think of our P-36.

Rudy took this assignment on the run, remembering that it was known, also, as Curtiss Export Model 75. One detail Rudy knew was that the landing gear retraction twist needed by the wheels was a Boeing patent, for which Curtiss paid a royalty fee, but he knew enough not to mention this just now. The plane first flew in the spring of 1935 and hit 281 mph. About two years later, with a different radial engine and other improvements, Curtiss had received a US Army Air Force contract for P-36 planes, and he'd heard that several other countries were interested in it, also. Right now, in April 1939, the rumor was that successfully combining the P-36 Airframe with the 1200 horsepower Allison V-12 liquid cooled engine could result in an even faster fighter plane, the (X)P-40 line. That would be a biggy, the guys in the engine design shop were saying!

When first designed, the P-36 needed more horsepower, plus a supercharger for higher altitudes, more than two machine guns, and some strengthening of the fuselage here and there. Continuing improvements had produced a popular modern fighter with high horsepower per square foot of wing size - called low wing loading, - Rudy added, with a resultant fast roll rate for quick maneuvering, plus an excellent rate of climb of 3,400 feet per minute. Its maximum speed had improved to 313 mph. That's why several other countries were getting in line to sign contracts.

(Note: Although no one at Rudy's meeting that day could have known, 900 RAF "Mohawks" and export "Model 75s" would eventually be purchased and used by a dozen other countries, especially France, in many variants, using several different engines, and with numerous gun and small bomb carrying provisions. Sale price in the 1930's was approximately $23,000 US. On December 7, 1941, at Pearl Harbor, Hawaii, four Curtiss P-36 "Hawks" were undamaged by the initial Japanese air attack and took off under fire, engaging eleven Japanese fighters. After shooting down one Japanese aircraft Lt. Philip M. Rasmussen was attacked by two Japanese A6M2 Zero fighters. Machine gun and cannon fire shattered his canopy, destroyed the radio and severed the P-36 hydraulic lines and rudder cable. Lt. Rasmussen flew into cloud cover and succeeded in landing at Wheeler Field without brakes, rudder, or tail-wheel, and with more than 500 bullet holes in the P-36. For his actions he was awarded the Silver Star.)

After answering several questions, Rudy praised the plane for its innovative features such as an added supercharger, extensive use of metal in construction, both nose and wing guns, light pressure controls at high speed, high power to weight ratio, ability to adopt to foreign instruments, gun sights, and reverse throttle positions as the French Air Force insisted, ability to take wing mounted bomb releases, the proven ability to be transported abroad by aircraft carriers as well as packed dismantled in large crates. They were capable of quick take off capability, and hopefully able to turn tighter than a Messerschmitt, with lighter control input than a Hawker Hurricane. "Of course," Rudy added, "the new XP should prove to have better performance and features, but I believe that export model P-36s - Model 75s - are available right now, off the production line, aren't they?"

"Indeed they are," said the Export Manager, "and available for timely delivery." He smiled at Rudy and nodded several times at Mr. Juddson, obviously sending a satisfactory message.

Rudy was sitting back down as he heard Mr. Juddson say, "Thank you three Curtiss gentlemen for giving me your time this morning. I'm going to call this meeting closed, allowing me to spend some time with Rudy, and to say a proper good-bye to our visitors. Be assured that I'll provide him with our reasons for this meeting, as we discussed them among ourselves, so he'll be thoroughly briefed. And Bob, if necessary, some folks you don't know yet will get together with you for up-to-date pricing and export delivery details, if that's OK? Otherwise, thank you all again on behalf of our Board of Directors and myself."

As the Curtiss executives left the conference room, Mr. Juddson turned to Rudy, saying, "Rudy, I apologize for the mystery surrounding this meeting, and for not introducing you right away to our visitors. I want to do that now, and I see they're coming up so that I can. Ladies first, always, so I want you to meet Miss Janice Townley, who has traveled all the way from England to help me understand some of the details concerning a new company, HRM Aircraft, being formed there. Next is Ed Whittaker. Ed, whom I first met some time ago, also is associated with this new company, although an American. I should add that he's very knowledgeable about the technical side of planes and their manufacturing, while Miss Townley knows the business and financial end of things. They've been filling me in on how they'd like to explore a friendly relationship with Curtiss, and I believe I, and they, should talk with you right now. Let's the four of us step into my private little meeting room, have a bit of lunch, and see what you think about the unusual idea that these too have, possibly involving you." Each of the visitors extended their hand to Rudy and expressed their interest in meeting him. Rudy answered appropriately and the group, led by Mr. Juddson, took a few steps and entered a smaller private meeting room.

CHAPTER 2

A SPECIAL PROJECT

April 1939

Executive Office, Curtiss Aircraft Company, Buffalo

AS Rudy and the visitors followed their host, he turned to Rudy. "Rudy, I have another apology and a confession to make to you. Because, as you'll soon learn, these discussions are absolutely confidential, I didn't want to call attention to either our meetings or our visitors. So, your invitation today came from the Site General Manager. As a matter of fact, he's spending the day at our corporate offices downtown, while I use his office. I really am the Curtiss President and CEO, as my vice-presidents, but apparently not Mr. Greene your supervisor, knew this morning. And my name is Phil Juddson, although I guess I'm not as well known by all our employees as my Board of Directors thinks I am. But let's sit and get you filled in on the rest of the mystery.

"In a way, today may bring a little bad news to Curtiss but good news to you. Before I turn to our guests from HRM, I'll explain that HRM Aircraft Ltd., which likely will start building specialized aircraft in Great Britain as soon as possible, has a subsidiary – HRM Aviation - which will assist nations friendly to England and the USA, such as France, Poland, and Norway among others, in the development of their air forces. It will do this by providing advice and guidance, and by actually selling or leasing various types of military planes to them, including, I hope, Curtiss model 75 Hawks, which HRM Aircraft would purchase directly from Curtiss.

"We will not have an exclusive agreement with HRM, and HRM undoubtedly will purchase readily available aircraft from other manufacturers in our country, and those in England, France, Poland, and possibly elsewhere. Examples might be PZL models from Poland, Koolhoven fighters from the Netherlands, which are just coming into production, and Seversky, Consolidated, and others over here. I would hope to include our new prototype, once it's fully in production. In a way, HRM Aviation will act as distributor for various aircraft manufacturers by obtaining military planes from them and reselling them to countries with an immediate need for those available types. The advantage to those countries, none aligned with the Nazis I should add, is that HRM has the financial backing to ease any financial difficulties the smaller buyers might have.

"The good news is that today you may be offered the position of full time principal consulting engineer, or whatever they'll call that position, for HRM Aviation. That's up to Ed and Janice. If you were to take that position, you would be leaving Curtiss, and we at Curtiss would consider that bad news for us. However, it likely would create additional and faster sales for us without having to continuously explain lengthy details to potential foreign customers and then, if a purchase agreement is reached, arrange for a variety of foreign financial exchanges. HRM's consulting engineer would do that, and a lot more, as he represented HRM. In summary, Rudy, we'd hate to see you leave Curtiss, but I can't discourage you from an exciting and broad-based job at this point in your career. Now, I've said enough, and as they bring in sandwiches, I'll leave you to these two for a full discussion." Rudy, near speechless at this news, merely said, "OK. Thank you, I think!"

Sandwiches quickly appeared, as did coffee, and Ed Whittaker, sitting across the table from Rudy, as did Janice Townley, launched a surprise of his own immediately. "Mr. Worth – Rudy – I'll begin by saying that I'm a Colonel in the United States Army Air Force, a pilot, as are you, and I currently am on direct assignment to provide every possible assistance to a brand new organization co-sponsored by the American government, as arranged by President Roosevelt through our Office of Strategic Services. The other governmental co-sponsors are the Royal Air Force representing the British War Cabinet, the French Conseil Supérieur de l'Air, and the Commander-in-Chief of Polish military aviation, the Lotnictwo Wokskowe. Each of the sponsors has a strong desire to stop, or at least slow down, Adolph Hitler's push toward what we consider to be European domination or more.

"Within each of our countries, large groups oppose overt moves against Nazi Germany at this time, hoping for a lasting peace. While all hope for lasting peace, we military types judge that a large scale war, never-the-less, will come quite soon. Really, none of the nations I mention is prepared for war, although we believe that Hitler and his likely allies are well prepared and ready. As a partial remedy for our lack of readiness, based on the belief that air superiority will be necessary for a war's success, we are moving as quickly as we can to strengthen our air resources.

"Based on that concern, HRM Aircraft, Ltd. has been formed, although, unlike Phil's view, it may well never go into aircraft production itself. Rather, I expect, it will stimulate existing manufacturers to design and produce more and more, faster and faster, and encourage our friendly nations to acquire suitable planes as quickly as possible, or sooner. The HRM subsidiary we are calling 'HRM Aviation' is the operational arm by which we intend to do that. The title, at least for now, by which our co-sponsors refer to the combined effort is 'Friends of the RAF'. We use that since the RAF is long standing and well known, and non-descriptive to the world at large of a broader international effort to strengthen the military air forces of democracies against Nazism."

Over sandwiches and coffee, Colonel Whittaker presented Rudy with a summary of some of the current European situation. His focus was on Germany's possible intentions toward adjoining and other countries, following Hitler's move into the Saar and Rhineland areas four years earlier and into Austria last year. "Plus, and most likely, into Czechoslovakia any day now." From 1936 to 1939, the Colonel went on explaining, Germany, Italy, and Russia had practiced ground and air tactics during the Spanish Civil War, and some important advancements had been made in their aircraft – for example, Germany's Messerschmitt 109 fighter and the now infamous Stuka dive bomber.

Rudy listened intently, learning that after invading Ethiopia in 1935, Italy, under Mussolini, had merged it with Eritrea and Somaliland to form Italian East Africa. So Italy had to be watched as well. Importantly, Mussolini also appeared to have a special interest in Malta as well as Gibraltar, which really frightens the British Navy. Even worse, Britain and the United States were neither prepared nor desirous to wage war with anybody, much less a well equipped Germany and friends.

The United Kingdom's 1938 "Munich Pact" with France, Germany, and Italy would result in a disaster for England, the Colonel predicted, and for France as well. So would England's strong desire for world stability under post World War I national boundary lines, coupled with the intent to hold on to all their entire Colonial empire. All of these, plus Mussolini's desire to expand into more of the Mediterranean area and Hitler's insatiable desire to rule ever larger areas of the world, would contribute to what likely will be a very large European war. The Colonel sounded doubtful our country could keep out of it.

"President Roosevelt," the Colonel emphasized, "has a very strong desire to somehow slow Hitler down, or stop him completely, and he wants to aid England and France, but is hampered by the strong feelings of so many Americans, and our Congress, to stay out of Europe's political and territorial problems. Further, a recognizable portion of Americans, especially in the mid-west, seem to be pro-German, if not neutral, including Lindbergh, America's aviation hero!

"However," Colonel Whittaker pointed out, "our President has already authorized a very large contract for the purchase of military planes, urged Congress to authorize $300 million for Western Hemisphere defense, and last October 14 told reporters he would ask Congress to give an additional half billion dollars for warplanes. We need modern fighters and bombers, as many as we can design and produce, and as quickly as they can roll off the production lines. Curtiss needs to move on this as quickly as it possibly can, as do Douglas and the other American aircraft companies."

"Rudy," Janice interjected, "Your President Roosevelt is hoping we can do something to assist his friend Winston Churchill, who will eventually become our Prime Minister, keep Malta safer than it now is from the hands of Hitler and Mussolini. Sicily is so close to Malta, which until very recently has been a headquarters of the British fleet. Last September an official state of emergency was declared by my British Government, and some planning began to strengthen Malta's defenses. But with pressing needs to strengthen British Gibraltar and the British controlled Suez Canal, well, not much at all, if anything, has been done on Malta. In fact, our RAF people are complaining that planes and pilots are being ordered out of Malta on a weekly basis. As we said, HRM is being asked to unofficially help Malta plan and prepare. You've heard the old saying, *hope for the best, but plan for the worst?* Well, that would be your first project.

"We're sending you there not so much to sell them some planes. Right now that decision will have to be made in London, once they're convinced war is truly coming and that Malta must be defended and retained as an English fort in the middle of the Mediterranean. Rather, we want you to size up Malta's defensive conditions and their even larger situation such as food and fuel supplies, to help them where you can, and to act as an intermediary for HRM to assist with our belief that Hitler can be stopped now only by a stronger England and France. After hearing Ed's summary I'm even more eager for you to leave for Malta no later than, lets say, June 1. We'll crate up whatever you'll need to continue your work on engine improvements over there and arrange to keep supplying you with whatever else we can to assist you in strengthening Malta's RAF outpost and your own engine improvement research. As you can see, we've learned a lot about your talents and interests in a short time. Agreed? Will you switch from Curtiss and join HRM Aviation Ltd.?

"I'm prepared and authorized, right now, as Vice President of The RAF Friends, to offer you five percent more above whatever Curtiss is paying you, plus all, and I mean all, expenses for transportation, conducting business, and personal living. We'll establish an account for you at a good Malta hotel and, upon your signature, we'll pay monthly all expenses directly to a Malta bank. We'll deposit your monthly salary, directly, to whichever bank or banks you choose. And I'll have you sent, immediately, by courier, a formal written contract for one year, renewable if both parties so desire. As you can see, we want you onboard immediately as HRM's Senior Engineer and we have sufficient funds ready. I should add that your goals have been described already in this meeting: Do all you can possibly do to strengthen Malta's RAF defenses for war, and assist in planning for the general welfare and security of Malta should war come as we anticipate. It must never be captured by Hitler! We will communicate with you personally, directly, and indirectly, on a frequent and regular basis."

Rudy hardly appeared to ponder over this question. He looked directly at Colonel Whittaker and then at Janice. "If I didn't want to see my family back in Watkins Glen, and if I already had a passport and knew how to get to Malta, I'd leave in the morning. Does that answer your question?"

"Rudy," Ed added, "before you even ask, the U.S. Department of State will arrange and get to you, right away, an official passport plus an official document explaining your overseas work on behalf of a U.S. Federal Agency, and your assigned absence from our Country. In a somewhat unusual way, you will be working for an American co-sponsored foreign corporation. I will continue as your direct American contact and, in a sense, your assignment administrator. Janice is assigned as your HRM administrator for business and finances. I add, here, that Phil Juddson's personal assistant, Mrs. Osborne, starting tomorrow, will be compensated by HRM for taking four or five work days off from Curtiss work, with Phil's approval, in order to assist you and take care off all of your personal and professional needs in leaving Curtiss and in preparing to get to Malta. She will transmit all of these related expenses to Janice's office for direct payment to those service companies. Additionally, you might want to visit your family, back home, for a few days before you leave for London and Malta.

"Ed," Janice asked, "will you let the President know that HRM, with Curtiss help, is pulling the stops out to assist in any possible way with strengthening Malta's defense, and will you communicate the same message to your RAF contacts? I want Rudy to slide right into a fully cooperative situation as soon as he lands."

"The President will be so informed,'" Colonel Whittaker responded, "but I'm concerned with all that Rudy needs to do before he leaves for Malta. I'll help by informing my RAF contacts and urging them to pave the way for Rudy in Malta, but couldn't your HRM resident man in London - what's his name - start making living, financial, and communication arrangements for Rudy to save start-up time in Malta? Rudy, I have a brief case with me filled with quite current information about Malta and the Mediterranean area, and I'll leave it for you to review before you leave. But you have to treat it confidentially, just as you do this meeting and what was said here. Just be very sure I get it from you before you leave.

And one more thing, while I think of it: The RAF has Friends in many governmental organizations in England, so you might find that one or more "friends" arrange to meet you, possibly even before you get over there, just to size you up. My advice is to act just as you would if you were going to Malta as a HRM Aviation, Ltd. salesman, to learn what you can, but not get very far into the kinds of things we touched on today. Mostly listen until you get there, I'd advise."

"HRM's man in London is named Ian Standish, Rudy, and he'll get going on your arrangements right away, and will meet you as you arrive in London," Janice interjected once again, and added, "I'd suggest you cross the pond, as we call it, by one of His Majesty's ocean liners. Just let Mrs. Osborne know I suggested that and Standish can arrange a flight from there to Malta, and can fill you in on the latest news when you meet him. He's an old timer in Europe's aviation business and you can count on him. He's with HRM all the way, as you Yankees say. I'll phone him tomorrow to set things up. All but the date you'll arrive. Here's my card, with two phone numbers, so you can keep me informed of your travel plans and dates, and I'll keep Ian informed. And let me know in two days if you don't get the contract. Tell my courier to wait while you read it. Sign the copy and tell the courier to return it to me at our Washington office. I'll have already signed it, and the copy you'll keep."

Both Ed and Janice told Rudy they would talk with him in the next couple of days. The Colonel added that Mr. Juddson had anticipated that Rudy would accept their offer, and had suggested that Rudy set himself up over the next several days right here at Curtiss Corporate Headquarters, next to Mrs. Osborne's office, in order to facilitate communication with her, Ed, and Janice. He had added that he wanted to wish Rudy well in his new job, also, before Rudy left for wherever they were sending him.

With the mysterious visitors departed and Mr. Juddson as well, Rudy was alone in the room. He contemplated the fate, as he termed it, he had selected for himself. All had to do, he thought, was save Malta and be sure HRM Aviation got not only the credit for that, but more gigantic contracts for new planes as well! Oh, thought Rudy then, although his new employers hadn't dwelled on it, they had mentioned that Rudy was to continue his work on 'engine improvements'. To Rudy's thinking that was frosting on his cake.

It did sound like a wonderful opportunity to Rudy's father, mother, and sister when he told them all about the new job and the English company a week after his big meeting. He had driven back to Watkins Glen and his family for a hasty trip to explain why he would be away for so long, "basking in the Mediterranean sun while still being paid and on a great expense account." His mother was a little anxious about his being gone, especially to Europe, while his sister quietly contemplated another year working closer to the family business with him far away and focused elsewhere. Rudy's father, who followed both domestic and world happenings, nodded understandingly as his son guessed out loud that the Malta Project, to some extent, was a trade-off for some future aircraft sales contracts, but a project which might make the world a bit safer from the bad guys like Adolph Hitler. "O.K.," his father judged, "if you can do something to slow-down the Nazis, do it. But don't get yourself killed, or your mother will kill me." Rudy drove his car back to Buffalo, soon to be readied for storage, put up on blocks, and safely stored at a Buffalo warehouse, which he later learned from Mrs. Osborne was owned by Curtiss. The final drive back to his soon to be vacated apartment flat followed four days back home and several elaborate examples of home-cooked meals.

Some time was spent during his return drive practicing how he might explain it all to a couple of young women he'd been dating in Buffalo. Fortunately, they were unaware of each other, so with luck he could use the same presentation to each in turn. His last day in Buffalo included an early and satisfying meeting with the Curtiss President, plus a long train ride to New York City on the New York Central and Delaware and Hudson Railroads. One night in a New York hotel was followed by a taxi ride to the city's piers and, as Janice Townley had suggested, His Majesty's Ship, the Queen Mary.

CHAPTER 3

ABOARD THE QUEEN MARY

Mid-Atlantic Ocean
June 1939

WITH mild weather, calm seas, and a stomach to match, Rudy sat comfortably ensconced in a deck chair, out of the morning wind on the starboard side of the Queen Mary, not having any idea just which deck he was enjoying, but with no hanging lifeboats to hamper his view of sky, clouds, and never ending waves. Actually he was thinking, but not about his upcoming HRM Aviation assignment, for which he mentally thanked Curtiss, and not even about the amazing and over-sized breakfast he had enjoyed in the stunning first class dining room. Rather, about how effortlessly Mrs. Osborne had handled all the arrangements for his leaving Buffalo and the United States. Perhaps, he dreamed, with whatever position he returned to upon his undoubtedly very successful work in Malta, a personal assistant would be assigned to his beck and call, as Mrs. Osborne was to President Juddson back at his former employment. Occasionally, his daydream switched to how attractive, efficient, and friendly the important Miss Townley had been during their meeting and the subsequent phone calls he'd had with her to confirm arrangements.

Mrs. Osborne had not been fazed in the least by having to make the arrangements for all of Rudy's personal things to be put into storage. She waltzed him without penalty out of his Buffalo apartment's lease agreement, supervised getting his passport, and booked his tickets all the way to Malta. She repeatedly assured him that English was widely spoken on British Malta and that Mr. Standish, the HRM representative in London, would meet him as he got off the boat in London and explain all the arrangements made for him. Rudy had never stopped thanking her for all

25

she was doing for him for him, and she always explained that this was all part of her temporary, brief assignment. Getting it for the first time in his life, he really did enjoy that level of service!

He judged that his several years of basic design work, in-depth familiarization, and engine research tasks at Curtiss with the P-36 had taught him more than all his college engineering courses combined. Flying the Hawk during the various upgrade periods had been thrilling, and certainly had helped him successfully race the little red Mercury plane. During the time he was preparing to leave, Rudy had learned a bit from a meeting with Bob McDonald, the Export Manager, although, unlike a typical sales manager's focus, Bob never seemed to emphasize actually closing on a sales agreement. Rather he seemed to emphasize the desirability of helping the British military on Malta: "Get them ready for whatever's coming," he advised. That recollection led Rudy to realize that what even the Curtiss Export Manager had suggested was pretty much what Janice Townley and Colonel Whittaker had emphasized during his orientation session.

The throbbing, rhythmic sounds of the huge ship cutting through the waves were pushed aside that moment as a man's voice, politely spoken with a distinct English accent, questioned if the deck chair at Rudy's left was available for use. Rudy answered affirmatively, looking up at the same time, and seeing what he immediately thought of as a shorter, heavier, and older version of Colonel Whittaker, but one who spoke British English rather than American English. The Englishman settled into the deckchair, turned to Rudy, smiled as politely as he had spoken a moment ago, and introduced himself as Gordon Astill, late of the British military, and returning to England following a most pleasant and fascinating visit to America.

"Well Mr. Astill," Rudy replied" "I'm Rudy Worth from Buffalo, New York, traveling to Europe for the first time, and very pleased to meet you. You sound like you had a good time in my country. Did you travel around seeing the sights? Where did you get to?"

"Ah, yes," Mr. Astill said, "I truly enjoyed my too brief holiday, spending my days up and down your east coast. Quite enjoyable, visiting with people who are not as alarmed as we English are - or most Europeans for that matter Mr. Worth - about what certainly appears to be a coming war.

However, I am interrupting your solitude, and I apologize. Rather, now that we've met and realized common interests, I suspect, may I suggest, unless you already have dining companions, that we have a drink before dinner this evening Mr. Worth, and continue our conversation then? Might we also enjoy each others company at dinner? I, myself, am traveling alone and am eager to hear a more fulsome account of America's views on European politics than I was able to obtain while moving about your great country. Would it be possible for us to get together, as you Americans say, this evening? Unless, of course, you are already engaged?"

"I'd be happy to have a drink and dinner with you tonight. I'm traveling alone also and would enjoy that." said Rudy. "I'd be interested in what you certainly could tell me about what's happening in Europe. I need to head back to my stateroom about now, anyway, but where and when should we meet this evening?

"I propose that we meet in the Observation Lounge adjacent to the first class dinning room at seven o'clock, if that suits you. Until then, I wish you a pleasant day on his Majesty's liner."

That evening, Rudy, on his way to Malta in June of 1939 and eager to learn all he could from a former British military man heard the bad news long before he arrived at his new territory. Over drinks in the Queen Mary's art deco Observation Lounge, his new shipboard acquaintance, who turned out to be a retired but still hale and hardy British major returning to London, provided a detailed accounting of why the British high command had already made a strategic decision not to strengthen Malta in anticipation of a new, foreseen European war likely beginning soon.

Rudy, having briefly, and somewhat inaccurately, described his position as an erstwhile aircraft salesman as well as an aeronautical engineer, listened to retired Major Astill put it rather bluntly. "So you see, my young friend, there very likely isn't anyone of sufficient authority left on the whole island to even listen to a sales presentation, much less sign a purchase order. Mark my words, the war is quickly coming! Anyone headed to Malta had best get there soon. But I sense you are a friend to our noble cause, and eager to arrive." He said this matter-of-factly, without even a knowing blink of his eye, but to a now alert and wondering Rudy.

To a dazed but attentive Rudy, his new English friend went on to explain, as he inked a few lines on a linen napkin to illustrate Mediterranean geography, that from British Gibraltar on the east to Alexandria and the vital British controlled Suez Canal on the west, the distance is almost 2,000 miles. And British Malta – only 17 miles long and 9 miles wide – lies about half way between, just 60 miles and fifteen flying minutes south of Sicily, and almost as close to north Africa. Certainly an important position for exercising control of the central Mediterranean, the Major observed, but much too exposed to the strong Italian fleet and aircraft on Sicily for the British to defend. "Should Herr Hitler persuade Signore Mussolini to join with him," he judged, "there will be the devil to pay."

And besides, Rudy learned, should Germany move against certain European countries – such as France or Poland – Britain was obligated by treaty to join in their defense, as well as stopping any attempt by an enemy to invade its home islands. "Everything military will be needed elsewhere, thus Malta and 250,000 Maltese may well be left with some few anti-aircraft guns and little else when the balloon goes up," the Major opined. " I imagine most of our fleet and planes have already gone off to Alexandria and Gibraltar." In the Major's opinion, based on his visit to the United States, America seemed as unprepared for war as did Britain, and, except for President Roosevelt, apparently totally unwilling to discuss getting involved in European policy or politics.

Rudy, while disheartened by what he was hearing, realized that he should learn all the Major would explain, while understanding that he was learning a military man's opinion and predictions, clearly similar to Colonel Whittaker's. However, he considered also that his new friend was very likely the type of RAF Friend he had been alerted to back at the Buffalo meeting, and that his meeting the Major was hardly by chance. Rudy had no trouble remembering that his assignment was to assist in Malta's planning and preparations, laid directly upon him by HRM Aviation and, exceedingly indirectly, by President Roosevelt. Two evenings later, with the Queen Mary's speed pushed by fear of German submarines operating in the Atlantic, Rudy and the Major regretted that they were sitting down to their last shipboard dinner together.

After coffee and brandy, a new experience for Rudy, on this final night of the crossing, the Major declared it a most enjoyable time spent with his new American acquaintance. Rudy certainly agreed, despite the dismal news provided him over the last three evenings. Early during their second dinner together, Rudy had been asked to address his new friend as Gordon, while he, in turn, would be called Rudolph. Now Gordon presented Rudy with his formal card, naming him as Major Gordon H. L. Astill, V.C. D.S.O. M.C.

"Rudolph," Major Astill said, "I have a surprise for you. I shall write on my card an introduction to an old friend of mine who, if what I hear is correct, may even now be waiting on Malta, most probably to be named its next Governor and Commander-in-Chief. He was my commander at the Royal School of Military Engineers. I was with him then and a following year, until I retired almost two years ago, when he was General Commanding an important region. He is the much decorated General H. J. Garrison, and I suggest you get this card to him when you finally arrive in Malta. It will introduce you as an American friend, an engineer on our side, there to help strengthen Malta's defenses, especially those of the vital RAF. I hope this might help you there, although I very much doubt in any role as an aeroplane salesman. Will you do that, Rudolph, and also give the General my fondest regards? Oh, and keep in mind, he is a religious man in all aspects, even war, clear thinking, and a good decision maker."

Rudy and the Major agreed they likely would not meet again, since the Queen Mary's fast crossing would put them at Southhampton wharf, London, early the next morning. The major would be "training to London", while Rudy was to be met on the dock by an acquaintance. Rudy left the Major with sincere appreciation for his time and friendship, and especially his willingness to prepare him for such an uncertain Malta. Rudy wondered what more he might learn tomorrow from Mr. Ian Standish of HRM, and just how confusing it would all prove to be. He thought that perhaps these few days, at HRM's expense on this beautiful ocean liner, would be the best part of the whole trip, which he never had asked for nor imagined, anyway!

Early next morning Rudy was handed a sealed envelope by a ship's steward. It had General Garrison's name written on it and the words Personal and Confidential, and it was wrapped in a note written late last evening by Major Astill asking Rudolph to kindly hand it directly to General Garrison as soon as he and the General met. Putting the envelope in his coat pocket, Rudy continued with his preparations to leave the liner as soon as he could after it was secured to the Southhampton pier. In less than an hour, lugging two bags, he walked down the Queen's gangway, searching for someone in the waiting crowd of greeters carrying a sign with his name on it. In a minute or two he spotted a stout, red faced man in a brown tweed jacket holding up a small sign inscribed with what looked like 'Mr. Worth.' Rudy pushed toward him through the continuing stream of debarking passengers and called out, "HRM?" "Yes, yes," was the answer. "Are you Mr. Rudolph Worth?"

"I am," responded Rudy, "and I see from the sign that you're the HRM man I'm to meet; our agent in Great Britain who will get me on my way to Malta."

"Well, I'm your man, although what sales can be achieved in Malta right now is rather a mystery. Pardon me for being so frank, Mr. Worth, but at least they did listen to me – or rather my several cables. Please, don't be concerned over any who might imagine that you're here to sell fighter planes to Malta – which is already saying good-bye to British ships, planes, submarines, and soldiers! There is a great deal of planning and preparation needed to be done, and as quickly as possible. Malta, including my friends there, are frightened by their weakened position so close to the Italian Air Force fields on Sicily, and even more by what they see as their abandonment by Britain after so many years of considering themselves loyal members of the British Commonwealth."

The HRM representative, clearly agitated, grew even more red faced as he apologized "Sorry, Mr. Worth, I'm Ian Standish and I'll do all I can to get you on your way. I do wish they'd sent you over with a couple of squadrons of Hawks however, each with its own experienced pilot, all ready for our RAF Malta. We're going to need them if the Nazi lunatics don't quiet down. Right now, Malta appears a lost cause, but I'll see you get there, don't fear."

Lifting one of Rudy's bags, Standish pointed toward a car parked along the long dock and told Rudy he had reserved hotel rooms for them a bit south of London, but in a good position to Heston Aerodrome, west of central London, in Middlesex, all of which meant nothing to Rudy. Rudy learned he was scheduled to begin his next leg tomorrow on a British Airways Ltd noontime flight. "But don't worry," Standish joked, "it's an American plane, a Lockheed 14."

CHAPTER 4

FLYING TO MALTA

Southampton, England
June 1939

IAN Standish explained that Rudy would hop, skip, and jump across France and then south to refueling in Italy, finally reaching Malta's Grand Harbour and the capital, Valletta. The plane, which could hold a dozen passengers and a bit of cargo, had a relatively short range without refueling, thus making it, as Standish observed, " A bit of a long trip." Rudy interrupted his guide with a cry of "Oh, Wait," quickly explaining that he had three crates of his engine research equipment on board that Mrs. Osborne had said would be transported all the way to Malta and were ticketed just as he was - the Queen Mary, and the rest of the way by air, to the airport in Valletta. He had forgotten about them and had disembarked with only his suitcases.

"Yes, yes," Standish said reassuringly, "She contacted me about them before you left New York, and I've already arranged for them to be carried by lorry to the airport you're leaving from. Don't worry, you'll see them when you arrive in Malta. She told me it's some engine research you're working on, so you will have to decide whether you want them sent to your hotel or put in storage at the airport until you set up a place to work. But no matter, they'll be safe until you need them. At any rate, there will be two additional crates flying with you tomorrow, but I'll explain that as we drive a bit today to a very nice little country inn. It's quite close to Heston Aerodrome, for tomorrow's noon flight on British Airways."

Rudy might expect refueling at one or two places he had never heard of, but, "The pilot will explain all that business," To make Rudy's trip sound even longer, Standish told him that British Imperial Airways was flying the London-Valletta route using AW27 Ensigns equipped with four engines and carrying 40 passengers, but they couldn't land safely at the same Malta airport as Rudy. Also, you could make the trip from Italy on a frequent basis with an Italian flying boat, which landed in Malta's harbor, but this, for some clouded reason Rudy couldn't grasp, apparently wasn't a good time for that route.

While in the car and headed north toward the hotel, though, Rudy began to learn from Standish why his air trip had been set up as it had. He described, as he termed it, the layout of Malta, especially the areas used by the British for flying and related activities. One area in particular seemed to hold an attraction , and that was the British flying boat base and the RAF Aircraft Repair Section at a place called Kalafrana. Rudy's special crates, plus two additional crates of miscellaneous parts useful to the technical people at the repair facility, were traveling under Rudy's name, an American from neutral America, whose luggage would not be questioned or opened at certain airports by Custom Officials. The two extra crates were obviously arranged for by Standish after learning about Rudy's assignment and travel dates. Rudy wondered if he'd be told what this was all about before tomorrow's flight?

Standish spoke haltingly as he drove, seeming to set out a topic to learn what his passenger's reaction would be, and then moving on to another related probe. He was quite interested in Rudy's research and work with the P-36 Hawk in his former position with the Curtiss Company, but even more, he circled around the topic of Rudy's personal feelings about the seeming isolationist spirit in the United States. He went so far as to question Lindbergh's openly stated positive impression with the German Luftwaffe and its military might, attempting to draw out a response. He certainly applauded President Roosevelt's desire to assist England and his friend Mr. Churchill in their stand against the Nazis, and waited through a few seconds of silence for Rudy's cautious concurrence.

Seemingly assured with Rudy's pro-American, anti-Nazi responses, Standish came to the point: Could Mr. Worth sympathize with Ian's efforts of locating and shipping absolutely necessary, but unavailable through regular channels, spare parts for his friends at the RAF repair facility, all done above board, with full RAF payment to the part's supplier? Standish continued, "Rudolph – may I call you that, Mr. Worth? Rudolph, can you understand that I'm unofficially helping the RAF, using my HRM Aviation and American contacts, but outside my official HRM duties in London, helping my friends at the Malta repair shop at this time of real need? I'm not getting any money from this, but I'm an experienced parts finder, and they need help! Besides, you might be wanting me to scout up things you would need for your own research, aircraft power plants and otherwise."

Partly confused with what he was – or was not – being told, Rudy responded that he understood Standish's patriotic spirit, and he especially understood Malta's serious need to prepare for its own defense, but really didn't want to learn anymore about locating certain equipment and seeing that it got to Malta's RAF repair shop. "Well said," replied an enthusiastic Standish, "then you won't be bothered by the extra crates that are being shipped with you directly to Malta by our friends at British Airways as part of your personal luggage. But please see that they get to the supervising man at Kalafrana. All right? His name is Foster Crayton, and he'll be looking for you when you land. It's just a little kit for an old Mercury engine on a Bristol Blenheim bomber, and the boys have needed that for a long time. Foster knows why you're assigned to Malta by HRM, and he'll get you and your luggage to the hotel I've booked you in, and also set you up with a semi-private working space at the Kalafrana facility. Until you learn otherwise, think of Foster Crayton as your guide and confidant in Malta."

Oh, boy, thought Rudy! What am I getting into? I'm not even on the plane yet, and I'm ferrying spare parts for an old British bomber. Malta's military resources are being pulled out by England. I have no sales prospects, and I'm headed for an island in a key position, about to get blasted in a new war. Oh, and to top it off, I now have a new contact person, apparently with an understanding of my full role in Malta, and a quick note from an old Brit I just met introducing me to an older Brit he hasn't seen in years and who may or may not have the top Malta job himself. Things are really looking up for me – I don't think!

Rudy's spirits lifted a bit, however, after he and Ian-as he was now beginning to think of him-checked into their rooms at a rather pleasant country roadhouse inn and met for a drink at its small bar. Rudy thought it looked just as he imagined an English country inn's bar should look, and the dinner menu chalked on a board made him feel even better. During their roast beef dinner, more 'well-done' than he preferred but still excellent, Ian presented him with an envelope and explained its contents.

"The Company has made provisions with a bank in Valletta to maintain a kind of line of credit in your name, and also to have your hotel bills covered weekly by the bank. I've had a reservation made in your name at the same resident hotel I used when I was last there. It's a nice enough place, with a good little restaurant and bar, and I suggest you have them place you on a running account and forward your weekly tab to the bank. All those papers are in the envelope."

"But a word of advice, Rudolph. If push comes to shove and shooting starts, remember that Valletta is a highly built up neighborhood, densely populated, with most of the port and key buildings located nearby. It's sure to be a prime target for enemy action, meaning I'd guess, bombers. So scout around for a hotel or rental place away from Valletta and the harbor, just in case. When you get there you will see what I mean! Foster and the boys at the repair facility can steer you in the right direction. Keep busy with your special project work. At least the big boss in HRM, and I'm told the bigger boss in Washington, are counting on it."

Ian next told Rudy he would speak a bit out-of-turn, just a private thought or two as they enjoyed their dinner without the Company looking over their shoulders. Rudy realized that Ian's next observations were meant to be both private and likely important to Rudy. If the advice and warning Rudy heard next from Ian had been told him back home in the United States by an American friend, Rudy would have heard: 'Do what you were sent to do, then get out of Dodge as quick as you can, 'cause there's no business here and the shooting is about to start!'

While Ian's message took longer and was more politely worded, Rudy realized the intent was the same: the RAF on Malta was thinning out rapidly. If any orders for planes for Malta were to materialize, they would come from RAF headquarters in London, and that was very unlikely to happen. Besides, they certainly would be for the newest fighters, Curtiss or otherwise, and most likely stimulated by the higher-ups of HRM Aircraft. Rudy might be well advised to spend what time on Malta was needed for planning, send a suitable report to HRM listing some brilliant ideas about how to improve on nothing, which is what they've got as resources , and go on to his next assignment!" While Rudy did not agree with Ian's observations, they were discouraging.

Later that night, with his head on a pillow, Rudy thought, here I am, an aeronautical engineer and pilot, sent to the RAF's Malta trouble spot by HRM, with a bunch of already built six gun, top out at 300 mph, Curtiss Hawks – at only 23,000 US dollars each – all ready in the U.S.A. to be loaded on the next freighter bound for Malta, assuming the shooting doesn't start immediately. The thing wrong with that simple solution, Rudy concluded, is that England's government has decided not to even try to defend Malta, but to take from it, as they already have, the resources there which they judge are more needed elsewhere.

Let's hold off a while, he planned to himself, and see exactly what the Malta and RAF situation really is. And just before he shut his eyes it occurred to him that this extra long, round-about trip to Malta plotted by Standish, along with the mysterious crates of parts for his friend at the so-called repair shop, might also be part of some bigger, more complex, story.

Next day at noon, with Standish on the tarmac at Heston Aerodrome waiving good-bye, Rudy's Lockheed twin engine flight took off on a north heading in what appeared to be great flying weather. In the third row of six, on the left side and looking out a window, Rudy, one of only five passengers, watched a rural countryside grow smaller as the plane gained altitude in a gentle right hand climb-out, the outskirts of London proper beginning to appear in the windows across the narrow aisle. Belted in directly across that aisle was a man in a blue uniform, looking a bit older than Rudy.

As he twisted in his seat, Rudy could see a a small corner of a colorful patch on the passenger's right shoulder that he supposed identified a British Airways Ltd employee. The man turned toward Rudy just then to tell him that, on this flight path, they really wouldn't see much of London City, but that Rudy would get to see a parts of France and Italy after they crossed the channel and before they got to Malta. Before Rudy could say anything, the man introduced himself: "James Conners, Mr. Worth, a Captain with British Airways – soon to combine with Imperial Airways – just hopping a ride this afternoon to take the left seat on our regular Paris to London late evening flight. Might have canceled this flight with so few passengers, but it's a special unscheduled flight, you see, that one of our boffins wanted flown. So Bob's your uncle, and here we both are. You are seen as an RAF Friend, you know, just as Colonel Whittaker, Major Astill, and Ian Standish are."

Without pause the now mysterious Captain Conners went on to a wide-eyed Rudy. "Your HRM man Ian, asked me to reassure you that you'll be in Malta before you know it, as will your bags and boxes, and those special crates of parts he's hunted up for our chaps over there. We've cooperated before, you know, in getting some replacement parts delivered to Malta unofficially. Especially for the old Swordfish torpedo planes.

"It's good of you to go down to Malta during this time of great anticipation. At least *I'm* anticipating being called back if a war does start, although I don't imagine I'll be up in my old SE-5 this round. Most likely a desk job if I'm unlucky! We'll appreciate anything you can do to help, though. Malta's in a precarious position, as I believe you've been told."

Rudy and the Captain, who apparently had flown a biplane fighter in the last war, talked as pilots do when they aren't up in the cockpit flying the plane themselves, and Rudy learned that, basically, what both Major Astill on the Queen Mary and Ian Standish had told him about Malta's situation, especially if Germany continued invading countries, and if Mussolini joined Hitler, was unhappily accurate. Then, Malta would likely go from the frying pan to the fire.

Captain Conners, while not entirely as pessimistic as Ian Standish, agreed that Britain could ill afford to defend Malta, at least initially, and perhaps for a long period, if Hitler would not cease his land grabbing. Another concern, heard again, was that Mussolini might be convinced to remain neutral if England would cede Malta to Italy, but "God forbid," the Captain exclaimed. "Something brilliant," he remarked as he looked directly at Rudy, "needs to be done!"

Captain Conners and Rudy wished each other well as the Captain left the plane at the Paris refueling, the Captain wishing Rudy good luck during his "Malta assignment," and commenting that they well might meet again. In fact, the Captain made it a point to note that, while Ian Standish could always get a communication to him, Rudy could contact him directly – night or day – by phoning the number on the card he was writing on at this moment, and saying that he wished Captain Conners to contact him as quickly as possible at the number he would give the dispatcher.

Rudy thanked the Captain, but thought that this certainly was a poorly scheduled airline, since the Captain of the Paris to London flight had to fly down from London to board his plane in Paris so he could fly it back to London. And he could be contacted day or night? Rudy now began to wish he had looked more closely at the patch on Captain Murrey's shoulder. After enjoying one of the dinners just brought on board, Rudy drifted off in an uneasy nap.

During the nap he heard repeated in his head what Ian Standish had confided to him earlier: without the crates of parts being smuggled into RAF Malta as part of Rudy's luggage, Rudy's trip on the bigger and faster Imperial Airways plane would have taken half the time and with fewer stops. Of course, as Rudy now realized, at any official airport stop in France or Italy with baggage inspection, Rudy, even as a neutral American citizen, would have had some explaining to do, and that might be, as Ian had remarked "A bit of an inconvenience."

But no matter; at this point all was going well. Rudy had learned from a brief conversation with his pilot during a fuel stop that they would land in Malta on time, and on a hard strip 'runway', surprisingly in the middle of a large grass field called "Hal Far", whatever that was, rather than a paved multi-runway type airport. Rudy was now beginning to wonder if HRM Aviation really knew what it was doing, sending him to Malta, on salary and all expenses paid, ostensibly to peddle some planes that everyone knew wouldn't be ordered for Malta, and help with the planning and getting ready for war phases. And him an experienced fighter plane engineer? The trip might well prove to be either ridiculous or a total waste? Or maybe, he thought, something else altogether?

CHAPTER 5

WELCOME TO MALTA

Kalafrana and Hal Far Airstrip, Malta
June 1939

RUDY'S first view of the Island, the complex shoreline of a harbor and a busy port, came as his plane lost altitude to enter the traffic pattern. It was obviously not Buffalo! In fact, it didn't look like anyplace in the United States Rudy had ever imagined. As far as he could see as the plane continued to descend, the built upon area consisted almost solely of dazzling white and cream color stone buildings, some quite large, looking very old and very tightly packed along narrow streets which climbed up, sometimes at steep angles, from this immense natural harbor.

As Rudy's plane lost even more altitude and banked to enter the left downwind leg of a landing pattern, his brief view of a larger area and very extensive port facilities, including working cranes and several ocean-going cargo ships as well as a couple of what might be warships, disappeared. The airstrip they were landing at was not far from a sheltered bay with what Rudy recognized as a flying boat ramp leading from the water toward several large workshop type structures. Many colorful small boats and a few larger ones were anchored or pulled up on the shore.

The growing tightness in Rudy's stomach made him even more aware of his anxiousness; his Malta assignment was about to really begin! For the third time in the last hour, Rudy pulled out the slip of paper in his shirt pocket to check the name of the man who, according to Ian Standish, would be waiting for him to deplane and who would be his guide: Foster Crayton. "O.K.," Rudy whispered aloud, "Foster, here I am." In a few moments the plane landed and taxied off the grass runway a short distance, toward a building. The pilot locked the left brake, revved the starboard engine, and the plane turned to face in the opposite direction as the engines wound down. The co-pilot's announcement was that the passengers could deplane as soon as he got the door opened and the stairs lowered in place. Hand luggage would be unloaded at the side of the plane, where it could be claimed. Other cargo would be unloaded shortly and carted to the small administration building for distribution.

Rudy was now in a hurry to meet Crayton, and so he moved quickly to be first in line at the plane's door. The door was opened and the co-pilot wished them a good day in sunny Malta. As Rudy started down the few steps to ground level, both the temperature and the glare gave a physical jolt, causing him to clutch the side railing and pause in his descent. Wow! Now he was sure this was very different from Buffalo in December. The next thing he noticed was a printed sign on the building welcoming passengers to RAF HAL FAR. In a moment a burly man dressed in a mechanic's grey one-piece jump suit came up and asked, "Are you Mr. Rudolph?"

"I'm Rudy Worth, Mr. Crayton, and I'm very happy to meet you and be here in Malta," Rudy replied.

The man greeting Rudy immediately said, "I'm not Crayton, I'm George. From the Shop. Crayton told me to get out here and get you and your stuff off the plane. He's left the Shops already today. Got a bug up his arse, I guess, but who knows what. You got anything besides a suitcase?"

"Oh." Rudy exclaimed. "I've got two suitcases and three crates of my work things, but there also are two crates for Mr. Crayton - plane parts I was told - that I was to see got to Mr. Crayton. They're parts that the shop has been waiting for, I think. Well, I'm off the plane, so where do I go with my things and how do I get there?"

"Cripe, sir, Crayton told me nothing else, but maybe the Shop Clerk knows. All those crates' will be OK here at the side of the building, so grab your suitcases and we'll get over to the Clerk's little office. Wait, I'll carry one of those. I guess you've had a long trip from England."

"Not England," Rudy replied in an agitated tone, "I've come all the way from America – for the HRM Aviation Company - and I need to talk to somebody, if not Foster Crayton, so I can get going on what I'm supposed to be doing!"

"Let's drive over to the Clerk, then. Maybe Crayton told him, and I'll go back and get your crates and the shop crates carted over to the Clerk's. He can figure it out."

A ride in an RAF truck down a short road toward a shop building got both of them and two suitcases to what apparently was the Clerk's office, and George turned around outside the door advising Rudy to go inside and tell his story to the Shop Clerk, while he went to see about the crates. Rudy stepped inside what turned out to be an office-type room inhabited by a young man typing behind a grey metal desk.

The man looked up and said, "You must be Mr. Worth, come all the way across the pond from HRM Aviation. Welcome, at last, to Malta Hal Far and Kalafrana's Shops. I'm Robert, the shop's clerk, and what passes as Foster Crayton's secretary and general factotum. I'm quite aware of your Malta assignment, or project, or whatever its going to be, and very pleased you've joined us. As I hope George told you, Foster was called to an unscheduled Kalafrana Wing Commander's staff meeting. Wing Commander Bartell, a good man, is relatively new in his assignment and still needs to get settled in on a routine. Foster was standing by to meet your flight, and was unhappy to be summoned away."

"If you can relieve me of the two crates which traveled under my name but are aircraft parts for the shop, and get me underway to my hotel, I'll be fine. Or should I wait here for Mr. Crayton? Oh, and then I've got a couple of crates of my own for wherever in the shop facility I can do my work."

"Let's get you underway, Mr. Worth, and I'll schedule you for a long session with Mr. Crayton first thing tomorrow morning. Who knows how long his meeting will last this afternoon. Ian Standish briefed me on the crates and your need for some out- of-the-way workspace, and I'll get your crates over there, waiting for you.

In the meantime, we've got a shop vehicle, such as it is, and I'll have George get you to the hotel Ian booked you in; it's a good choice, and I'll pick you up there myself tomorrow morning on my way in. Let's say at 8:30 in front of the hotel? We'll have coffee and tea and biscuits here for your meeting with Foster. Go and unpack and rest up. We have a great deal to do here at the Shops and, indeed, all of Malta itself, including our small Gozo, the island just to our north."

Rudy left as soon as George returned and received his instructions from Robert concerning Rudy's hotel, the *Palazzo Arja Ocean*, located on *Trig Summit* in *Birzebbuga*, a community on *Marsaxlokk Bay*, which George said was better called *Marsa Scirocco*. The hotel was two miles from the airstrip at Hal Far, only one mile from the aircraft repair facility at Kalafrana, and was on a public motor bus route. To Rudy, that sounded fine, although he cringed at his inability to understand the names, by George in the Maltese language.

With his suitcases in the back of the small truck, Rudy sat next to George and asked a couple of questions on the short trip. Rudy learned from George that, "If you want work at the RAF, or anywhere else on Malta for the English, you had better learn English language in school, or pick it up on your own." Besides Maltese, the next languages were Italian, since Sicily was only 60 miles to the north, and English, since Malta's military and foreign affairs were controlled by Britain since 1921, with only local business conducted by a Maltese parliament. Rudy learned also that in his American language, as George called it, his hotel was the Ocean Air, located on Summit Avenue in a community pronounced *beer-zeb-boor-jah*. Rudy began to relax. He felt even better when George pulled up in front of a four story very nice looking hotel building with three upper stories of balconies spreading across the width of the building, each looking out at the colorful bay.

Rudy got out of the truck, pulled both suitcases from the back, called his thanks to George for the trip and the language lesson, and walked through the hotel entrance doors which were being held open for him by an alert, formally dressed man calling out, "Welcome, welcome Mr. Worth, welcome to the Palazzo *Arja Ocean*." Another man, this one uniformed, relieved Rudy of his luggage while Rudy was being ushered into a beautifully furnished office by his greeter. "I'm Mr. Farinacci, the Palazzo's Manager, and I extend the warmest welcome to you, Mr. Worth. I have a mailing from America which awaits your arrival. All of this was said in perfect English as an envelope from Mrs. Osborne was presented. Mr. Farinacci told Rudy his bags would be brought directly to his rooms on the second floor, the balcony of which faced not the noisy, busy street, but the park at the rear of the hotel. Meantime, he would like to review the arrangements between the hotel and HRM Aviation, as 'organized' by Mr.

Standish and a Miss Townley of HRM Aircraft, Ltd. in Washington, America.

The financial arrangements were as Standish and Janice Townley had described them: all Hotel charges would be sent to the local Banco Malta for coverage from HRM. All of Rudy's personal charges in restaurants and shops would be covered, and Rudy should simply charge everything to his account at the Palazzo. Mr. Farinacci would arrange for prompt payment from Rudy's bank, and in turn from Miss Townley. When Rudy later opened his mail from Mrs. Osborne, he found a written note explaining the enclosed was a generous money order for Rudy's incidental pocket expenses in the local Maltese currency, or British pounds, sent by her as the last task in her temporary HRM work, and would be repeated every three months directly from the HRM business office, either Washington or London based. She wrote a fond good-bye to Rudy, wished him very well, told him to keep safe, and said perhaps they would meet again. Rudy was momentarily overcome by very early home-sickness, and especially the financial arrangement. From his perspective, it would help assure all the HRM co-sponsors that he'd do his best not to fail, he silently promised.

Mr. Farinacci told Rudy that he would always be available for any questions or recommendations Rudy desired for anything, including evening activities and entertainment, which prompted Rudy to cast his eyes downward and mumble a 'thank you'. This was followed by a description of the Palazzo's restaurant and bar and certain nearby recommended restaurants, plus an apology that the Palazzo was still awaiting the installation of a modern elevator for guest use. In closing, as a good salesman, the Manager told Rudy how pleased he was to have, first, Mr. Standish as a guest, and how very pleased now to have Rudy, also from the famous HRM Company, as a long time guest under these very fine business arrangements, and how happy he would be to serve any future guests from the HRM Company. At this, both stood and the Manager walked Rudy to the ornate stairway leading to the upper floors and his second floor Suite #15. Rudy gave his genuine thanks and soon learned, as a typical American, that Maltese buildings, like those in England, did not consider the ground floor to be what in America is the 'first' floor, but rather the *ground floor*. Thus Rudy walked up two flights of stairs, rather than one, to get to his second floor suite.

The door to his 'en suite' room was open, and Rudy found his suitcases placed by the balcony doors. He looked out over a little park and quiet street below, then walked through a side door past a large clothes closet and into a large, ornate marble walled bathroom containing a huge free-standing, curtained-off bathtub. That sight prompted him to unpack quickly, shed his clothes, turn on the water to the tub, step over its high side, close the shower curtain, and encounter a strange hose-connected mobile shower head looking very like a telephone handset. Undaunted, he used it to shower, stepped into a thick terrycloth bathrobe hanging on a wall hook, dried off and promptly tried out his bed, following Robert's suggestion to 'rest up'. Fortunately, the hotel dining room served dinner on the later European time schedule, so his extra long nap did not interfere with his timely arrival downstairs in a splendid – he thought – restaurant. Seated alone, he requested a 'typical Maltese meal', and thus enjoyed, for his first time, a braised rabbit dinner and an Italian cannelloni with coffee for desert. And, happily, the waiter spoke English. Doing pretty well, he judged, for a young man from Watkins Glen.

Next morning, right on time at 8:30, Robert stopped in front of the hotel driving a small Fiat sedan. Rudy, waiting on a busy sidewalk, recognized him and quickly went to the right side front door and grasped the handle, wondering why Robert was sitting in the passenger seat. Mr. Worth," Robert smiled, "Malta is like England; we drive on the wrong side of the road, as you Americans would say! Our cars are built this way. Go around or jump in the back, as you please, and we're off to Kalafrana and your meeting with Foster.

In just a few minutes, Robert was parking next to a side door at the shop building. He led Rudy through it and into an office, where a tall man, looking to be in his early fifties but already slightly balding, and dressed well with a white shirt and striped tie, awaited them. "Mr. Worth," he said, "I'm most pleased to meet you, with apologies for not being here to greet you at your arrival yesterday. Please come in and we'll have a light breakfast while we sit and talk.

"Mr. Crayton, I'm happy to be here. Robert has been very kind and I'm settled in at my hotel, so I look forward to learning how I might be of help to you and your preparations for a possible war. Or whatever is going to happen. And may I ask that you all call me Rudy, as they do back home?"

With niceties dispensed with, and with coffee and English 'biscuits' brought in by Robert, who apparently was not to sit-in during the discussion, Foster Crayton began on an unhappy note: Rudy's assignment to Malta was not well understood by Wing Commander Bartell, Commanding Officer, Kalafrana, who had wondered at yesterday's staff meeting just what he was supposed to do with an American salesman with no military experience who was here to "help the British defend Malta", sent by a company whose planes we didn't have, and whose assignment was a mystery to both himself and even Malta's Commander in Chief?

"You must understand, Rudy, that while I'm recently retired RAF, where I was assigned several years ago as Officer-in-Charge of the Aircraft Repair Section at Kalafrana, I'm now just a civilian employee put back into the same job because most military resources including the fleet and the planes, plus vast numbers of military personnel, have been pulled out and reassigned elsewhere. I don't swing much weight here, to coin a phrase, with those few left in the higher echelons. However, I understand from Ian Standish and from James Murrey, an old RAF acquaintance, that there is a bit more to this than meets the eye, and I suspect that the identification of you as a special 'Friend of the RAF' will soon make its way to my Commanding Officer and others above him who also may not understand."

Without giving Rudy a chance to reply, Crayton continued, "Therefore, I suggest that we get you situated in a private workspace here in the Shops where you can continue with your engine research experiments, while I brief you on the RAF's situation in Malta, and we allow a little time for the word from RAF headquarters to reach our several Commanding Officers, Air and otherwise. And now I would like to show you a map of both Hal Far and Kalafrana, explain what we have here, and then take you for a little tour of our area, if that's agreeable?"

Rudy, made uneasy by this news, and seated on the edge of his chair, simply nodded his understanding and agreement. "That's fine with me." he added. "Where can I set up? Or do you think it's better for me to wait until things are clearer? I don't want you to have a problem with the Commander because of this."

"No, no," Foster replied, "it will all be handled quickly; just a delay in local communication. Let's get you working at your assignment right away, but let us take a little tour of what we have here first, so you'll know the scope of services we provide as a unit of the RAF."

CHAPTER 6

THE PROJECT BEGINS

RAF Kalafrana Aircraft Repair Shops
June 1939

RUDY'S tour of the Kalafrana shops, with Foster Crayton as his guide, impressed Rudy with the size and equipment available for both engine and air frame maintenance and repair. He was impressed even more with the skilled workers, most of whom were Maltese technicians, many with more than twenty years of aircraft experience, plus the few remaining RAF personnel. During the tour Rudy was introduced by Crayton as "a friend", which appeared to raise no questioning glances from the workers. Rudy spoke little, but smiled and nodded a lot; the language spoken was English with a British twist. All he was introduced to were openly very welcoming in their greetings, in their body language, and often in offering a handshake.

When they came to a space set apart by what looked like recently erected wooden walls and a large, lockable double-wide entry door, Crayton led Rudy through the door and swept his hand with obvious pride at sturdy work benches built against two of the walls, a heavy rolling engine hoist stored in a corner, a grinding wheel and large vise mounted on one of the workbenches, and numerous hand tools hanging on wall pegs.

"We can bring in more spanners - what you call wrenches, I think - and any small machine tooling equipment you might need, or we can do larger tooling on the machines in the outer shops. With most of the planes already having left the island, and the four patrol flying boats going to be reassigned to Gibraltar very soon, we've got some time to spare in your assistance. I don't especially want to give anyone the impression that you're doing some type of secret work in here, but I'll give you a key to the door should you want to lock up any time.

"Just let me know what else you need by way of equipment, and if you want assistance from any of the technicians. They are very good at improvising when needed. In fact, if you like, I can assign one of them to assist you full time once you get started. We still have a fair inventory of spare parts, and we do have a couple of good engine testing benches out in the yard. And don't be surprised at what you see the lads working on, since we take care of the big rescue launch and most of the RAF lorries."

Rudy was not only pleased, but overwhelmed with the great setup already in place for him, and with the more than generous treatment being offered by Foster Crayton. Later he would learn how far out on a limb Foster had placed himself without official approval from the RAF officialdom on Malta, and just how that approval finally had been brought about. For the moment, however, he was happy to begin unpacking his three crates and to ask Robert where he might get a small table or desk, plus a chair, for his paper and pencil type work. Robert promised to meet that need, and suggested that Rudy finish his unpacking and allow him to explain the bus schedule to get Rudy back and forth from the hotel. Robert also recommended asking the hotel to pack a lunch for Rudy to take to work each day; there would be room for it in the small cooler in the office, and Rudy could set his own schedule. For today, Robert would work on his own tasks to finish the morning, and then drive Rudy back to the hotel, explaining the bus business on the way, and allowing Rudy to get a midday meal at the hotel or one of the nearby eating places, and to explore the commercial area around the hotel.

What Rudy didn't know was that Robert's task that morning, assigned by Foster, was to find Captain James Conners by telephone, and to connect Foster as soon as possible. As Rudy left the office, Robert dialed the same number the Captain had given Rudy during the plane ride, and told the dispatcher what was needed. In a quarter hour Foster was on the phone with James Conners.

"Jim, Foster Crayton here," went the brief conversation. "Friend Rudy is here and unpacking his gear in the private shop we set up for him. Unfortunately, the wicket has gotten a bit sticky, to use a phrase, since neither my Kalafrana Officer-in-Charge, Wing Commander Bartell, nor- I'm told - the Malta Governor, General Sir Bonham-Carter, have either not received the necessary information, or do not understand it. I'm keeping Rudy on a short tether and myself a bit out of Bartell's sight since yesterday's staff meeting, when my RAF boss wondered out loud what the hell this 'Mr. Worth, the American' business was all about. Can you get the powers-that- be to take care of this, and right away?"

James Conners' answer came quickly: "I'll take care of it immediately. I suspect that the message will arrive to the Governor from the Minister's Office, and to your Wing Commander from high in the RAF, likely the Air Officer Commanding Mediterranean, who is Air Commodore Fairthorpe. I'm looking up your Wing Commander Bartell as we speak. Yes, this would be J.R. Bartell. All right, Foster, I'll move on this immediately; thanks for phoning, and I'll send word when you can raise your head down there. Good Bye."

Three days later the Wing Commander walked into Rudy's workshop for the first time, greeted Rudy as though they were old acquaintances, and asked him how his aircraft engine experiments were progressing. Rudy was flabbergasted and fearful of being ejected, but was calm enough to respond warmly and to explain that he was working on a few relatively new but simple ways to increase the horsepower output of engines without engaging in extensive, time consuming engineering modifications. Examples Rudy listed included increasing the octane rating of the gasoline fuel, converting single stage supercharger blowers to two stage, and injecting water mist or a combination of water and methanol alcohol mist into the fuel and air intake of the engine to reduce temperature, and switching to three bladed propellers.

Rudy was about to provide some details of the gains in horsepower when Bartell almost cried out in desperation, "Without any planes left to us, and with no realistic hope of our seeing any in the near future, your methods – no matter how successful – will be of naught assistance to keeping the enemy at bay. I shall be expected to wage war in defense of this island without a fighter plane to send aloft, much less a squadron or a wing. I am already a Wing Commander without a wing, and in a few days our four old flying boats are ordered to Gibraltar, and that's the end of it."

Even though Rudy had heard a generalized version of this lament as recently as his Queen Mary voyage, he began to mumble words of encouragement which were at least optimistic regarding a relief flight of British fighter planes – Hurricanes most likely – coming in soon. "No." Bartell replied. "Defense of our treaty allies and, God forbid, the Home Islands must and shall come first! We simply are ill prepared for the war that so many think will soon be upon us! And before long one of our flat tops will stop by to pick up the few crates of planes that were left temporarily with us on their way to Egypt, and there's the very end of it. Search lights and ant-aircraft guns will be it!" Rudy realized later that the operative word uttered unknowingly by Bartell was *crates,* but that knowledge would come later, brought to light by an off-hand remark from a Shop technician.

Rudy had already learned, however, that many Maltese citizens were now foreseeing abandonment by the English, should Hitler and Mussolini desire Malta in their future acquisitions, and were both fearful and angry. In fact, this information had been voiced during Rudy's lunch with Mr. Farinacci back at the hotel, just three days ago. Robert had driven him back early on that first day, allowing him time to explore the hotel neighborhood and finish unpacking. But rather than allow Rudy to seek lunch elsewhere, the hotel manager had invited him to be his guest in the hotel dining room. With his lunch, he heard an earful. Mr. Farinacci seemed well-informed concerning local feelings and, while not speaking directly against what appeared to be current British policy, voiced high concern over "British lack of understanding of Herr Hitler's true intent." This he coupled with the fact that Malta was so close to Italy in several ways, including, of course, geography. What did Rudy think about this, Mr. Farinacci wondered? And could he sympathize with the growing Maltese anger at the British? Wisely, Rudy voiced no thoughts on this subject, although his host obviously wanted to draw him out.

Several days after the Wing Commander's surprise visit to Rudy's workshop, Robert delivered mail, a plain envelope for Rudy marked 'Personal and Confidential' and postmarked from London. There was no return address evident, causing Robert to remark, "She's found out where you went, I think." This was followed by a laughing snicker. "What?" a puzzled Rudy exclaimed. "Where did this come from?" As the still laughing Robert left the workshop, Rudy slit the envelope open, revealing a brief note on a plain sheet from Ian Standish, his London based HRM Aviation contact.

The note, handwritten, explained that Ian, after talking with Colonel Whittaker by phone, had phoned Bob McDonald, the Curtiss Export Manager in Buffalo the day after Rudy had flown from England. Ian pointed out that one of the crated export model 75 Hawks, already slated for a sale to the French, would be extremely useful to HRM Aviation on Malta. McDonald had agreed with Ian that Rudy could hardly even describe export Hawks if he didn't have an actual plane to show the product with which he was so familiar. Therefore, with McDonald's assistance, Ian had arranged for one plane among export models already crated for delivery to France from a certain UK port on an English cargo ship to be mislabeled to Worth Engineering Company, LTD, Valletta, Malta. The note stated that the manifest identifies contents as *"XF3B Buffalo Equipment shipped from* C. Wright *Manf. Co. Buffalo, NY, USA. Content Weight 2,150 Kg."* A postscript added that *"Small additional contents for approval inspection. Crate carried by MV Empire Ellesmere due Valletta Port via Gibraltar on or about 19 June."*

Rudy's immediate thought was that he had only a couple of days to check the inbound ship list for Valletta. His second thought was to get immediately to Foster Crayton and ask what needed to be done to get the huge crate from an English cargo vessel to the Kalafrana Shops. His third was to thank Bob McDonald somehow, sometime, but Ian Standish most of all. One real fighter plane!

Crayton's reaction to Rudy's news was puzzled enthusiasm. Yes, one or even two large crates could be transported to the shop area from the ship unloading dock. This had been done before, but it would take some arranging and possibly some subterfuge. However, Commander Bartell would now undoubtedly approve once the cargo ship's arrival date was confirmed by the Harbourmaster's office. But where should the crate or crates be stored, and what would Rudy do with the contents? That got Rudy's quick answer: "Out of sight inside a hangar or shop building with a forty foot wide door opening; we're going to put it together!" A check with the Harbourmaster's office showed the *Empire Ellesmere* due for docking three days hence, and Crayton, after confirming with Commander Bartell, began making the off-loading and transport arrangements. The large shop building directly behind Rudy's workspace had space cleared for assembly, and Rudy began planning what kind of assistance he would need to get it together and tested.

The next big surprise came not just to Rudy, but to Foster Crayton and eventually to Commander Bartell as well. It was delivered by the very same workman, "George from the shop", who had met Rudy as he deplaned at Hal Far airstrip. George had been tasked by Crayton with arranging to get the crated plane from the dock to the Kalafrana shops, and he stopped by to confer with Rudy and Crayton. When Rudy apologized to George about the challenge of transporting the crate George replied, "Not a problem. It can't be much bigger than the eight or ten crated old two wingers stuck down in the back of everything at the docks, waiting to get picked up by the *Glorious* or some other flattop." "What?" Crayton and Rudy exclaimed in unison. "What two wingers and where are they stacked? And who owns them?"

"If you don't know, Mr. Crayton, I sure don't. Ask the Dock Master, I suppose. They been there for weeks. Nobody pays any mind to them. *Mhux in-negozju tieghi*, as the boys down on the docks say; not my business!"

"Okay, George. I'll check them out. And thank you. In the meantime, let me know if you expect any trouble with the transport of the crate coming in," Crayton said. Turning to Rudy, he said, "I'll check with Commander Bartell and let you know what this new one is all about. Eight or ten biplanes? If we're lucky, they're Sea Gladiators and everyone has forgotten about them. Maybe they're written off? Wouldn't it be fine if they're really Hurricanes and labeled incorrectly, as is your Hawk mislabeled as a Brewster Buffalo? Or did you think I couldn't figure that one out?"

In a few days, thanks to Commander Bartell's inquiries, all three suspected the forgotten crates housed ten Gloster Sea Gladiator biplanes. Originally they were to be picked up by the British carrier *Glorious* at the Kalafrana slipway for transport as reserves to the north Atlantic from Alexandria. They were left on the Malta docks by error, and appeared to be still registered to the Royal Navy. Both Bartell and Foster Crayton had learned, in no uncertain terms, that this valued property of the Royal Navy was, under no circumstances, going to be be transferred to the Royal Air Force. And that stern, official statement, had been verified by Captain

Donalds on Malta and Commander Fairthorpe all the way from London. Rudy could hardly believe what he felt was the absolute stupidity of this inter-service lack of cooperation. And with such dire possible results! Foster assured him that they had heard the final word, and he refused to discuss it further.

Through some quiet Curtiss research, Rudy learned that what he hoped was in the Buffalo crate was one of many export models of the P-36 identified for export purposes as the Hawk 75 A-2/3, ordered by France from Curtiss in late 1938 and scheduled for delivery starting in May, 1939. With some improvements in engine horsepower and the number of wing guns, beginning with number 48 coming off the Buffalo production line, 135 models designated as A-3 were ordered, but only 133 were ever officially delivered. Of the various models, from A-3 to A-4, only some reached the French Air Force, with the remainder diverted to Britain, including, Rudy guessed, the one shipped to Worth Engineering, Valletta, Malta.

While a sensible solution to the crated planes left at the port docks might never emerge from the bureaucratic British military quagmire, Rudy and his two allies at Kalafrana hoped to know a lot more about the contents of the surprise sent from Buffalo in just a few more days.

CHAPTER 7

LIGHTNING STRIKES

Malta

Summer 1939

LIKE most Americans during the 1930s, Rudy Worth knew scant details concerning the trials and tribulations of European politics and the broader events that were leading to a world war eventually involving his own country. And even as he began his HRM sponsored 'Malta Assignment', almost everything he had been told focused on Malta and its unique, precarious situation. His recent education, provided by Colonel Whittaker in Buffalo, Major Astill aboard the Queen Mary, Ian Standish in England, Captain Conners on the plane, and Mr. Farinacci in the hotel dining room had all been filtered through Malta's current situation and needs.

Key European events, including Hitler's rise to the Chancellorship of Germany and his annexation of selected areas in central Europe, and Italy's Ethiopian war and north African empire building under Mussolini were not much noticed by typical Americans. Neither were the Nationalist's success in the Spanish Civil War by Francisco Franco (with help from Germany and Italy), nor Spain's immediately joining the Anti-Comintern Pact uniting Germany, Italy, Spain, and Japan, all pledging anti-communism policy. And although met with praise, the Munich Agreement of September 1938, signed by Germany, Italy, France, and the United Kingdom, which soon resulted in the fall of Czechoslovakia to Germany, all pointed not toward the "Peace in our time" imagined by England's Prime Minister Chamberlain, but the division of much of the world into two warring factions.

Rudy was unaware that the 1938 fall of Czechoslovakia resulted in high concern among many in Britain, and a special focus on British military readiness. In Malta, however, despite a timely decision by a committee of England's Parliament, the initial promise of much needed additional anti-aircraft guns and searchlights to be sent to Malta was not fulfilled. Adding further demoralization to an apprehensive citizenry, a large group of artillery soldiers were transferred away to Alexandria from their posts on Malta.

Additionally, Rudy quickly realized that there truly were no fighter planes left on Malta. He learned later also that the famed British warships, the Mediterranean Fleet, had followed the planes to either Alexandria, Gibraltar, or the Home Islands. Apparently the British government's decision not to defend and hold Malta against any attempted invasion was being implemented by the withdrawal of their military resources. Mr. Farinacci, in his eagerness to teach Rudy a bit of Maltese, had him repeat *Dak juri dak li hu verament importanti gh all-ingilterra.* He then told Rudy it meant "That shows what is really important to England." But until that time to come, when Hitler's Germany would invade Poland on September 1, 1939, Rudy spent little time pondering what might be Malta's future. Instead, he worked long hours daily, especially focused on getting the P-36 ready for flight, but also on ways of improving engine performance and learning about Gloster Gladiators, all of which fascinated him. Or not quite *all* his attention, as we shall learn.

During the summer, he established a telephone link with Ian Standish, and one with Janice Townley at her London office. Each of these brought him shipments containing his requests for certain engine enhancement equipment, plus supplies and encouragement to continue his efforts to strengthen the exceedingly limited aviation resources left on the Island. Several times he wondered to Janice if what he saw as meager efforts were worth the cost, but she said the HRM group never wavered in its determination to aid these quiet efforts to slow-down Hitler.

During one particular phone conversation near the end of July, Ian asked for the status of the P-36 aircraft. Rudy was eager to describe how the huge crate was craned onto a large flatbed trailer and towed by a tractor to a Shop building which had been made ready. There a mobile crane positioned the crate while shop workman, led by George, unfastened the crate's front panel, hinged at the bottom edge, and lowered it to the ground.

The entire aircraft had been cleverly disassembled, packed specially for storage, and secured into the crate, major section by major section, wings behind the fuselage along with the horizontal stabilizer and elevator assembly, rudder and propeller, engine still bolted to the fuselage, and miscellaneous small elements secured to the crate's bottom. Among these were two 20mm aircraft cannon, complete with loaded circular magazines and a note which said, "Try these." As Foster commented to Rudy, such crating of aircraft to be delivered abroad was not as unusual as Rudy had thought, although the cannon as possibilities for a Curtiss Hawk were a surprise.

With much assistance from two technicians and George, each assigned full time by Foster Crayton to aid Rudy, the P-36 was completely assembled, the engine filled with all necessary fluids and run up, and all controls tested and adjusted. At least that was the quick summary provided to Ian, without mention of the volume of work involved, nor a description of how the wings would now have to be taken off so the plane could be towed to the Hal Far field over the narrow mile long road connecting it with the Kalafrana shops. There were a few small hangars at Hal Far, and the new plane would be completed with the wings attached, and all systems tested again, along with a couple of taxi trials before any flight. Rudy thought it might be another month before someone, hopefully Rudy himself, could try a short test flight.

To Colonel Whittaker's earlier request for information to pass on to the HRM executives concerning his experiments, Rudy was quick to list the 50/50 water and methanol mist injection into the plane's supercharger boost system, an increase in the fuel octane rating, an adjustment in the engine timing to recognize a lower running temperature, and the upgrade from single to a double stage supercharger. All of these efforts, Rudy was finding on a Gladiator type test engine taken from an older Bristol bomber stored at HAL FAR, resulted in measurably higher horsepower outputs with longer permitted boost times designed to improve climb rates and thus, hopefully, actual dogfight speed and effectiveness.

Amazingly, the only people thinking about the crated Gloster Gladiators were Wing Commander Bartell, still without any planes and pilots to command, Foster Crayton, who itched to pry open one of the ten *Sea Gladiator* crates he had verified, half-hidden down in the dock and ramp area, and Rudy, whose single-minded focus on the P-36 was now beginning to ease off as he began to realize that, if the Hawk's flight tests were successful, Malta would have a lone modern fighter plane, although minus an experienced fighter pilot.

There was one other interest which had developed rather quickly in Rudy's daily thinking and which caused him some disquiet. It was nothing he cared to mention to Ian Standish, or even to Foster Crayton - as much as Rudy liked him - and certainly not to Robert. Indeed, Robert was mostly responsible for Rudy's disquieting new interest, due to Robert's urging to, as he argued, "Get out of this constant, all consuming engineering work, see the amazing sights of Malta, and do some unwinding!"

As a result of Robert's insistence, Rudy did indeed get to view what to him *was* a most amazing sight. This occurred on July 2, and continued unabated as Rudy puzzled over how to proceed with his now very strong interest in a fascinating young woman he had seen walking with two others along Mellieha Beach. Robert had brought him there that Sunday afternoon, providing a day of leisure. Through blind chance he learned her name was Ana Boiano, and as the French would say, he was *Coup de Fodre*. Struck by lightning!

Later, when he described his situation to Mr. Farinacci, he learned that in this case, since Boiano was an Italian name, he might memorize the words *colpo di fulmine*, and use these at an appropriate time. (Rudy asked if he could learn to say it in Maltese, but Mr. Farinacci told him that *Imhabba mad-dagga t'ghajn* perhaps wouldn't sound quite as romantic.)

Fifteen minutes after the three women had strolled by the young men's beach chairs, they strolled back past them again. One of the young woman paused for a moment and stepped closer to say, "Robert, how nice to see you, but don't get sunburned. It is a beautiful day, but I didn't know you came up this way just to get some sun." Robert didn't even get up from his chair, but shielding his eyes with his hand replied, "Ah, Nina, I'm just showing my American friend from work a little of the Island. Rudy stood as Robert said, "This is my colleague, an engineer from America, here for the year, Mr. Worth."

Rudy smiled and said, "I'm very happy to meet you. I'm Rudy Worth from HRM Aviation Company in America, and I do love your beautiful weather and fascinating island."

All in perfect British accented English, Nina said a few friendly words to Rudy, good-bye to Robert, and excused herself to keep up with her friends who had continued to slowly stroll. Robert turned to Rudy and said, "I went to school with her. She's nice enough, and popular, but not my type. Rudy, Rudy, did you hear me? Stop staring at them, pull in your tongue, and close your mouth. I know which back you're looking at; forget it! That's the untouchable Ana Boiano, who is far above our station in life.

"The Boianos live near here in Sliema. She spent a few years in Italy at a university, and has been back in Malta because her father needs her here full time. Now let's walk over to that kiosk and get a gelato. Otherwise I'll drop you off on Strait Street in Valletta where the bars and nightspots are, but leave your wallet with me." Rudy settled for the gelato, but filed the Strait Street name away for possible future reference, just in case.

A couple of evenings later Rudy found Mr. Farinacci standing outside his office, and asked if he had a moment for a quick question. The hotel manager immediately pulled Rudy into his office, indicated a chair, sat down at his desk, and spread his arms as a welcoming indication. Rudy said, "Mr. Boiano?" in a questioning way.

Mr. Farinacci quickly asked if Rudy had a question about his business with the Malta bank, since all was going smoothly as far as he knew. Before a puzzled Rudy could answer, Mr. Farinacci added that Mr. Boiano was the bank's President. "No, no," Rudy said. "Not that kind of question. I mean the Boiano family in general. They live in Sliema? I was just wondering about Mr. and Mrs. Boiano and their family."

Mr. Farinacci looked questioningly at Rudy and explained that unfortunately Mrs. Boiano had died some years ago while in Europe, of an illness. The family, as it has been for several years, consists only of Mr. Boiano and his daughter Ana, who have always lived in a very nice home in Sliema. The daughter studied at the University of Bologna, in management and international business, but is a true Maltese and returned from the University as soon as she graduated, or perhaps shortly before that. She has lived with her father and runs the family household and represents its activities as well as acting as her father's personal assistant. She is highly intelligent, known in the community, "And Rudy, if you would see her you would understand that she is one of the most beautiful young women in

57

Malta, but thus far not one of our would-be suiters has captured her attention. But perhaps you have asked about the family because *you have already seen her?*"

It occurred to Rudy, once again, that Mr. Farinacci was a pretty smart old man. "Well yes, but only as she and her friends walked by at the beach last Sunday. One of her friends stopped to chat with my work colleague, but Miss Boiano only strolled by. I had a very brief look, but I think she certainly is a very attractive woman!"

"Ah, Rudy Worth," Mr. Farinacci said, "good luck to you. I think you have a little *fallen in love at first sight?* If the right time ever comes, I know Mr. Boiano and could put in a good word. But from what I have heard about the daughter, she is difficult to approach. At first you will need to be properly introduced. But, Rudy, proceed carefully and slowly, I advise you. Learn all you can about her, consider carefully, and then devise whatever your next step is to be. But tread slowly, I advise you. I earnestly advise you."

Rudy nodded slowly, almost as if he understood what this local wise man was telling him.

CHAPTER 8

THE INTRODUCTION

Sliema
Two Weeks Later

A few days after Rudy's conversation with Mr. Farinacci concerning his chance sighting of the devastating Miss Boiano, Rudy was cornered by one of the technicians assigned to assist with assembling the P-36. Paul Lafessi explained that he is the brother of Nina, who had talked briefly with Rudy at the beach two weeks ago. He was inviting Rudy to Sunday dinner at the request of himself and Nina, but especially his mother, who strongly insists that the American engineer must have a proper home-cooked Malta dinner. The family lives near Sliema, and Paul will get Rudy at the hotel, on his motorbike, next Sunday at one o'clock.

Rudy agreed with thanks, not only in anticipation of a family meal, but thinking that perhaps he could skillfully learn more about Ana from Paul's sister. After all, he mused, when the Curtiss executives had questioned him about any ties to Buffalo, he successfully minimized his balancing act of several girlfriends from Buffalo and Penn Yan. Or perhaps, at that interview, he had forgotten entirely to mention this? Thus he should be able to subtly raise a couple of questions with Nina about her activities and friends in Malta without even revealing his actual purpose.

He is, he judged, a bit more sophisticated than he lets on to others, and the time has come to use his older male experience!

Thus, early on a warm Sunday afternoon, Rudy found himself on Paul's motorbike, headed to a home-cooked meal, and clutching both a wrapped bouquet of flowers for Mrs. Lafessi and the back of Paul's belt to keep from falling sideways on the tight turns north of Valletta. Heading at speed toward neighboring Sliema, Paul skirted west around the large and complex Marsamxett Harbour, past the bridge to Manoel Island, and pulled into a short gravel driveway in front of a tidy cream colored stone-block two story house. The engine was shut down, the kickstand dropped in place, and Paul, Rudy, and the bouquet slid off the bike and entered into the welcoming arms of Mrs. Lafessi.

In passable English she told Rudy how happy she was to meet Mr. Worth, the engineer her son so admired, and to finally have him in her home. Nina, in a perfect British accent, reached over to take the bouquet and to welcome Rudy, thanking him for the flowers and promising a true Maltese family dinner. She hoped he was hungry! Rudy was introduced to Nina's younger sister Mila who, he learned, was preparing to enter her first year of college here on Malta.

On the trip up from the hotel, Paul had yelled back to Rudy that his grandmother, who lived on the smaller nearby island of Gozo, was ill, and that his father had been up there to stay with her since Friday. He would miss today's dinner, but is eager to meet Rudy. He, like Paul, is a shop technician, but in a senior position, with many more years experience with RAF planes.

After glasses of Maltese wine for all in the sitting room, Mrs. Lafessi instructed them to be seated in the dining room while she brought in the first course. Following the *Minestra* soup of vegetables topped with a spoonful of ricotta cheese and accompanied by bread brushed with olive oil, sweetened tomato paste, onions, olives, and capers – called, they told him, *hobz-biz-zejt* – she brought in a small slice for each of a locally prized *Torta Tal-lampuki* fish combined with walnuts, olives and raisins.

This was followed by a main course of braised veal stuffed with ham, cheese, and herbs. Rudy, from his experiences in Buffalo's Italian restaurants, saw this delicious dish as similar to beef bracciole or veal rollantini. It was accompanied by roasted potatoes, and called *bragioli* in Maltese.

Along with wine, Rudy was greatly impressed with both Maltese cuisine and the amount of food he had consumed. Still, he answered Paul's question regarding room for dessert with a firm "Yes," but at the same time that a noise in the driveway caused Nina to suddenly stand and say she would "See who that might be!"

As the noise shifted from the driveway to the front door and then toward the dining room entry, Rudy, still thinking about the promised dessert, did not notice the sly smile and soft giggle thrown in his direction by Mila, the younger sister. "Oh, said Mrs. Lafessi, "it looks like Nina's friend has stopped by. Please come in my dear; you are just in time to join us for *Qubbajt* and coffee. And to meet Paul's colleague at work, all the way from America!" Realizing that Nina and someone else were coming into the room, Rudy turned his head in that direction.

As they entered, Nina turned to her friend and said, "And this is Paul's American aeronautical engineer work friend, Rudy Worth. Rudy, this is my friend Ana Boiano.

Whereupon, Rudy, a self-described sophisticated adult male American, boasting much experience with women, leaped up, forcing his chair to be knocked backwards to the floor, his water goblet set to rocking, and Mila set to giggling. Paul rushed to right the chair while Miss Boiano said, "I'm so pleased to meet our American visitor. Are you enjoying our country, even in these trying times?"

Rudy could hardly stammer a sensible reply as he now fully realized that this most entrancing woman stood before him in Mrs. Lafessi's dining room, addressing him in the softest, most entrancing voice, and with the most enticing accent – later identified by Mr. Farinacci as Itlo/Maltese/English, probably practiced for the occasion.

Mila had stopped giggling, prompted by a glare from Mrs. Lafessi, who then ordered Paul to place a chair for Ana. Mila would set places for dessert and coffee, the dessert being home-made *Imqaret*, telling Rudy these were deep fried sweet pastry filled with her secret mixture of dates and spices. The coffee would be Italian. Ana was carrying two books and offered them to Mila, now seated next to her, commenting that these had served well as beginning texts in business subjects when she was at University, and perhaps Mila could now benefit from them in her upcoming college classes.

Mila gave voluminous thanks, somewhat cut short by Nina's observation that, "it was so nice of you Ana, to stop by chance on a Sunday afternoon just to drop them off. But we're delighted that you did, and just when we have our American guest trying some of my mother's Maltese recipes."

"It's no bother, since I want Mila to have a head-start on her first year at college. And how nice to meet an American. Will you be here for very long, Mr. Worth? Rudy's answer to Ana sounded like, "I hope so, very much, because I'm overcome by the beauty!" It was added to by Paul, who said, "Rudy is here representing American President Roosevelt, and is conducting secret projects to aid Malta, just in case the worst thing happens!"

Rudy pulled himself together, gazing across the pastry and coffee cups to Ana, and explained his small contribution to making Malta safer by conducting a project for the HRM Aviation company, in concert with the RAF. "So, Miss Boiano, I believe that I'll be working here for at least a year."

"Well," Ana replied, looking directly at Rudy, "as does my Country, I certainly appreciate anything you can do to safeguard us. I think my father believes the worst will come about, and quickly, and I would like to know more about your project, but as Paul said, this is secret, so I understand. But I must say, Mrs. Lafessi, you are the best pastry chef in Malta. This dessert is the best I've had. It has to be your secret mixture! Two secrets on the same afternoon!"

After a few more minutes of conversation, with Rudy's heartbeat slowing down and his ability to respond calmly and intelligently to Miss Boiano improving, Paul remarked that he and Rudy should begin to think about getting back to the hotel, since tomorrow would be a full workday at Kalafrana and the ride back to Rudy's hotel should be taken in good daylight.

Instantly, and as with one voice, Ana said she had her car outside and was heading south on another errand anyway and could easily drop Mr. Worth at his hotel, Nina said that was so nice to offer, and Mrs. Lafessi, looking sternly at her son, said, "That's a very good idea, Paul, because tonight you can then fix Mila's desk lamp in her room so she can look through those text books Ana brought her." Mila instantly said, "Yes Paul, I'll need that light working tonight!"

Paul, somewhat bewildered, noticed Rudy's slight nodding smile, and agreed that a car ride did sound better than a motorbike.

Following good-byes and thank yous, and genuine praise from Rudy for a spectacular meal, Ana and Rudy walked a few steps to her car, a Fiat but a different model from Robert's. Rudy judged it very much newer than Robert's, understandably a function of economics. As soon as she started the motor, a powerful one, Ana backed skillfully onto the road, shifted into first gear, and asked Rudy if he minded riding with a woman driver. Before he could answer, she slid into second gear, gunned the engine a bit, and smoothly dropped into third.

Rudy, by now assured, told her that his sister drove as well as any man and that his family owned a busy vehicle center in Watkins Glenn, New York, very near a famous race car track. He was quite accustomed to excellent women drivers.

During the drive to Rudy's Palazzo Hotel, Ana talked about the many places and sites of interest on both islands – Malta and Gozo – and explained that the tiny island called Comino, lying between Malta and Gozo and site of the magical Blue Lagoon, had only a few residents and was largely unsettled. Rudy did his best to respond in an intelligent, interested, and sophisticated way, while even on the tightest turns of the road never taking his eyes off his driver.

All too soon, he realized, Ana had pulled to the front of the hotel. Rudy, thinking this might be his last chance, turned toward her and started to say how much he...but was stopped abruptly by her turning to him, touching his cheek with her hand, and saying, "Rudy, stop. Don't say more. I know, I know. But let's wait and see what may come now that we're officially introduced. I saw you when you were introduced to Nina by Robert and wondered what type of man this American visitor might be, so as you perhaps recognize, our meeting today was prearranged by my friend and her family, even young Mila. All except Paul, who, I'm sure, is still wondering how that little act about the ride back happened so quickly.

"But I must tell you that there is a more pressing reason for my wanting to meet you today. As you may know, my father is the head of Banco Malta, where all of your financial arrangements are conducted. Your reasons for being here are no secret to him. And, he suspects, no secret to the group of pro-Italian Maltese who have their own agenda. My father is a strong Maltese patriot and serves as chairman of a committee of like minded who are pushing our English Governor, General Bonham-Carter, to quickly approve an action plan in preparation for a possible war or attempted takeover of Malta by Benito Mussolini.

He has been talking to me about this, since I organize and file the notes of his committee meetings. When he said that he was looking for a good reason to talk with you about their goals, I volunteered to speak informally with you first. And here I am, now doing that. Would you be willing to meet privately with him?"

Rudy immediately agreed, and as he did Ana told him he would quickly receive a message from her father. Hand on the gear shift, she added, "Wonderful! I'll pick you up next Saturday at ten for sightseeing. Please ask the hotel to prepare a picnic lunch for two and I'll see you then." An astounded but very pleased Rudy had no choice but to slide out and push the door shut, as she gunned the Fiat away from the curb.

CHAPTER 9

THE WING COMMANDER'S MEETING

RAF Kalafrana Workshops
July 1939

THE day following his official introduction to Ana Boiano, Rudy was snapped from his girl-of-my-dreams musings by Foster's announcement that they were both going to a meeting just called by the RAF boss of the Kalafrana Aircraft Shops, Wing Commander Bartell, agenda not yet revealed. "First time he's done it this way, with no pre-alert and no agenda items even hinted at," complained Foster.

In the meeting room were several RAF administrative officer types, one of whom Rudy had already met in passing. Although he couldn't recall the name, he remembered the man had been described as both a pilot and an experienced engineer. Three civilians were already seated at the table, one of whom, Foster whispered to Rudy, "Is the new aide to Malta's Governor, General Sir Bonham-Carter. I imagine that's why this quick hurry-up meeting. And that RAF Captain, the tall chap standing near the last chair at the side of the table, is the Administrative Deputy to our new and not-yet-arrived Air Commodore Fairthorpe, soon to be Bartell's boss. Something's up!"

As Foster and Rudy pushed toward adjacent seats, Wing Commander Bartell strode into the room and headed for the chair at the head of the table. While Rudy quickly claimed a chair, he saw that all of the RAF uniformed personnel, and even Foster, now a civilian, remained standing until Wing Commander Bartell took his seat. The group was thanked by Bartell for attending on short notice, the reason being that Malta's Governor only yesterday ordered an up-to-date estimate of air protection for possible defense of Malta.

"The Governor," Bartell said, "is represented here by Mr. Francis Simmons, recently appointed as the Governor's Special Aide for War Measures Planning." Mr. Simmons half-smiled and nodded at those others around the table. Dressed for a business meeting, he opened a brief case from which he extracted a pad and pen which he set before him on the table. Looking around the group, he sat back and smiled again at each, most especially at those in uniform, especially including Captain Donalds, who nodded recognition in return. Apparently they had met before, thought Rudy, watching the interchange. The purpose of this gathering obviously was not a total surprise to all, so Rudy became even more observant, alert to his HRM charge to assist not only with preparation for an air war, but to render assistance to overall war planning.

Bartell went on to say that the attendees would provide the necessary information as each reported during this meeting, and Mr. Simmons would compile a draft RAF/Air Protection report for review, emendations, and final concurrence by this same group. A similar process would be followed with the two other key groups, one representing naval forces and the other ground defense forces. The latter would have anti-invasion and anti-aircraft defenses in its purview.

After further consultation with key staff and the Air, Naval, and Ground Forces Commanders themselves and, of course, the London War Office and Committee of Imperial Defence, the Governor, as Commander-in-Chief of Malta, would soon issue a Combined Action Plan. Steps to be taken for the protection and well-being of the Island's population, should bombing ever occur, would be recommended separately by the new Special Constabulary, headed by the respected Dr. Albert Laferla, who is also the Island's Director of Education.

Wing Commander Bartell was hosting this meeting, he explained, because his Shop facility was convenient to Hal Far air group, the naval personnel offices, and the Kalafrana technical support and air personnel. He then relinquished the chair to RAF Captain Donalds, Administrative Officer to Air Commodore Fairthorpe, who has already been appointed by the Air Ministry as Air Officer Commanding Malta, but not arriving until November. "Fortunately," Bartell observed, "Captain Donalds is well acquainted with the current situation on Malta, and is in very frequent contact with our absent Air Commodore, who is completing his duties at Air Ministry."

When introduced as leader of the assembled group, Captain Donalds stood and, as Foster later commented to Rudy, illustrated his keen awareness of the current air protection situation for Malta by stating that the planning work of the group should hardly be oppressive, since now, getting toward the end of July 1939, almost all of the military aircraft previously stationed on Malta with their pilots had already been flown off to Royal Navy carriers, Gibraltar, or Alexandra.

Further, since a Home Office decision not to try to defend Malta should war erupt with Italy already appeared to have been made, any remaining aircraft likely would depart Malta quite soon.

This clear but unexpected statement elicited a cry of "Hear! Hear!" from some RAF attendees, and frowns from two of the civilian attendees who, as Rudy now gathered, represented the British Government and the Malta Governor's position that Britain's foreign treaty obligations with such as France and Poland, and, certainly, defense of the Home Island, must be held paramount.

Rudy was surprised when Mr. Simmons spoke up and revealed that thus far in the current fiscal year, Malta's government had spent only a small fraction of one percent of its total budget on what might be termed "civil defense", while at the same time military strength apparently was being diminished significantly, if not totally, in many aspects.

The meeting had hardly progressed beyond Captain Donalds' opening pessimism when Foster slid a scrap of paper under Rudy's hand. Rudy paused a moment and then, clear of others' eyes, glanced down to read "Not a word about our crate." He nodded his understanding just as Mr. Simmons asked the group if he could at least record two possible air protection strengths: the status of Malta's airfields, and the rumor he had heard that quite a number of crated aircraft were waiting at the docks or elsewhere on Malta for pick-up by a Royal Navy aircraft carrier?

With an urging lifted chin from Captain Donalds, "Certainly," answered one of the RAF Officers whom Rudy recognized as the engineer/pilot, identified now as Squadron Leader, F.D. Slingerland the Command Engineer Officer. "In for a penny, in for a pound concerning our flying fields. Well, the oldest is Hal Far, opened shortly after World War I as a land base for the Fleet Air Arm, and still a single grass covered runway susceptible to rain caused mud and regularized resultant closings, plus strong crosswinds which challenge takeoffs and landings. New pilots quickly understand that, while one may choose not to take off, landing is quite another matter." This drew an inadvertent guffaw from Rudy, who, embarrassed, quickly looked down at the table top, avoiding Foster's glance in his direction.

"You all know it's near the Port, sometimes referred to as Marsa Scirocco," Slingerland continued, "with some hangars and repair facilities, and is connected by a fairly narrow dirt road, about a mile in length, extending to Hal Far from the seaplane slip and these Kalafrana Shops to its south. Typically, aircraft which must be towed from the Shops to the Hal Far strip must be towed with wings folded when so designed, or simply removed for others.

"About eight miles northwest is Takali, located on a wide and level grassland, once the basin of an ancient lake. The nearby hills and wind currents make for tricky landings, and during the wet season it's often not usable, since like Hal Far, it has no hard surfaced runway.

"Our third, and only other airfield, Luqa, is approximately half way between Hal Far and Takali, but is still very much under construction. It was begun last year and, when completed, will boast cross runways and taxiways, tarmac covered. But right now it's only a bit more than half completed, I would judge, with runways still awaiting their intended, necessary full length. And that's about it! Should we be happily swamped with Hurricanes and Spitfires come to save us, we'll be hard pressed to handle their arrival, their landing, and their on-the-ground protection, given the current lack of preparation and material resources."

"Thank you for that important information Squadron Leader Slingerland ," Captain Donalds said, as he looked toward Mr. Simmons. "Your second question was about some number of crated aircraft, possibly stored down at the docks or slip area, owned by the Royal Navy, and awaiting transport elsewhere by a carrier. I believe Wing Commander Bartell may have some information about that?"

It was Bartell who now stood, a note card in hand obviously in preparation for this question which reflected the somewhat widespread, optimistic rumor floating around the military personnel. "I do have some information, but I must point out that whatever are the actual facts concerning these crates and their history – and exactly how many and what they may contain – are a bit difficult to ascertain. There are several rumors concerning them circulating among us, so I ask you to understand that some details of what I shall now recite may not, in time, be proven entirely accurate. About three months ago, April of this year, 1939, 20 or more aircraft, biplane fighters called Sea Gladiators, designed during the mid 30's but constructed by the Gloster Company more recently than that, and possibly with some armament and other variations, were crated in England– not at all unusual – for transport by freighter here to Malta.

"Six or so of the crated aircraft were quickly transferred for use in the Middle East, and the remaining were assembled at Hal Far for use by a squadron aboard *HMS Glorious*, which was normally stationed at Alexandria. A month later, *Glorious* brought three of the crated Gladiators back here from the Middle East for assembly. They were assembled also at Hal Far and became part of the carrier's squadron.

"The squadron, #802, flying from Hal Far, then participated in a training exercise, a simulated Malta invasion, during which one of the planes went into the sea several miles south of here near a small island which is part of the Malta archipelago.

"Those remaining – all but that unfortunate one – formed the squadron and were flown from Hal Far to the *Glorious* on 6 June last, and currently thus, are not stored here on Malta. I cannot say what may transpire in future months, but they currently are not here on Malta. The rumors of their presence here, in July of 1939, are historical. Hence, at this time, they cannot be counted as resident protectors of Malta in Mr. Simmons's report. There are no longer any crated Royal Navy aircraft on Malta to the best of my knowledge and the confusing records I have located."

Before a breath or question sounded in the hushed audience, Captain Donalds thanked Wing Commander Bartell and observed that the forthcoming air preparedness report might be rather brief, although the assembled group should identify the very few RAF military aircraft remaining on Malta today and list them for Mr. Simmons. At that, in almost but not quite a whisper, someone said, "Let's not forget the Queen Bee!"

Immediately Captain Donalds turned again to Mr. Simmons, saying, "If you jotted that down, Mr. Simmons, we do have one unarmed radio-controlled, pilotless aircraft, capable of 100 miles per hour when towing a target for gunners. It is, I recall, a variant of the old Tiger Moth, but called the Queen Bee. We really should not credit it. However because Hal Far has been, and still is, a designated RAF Station, over the last decade it has been used as the land base for the squadrons of whichever Royal Navy carriers would visit Malta.

"As a result, several carrier type planes – from the old Hawker Demons to more recent Fairey Swordfish -- have, over the years, been in and out of Hal Far quite often. Unfortunately for us, they and the now much desired Hawker Hurricanes apparently are not available in these uncertain times." Mr. Simmons nodded his appreciation, while Rudy whispered to Foster his praise for Bartell's account of the mysterious crates. Foster nodded his agreement, recognizing that Bartell had referred only to RAF and Navy aircraft and not a certain P-36 painted in the colors of the French Armée de l'Air.

Captain Donalds gave the several raised hands an opportunity to speak opinions, raise questions, and generally lament their worrisome situation, and then called the meeting closed. He was speaking privately to Mr. Simmons as the others filed out, except for Foster and Rudy, who were beckoned to one corner by Bartell. "Captain Donalds wants a word with the three of us, so hang back a moment, please. Ah, here he comes."

The Captain indicated chairs at the corner of the table, they all sat, and Captain Donalds reached to offer his hand to Rudy. "We've not yet met, but I do welcome you – and HRM Aviation Company – as special friends of the RAF. According to my colleagues at the Air Ministry, we are going to be needing all the friends we can get, and quickly. So I ask, where are you with your experimental engine work, how can we use your findings, and what about the contents of your mysterious delivery?"

Rudy was eager to respond. "Last query first, Captain Donalds. The Curtiss P-36 fighter is ready for taxi tests and flying, but I have a thought about that. However, it's ready, armed, and fueled – with 100 octane, and that's another challenge. I've thought that we should keep its presence secret, and I want to discuss that with you as well. Men at the shops often say that the sometimes daily commercial Italian planes flying to Malta enable their pilots to photograph anything of military interest here on the Island.

"The crate containing the fighter also contained two wing cannon which possibly could replace the wing machine guns, but we'll need 20mm cannon shells for them in addition to .303 ammo for the two nose machine guns. I probably should pull the two wing machine guns and replace them with the cannon anyway, and keep my fingers crossed that we get some 20mm shells for them. Without the Gladiators, though, it looks like one P-36, unless we get some Hurricanes flown in, which you all seem very doubtful of. If we can quietly arrange for a secret airstrip or hangar someplace, I'll fly the Hawk there, complete with the French colors it arrived in, and hide it until needed!

"Concerning the engine experimentation, I've worked on the Bristol Mercury engine in the shop's test block and calculate a significant improvement in horsepower through the use of 100 octane fuel, a two stage blower rather than the existing one stage, and a helpful change in timing allowed by a reduction in engine temperature through the use of a methanol-water fuel injector. Foster knows as much as I do about where we are with that business, and our man in England sent along two injection kits for Bristol engines, which arrived on the plane that delivered me here. We may also be able to locate a couple of usable metal three bladed props as well.

"Also, we would want to fit all the biplanes with three bladed metal props, rather than the wooden two bladers, and get some decent spinners on the prop shaft ends. If we can find a more streamlined engine cowl that will work, we'd try that too. Over the several years of its development, Gladiator upgrades have improved its fly-ability and performance, and I believe we could continue that increase in performance and make a recognizable difference. Many of the Shop technicians are very familiar with Gladiators and are eager to see what we can accomplish with them.

"Some research by RAF Friends appears to indicate that one or more Gladiators were factory built complete with two additional universal machine gun mounts for pods under the main upper wing, in addition to the two fuselage guns and the two lower wing gun pods. One suspected serial number for this addition to the craft's fire power is 8042. This possibly could mean that, had we any Gladiators here, we could see whether a minor structural improvement to the inboard sections of the top wing could be so made and equipped, or if any wing modifications were even necessary other than actually using the upper pods as they were intended. I'm aware of the high performance of the newer Polish PZL fighters, and I've seen a couple of photos of their top wing cannon. I'd hope we could match them!

"Of course I'm concerned about total aircraft weight, since the more effective blower and the added fuel injection system obviously will add some pounds. We would, of course, if we end up with Sea Gladiators, remove the carrier arresting hooks and the inflatable lifeboat pods, and that would help us with a weight problem. However, if Gladiators can't climb fast enough, or fly fast enough to be effective, the number of guns won't make any difference in their usefulness. It's difficult to judge improvement trade-offs when we don't have an example to work with, as you know. Without any planes' engines to improve, we're stymied. If we are attacked, as they would say in Buffalo, we're likely up the creek without a paddle!" To which Captain Donalds responded, "Indeed," while Foster asked, "What's the name of that Buffalo Creek?"

Wing Commander Bartell who, as he once proclaimed to Rudy, currently was an RAF Commander with no planes to command, suggested that the several still open questions concerning the P-36 would be discussed by Rudy, Foster, and himself, and he would report back as soon as possible to the Captain with their suggestions.

Donalds agreed, and complemented Bartell: "That was skillful handling of the crated aircraft question raised by our Mr. Simmons, never wavering from the Royal Navy ownership of those crates, and no other. Although I expect that many, if not all, of the RAF in the room are well aware of what our American friend here has been putting together. But I also expect that there will be no spreading of that information by our people.

"To misquote an American – Mr. Franklin, I believe – who said we must all hang together, else we shall all be looking up at Italy's Reggia

Aeronautica on a Malta bombing run? Or something like that, Rudy? But bad pun's aside, you three, I expect that more likely the jockeying among our few remaining flying officer pilots has already begun concerning just who will be assigned to the P-39, should the proverbial balloon go up and those daily commercial Italian flying boats coming to Malta are replaced by Caproni bombers!

"Please do let me know your collective thoughts about our challenges, as I will have my bi-monthly situation report due Air Commodore Fairthorpe in a fortnight. Thank you all." With that, Captain Donalds strode off toward his office, and Bartell toward his.

As Rudy and Foster continued their way, Foster turned to Rudy in praise and some wonderment. "We'll, you certainly handled our activity report to Captain Donalds beautifully! Short and accurate, to the point and honest. And I believe he appreciated your quickly stating our pluses and minuses. Especially about hiding the plane until its really needed – great idea; just tell me where? And what a change in your *persona*--if that's the word-- as you responded to him. Decisive and...how do I describe it?"

"I think mature, experienced, clear thinking, decisive, and older-seem- ing than my young age would do it," said Rudy, "but that's more like the real me than the wide-eyed young man who wandered off the plane at a strange grass strip on a, please forgive me, strange island, and with a very strange assignment, less than two months ago.

But I should mention, first, that I've been thinking that I would be fly- ing the P-36, not some local pilot who's never been near a P-36 or even seen one before, and also, I've recently had what might perhaps, possibly turn out to be a life changing experience. So I've changed gears to a new but real me. Period!"

"Oh'" said Foster, "that explains it then. And I was thinking it might have been my example of a super, brilliant friend. But anyway, let me think about who should be our fighter pilot if the need arises at shooting time, and you give me some idea of where we might hide the plane after you test it out in the air, unobserved. And, don't forget, we must keep the good Captain's bi-monthly report in mind."

Late that same afternoon, when Rudy returned to his hotel, the young woman at the reception desk displayed her usual smile and handed him his room key. But this time she added an envelope, saying it had been delivered by messenger an hour ago. In very precisely written script it was addressed to Mr. Rudolph Worth, Eng. Just below his name and the added reference to Engineer was the word *Personal.* Rudy quickly took the envelope, his room key, and an anxious feeling in his stomach up the marble stairway to his floor. As he stepped into his room he tore open the glued flap and pulled out a half sheet of heavy watermarked bond. The top was embossed with a name in dark blue formal script.

CHAPTER 10

A DILEMMA

*A Private Dining Room at the Palazzo Arja Ocean Hotel
July 1939*

THE name embossed at the top of the few handwritten lines of the message was *Anthony R. Boiano*, causing Rudy to instantly recall Ana's question: "Would you be willing to meet privately with him?"

The message from Bank President Boiano was brief and to the point:

Mr. Worth, would you allow me the pleasure of your company as my guest at dinner tomorrow evening, Tuesday, at 7:00. This would allow us to discuss, informally, your impressions thus far of Malta, as well as our concerns over the current troubling world situation and the need for a thoughtful plan. If you are agreeable, simply inform Mr. Farinacci and he will send word to me tomorrow morning and prepare a special menu for the two of us in the small private dining room at the hotel. I very much look forward to meeting with you.'

Well, Rudy thought, he doesn't give me much choice, but I'd be crazy if I said no to such a prominent citizen and chair of the committee pushing for the Action Plan. Besides, this could be a chance to impress the old man with my personal suitability. Note in hand, Rudy rushed down to the hotel's lobby to see if he could catch Mr. Farinacci and get tomorrow's dinner set up tonight. No sense wasting time, he thought, thinking more of his interest in Ana than the Governor's directive about a needed plan for possible war.

The next morning at the Shops, Rudy consulted Foster about getting the P-36 up the road from the Shops to the Hal Far field. They would need to detach the wings, get a tow, and, once there, get the plane quickly into a closed hangar out of sight, so the wings could be reattached, wing machine guns switched for the two 20mm cannon, if possible, and a final check made.

Then, at a time when no Italian commercial flights were coming in and relatively few people were about, Rudy would do a couple of taxi tests and a take-off and go-around He really didn't know if Hal Far was long enough for touch-and-goes for the 36, but it had already occurred to him that he needed to measure out the length needed to safely take off. Likewise, he needed to judge what would be needed for a grass field landing, with full flaps or maybe a side slip to help.

Very important was the fact that 100 octane aviation gas was almost non-existent on the Island. He realized, also, that if he bent this plane out of shape he might as well take the next freighter back to Watkins Glen and see if his sister would hire him.

With thoughts of runway length needed, a secret hangar, and 100 octane fuel, he walked through the shop, stopping as he saw Paul. Paul greeted him, and as an aside, said to the older man he had been talking to, "Missier, this is the American engineer I've been telling you about, Rudy Worth, who is working to help us. Rudy, this is my father, Vincent. You didn't get to meet him at our dinner because he was checking on my grand-mother that Sunday."

"Mr. Lafessi," Rudy said, "I'm very happy to meet you. Paul is doing a great job on our project; you can be proud of him. I hope your mother on Gozo is feeling OK? I remember that you were in Gozo to help her when I had dinner at your home."

"Thank you for asking about her, Mr. Worth, but she's fine now and back, busy as ever, trying to get some light farming done using hired help. But you know how that is. I'm trying to convince her to at least slow down. I've told her, keep the old farmhouse and the best barn plus an *ettaru* or two for her garden, but sell the rest and start taking it easy. Without my father, who passed away several years ago, she just can't keep up with things. And I'm busy here at my job and can't get up there as much as she wants me to.

"Oh, I just used our Maltese word *ettaru* for the English hectare. If she kept only two hectares and sold the rest to neighboring farms, that would still give her about five acres, as you Americans would say, and that's more than she needs for her vegetables and a few chickens or rabbits. It's nice flat land pretty much, and for Malta, good soil for certain crops. There's a local farmer who would really like to buy those fields. My father never liked our common rock walls and spent years taking them down and clearing the surface. But if I know her, she's quietly in the process of signing over all of it to me, and staying right there and doing what she wants to do!"

"I really do want to visit Gozo," Rudy said, "and I hope to go up soon, perhaps this weekend. Where on Gozo is the farm? Does she have a lot of land?"

"Well you should get to Gozo, Mr. Worth. There's a great deal to see—a lot of historical and beautiful sights like the Calypso Cave, and especially the Citadel. My mother owns at least fifteen hectares, I would think. You'll drive right along them if you head toward The Citadel, which the British call Victoria.

"In fact, there's an ancient horse racetrack up there, on the road just southeast of a little place called Naghla, before you get to Victoria. When you get off the ferry, outside Mgarr, head north toward Nadur and keep going west toward Naghla, and then Victoria. That's the more scenic upper road. But I suggest a car, rather than a motorbike, or you'll be eating dust all the way. I'm always working here at the Shops or up at Hal Far, so let me know how you like Gozo. And I wish you the best with the Project. And thanks for the good words about Paul."

Rudy expressed his thanks for the directions, and said he expected they would soon have the chance for another conversation. He continued his search for Foster and found him instructing a technician on how to set the controls on a milling machine for a special repair job on the engine of the fast rescue boat usually stationed at the slipway.

"Oh, by the way, Foster, I think you said I should let you know when I discovered a good hiding place for the plane. I may have! What do you think of a stretch of farmland with a barn, up near the old racetrack, on Gozo? And it didn't take me all day to find it, either!"

Foster looked askance at Rudy. "You've been up there already?"

"No, but I intend to check it out on Saturday. I'm getting a ride to Gozo. Can we talk now about getting the plane up to Hal Far and into a closed hangar? We're ready to pull the wings back off, tow it up the road and hangar it. I'm eager to try a taxi run and then to get it off the ground and in the air when no one's looking. And don't tell me that's at 1:00AM. I once heard that only birds and fools fly, and birds don't fly at night."

"Do you also have one of those witty American sayings about our shortage of 100 octane?"

"Sure," said Rudy. "The only time you have too much fuel is when you're on fire. Ha, Ha! Seriously, do you think we might not get enough to actually use the plane if needed? Could we, instead, get octane booster additive to bring what gas we can get up to a higher no-knock level?"

"If we can't get the 100 in sufficient quantity brought in by a tanker ship or a cargo sub do you think your HRM man in England can ship us octane booster?" Foster had such a serious, semi-depressed look as he considered the fuel problem that Rudy wondered if all the work was going to be for naught, anyway.

With that depressing notion on his mind, Rudy took the earlier bus back to the hotel, thinking he had better look his best for tonight's dinner.

A minute or two before 7:00 Rudy reached the door to the small executive dining room Mr. Farinacci had pointed out the night before. Rudy looked in just as a short, stocky, quite distinguished looking older man in a tailored suit looked out the open door and strode to Rudy from the room, holding out his hand. "Ah, Mr. Worth. Welcome and thank you for coming here so that we can at last meet. I'm Anthony Boiano."

I've been wanting to meet you, Mr. Boiano, and I'm grateful for your invitation. I, too, am concerned about Malta's readiness for war, and I'm here to help with preparations in any way I can. And please call me Rudy."

"Rudy, then, let us sit, see what this fine hotel has prepared for us, and begin our discussion. My daughter has spoken well of you, as does Mr. Farinacci. By-the-way, he's a member of my Preparedness Plan Committee, which has great concern but not much of the British ear. We seem to generate noise, but little action from the Governor. Also, whenever the Committee reaches an agreement to move forward, even with a very small sub-project, to strengthen Malta, either or both the pro-Italy,or pro-Fascist group here on Malta has already moved politically to hinder us.

Nothing, I think, can be a secret on Malta! Perhaps with your insider's view, however, you can ease my fears?"

"I'm afraid not," Rudy responded, "since there are very few military resources left on Malta. Planning has only just last week gotten underway by the Governor's directive, and perhaps that will at last lead to some useful steps to safeguard the civilian population. But unless the British can free up some ships, planes, and pilots, there seems little can be done. I've learned only that a very, very small amount of your Malta budget has been spent on what we in America call 'self defense'. Why doesn't the Governor act as you believe he should?"

"Ah Rudy, I know you are not an innocent in these things, but add to that more anti aircraft guns and gunners," Mr. Boiano replied, "more search lights, and well equipped soldiers to hold back an invading force. Imagine what would happen if an enemy came by gliders or parachute? Even if they came by sea, all we have is a little barbed wire and a few cement bunkers. The English are worried about their so-called Home Island. Wonderful, but what about *our* Home Island right here in the middle of the Mediterranean and a few miles from Mussolini's boot! Even many English living here on Malta speak about returning to England now, before hostilities begin, and while passenger ships are still sailing. But to answer your question directly, for many reasons, all quite understandable, our Governor is incapable of varying from the dictates of British Parliament. After all, he is a long time, true Englishman, assigned here to govern as his higher power directs. I do not fault him for that, but I question the common sense, I think you call it, behind the decisions handed to him as a *fait accompli*."

As his host spoke, Rudy could see Mr. Boiano's face grow redder with anger and hear the bitterness in his voice. Rudy sensed he was in for a tricky evening's discussion he was ill equipped to manage. But Mr. Boiano obviously was trying to calm down, and forced himself to sit back in his chair and stop speaking, as a waiter served them a first course antipasto.

"Mr. Worth – Rudy – please understand that Malta has lived under the British flag for more than one hundred years. The British helped us drive out Napoleon, and not long after 1800 they took us on as a type of protectorate. Obviously, they realized how geography had made us a most valuable Mediterranean asset in what they saw as a profitable inland sea. As time passed, and especially after 1918 and the end of the war, the Treaty of Versailles' redistribution to England of much of the territory from Morocco east to Egypt caused Malta's importance to grow. As you know, we became the large, permanent British naval and air base between Gibraltar and Egypt. Vital, but not now, when compared with certain other needs of Great Britain at this time in history.

"But, perhaps more important, we became this part of the world's shipping and commercial center, with the profits of all that trade going - where would you think - toward England of course. As you can imagine, however, many, many Maltese looked not to England as our cultural, emotional, and ancestral home, but instead to Italy. And a high percentage of our quarter million population still see it that way. Now, with the world's important countries seeming to pick sides, our island contains a large percentage of pro-Italian Maltese. Add to this the fact that those Maltese who still entertain strong, favorable feelings toward the British Crown are becoming more and more dismayed at the withdrawal of our defenses, while the larger number of our people, seeing the same weakening, can only hope and pray that a war will bypass Malta, or that if Italy goes against England, Mussolini will respect a Maltese neutrality and our long-term friendship and relationship with his country.

"I know of no citizen here in Malta who has positive feelings for Hitler, but I understand that in America your President struggles against distinct pro-German citizen groups who have some political strength, thus he is limited in the material aid he can send us. But he, and others, Rudy, through HRM Aircraft Ltd., or more accurately for our discussion this evening, the operational arm called HRM Aviation, your President and others have quietly sent you here to aid us and, I know, to help keep us with England, not an uncertain Mussolini, and certainly not Fascist Germany.

"As an aside, as you can see, I am aware of the mission of HRM Aircraft, Ltd., and, as well, its operational subsidiary for which you labor, HRM Aviation. One controls the other's field operations and projects, so in Italy HRM Aviation might be categorized as an S.A. Organization – *Sociata Autonima*. I also know that our Governor firmly believes that all military resources possible must be kept available for defending not Malta, but England, France, and God knows which additional countries in Europe more important to the Crown than we 250,000 Maltese crowded onto this tiny island. What few troops we have – and believe me, they are few in number – and the few small, coastal ships we have with any armament, are here under English control and obliged to follow British policy and task directives.

"Mr. Worth, I ask you, I implore you! Can HRM Aircraft Company send us the planes and pilots we would need to defend us? Oh, I know that is impossible, but tell me, what can be done? What can you do in your role? Can you quickly build us fighter airplanes and find pilots for them? Is the secret plane I've heard about really your secret weapon? Can you change the Governor's thinking and reverse the outward flow of our soldiers needed to safeguard our shoreline? Are there not crates of fighter planes stored here and waiting to be assembled? Is there not a small group of influential RAF officers who want to get Malta at least more ready for a war, and are you not seen by them as a resource? Please forgive me, Rudy, for my carrying-on. I know how impossible Malta's current situation is, and yours also. Perhaps my best question really is, in your judgment, what can my Maltese Preparedness Planning Committee do to get some real action?"

Rudy's response was silence for almost a full half minute as he puzzled over just what his position in Malta's politics should be. Of course, he thought, this man has at least three roles in my life as an American in Malta: As head of the Banco Malta he manages my financial support from HRM; he runs a key citizens' war planning group; and he's Ana's father.

"I'm on Malta's side against the bad guys. I'm here representing the HRM Aviation's interest in helping the British prepare for a possible war. I realize, now that I've been here listening to others for two months, that many British officers and civilians are very concerned over leaving Malta defenseless. A 'Friends' group, of which I'm a member, was formed, and some of the people I've met also are 'Friends'. Tell me, Mr. Boiano, have you heard any talk about the Governor being replaced? Would a stronger Governor be able to improve your situation? Can pressure be put on the Home Office to bring that about?"

Mr. Boiano looked directly at Rudy and said, "Not only my committee, but several of our English residents with key contacts in London have moved to bring that about, and we are hopeful that a new Governor may be appointed very quickly, but who can tell? And such a person may be even less strong a leader than the current man!"

"OK," Rudy responded finally, "Give me just a couple of days, and I'll do my best to have some answers and recommendations for you. I'm here from HRM Aviation, under an RAF flag so-to-speak, and I'm here to do all I can to help Malta. But I need a couple of days to get some sensible ideas for a plan to you. Is that OK with you? I hope it is."

"Yes, Rudy, it certainly is, and I apologize for my approach to you. I know you'll do all you can. Simply let me know as soon as you're ready. Now let's finish this dinner, or I'll hear about it from Mr. Farinacci! Oh, before I forget, Ana asked me to give you an important message: 'don't forget to order the picnic lunch for Saturday.' Does that make sense to you?"

"Oh yes, And please give her a very important message from me: I must get to see Gozo on Saturday, so be prepared for sightseeing up there. It's most important. And thank you very much, Mr. Boiano. I learned a lot tonight! Let's hope something will come from our efforts, and those of your committee. With a few more pleasant words, the dinner and the discussion finished, Mr. Boiano went to his waiting car, and Rudy to an uneasy night's sleep.

CHAPTER 11

GOZO

August 1939

FOLLOWING his meeting with Mr. Boiano on Tuesday evening, Rudy spent the next three days thinking, listing available resources, and discussing ideas for additional resources with Foster. Despite what he had heard at the recent meeting of the Governor's War Measures Planning Group, he still was surprised at how short his list of military resources was proving to be. Fortunately, he thought, war would not come soon, and, hopefully, not at all.

If there had been any enjoyment in this exercise, it was during the time he spent in listing what, with a little imagination and a lot of luck, might be developed over the next year or so of his assignment. In fact, Rudy smiled at the prospect of a long stay on Malta. Along with his daydream of moving into a more prominent and heroic role, flashed a mental view of the blond haired, blue eyed, curvaceous and captivating Ana.

On Thursday morning Rudy stood talking with Foster in the outer office, near Robert's busy typewriter being pounded by the office clerk. Rudy had just finished describing how, on the coming Saturday, he was being driven by Miss Boiano to Gozo, where he would check out the possibility of establishing a semi-hidden airstrip, barn-type hangar, and work shed for the soon to be flown P-36 Hawk. Foster inquired if Miss Boiano had already agreed to provide Rudy's needed transportation, when Robert began to struggle between coughing and loud laughter. "Oh good grief, Foster, half the population of Valletta knows that our friend Rudy here and the lovely Miss Boiano are already an item, having met only last week! Where have you been with the local gossip?"

"Yes, yes," replied Foster. "I caught-on when Rudy told me he'd met privately with Mr. Boiano."

"Hold on a minute," Robert squawked, "are you saying that the romance has progressed that far after just one week?"

"Calm down, both of you." Rudy jumped in, "That was a meeting about Mr. Boiano's Preparedness Planning Committee. We hardly even mentioned his daughter."

"I'll bet," Robert threw in, "but this reminds me, Rudy. Don't take the bus back to your hotel this afternoon. Ride with me; I need to check something with you and we can talk as I drive. We can leave whenever you're ready."

Not much later, while bouncing along in the old Fiat, Robert suggested that Rudy join him for a drink at the Hotel's small bar. "Sure," answered Rudy. "A cold beer would be nice on a hot day. Park this thing and the beer's on me!"

In fifteen minutes, both were seated at a corner table for two in the lounge of the Hotel Palazzo, each having taken the first sip of a cold Cisx lager, Malta's favorite beer. Robert opened the conversation by asking if Rudy's hotel and financial arrangements were working out.

"Fine." the American said. "This place is great, the Manager is really helpful, and HRM is following through just as they said they would. I've no complaints, and the arrangements you and Foster made for me at the Shops are really outstanding. What do you need to check with me about today, as you said?"

"Rudy, I apologize for bringing up something that relates to your personal life here in Malta, but I feel I should, since I'm a little bit responsible for what I think I should mention. After all, I'm the one who pointed out Ana Boiano to you, that Sunday afternoon at the beach."

"I'm glad you did, Robert, I'm really glad. Is something wrong? What's up?"

"No, nothing's really wrong, but what I mentioned about Ana that afternoon – about her university in Italy and coming home to help her father's business – that stuff. You remember? I really didn't mention the whole story about her coming home. Didn't even occur to me. Just gossip, anyway, but since you've gotten semi-serious about her? Anyway, there may not be anything to it, but the rumors at the time were that there was some kind of a problem about a professor who was supposed to be there on some kind of exchange from America. Never any details, probably just a bunch of jealous girls here who...well, I just thought you, being from America and all, should be alert in case some busy-body here brings it up, or maybe some local guy who couldn't get anywhere with her and has a grudge against you. So that's it, and I only want to alert you, just in case!"

"Oh Boy," came softly from Rudy. "Oh Boy," even more softly. A long breath, quietly expelled followed both, and that was followed by a tightened mouth and a "What the hell could that mean?"

"I'm sorry, Rudy. I never should have brought it up. I'm sorry, and I emphasize it was just a bunch of empty gossip. I never should have repeated it!"

"Don't fret, Robert. I've not had the chance to learn anything at all about her, but this Saturday I shall. And she'll learn some things about me. How old would you say she is? I've been thinking maybe 23 or 24. That puts me five or six years older, at least. Being assigned here by HRM Aviation is the most complicated thing that's happened so far in my life. I guess I'd better find out about hers. I suppose I got interested in her based on her looks. I've never really met a woman who affected me this quickly or this way before. Cripe! OK, I'm OK and ready for Saturday. Do you want another beer? I do."

After Robert left, speaking not a word other than a quiet goodbye, it occurred to Rudy that he'd better order Saturday's picnic lunch, stop imagining the worst concerning Ana, and get his mind focused on the report he promised to Mr. Boiano - Ana's father and Chairman of the Preparedness Committee.

Fortunately, Foster really was interested in the Gozo airstrip idea, and had checked the Malta to Gozo ferry schedule for Saturday. Learning that a 10:00 am pick-up at the hotel would not get them to the Malta ferry slip in time for the 10:30 ferry, Rudy, thinking he should get word to Ana, was spared a problem when the hotel receptionist told him Friday morning that there was a message saying his Saturday morning pick-up would be at 9:15, and his lunch basket would be at the front desk by 9:00. Apparently, Ana had gotten Rudy's message and was planing ahead. So was Rudy, for his upcoming conversation with her.

Friday morning, at the desk in his workroom at the Kalafrana shop, Rudy see-sawed between writing out for Mr. Boiano's committee a list of the extremely limited aviation resources still available on the island, and mentally listing the topics and sub-topics to be fitted into Saturday's trip with Miss Boiano-- as he now began to think of her, unconsciously prompted by Robert's gossip. All of this was interrupted by the same Robert, who seemed to fly into the room.

"Rudy, I've just learned that Paul Lafessi has his eye on a real motor-cycle, a Ducatti, that's up for sale by a guy in Birgu. But he can't buy it until he sells his little bike; you know, the one you had a ride on up to his house. That's a great little bike, Rudy. It's an English Vincent – the Rapide model, the one with a V-twin engine. Paul's really taken great care of it, and, you know, it will carry two and still move right along. That bike would save you bus fare every day and get you wherever you want to go. You wouldn't need a license to drive it, and I'll show you how to transfer ownership and get a new tag for it! You really should get to Paul right now, before somebody else in the shop gets it. I know he'd give you a good deal! He bought it from a UK officer who was being transferred. I'm thinking it was in '37, and I believe he paid just under 100 pounds for it."

"You think so? I rode a motorcycle back home, and I guess I could learn to ride on the left side of the road here. I could set a better time schedule for work than I can riding the bus, and begin to see more of Malta than just walking Valletta streets, that's for sure. I wonder what he wants for it? I could probably keep it just under my window, out back of the hotel; it must have some kind of a lock, I would think."

"Ask him, Rudy. He was just behind me coming into the shops and he's just out in the main area. He really thinks highly of you and I just know he'd give you a better than fair price. And you can afford it, for heaven's sake!"

So in less than fifteen minutes Rudy became the proud owner of Paul's former Vincent Rapide motorcycle for 94 British Pounds, or about 450 US dollars. Paul went off to close the Ducatti purchase, and Robert began telling Rudy about where they would go today to switch ownership and get a new tag for the back end. "But," asked Rudy, "don't I need to get some kind of insurance first," thinking of how things worked back in Buffalo?

"Please, Rudy," Paul answered, "Let's get the bike registered and have you ride it back to the hotel and get it parked wherever your friend the Manager wants. Paul gave you the keys, so park and lock it, and forget it until Sunday. Remember, tomorrow's a big day for you. I'll follow you in the Fiat and we'll come back here to the Shops and finish up our work. Then I'll drive you back to the Palazzo for the last time and you can plan your wardrobe for the big day."

Wardrobe was the operative word in Robert's suggested plan for the remainder of the day, as far as Rudy was concerned. Thus, on being returned to the hotel, Rudy went immediately to his room and dug through every item of clothing he could find, searching for choices that would lend him an aura of sophisticated, urbane charm tomorrow. Oh, and strength of character and intelligence as well. They could be very important, he chided himself, as he resolved for the tenth time to totally forget the visiting American Professor.

The next morning, in front of the Hotel clutching a picnic basket, and bouncing from one foot to the other in a nervous rhythm, Rudy peered down the street. Ana's Fiat arrived from the other direction and glided to a stop at the curb "Hello there," she called, leaning over to unlatch the passenger door. "You can set that beautiful basket on the rear seat, and we're off to the Gozo Ferry".

"Hello to you, and thank you for changing our plans and for spending the day checking out an important possibility in my personal planning. And thank you for looking so beautiful! I mean, you always look beautiful. I mean...oh,I hope you know what I mean?

"Thank you, Rudy. You look rather splendid yourself, dressed for an adventure on such a nice day. I'm glad we're getting to Gozo, no matter the reason. It's going to be a spectacular day for touring. While I get us to the ten o'clock ferry, perhaps we could get to know each other? I know you're an American sent here, my father insists, to play a key role in getting us ready for a likely war. Malta needs to hope for the best but plan for the worst, he recites daily. But beyond that, I'd love to know more about you, your family in America, your aviation work, and what you think of our little island. And certainly all you're doing to get us better prepared for a possible war." All of this was said as she smiled frequently at her passenger and tooled the Fiat through the traffic and up the hills away from the bay.

Obligingly, and missing the opportunity to ask the same of her, Rudy talked through much of the personal and professional history he had presented three months earlier to the Curtiss and HRM executives in Buffalo, but never getting near his switching to HRM Aviation, or the special briefings he had received before, during, and after his getting to Malta. Rather, general research in improving aircraft engine performance was as far as he thought he should get in his description of professional work. After all, he realized, if she runs the files system for her father's committee, she'll get some details from his reporting session. But I've got better stuff to talk about with her besides how bad things look for Malta if shooting really starts.

It occurred to him at that exact moment, also, that any detailed business of the P-36 should remain within the RAF circle until others needed to know, although her father apparently had a strong suspicion. Today's scouting of Gozo would have to reveal a personal flying interest in creating a small airstrip on that tiny island, away from the congestion and bustle of the main island. Rudy had already described his flying activities back at Penn Yan with the little Mercury racer, and how much he missed that kind of week-end enjoyment. Naturally, he reasoned to himself, having the invitation offered to him of a car and fascinating driver on a seldom free Saturday couldn't be missed. And it would be reasonable for Ana, or anyone else, to assume he was intending to get an older small, used plane for his spare time enjoyment, with occasional week-end flights based on Gozo Island.

Once Rudy had finished describing himself and his work interests, he stopped to catch his breath, giving Ana the opportunity to ask, "So, Rudy, you have left your mother and father and your other loved ones back in the

United States? Although, you didn't say that your former position at the Curtiss Corporation in Buffalo remains open for your return from your new HRM position and assignment. So naturally I wonder about your future. After all, you're still a young man. But what about your friends in Buffalo? You must miss them?"

Rudy, baffled over possible hidden reasons for that question, still had a ready answer: "No, not really! There's only my sister at home in Watkins Glen with my parents, and the guys – I mean the men I worked with when I was with Curtiss, and the men I flew with on most weekends – and I can easily live without them for a year. I do send a note to my parents and sister about once a month. I had a few dates with some young women in Buffalo, but my job at Curtiss was very time demanding, and I certainly don't hear from any of them.

"No, I'm not corresponding with anyone back there in the States, except my HRM contact, and that's only once a month. So while I may get a bit homesick occasionally, I'm really fully into my life here, as work oriented as it is, but I'm hoping to change that. Yesterday I bought a small motorcycle, so beginning next week I 'll be able to get around without having to depend on the bus schedule, even to get to and from work, or to do other things."

"So, I'm happy to learn that there will be some *things*, as you call them, in place of your professional assignment. How interesting! What might they include, and just what kind of engineering projects are you conducting at Kalafrana?"

"Well, they certainly might include my strong interest in a stunning new acquaintance, one who has a very nice Fiat convertible and a father who has pushed me into a bit of a dilemma. She's also very intelligent, I might add, since she has already gotten me to recite my life's history without my knowing even where she lives."

"Well, you fool, if you're good I might drive you by where I live with the father you speak of, in Sliema, but what is this dilemma he's handed to you? Has he been getting into his favorite history of the pro-British Constitutional Party versus the Nationalist Party. You know, I expect, that he's a Maltese patriot who is torn between his respect for what the British have provided his beloved Malta over many decades, and his desire for

Malta's self rule. And I should add, his natural fondness for Italy, with which we all, and certainly including myself, naturally feel a very strong cultural kinship, or so the Nationalists say."

"My dilemma," Rudy responded, "has me torn by the knowledge that the British government deliberately and perhaps heartlessly appears to be leaving Malta and its people high and dry, as they say in Buffalo, and my HRM assignment to help the almost non-existent Royal Air Force left in Malta. By-the-way, I complement you on your ability to change the subject. That slick-switch from my history to yours was well done. Does my now favorite street in Sliema have a name? What else may I learn about you?"

"Give me a moment to drive what you say is your favorite auto onto the ferry and I'll tell you about me, or at least the basics. The autos in line ahead of us appear to be moving, so here we go to the island of Gozo."

With that, Ana slowly followed the two cars ahead of her onto the ferry, stopped where the attendant pointed, shut off the motor, and pulled on the hand brake, as instructed by the signs fastened every several feet along the boat's side rails. "Come on," Rudy. "it's required to leave your auto and go out to the stern, where the benches are. Let's get some sunshine!"

Well, thought Rudy, now let's see what she finally has to say about herself. This could be interesting, but could the visiting professor business really be a deal breaker to me? I'll have to learn more about it before I get off this bus ride she's got me jumping on. After all, there was what's-hername back in Buffalo, and the other whats-their-names, too, and I hardly remember them now.

Slightly uneasy, whether from the memory of his Buffalo adventures, or in anticipation of the next few minutes, Rudy followed Ana to an empty bench seat. "OK", he said, "it's your turn."

"This won't take as long, since I'm only 24," Ana started, seemingly in jest, but given away by her own shaky voice. "I was born into a loving and comfortably well-off family in Malta. My father has always been in business and finance, and we - my father and I - still live in the house on Amery Court, not far from Tower Road, where I lived as a child in Sliema. I went to a Catholic girls school and had a nice childhood, but just before

I finished my academy education, very sadly, my mother took a short trip to Italy to visit some distant relatives who lived near Padua, caught some kind of a sickness, perhaps a flu, was put in hospital, and passed away within four days.

My father was devastated! I was devastated! As you may know, my father has not remarried, but has counted on me since then, although for the first three years or so I, too, was in Italy for months at a time, to the highly respected University of Bologna. With my father's funding, and at his urging, I studied management and finance and did well in my studies, at least for the first two and a half years." With those words, Ana began to tremble and hesitate with words, but after a long pause and an obvious gulp of air, she continued in a strained voice, uttering almost each phrase slowly.

"I began to realize that my father saw me returning with my degree, and functioning as his personal assistant, I missed my mother terribly, I missed my home and Malta, and I know now that I was rebelling against those several forces I couldn't control. Somehow I became friendly, overly friendly, with a visiting instructor who was teaching in the business school as part of an American exchange program. He was very attentive to me, more than sympathetic and understanding, and I was more than stupid and naive. This continued for three months, but it all caught up with me, for both better and worse, when his American wife came over for an unannounced visit. It took her less than a day to learn what was happening, for a blowup to capture much attention, and about three days for the head of the business program to fire the American and call me in for a very terrible and humiliating session.

"I was more than embarrassed. I was more than humiliated. I was identified as Miss Idiot, and worse, a naive, immature, stupid girl from Malta. I knew that the several other students from Malta would spread the story, probably with embellishments, quickly back to here. The only good news was that I knew I probably wasn't going to be pregnant, no matter what the gossip speculated. To shorten a long story, the Dean un-enrolled me and I returned home.

"For weeks I wouldn't even leave the house in daylight, but that didn't matter, since the role of father's personal assistant became my salvation.

That and very helpful private sessions with a counseling physician friend of my father's, are the only reasons, even now, that I can tell you this without collapsing." At this, Ana's voice and body were shaken by several sobs. There were no tears, but Rudy was overcome with Ana's obvious emotion and with the sense that he possibly was the only person other than the physician to have heard this directly from her."

She spoke again: "Rudy, tell me the truth. Had you already heard this awful story about me? Is that why you were so careful to tell me that you're not married to a woman in America? No, don't answer! I don't care! What matters is that I'm very afraid of...No. Don't reach out. Don't touch me! I'll learn how you feel about me soon enough. And I'll know what I might feel for you. Maybe I'm just afraid of American men, and that's why I asked those probing questions?

"I can't tell yet. Let's just return to the car and find that little airstrip for your piloting hobby, or whatever it's called. Isn't that why you got me to drive you up here? So you can have your week-end fun with some little airplane you've got your eye on? While my father thinks you're trying to save his country?

And please don't do or say anything. We'll both know soon enough if we want to happen what might happen between us. We'll drive straight up to the center of Gozo's farmland now, while you look for a suitable whatever it is you're looking for. Just nod *yes* if you agree."

Rudy, wisely, simply nodded his head, mouth shut, and hands at his sides. And so the hunt for a suitable place for Rudy's next venture went on with no further talk of Ana's obviously upsetting university incident. Without much of a plan, and without much conversation, they drove right by the farm property described to Rudy by Vincent Lafessi. Rudy judged as much, having noticed the old racetrack, the flat fields, the absence of stone walls, and the large barn as they drove closer to Victoria on the northern route. Without knowing exactly why, Rudy never commented to Ana that he was looking directly at a splendid potential site for the Hawk.

CHAPTER 12

WAR NEWS

Malta
August 1939

RUDY'S thoughts on the quiet Sunday spent alone, the day after his scouting trip to Gozo, the trip which had been made momentous by Ana's disconsolate recounting of her University misadventure, brought no happiness to him. Yes, he knew, the Lafessi farm on Gozo was as ideal as he could find for a hidden-away airstrip. A grass runway on long, flat, well-drained earth with no stone fences could easily be mowed, and an oversize barn plus a couple of smaller ones were already in place. But today that didn't matter, since Ana's still lingering trauma and self-recrimination obviously had not been set aside by her sense of Rudy's feelings for her.

Not surprisingly, she thought he was using her to get to Gozo so he could find a suitable place for a small private plane he wanted to buy so he could play week-end pilot. He could think of little else. Whether she would, or could, ever respond to him seemed doubtful. He spent the day in depression, his hopes of reciprocated romance with the girl of his short lived dreams lay shattered, and, more important, that young woman was in abject misery. Thank heavens he wasn't responsible for it; he had only restarted her great sadness by pushing a possible relationship too quickly. How he'd love to meet that visiting American professor bastard!

When Rudy arrived at the shops on Monday morning, having ridden his new motorcycle from the hotel for the first time, he found the office area pulsing with excitement. Surprisingly, both Wing Commander Bartell and RAF Captain Donalds, the Administrative Officer, were both there, deep in discussion with Foster. Robert was at his typewriter, but leaning in the direction of the group, not wanting to miss a word. Foster's voice was about two notches above his normal volume and almost vibrating with some emotion Rudy couldn't decipher. Seeing Rudy, Foster called out: "Rudy, glad you're here. Much is happening already. Come on over and hear the news; it certainly affects you! We're getting some important visitors today."

"Oh," said Rudy, "anyone I know?"

"Both of them," responded Bartell. "At least you've met them. One in America, the other on a plane coming here: Colonel Whittaker of the United States Army Air Force, an air war adviser to HRM and, even more importantly, to your President Roosevelt, and our Air Vice Marshal James Conners, RAF, whom you met suited up as a British Airline Captain on your flight to Malta. Among other duties, James serves as the coordinator of an unofficial, but internally recognized group known as Friends of the RAF, of which you, Mr. Worth, are a member, as you know. Both are due to arrive on the late afternoon BA flight today, and will depart tomorrow the same way. Captain Donalds is seeing to their lodgings for tonight and is arranging meetings, including a dinner meeting this evening for all of us. And that includes you, Robert, as note taker."

Captain Donalds, looking at Rudy, turned directly to business and said, "Could you bring us up-to-date on your work, and also include what you learned from Mr. Boiano concerning his preparedness committee. Foster says that you've met with him, at his request."As Rudy nodded and began to agree, the Captain turned to Foster, asking, "Don't you have a small conference room we could move to for a preliminary session before they arrive?" Foster nodded while pointing over his shoulder, and swung his arm to point the others toward a closed door. "Robert," the Captain continued, "we won't need notes for this little session, but we certainly will at tonight's dinner meeting. We'll meet at six in a private dining room at the Palazzo Ocean Air hotel, and I'll have my driver for any needed transportation to and from."

Very quickly, all were seated on folding chairs around a table in the small conference room, and Rudy found the others looking at him to begin. "First, the easy one: Mr. Boiano is Chair of what is called The Maltese Preparedness Planning Committee, citizen members only as I understand it, and which he said is greatly concerned over the local lack of readiness for a war, but which has found no interest on the part of the Governor or other authorities. He says their worries are generating noise, but no action. He said, also, that what they discuss is hardly a secret for more than a day or so to the local pro-Italy group.

"He asked me, as an outsider, for my impressions of Malta's state of preparedness, but I have not yet responded. Please give me some guidance. I caution you that he appears to be a strong Maltese patriot who, while recognizing England's long support of Malta and is grateful for that, is very dismayed over what he sees as the Homeland's decision to assist countries such as France and Poland, while pulling out such a volume of military resources from Malta.

"He certainly believes that what he calls *The Crown* has decided that Malta and its quarter million population will be left hanging – as we say in the States – should war come. He pointed out that Malta still has a large pro-Italian leaning, even while Mussolini is not highly thought of. I judge him to be pro-Maltese rather than pro-British Crown, and anti-Fascist. He certainly is afraid that, should Mussolini decide to take Malta and its key location in the Mediterranean, there is neither an action plan nor sufficient resources to stop him.

"He is a prominent citizen, head of the Banco Malta, intelligent, and certainly no fool. I say that because in his impassioned presentation at our meeting, where he deliberately, I'm sure, revealed that he knows quite a bit about what's happening here. For example, he called for help in my 'HRM role', asked could not the Curtiss Company build planes for Malta and find pilots for them, convince the Governor to acquire more ground troops to defend the shoreline, and admit that we have crated fighter planes stored here waiting to be assembled. Also, and I should not have been surprised at this, he inquired about what he called a secret weapon, as well as a small group of influential RAF officers' wanting to get Malta better prepared for war. He seems to know, as well as I, the available military resources, including the Hawk. I hardly know what I can add to his knowledge base in my expected report to him."

Following a minute's silence by all, used by Rudy to catch his breath, Captain Donalds pushed back in his chair from a position which had grown more rigid as Rudy went on to depict the pro-Malta thinking. "Well, Rudy, that puts you, and us I expect, in a bloody awkward position, pardon my verbiage. At least we RAF types are expected, and required, I might add, to show loyalty to the official policy, positions, and actions of our government. Our challenge here, possibly, is to determine actions which are appropriate, not to London's pronounced formal policy concerning Malta, but to implied policy – implied by the systematic reassignment of ships, planes, and personnel from Malta to far removed locations.

"I believe for the moment my advice to you, as our American RAF Friend is: if you are obliged to report to Mr. Boiano today, you advise him that you are quickly checking with several sources, including the Curtiss Company as well as other possible, but not very likely, aircraft sources for a technical response. In the meantime, let us all see what we can learn from our visitors this evening that would bear on this. By-the-by, you may all be sure that each day in my current assignment as Deputy, I wish more and more for Air Commodore Fairthorpe, my senior officer, to be released from his duties at Air Ministry, allowed to transit to Malta, and take top decision making command." This was followed by subdued, knowing laughter around the table.

"Now, Rudy, please catch us up with your current HRM assignment," Wing Commander Bartell asked, "and don't forget your secret weapon, courtesy of friend Mr. Standish in England."

Rudy pushed back in his chair, put both hands flat on the table, cleared his throat, and said, "Considering that my assignment, ostensibly, was to encourage the acquisition of additional aircraft to the RAF on Malta, and to improve as much as possible the performance of already available planes, since our man in London, Ian Standish, could send us only one, I'm reminded of the airline pilot who announced bad news and good news to the passengers. The bad news, he said, is that we're hopelessly lost, but the good news is that we're making very good time! Our time is marching swiftly ahead, but we have very little, if anything, with which to work. We desperately need some additional planes!

"Unless someone sends us some fighter-interceptors and experienced fighter pilots to match, if the balloon goes up, as you Brits say, Malta is going to need a lot more anti-aircraft guns and gunners than it has. Still, yes, thanks to Ian's help in misdirecting a brand new, crated Curtiss P-36 Hawk to us – soon to be assembled, hopefully, with a 20mm cannon in each wing as an experiment, plus two machine guns in the engine cowling – we do have one fighter plane on the Island as our secret weapon. And it does have a tremendous rate of climb, 3,400 feet per minute. Oh, and as you would understand, it's painted in the colors of the French Armée de l'Air, which is perhaps wondering why its order was one plane short!"

"To that rate of climb point," Captain Donalds interrupted, "We did get our Radio Directional Finder early warning system installed at Dingli Cliffs last March, so we should get alerts announced before we're hit by aircraft. I expect it will work better than our decade-old 200 foot parabolic acoustic mirror type of hearing aid up at Maghtab, the only one of its type outside of Kent. Of course, Dingli's new RDF device, the first installed abroad by Air Ministry, is still in the experimental stage. But pessimistically, with only one interceptor plane at our disposal, as Rudy might say, so what."

"As you all realize," Rudy continued, "my core HRM assignment is to assist the RAF in any way I can to strengthen the defense of Malta and help keep it safe from Fascist control. To that end, I offer you my thoughts. I would hardly term them recommendations, since most only build upon obtaining additional fighter aircraft we don't have. However, I do recommend that, after quick flight testing at Hal Far, we transfer the Hawk to an, as yet, unprepared airstrip and hidden hangar in central Gozo I have identified. It is owned by the mother of a long-time Shop employee and I believe an agreement could be worked out by the family and, for example, Mr. Boiano, with Banco Malta footing the immediate costs and named in a rental or lease agreement, if that's necessary. If not, we should keep this as quiet as possible and handle it all among ourselves.

"I am well checked out on the Hawk and have flown several hours with a Curtiss war-experienced pilot. Therefore, outside of my Curtiss affiliation, I would expect to pilot the Hawk in the Island's defense against, I'm assuming, Italian bombers, should it come to that."

"Thank you, Rudy. I and my colleagues are touched by your willingness to pledge in Malta's defense, and we shall keep that well in mind, 'should it come to that', as you say. I do believe that the plane should be considered as a full RAF aircraft, rather than simply loaned through the lend-lease naval agreement, however, for whatever that may mean. But I thank you most sincerely, and also for your obviously intelligent recommendation for deployment to Gozo. Now, please brief us on your additional thoughts, no matter the seeming impossibility of bringing them to fruition."

Accepting that the British almost always spoke in carefully selected words and in formal tones, Rudy nodded agreement to continue, but kept tucked away his strong desire to be the Hawk's pilot no matter what!

"My research activities here in the Shops have been facilitated, aided, and made possible by Foster, and by Wing Commander Bartell's continuous support, and also by the excellent aid extended by the Shop's very skilled mechanics. As a result, while hoping against hope for a squadron of Hawker Hurricane fighters and their pilots to be assigned and transported here quickly, I, and I think Foster, believe that we could improve noticeably on the performance of older fighter planes such as the oft-mentioned Gloster Gladiator, as you've heard, by the installation of available three bladed metal propellers and two stage superchargers, and by the use of both 100 octane fuel and pump driven water-methane fuel injection systems. Thus, without changing to larger engines, horsepower would be significantly increased while engine operating temperature would remain within safe limits. The ability of a Gladiator to climb more rapidly and to attack, escape, and fight against faster planes – bombers and fighters – would be increased. There are other possible improvements as well.

"Perhaps you can anticipate, Captain Donalds, what I am suggesting? As a tactic, should Malta become the target of bombers and escorting fighters – as was done elsewhere in the last war-- improved Gladiators, alerted by RDF, could climb rapidly enough to be at a higher altitude for a diving machine gun attack, with totally unexpected follow-up by the faster Hawk with its cannon.

"Without the added speed of enhanced biplane fighters, we judge that modern bombers could outrun the biplanes, which is an excellent example of the value of Hurricanes, Spitfires, and even Hawks for that matter. However, I don't need to point out that the Kalafrana Shops and the personnel operating them are top notch, and I would include there the Maltese mechanics and technicians, Mr. Crayton doing his wonders, and the RAF staff such as Squadron Leader Slingerland and the non-commissioned sergeant supervisors. In the sad absence of Hurricanes, the Kalafrana and Hal Far team could create some amazing improvements on a few Gladiators."

"Thank you, Rudy, and you two stalwarts as well," said the Captain. "Please tell me if you need transport to and from tonight's dinner, and I look forward to seeing you all, plus Robert, this evening at six. I'll handle introductions, but let our visitors set the agenda, and stand ready to present your best thinking regarding the existing situation and Malta's needs and future, as Rudy did for us.

So with just enough time to shower, shave, and dress for the dinner meeting, thinking it important to have the visitors impressed with his rather new persona, Rudy stood in the entrance of the Palazzo waiting for the arrival of Colonel Whittaker, Air Vice Marshal Conners, Captain Donalds, Wing Commander Bartell, Foster Crayton, and Robert, the appointed recorder for what should be an eventful session. He might well have looked earlier into the small, cozy tap room of the hotel first, for that is where he, Foster, and Robert found the visitors with Donalds and Bartell fifteen minutes later, following the arrival of his two co-workers in Robert's old Fiat.

As soon as Rudy appeared in the bar's entrance he was spotted by Captain Donalds, who alerted the others that it was time to proceed to the executive dining room. And so the seven, with Rudy leading the way, strode to the special dining room for dinner and discussion. Colonel Whittaker was eager to greet Rudy, and did so, with enthusiasm as they entered the attractive room, as did James Conners. Rudy still thought of Conners more as an airline captain than a highly ranked RAF officer, but instantly decided to ignore the circumstances of their earlier flight together and recognize him as the highest ranking RAF officer he had met thus far. Small printed place cards indicated that, while seating mingled the diners, Robert was to record proceedings, placed at Captain Donalds' left. Rudy was placed between the two special visitors as part of their host's plan, he guessed.

A first course had already been placed on the table, and Captain Donalds encouraged all to begin enjoying the meal, but cautioned that all but cursory conversation should halt while waiters were in the room. He then introduced Colonel Edgar Whittaker to Foster and Robert and observed, "Now we are all acquainted with each other." Rudy looked around and realized that was an accurate statement. "Rudy," spoke Captain Donalds, "your presentation this afternoon already has been summarized for our visitors, and they are fully aware of the current state of affairs regarding the reduction of Malta's military resources. Colonel Whittaker will begin tonight's session by summarizing the relevant situation in the States."

"I can do that by stating that President Roosevelt has only increased his desire to lessen, or bring to a complete halt, any further aggrandizement by Hitler. He is in accord with his friend Mr. Churchill's sense of the Nazis. He has, and still is, cautiously moving to bring as many military resources as possible within your reach, given the still strong anti-war and isolationistic position of many of our citizens. Further, he has made huge strides toward increasing our own military strength, especially that of our air force. He is well aware and supportive of the HRM Aircraft and Aviation assignment of Mr. Worth, formerly of the Curtiss Company, who is here in our desire to help your Island and the RAF in any way realistically possible at this time. And, Rudy, the Curtiss Company is fully committed to supporting you and your efforts here. Its Board of Directors and its chief officers as well, including Mr. Juddson, only wish that a large number of fighter planes could be miss-delivered immediately, as was that mysterious single one destined for France. And, Rudy, Mr. Juddson asked me to tell you that a future Curtiss position stands firm, as discussed.

"Further, the HRM representative and Friend in London, Mr. Standish, *is* able, I understand, to ship immediately to the Worth Engineering Company in Valletta, Malta a non-bill of lading order for engine improvement parts such as several advanced superchargers and water/methane injector systems, plus both methane and octane booster secure containers. A cryptic telephone order tomorrow to him, with any other unmentionables such as MG and 20mm ammo would be in order. I must note that time is of the essence, since all private indicators point toward immediate hostilities for Malta, and I emphasize immediate. My information is that some in your Parliament are now absolutely adamant that negotiations with Hitler conducted by an Italian official, and leading, possibly, to a transfer to Italy of Malta, must never take place. That would appear to imply that, as soon as possible, some provisions to defend Malta might well be made. But I do emphasize *as soon as possible*! I am asked, also, to indicate that an immediate and appropriately routed air shipment, rather than by cargo vessel, is strongly advised. I hope, Jim Conners, that various other Friends of the RAF could advise on the most expeditious air carrier and routing for a special order? Ah, I see a nod! Good. Excellent, in fact."

"Thank you, Ed, for all of that," said Captain Donalds. "We are, you may report back home, most sincerely grateful, and our Friend Mr. Churchill will be so advised. I now call upon Air Vice Marshal Jim Conners."

"Ed, I personally, and on behalf of the RAF, thank you for all you and President Roosevelt are doing in what likely will be my country's time of greatest danger and need for true friends. Your sense of immediate hostilities is, we concur, unfortunately accurate. We are about to be caught, we greatly fear, unprepared. Courageous and brave for sure, but almost totally unprepared both militarily and politically. And I shall deny ever saying that, should it be repeated!

"Now, based on all that I've heard today, coupled with what I've learned in the past fortnight, I predict a Nazi advance in eastern Europe very, very soon. That likely means that France and my England will soon be most seriously involved. No matter that our government may quickly realize that Malta must be defended, and some modicum of air cover will be necessary, the first act, certainly, will have to be managed locally.

"That means, I now realize, that the RAF must either beg, borrow, or steal some Gloster Gladiators from our Royal Navy, and very quickly. So, Friend Rudy, when you phone tomorrow, please specify that the engine parts and MG ammo will be for whatever powers Navy Gladiators. Foster, here, will know the details of that, and likely Sea Gladiators if there is an engine difference. It will be up to me and some selected Royal Navy Friends of the RAF to manage the cutting loose and shipping to Kalafrana of a modest number of Gladiators. It will be up to you Kalafrana types to get them ready, and up to you, Captain Donalds, to gather some volunteer pilots from your remaining few and get them up to speed on general battle tactics, until we can get them some planes with which to practice.

"Rudy, my friend, get the Hawk tested and hidden away, ready for action, on that field up on Gozo. Your RAF colleagues here, and perhaps Mr. Patriot Boiano, can figure out managing the lease or rent or whatever is necessary for the land. If it's owned by a Kalafrana Shop family, Foster could talk to them about the quick and quiet need for the good of Malta. You understand what I mean: we need the Hawk fueled, armed, and ready to go, probably even before any Gladiators start their supercharged, boosted engines. And then you get ready to install your magical fuel/methane injectors, and so on on the Glads. I should have had that business on my old SE-5, back in the so-called Great War. I ask you, if that was the 'War to End Wars', why have the London newspapers already given it a number?

"One more news item before I turn this great dinner back to our host: Your Governor, General Sir Charles Bonham-Carter, God bless him and his good work, is being relieved of his duties because of a greatly weakened heart, and is being replaced by...Rudy, pay attention... Lieutenant-General H. J. Garrison. I have alerted Rudy, because while enjoying himself on the HRH Queen Mary from New York to Southhampton, he also enjoyed meeting an RAF Friend recently retired from the Royal Engineers, Major Gordon Astill, who gave Rudy a letter of introduction to General Garrison, who even then was being primed for Malta. So Rudy, stand by for an important contact." With that surprise ending, Air Vice Marshal Conners sat, picked up his spoon, and addressed what he termed 'a very proper pudding'.

After thanking Jim Conners, Captain Carter suggested that all should enjoy the last course before the cheese board, and that the Kalafrana group meet with him tomorrow morning at 10:30 in his office to confirm their internal and immediate action steps. Prior to that he would see the visiting guests off to their scheduled morning flight.

Only a little later, after giving his thanks and best regards to the visitors, plus his promise of quick and effective work along their recommended lines, and after thanking his host, Captain Donalds for including him, and saying good night to his colleagues, Rudy went up to his room. He was thinking not of Ana, but of the Hawk and his plans for it.

CHAPTER 13

THE FLIGHT TEST

Malta

August

RUDY rode his motorcycle to the Shops early the next morning, primed not just for the 10:30 meeting, but for real action. He recited to himself the steps needed immediately, as urged by Jim Conners, before war and Malta's involvement in it proved them too late. He calculated these steps to be: phone Ian immediately for a quick air shipment of necessary items; get the Lafessi family to agree to special use of a small portion of their Gozo farm; prepare a brief sanitized status report for Mr. Boiano and his citizens committee and hope for the best from Mr. Boiano; seek Banco Malta's financial support should Gozo airstrip costs need covering; flight test the Hawk; and prepare to move it to Gozo. Before he, Foster, and Robert left the Shop for Captain Donalds' meeting, Rudy had already composed a summary response for the citizens committee. It was accurate concerning the very limited aircraft resources currently located on Malta, except that it did not list the Hawk P-36, Remembering last night's prediction of war soon, he was determined to advance his assignment to help Malta's defense, and he had already decided with Foster the steps required for testing the Hawk's air worthiness.

Captain Donalds' requested meeting, with Wing Commander Bartell present, moved quickly to individual assignments. Rudy was asked what he would request in a phone call to Ian Standish in London, and responded using Colonel Whittaker's list in addition to his own: "Since we have ideas about obtaining some number of Gladiators, and after checking the Shop's available parts inventory, I'll ask for six variable pitch three bladed metal props for Mercury VIII engines, if Foster says they're suitable, six two-stage superchargers, or single stages if that's all that can be fitted, four more water/methane injector kits added to the three I brought with me for experimentation, and as many cylinders of methane liquid as he can get, along with the same of octane booster liquid. We'll also need a spare 20mm wing canon and as many rounds as he can obtain, all for the Hawk. I assume we already have sufficient .303 and .45 caliber ammo, but I'll check to see before I call. Also, I'd probably better have that call to him placed over a secure line, if there is such a thing here?"

At that point Foster said, "Rudy and I are in agreement concerning when and how to flight test the P-36 this week, and what we'll need up in Gozo if, and when, we'll want the plane hidden safely away up there as the wise thing to do. I'll speak to Vincent Lafessi, one of our senior shop technicians, about our interest in using a bit of his mother's Gozo farm, and get up there myself to see what we'd need to convert one of the barns to a hangar and mow a grass strip. I'll report my findings and also what level of funding, if any, will be needed. By the way, Rudy, if our parts shelves have spare metal props for a two engine Bristol Blenheim bomber, they should fit the Gladiators. But do put some proper prop spinners on your list to help with streamlining."

Captain Donalds shifted attention to the, as yet, unannounced change in the Island's Governor, as they learned last night. "Rudy, let's wait for the official announcement before we plan how best to use your letter of introduction. I would hope the least it can provide for our cause is the agreement of General Garrison to our need to somehow obtain and properly outfit some Gloster Sea Gladiators for our would-be Fighter Flight. Which reminds me, Bartell, to inquire about what you see as a source for pilots?"

Bartell's response was not as humorous as it might sound to an outsider. "If you mean experienced fighter pilots, aside from anyone left over from the Spads and Fokkers of the last war, I haven't located any. However, we do have a couple of the younger RAF administrative staff who have some flying experience, and there likely will be a couple of pilots remaining on the Island when the flying boats are reassigned elsewhere. We also may have remaining one or more Swordfish pilots from that group, but it's impossible right now to know exactly. Friend Rudy certainly has flying experience, as do I, but I would hardly know how to classify his presence here as an RAF officer engaged in shooting at enemy planes. However, I shall continue to search and to hope for a flight of Hurricanes and pilots to be assigned to us at the last minute."

"Not likely very soon to be Hurricanes, but tell me, Bartell," Donalds asked, "do we have any Gladiators hidden away in crates or expected on a scheduled aircraft carrier inbound to Malta? If not, it's up to Jim Conners to wave a magic wand. Otherwise you'll need to mount a shotgun on the old Queen Bee, if it's still flyable."

"Unfortunately," Bartell responded, "our Royal Navy appears to have entered a chess game with our London decision makers. London changes the Navy's disposition of carriers and thus their Gladiators on a seeming weekly basis, and the Navy is forced to respond by diverting those ships and their flights and squadrons from Alexandria to Gibraltar and back again. I'm thinking that if James Conners, with his contacts, can entice one of the carriers to stop here and off load a few crates of spare planes, we could get them assembled and form a land based defensive group in short order, selecting our most appropriate pilots. But, as we know from experience, often the Royal Navy chooses to overlook the needs of the other military. You may be sure, though, that I'll be keeping my eyes open."

With that, Captain Donalds said he would wait one day and then phone Jim Conners to spur him on. He thanked the group and dismissed them to carry out their assignments. Rudy asked if the Captain would review a draft of his brief report to Mr. Boiano before it was sent, and that was agreed, with Robert bringing it over for review.

As soon as he got back to the Shops, Rudy hunted up Paul Lafessi and George, asking them to make arrangements to get the Hawk ready to be towed to an empty hangar at Hal Far as soon as possible this week, to do what was needed to the wings so that it would fit on the narrow road leading from the Shops while being towed, and to get the wings back on the plane after it was parked safely inside the hangar. If more help were needed to do this, Rudy would provide it himself. The plane would then be rechecked, and the engine run up, all in preparation for taxiing and flight testing. He then went off to tell Foster what he had just arranged, and to promise his working support for creating a Gozo airstrip once Foster agreed with Rudy's chosen location and gotten an agreement from Mrs. Lafessi and her son, Vincent. If that arrangement proved impossible, then another reconnaissance of Gozo Island would be needed, or perhaps of northern Malta Island itself, even with all its stone fences and hills.

"And Foster," Rudy remembered to say as he turned toward his private workshop, "once I have the Hawk up in the air and tested its flyability, I'll go further out a bit and see if the wing canons fire OK, and the two machine guns. How far out do you think I should get? I don't think the wings will fall off when I check the guns, but I don't want the gun noise to carry way back here."

"Please, my friend, let's worry about that on flying day. I'm going to find Vincent Lafessi right now and launch the big question. If he's at all cooperative, we'll see who should approach his mother with the details. I'm hoping he'll be on our side. After all, we'd locate up there only if we need to, right?"

Three days later, Saturday afternoon found Rudy, Paul Lafessi, and George, who was working overtime, in a hangar just off the airstrip runway at Hal Far. They were standing back from the Hawk, admiring their now completely assembled and twice checked over plane. "It's beautiful," Paul exclaimed, "shall we see if the engine starts? It's filled with oil and the hundred octane gas we stole from the tank down at the seaplane ramp, and we've already run it once down at the shop's test bed and twice after we reinstalled it, and once yesterday after we got it here. Instruments are OK, all the fasteners are in place, compressed air's OK. What do you say, boss?"

"I agree it's ready to taxi, and fly as well, but I'm going to check with Foster and Bartell later today and see if they'll be here tomorrow. They both said a Sunday is the best time to avoid lots of eyes. All we're looking for is to make sure it stays together up there at speed, handles the way its supposed to, doesn't lose its prop, collapse its wheels, or shake the wings off when the guns fire a couple of rounds. I'll wear a chute, although I've never used one, but all the fancy stuff will come later on, after we know it can go up and down, fly straight and level, and bank and turn without going into a flat spin. Ha, Ha!"

Sunday Morning had not only Rudy and Paul, along with George - "On me own time," as he said, "cause I wouldn't miss this fer naught." - but Foster also, as well as the Wing Commander, standing in the sunshine outside the hangar at Hal Far. Rudy had written out a check list and was busy with Paul going over the plane, even including draining a couple of ounces of the precious 100 octane into a clear glass jar to check for water in the gas. This was explained by Rudy as, "What we always did back at Penn Yan, where we bought our gas in five gallon Jerry cans from the local gas station down in the village." Well here, thought Paul, we stole the gas from the flying boat fuel tanks, and we didn't even pay for it!

After twenty more minutes of checking, Rudy, minus the forgotten parachute he had promised yesterday , climbed into the cockpit, settled into the single seat and, assisted by Paul – momentarily standing on the wing - buckled into the harness. He still clutched his checklist and was watched by the others as he wiggled the stick and rudder pedals while turning to see that the control surfaces were working properly and that both of the wing flaps went down and then back up together. He pushed the primer knob four times, checked his mixture and prop controls, advanced the throttle knob just a tiny bit, smiled as he thought of how they had reversed the throttle linkage from French pull to English push, pulled the stick full back, stepped on the toe brakes as a precaution, yelled 'Clear prop', and waved a rotating signal to Paul on the ground with George, to energize the starter.

With smoke and a sudden roar, the engine started, the propeller spun rather quickly, but as the engine slowed a little, the bystanders saw the many small engine cowl cooling flaps open. Rudy signaled again, and both George and Paul, one on either side of the plane and safe from the now blurred spin of the prop, yanked the wheel chock ropes, freeing the two wheels. Foster began to speak out loud but seemingly to himself, as he gave his interpretation of what they were anxiously watching, without ever turning to the others. Each of the four appeared to rock back and forth almost in unison, as though urging the Hawk to do what it should do, and nothing else.

Now the Hawk, pulled by a faster spinning prop and louder engine, began to roll forward. Even with the cockpit canopy not yet slid forward to enclose Rudy, the Hawk stood almost ten feet high. Its 37 foot wingspan was eight feet longer than its length, and the experimental canon barrel protruding from each wing looked ominous, as did the two machine gun ports atop the engine cowl. "It's OK," Foster narrated to himself, "He's first only going to taxi it a few times to see how it handles on the ground. The engine sounds good. It's much more horsepower than our Swordfish. He's not even wearing a pair of goggles, but for taxiing he's OK. Why is he stopping? Oh, he's running it up to check oil pressure and temp, and test the dual magnetos for an RPM drop. Now he's giving it more RPM; where's he going? Up to the end of the strip? Ah, he'll try a fast taxi into the wind. When we're through with a flight test later this week, Wing Commander, I think we should get Captain Roberts to declare this plane an official RAF aircraft and start looking for a couple of potential pilots for it, just in case it's ever needed. Sound right to you?"

Wing Commander Bartell told Foster much later that just as he was to agree with his plan for the plane, Foster interrupted with a loud yell. His, "Oh my God, he's turning onto the strip and lowering his flaps. He's gunning it! He's starting a take-off run into the wind, No, He said only taxiing today, No, by God, he's got his tail wheel up. There he goes!... He's up and starting to climb. Wheels going up. I hope he bloody well knows what he's doing. But he must; he helped design it and he's flown one back at the plant. I can't look. I think I'm furious. He'll get it from me if he gets back in one piece."

"Oh, Clayton, get off it. He knows what he's doing," Bartell said loudly, "I'd do just what he's done, and so would you, if we had the chance. He's trusting himself and the Shop's good men. And they've checked it out time and again. He'll fly it and get down safely right here."

"You don't know it, but he's going to test fire the guns out to sea, beyond our sight and hearing, but I hope you're right about getting back here safely," Foster said , followed by, "Sir."

Paul and George, neither wanting to enter their bosses' loud discussion, inched sideways a few feet more away from Foster, and peered into the distant sky, aiming toward the direction in which Rudy had set off. The silence now among the four was unsettling until George shouted, "Here he comes!" and pointed to a dark spec low on the horizon, growing larger by the second. In what seemed like an instant in time and 50 feet over their heads, the Hawk did a low level, high speed fly-over, followed by a turning climb leading into a downwind entry off to the side of the landing strip. "Get your wheels down," shouted Foster, "and the flaps," just as a wheel lowered from under each wing, as did a flap. The Hawk's speed seemed to slow a bit, even as it descended faster, now on a short final approach. In less than a minute, Rudy was taxiing the Hawk toward them and the hangar.

As the four began to move in what they hoped was the right direction, the plane stopped and wheeled around, tail pointed toward the quite close and wide open hangar door. The engine shut down, the prop turned to a standstill, and Rudy slid back the now closed cockpit canopy and waved jubilantly. "I don't know whether to congratulate him or let him know how angry I was when he took off," muttered Foster to himself."

"Save it for later," Paul brashly suggested, "and let's get the tractor hooked up and get it into the hangar and out of sight as soon as he climbs down. Just don't go too near the exhaust stack or the engine. They'll be hot. And be sure the gun switches are safetied." In less than thirty minutes, cheers and congratulations finished, both the Hawk and the hangar door were each secured. Bartell's invitation to stand lunch for all, where Rudy would tell them everything, was accepted with thanks, and the now much relaxed and happy five departed Hal Far.

Foster and the others heard, in perhaps more detail than they thought necessary, all about the limited taxi and surprise flight tests at Sunday's luncheon, which was paid for courtesy of the Wing Commander. The plane flew beautifully, the guns, canon included, fired their few rounds without problems. Rudy was very pleased with his ability to pilot the Hawk unerringly, as he judged it. "So far, so good," he pronounced, looking especially at Paul and George. "Oh Gawd," mumbled George to Paul, "what will he want next?"

By noon time on Monday, Rudy was beginning to direct his attention to the call he had placed to Ian in London and to learn if Ian had responded, or even received the message he had left with Ian's colleague in the London HRM office. At his desk he quickly learned. "*Yes, from Ian.*" Robert had written on a pad left for Rudy, time-stamped 11:00. "*All being shipped air freight. Expect this week on BA flight. Ian says events moving fast. Good Luck."* Robert had added the news that, *"Mrs. Lafessi agrees to Gozo project. Foster meeting now with Bartell. He asks you prepare list of what's needed up there. Check later today."*

Rudy immediately sat and began to scribble a list on Robert's pad: 1) Narrow mowed runway not obvious from air. Disguise with other short mows?; 2) Big barn with 40 foot barn door sliders. Provide and install sliders?; 3) Small structure for pilot and mechanic sleeping, eating, water, etc. Use other barn? Disguise smaller items as stacked hay or keep them in other barn? 4) Radio/phone to house. Alerts?; 5) Fuel tank and pump. Disguise, or refuel always at Shops?; 6) Transportation for personnel. Motorcycle? He tore off the sheet, pocketed it, and strode off to find Foster. Keeping a plane ready to take off immediately from Gozo was a little more complicated than he had imagined, but it all would be worked out. While walking, he thought about how to use Ian's promised early Christmas present of delivered necessities. For Rudy and the others, Monday, August 28, 1939 was proving to be a very busy day. Hopefully, the remainder of the week would allow him time for planning. Was it too soon, he wondered, to maybe call Ana? Perhaps they could see each other over the quiet coming weekend.

CHAPTER 14

BLITZKRIEG

August 29 – August 31, 1939

THE British Air flight Rudy was anticipating on Tuesday arrived at 4:00 pm, unusually late, and Robert had to cajole George to get the crates off the plane and stored in Rudy's workshop before leaving for the day. George, aided by three other hastily recruited Shop workers, plus the old truck, grudgingly obliged. The six wooden crates were heavy, and there were some mumbled comments heard from the four as they lifted and shoved the crates from the truck into the Shop, having already pulled them from the plane's storage area. Rudy and Foster quickly went to work prying the lids off the crates as soon as they were moved into what Rudy sometimes thought of as his laboratory, while Robert, clipboard in hand, checked off the contents from the wish list sent to Ian Standish. As George was retreating from the Shop to head home, Robert called to him, "Were there any three bladed props?" No answer from George prompted Foster to jog outside the Shop's still open hangar door and spot them, leaning against the Shop's outer wall, each blade wrapped in heavy brown paper.

"They're out here," yelled Foster. "We'll bring them in tomorrow; they'll be safe enough out here and I'll get George to finish the job. We'll have to see if we need them or not. Let's check what's in the last two crates, lock up and call it a day! Rudy, now that we've got some parts to work with, the two of us can talk tomorrow first thing, pull the canon ammo aside for the Hawk, and get going on moving the plane up to Gozo once the strip is mowed and we can get it into and out of the barn. You'll need to get up there quickly this week and mark where you want the grass and weeds cut. Once it's up there you can always fly it back here for refueling."

Where and how Ian had obtained them, Rudy could not imagine, but the two remaining crates contained metal cylinders of octane booster and of methane. The cylinders were held tightly in place by partitions which had been carefully built into the crates. When he exclaimed his happy amazement over the contents, Foster smilingly said, "I've learned that, with Ian, one should say 'Many thanks, my friend', but never inquire concerning details. Typically we would get an invoice from some parts supply house, which we would pay. But this time, with the magic of HRM Aviation or HRM Aircraft, Ltd., whichever is doing this good work for us, and your President Roosevelt, I believe we should not look this gift horse in the mouth."

The next day, Wednesday, began with the Gozo meeting Foster wanted. He had invited both Paul Lafessi, Rudy's young Shop technician assistant, and Paul's father, Vincent, a Shop supervisor. "Rudy," Foster began, "When I talked with Mr. Lafessi about our Gozo project the other day, he agreed immediately, and explained that his mother had signed all of the Gozo farm property over to him, anyway, since his father passed away. He'll handle the arrangement and explain things to his mother, who, as you know, still lives up in the old farmhouse near the barns. He believes that the idea of hiding our plane up there in case it's ever needed makes sense, and the property is ideal for a make-shift grass strip and hangar-barn. Is that correct, Vincent?"

"Yes, as I told you, Mr. Crayton, what Paul tells me about this fighter plane gives comfort that we would have at least a little protection if that bastard, Mussolini, throws in with the Nazis. If you can arrange for the big barn to be cleaned out and get a long sliding door installed for the plane, I can get a disguised grass strip cut by a neighboring farmer who rents a bit of our land, and we'll be set. Oh, I hope we don't get into another war, but if we do, you'll probably want a couple of our people to live up there on some sort of shift arrangement, with a radio set-up to alert the pilot. The farmhouse could handle that. From my experience with the big, slow Fairey Swordfish, which we still have a couple of in the old hangar, and even with Gladiators, which we don't have, this new plane – the Hawk, as Paul calls it – is the only thing that could climb fast enough or really do anything to help."

"Mr. Lafessi," Rudy exclaimed, "you are exactly right in everything you've said. Thank you, thank you! I'll go up there tomorrow, check out the barns, the prevailing wind – if there is one – and figure out where a strip could be mowed. I'll make a rough layout on paper and have it back here on Thursday for Foster and you." With that, the meeting was over and Foster, beckoning to Rudy to follow, headed off toward the six crates and the propellers, still leaning against the Shop wall outside. Paul motioned to Rudy that he needed a word, so Rudy stopped.

"Rudy, I think the idea is great, and whatever I can do to assist, just tell me. I know the old farm pretty well; Nina and I would go up there to visit the old folks and get out of the city. The wind usually is out of the northwest, and one of the barns is really big enough for the wingspan of the Hawk. There's a Gozo local builder in Victoria who could do the sliding barn door thing using supporting uprights for the ends and a crossbeam for the top span. Even a metal beam rather than a wooden one, for the thirty-some feet. Those long sliders have little wheel brackets on top which roll on a long track. We could build a towing dolly for the nose wheel and get a used tractor from somewhere on Gozo to tow the Hawk in and out. Let me know what you want me to do, OK? I can get going on what I just mentioned right away.

"Oh, before I forget, my sister Nina wants to go up and check on our grandmother. If you're going up tomorrow on your motorcycle, I could tell her to take the bus from right near our house in Sliema to the Malta ferry dock and hitch a ride with you to the farm. She's used to riding on my old machine and could show you the barns and things. If that's OK, would you want her to be up at the ferry dock for the noon-time ferry to Gozo, or earlier?"

"Sure," Rudy responded, "I remember her from that great dinner at your house. But make it the 10:30 ferry. We'll get a quick lunch at the restaurant at the Gozo end of the boat ride, then straight up to the farm, I'll look it over, make a sketch, and back for the afternoon ferry to Malta. I can drop her off home on my way to the hotel. You're sure she'll be OK riding the bike? If so, tell her to look for me around 10:15 at the ferry dock." With that, Rudy ran off to the crates and a day of inspecting their contents and planning in detail what would be used to enhance the Hawk. The remainder would be held in the unlikely event that Jim Conners could obtain a few crated Sea Gladiators to be left at the Malta docks by some passing British ship.

Rather than the quiet last week of August Rudy had hoped for, early Thursday morning had him on his motorcycle headed north from the Palazzo Hotel toward the Malta ferry dock at the very north end of the island. The motorcycle's gas tank was full, and he was dressed for a warm summer's ride in shorts and a light shirt on this, the last day of August. In the small saddle bag he had stuffed a bottle of water, a couple of pencils, a pad, and a map which showed both Malta's and Gozo's road network and small communities. He had taken this drive north not long ago in Ana's convertible, of course, and although he was cruising again through some remarkable scenery, his thoughts kept switching from attention to the road back to her and his utter confusion and torment. Nothing he thought of, however, did a thing to clarify what he had heard and experienced on that remarkable day.

In truth, he didn't know what to do to make her feel better about him and what he still wanted: that their meeting would be the beginning of, to put it politely, a wonderful romantic relationship. Had it all truly ended before it had hardly begun? No, he considered, with time she'll conquer those horrible events at the Italian University and back home in Malta when she returned. Now he began to alternately rage with jealousy over what he imagined had transpired between naive Ana and the visiting professor, and the mental push those thoughts gave him toward warmly recalling the years of experiences he had enjoyed in Buffalo with good-looking young women. Alternating his thoughts between those two somewhat related scenarios unsettled him even more, distracting his attention from the perils of driving a motorcycle safely over the twisting Maltese roads.

Hell, he fumed, I've been here almost three months, and I never even held hands with her, or anybody else, much less...He narrowly missed a small farm wagon filled with crates of chickens, which led to a vision of several crates of bi-wing fighter planes, which brought him back to focusing on his mission today. But realizing he had just almost hit two people walking on the road's edge by one of those damn rock walls, he shook his head, put his unsettling thoughts aside, and focused on getting safely to the ferry dock and...wait. He tried to remember, at the Sunday dinner, was Nina the young girl getting ready for college, or the other one, whom

Robert had introduced him to at the beach as he stared at Ana walking by. Yes, for sure, it was the teenager getting ready for college, wasn't it? Well, he'd know shortly. What's the difference? Ana was just so good looking...

Arriving at the Gozo ferry slip five minutes late, Rudy parked the motorcycle in line just behind a truck and started walking toward the ticket booth. This was quite a crowd, he thought. Gozo must be quite popular. While sliding sideways through the crowd and looking for a teen aged girl, he almost bumped two older men who were laughing quietly while looking at a nearby younger man being loudly berated by a woman. "Don't walk between those two, lad, or you'll catch it from the wife too. He made a fatal error." said the first, speaking excellent English. "He certainly did," added the second, "because while you may look, you can't be so obvious about it!" "Or take a loud, deep breath at the same time you're looking," added the first.

Still smiling knowingly, both men turned slightly and pointed with their chins toward the slender, shapely back of a woman standing at the edge of the crowd and looking back toward the road. "But you know," observed the first, still in excellent English, "I think that one's worth catching hell for. I noticed her earlier. She's gorgeous from the front as well as the back!"

Rudy was staggered, as were the two men, when the young woman turned and, seeing him so close, waved with a ticket in her hand to motion him toward the ticket booth. "Oh Gawd.'" said the first man, "No offense meant, lad. Your lucky day!" Both men then turned and hurried away toward the still docked ferry. Rudy his stomach tightening, waved back to Nina, pushed off to get his ticket, and thought: It certainly looks like it!

Ticket in hand, Rudy was torn between striding toward Nina or getting to his motorcycle so he could push it onboard the boat, now shaking in the water a bit from its just started engine. No decision was needed, since this stunning, dark haired beauty, looking as though she had been poured into her tight slacks and tighter sweater, strode to him and clutched his arm. "Hello Rudy, or should I say Mr. Engineer Worth? I'm very happy you made it. I certainly didn't want to hike up to the farm without you. Well, we have our tickets, so let's push Paul's old motorized rattletrap up the ramp and grab a bench in the shade so we can get acquainted during our half hour ride. Rudy couldn't tell whose hands reached the cycle's hand grips first, but when Nina began to push toward the ramp he simply said, "Please, call me Rudy, and thanks for making this trip on the same day I had to get to Gozo." He then pushed atop her hands, almost afraid to look at her as they bent to the task.

Once the cycle was safely in place Nina said "To a shady bench", grabbed his hand and tugged him toward a bench facing the railing. "This way I can point out the tourist sights, like the Blue Lagoon on little Comino island. Or," she said in a teasing voice, "did you get to see all the sights when you were up here on your first trip?"

Rudy was taking a chance, he knew, when he answered, "I believe I've forgotten about that trip, so just tell me about yourself, Nina, and show me whatever you think I should see. I must confess as an American outsider, I was nervous when I had that wonderful Sunday dinner at your house, and that arrangement, which had Ana showing up to drive me back to the hotel, really threw me off. You and I never had a chance to talk that afternoon and I want to make up for that today. I haven't seen nor spoken with Ana since the car ride up to Gozo the Saturday after the dinner, and while I guess I'm impressed with her, I have no plans for further contact with her. That trip up here to Gozo with her didn't help, believe me.

"I'm just grateful it's you rather than your sister or your brother, who needs to check on your grandmother today. And, by-the-way, you look spectacular. Did you dress down on the day of the dinner because Ana had gotten you into her little plan? You had that poor man on the dock almost beaten by his wife for even looking at you, and I can understand why."

"Rudy, women love to play games, but apparently you're on to us. And you probably have noticed that, with you, I'm better at American English than I am at sounding like a Brit. I really loved meeting you on the beach that day. You were so formal, and so taken up with Ana's swaying up and down the sands. She wanted to meet you, the American engineer, you know, before she even saw you with Robert that day. I still don't know what that was all about, but never mind. We're here and she's been out of sight, back up in Italy so the rumor is, at her former university. So let's get to know each other, if you want." That proclamation was immediately followed by Nina moving sideways on the bench against him while shivering, as she said, from the colder ocean breeze. Rudy realized he was shaking as well, but likely not from the breeze.

Their boat ride to Gozo lasted only long enough for Rudy to realize that Nina was not only gorgeous and openly flirtatious with him, but intelligent and with a quick sense of humor. She had mentioned that she had become practiced in what she called American English by reading as many American magazines as she could, and watching the few American movies that played occasionally in Valletta. She wanted to practice with Rudy as often as she could, she said, or as often as he could stand her. She had completed college at the local university, having majored in maths, as the Brits termed it - unusual for a Maltese female - and minored in geography. Languages came rather easily to her, and she spoke both Italian and Spanish, as well as English and her own Maltese.

She had just turned 24 years old, five years younger than himself, he realized, but quickly forgot about. Nina worked as the Port of Valletta office manager for an international shipping firm, but was growing bored and restless, and thinking about a change. She had never been married, but had once been engaged for two or three months. Although she dated, she said she was bored with the men she met. Yet at least so far, she judged aloud, Rudy was not yet in that category. Also, she added, she quite often was called upon to model clothes for Maltese shops and occasionally for an Italian clothing design firm located in Milan, and with a popular retail shop in Valletta.

Rudy, when his turn arrived, presented a concise version of what he had recited to the Curtiss and HRM executives, and spent as little time describing his dating history to Nina as he did back at the Buffalo interview. It was apparent that Nina had benefited from her brother Paul's very positive experiences with Rudy, and with her father Vincent's high regard for the brilliant American Aeronautical Engineer sent by President Roosevelt to help save Malta. There also had occurred a one time brief conversation with Mr. Farinacci, whose wife admired Nina's appearance as a model for women's clothing she herself could seldom fit into, and who occasionally was accompanied by her husband at Valletta fashion shows. Mr. Farinacci respected Rudy's previous work with the great Curtiss Corporation, he had said, and now with HRM Aviation which has sent him to help Malta. Nina's mother, as Nina expected, had been greatly impressed with Rudy's charm and politeness.

Putting it all together, Nina judged Rudy to be a genuine, good looking, tall enough at five feet eleven inches not counting a full head of sandy colored hair, blue eyed, intelligent, well-spoken, more interested in women than he let on, high earning professional. With his sense of humor and his return to America assured, she wondered, what else could possibly be added? Well, she thought, I'm being honest with myself and with him. I'm not a gold digger, and I'm not overcome with desire to go to America. My family is here. And I'm under no pressure from my father, mother, or myself to get a husband. So let's see what Miss Ana Boiano does with some competition or, more interesting, what the hell she's up to with our favorite aeronautical wonder!

With all of these thoughts behind her, and with Rudy's hormones and brain competing for first place in his head, the ferry pulled into Mgaar Harbour, Gozo, and docked. Rudy insisted in leading the motorcycle down the off ramp, and it was just a quick ride to a food kiosk where sandwiches and bottles of water sufficed. Off the couple went, with Nina holding on tight to Rudy's back. Following her directions, they headed northwest on the main toward Victoria, but with a turn coming up to put them on a parallel road that would take them to the farm before it, also, led to Victoria and the old walled Citadel.

As they neared the important turn off, Nina tightened her arms around Rudy's back, leaned even closer than she had been riding, pushing herself tight against him, moved her hands fully across his stomach, leaned her head forward, pushing her mouth against his left ear, and whispered above the engine noise, "The turn to the right is coming up, just past the end of the stone wall we're alongside right now. Is my holding on so tight OK? The road is so bumpy I'm afraid I might fall off if I don't hang on to my pilot." She kept her mouth against Rudy's ear and her arms and hands tight around him. Rudy could only nod yes, yes and wonder if he might explode, or possibly implode, before they reached the farm. Slowdown a little, he told himself, look for more bumps in the road to bounce us over, and enjoy her and the ride! Nina instructed Rudy's ear to turn left when they reached the road which would pass the farm, and before his explosion-implosion theory could be tested, she said, rather sadly, "This is it.

We're here. Grandma's house is coming up on the right. Stop here for a minute, will you?"

He stopped, and Nina hopped off the back of the seat, came around to Rudy's face, and drew close. Rudy had imagined this was the moment, and putting Ana Boiano, Malta, and even President Roosevelt out of his mind, he was misled when he saw that she had deliberately spilled a half bottle of water on the tail of her shirt front in order to wipe the accumulated sand from his face. As she wiped, she said, "This motorcycle is ridiculous for dirt roads. Let's either get helmets and goggles, or trade this thing in on a used car! That is, if we're going to do this again. Or is this our last date? The barns are up ahead on the right, and just about all you can see belongs to us. Go do your thing and then get back here to meet Grandma and pick me up for a ride back to the ferry and Sliema. The afternoon ferry is at 3:30, and you're dropping me off at my house."

And at that she leaned into him, he still sitting on the motorcycle, and quickly kissed his cheek. Just before he imploded he stuttered, "I'll be back in thirty minutes to meet Grandma. Let's talk about a car. Maybe I could rent one or borrow one. I'll keep the bike at the shops for emergencies." As he tried to say something more sophisticated, he realized that she was already headed toward the farmhouse. Wisely he stopped talking to himself and headed the motorcycle up the road toward the barn area.

Rudy found the land flat and clear of stone fences, typically found criss-crossing every field in Malta. There were no tall trees, only an occasional clump of bushes, so all could be mowed or cut down low enough and long enough for a take-off run leading from the largest barn's area. It would head into what Paul said was the usual wind from the northwest. A couple of short mows crossing the strip and heading nowhere, or toward one of two smaller barns, would detract from its runway appearance.

He drew his approximate sketch for the strip and paced off two sides side of the longest and widest barn. It would do to provide complete cover for the Hawk, and a pair of closed twenty foot long sliding barn doors would look like the old barn siding were still in place. This would do the trick, Rudy thought, even if each of the slide rails were supported by a post at its end, out past the barn's two sides. He paced off what was needed, and sketched out the Hawk's new hangar.

Still smoldering internally, Rudy rode the short distance back to the farmhouse, got off, and went inside to greet Nina's Grandmother. She and Nina were in the kitchen of a pleasant looking farm home, and Nina described Rudy as Paul's boss back at the Shops, and the person who had given her a lift to the farm to measure for the new project. Grandma thanked Rudy for bringing Nina to her, Rudy said he likely would see her again soon, and the two went out to begin their ride back to the ferry and the big island. "Do you want to spend a minute seeing where I think the grass strip should go, and the barn we'll convert to a hangar?" questioned Rudy as they got back on.

Nina's response came quickly, "Rudy, if we go back to look at the barn we'll never make the ferry!" Rudy understood, he thought, nodded his reluctant agreement, started the motorcycle's engine, and hoped the return trip would be as interesting as the morning ride. Perhaps, he smiled, tomorrow, September 1, might turn out to be another fascinating day. Who knows?

CHAPTER 15

IT'S POLAND'S TURN!

Friday, September 1, 1939

RUDY slept a bit later than usual on Friday morning, and spent a couple of additional minutes, eyes still closed, half dreaming about yesterday's experience. And what a wonderful experience it was, even though he may have overplayed it a bit, he judged, by inviting Nina to examine her own grandmother's barn with him as guide. He realized now, although still excited by his obvious attempt yesterday to be alone with her, that she had handled him and his eagerness in a sensible, yet promising way. At least he hoped it was promising? Ye gads, he thought, he had acted like a hormone inflamed teenager from Buffalo! But he'd do better the next time. Hadn't she suggested a next time? Hadn't she suggested he get a car? That must mean something!

By now he was fully awake and thinking about getting up and ready for work, when a hurried rain of knocks on his hotel door was followed by a loud and shaky "Mr. Worth, sir, there has been a phone call for you from Mr. Crayton. He says you must get to the Shops as quickly as you can. Germany is invading Poland! Can you hear me, Mr. Worth?"

"What," yelled Rudy, What did you say? OK, I heard you. I'm on my way. Thank you!" In less than fifteen minutes he ran down the hotel stairway, waved an arm running by the two employees tuning a small radio on the reception desk, unlocked and started his motorcycle, and gunned the machine down the street toward the Kalafrana road. He was going so fast when he reached the Shops that he almost lost it, skidding to a stop on the gravel next to the building's entry. Leaning the bike against the building, he yanked the door and raced inside to see almost the same sight he had seen just minutes before at the hotel desk. Foster, Robert, and several RAF uniformed officers were bent over a civilian type radio listening to an excited London broadcaster speaking so fast Rudy could scarcely understand what was being said.

Foster looked up and, seeing Rudy, spoke louder than needed in a trembling voice. "Rudy," he yelled, "you and Robert get that Hawk flown up to Gozo someplace. Cover it with hay or something, and get back here as soon as you can. This is IT! I'm waiting for Bartell or somebody to officially get this place going. Everybody knows England has an agreement with France to go to war if Poland is invaded. According to this newsman in London, Hitler has sent a million and a half men into Poland from three different directions, one and a half million German soldiers. He says that's three times the size of the Polish army. Lots of tanks and planes. Britain and France have ordered total mobilization, and I'll bet Italy will join right in. Damn it, you can guess what side they'll be on. We need to do all we can to get ready right now. We are at war!"

One of the RAF officers, Squadron Leader Slingerland, added, "We need to immediately get the few remaining Swordfish Stringbags into whichever hangar is farthest from the runway. The first bombers will go for them, sitting alongside the runway as they have been." Robert added, "And they still are, but shouldn't we wait for Captain Donalds and Commander Bartell to give us our marching orders?"

As if on cue, both the Captain and the Wing Commander burst into the office, out-of-breath, red-faces caused by a hurried trip from their communications room, and with radioed news from the outside world. It was Rudy's impression that, while Captain Donalds was attempting to provide the others with news from the Air Ministry in London, Wing Commander Bartell was issuing orders to safeguard the very few RAF planes left on the Island, including what he now identified as 'our Warhawk'. Actually, Rudy thought, the news from RAF Air Ministry was even less informative than what the London announcer was stumbling through. For all the local talk about needing plans for this kind of news, Malta is a sitting duck, thanks to the higher-up decision to pull out all usable resources!

All knew of the treaty to protect Poland if it were invaded, but aside the mobilization order issued by Parliament, nothing positive relating to Poland - or Malta, for that matter- had been done nor even suggested by

Prime Minister Chamberlain and the British Cabinet. Using one set of words or another, each in Crayton's now crowded office voiced agreement that Malta's future was dependent on Benito Mussolini and his *Regia Aeronautica.* This was reported as 1500 combat aircraft strong. Happily for Malta, although just fifteen minutes flying time to Valletta from the Regia's airfields on Sicily, that air force is, for now, in a neutral, non-combative mode. But how long would that last? Italy would certainly join hands with Germany, now that Hitler has made this definitive move in Europe.

Captain Donalds knocked on the table to get everyone's attention and silence, and in his most serious voice declared that he would quickly assign team leaders to certain tasks in preparation for what was certain to come to Malta, perhaps as soon as this evening or tomorrow morning, should Mussolini so decide. "Prioritization of effort," he urged, "is most import-ant, as is the obvious necessity to engage and explain the situation and the goals to our key people, both RAF and civilian, and assign them to our task groups.

"In the absence of our appointed but absent Commanding Officer, Air Commodore Fairthorpe, I shall continue to coordinate our efforts and to communicate daily, both up and down our chain of command. One of our most important goals is to obtain fighter planes for our defense against the Italian bombers we anticipate, preferably Hurricanes, but Gladiators if need be. The couple of Swordfish torpedo planes still located here should be safeguarded until we move to an offense mode. But we need planes and pilots, and Wing Commander Bartell, aided by the several RAF officers in this room and, hopefully our friend Captain Murrey, will find a source and establish a pilot corps, an operating RAF Station, and a communication system.

"And Rudy, I am declaring the Hawk to be an RAF fighter plane dressed in French colours, but I do recognize its source, and the fact that you are the only person on Malta who even knows how to start its engine properly, much less take it aloft. Get it safely hidden away this morning, if possible, and function as Task Force Leader to make your special remote airstrip plans a quick reality. Pick whomever is needed as your team, but for the sake of secrecy keep it small. At this time the Hawk is, as you Americans would point out, our only 'ace-in-the-hole'.

"To you, Mr. Crayton, goes the task of maintaining a viable repair station and shop facility, plus a sufficient workforce of excellent mechanics and technicians as we currently enjoy, and which will continue to operate as we now do. Further, because of the Shops location, open exposure, and structural design with so many glass windows, a plan is needed to remove the necessary repair facility and personnel to, hopefully, a new close-by location much less exposed to bombs and warship guns. In order to properly coordinate our efforts, I want Bartell, Crayton, and Rudy to meet each morning in my office at ten for briefing and reporting, whenever possible. Thank you. I urge you now to get to it!" With a somewhat dramatic flair, Captain Donalds, as adjutant to Malta's still in London Air Commander, turned and hurried from the room. In less than a minute or two, Foster Crayton's office was empty of all but Robert, typing his notes of the just ended meeting, and Foster, who searched around for a pad and pencil.

Rudy headed immediately to the Shops looking for Paul Lafessi and his father, but stopped short when he caught up with RAF Officer Slingerland. "Squadron Leader," Rudy called out, "Can the Swordfish carry a pilot and two passengers, if need be? That would really help get the single seat Hawk to Gozo, following a Swordfish with Paul Lafessi as spotter, leading me to what I hope will be a soon mowed grass strip on the Lafessi farm. I'd land, get the Hawk camouflaged some way, and your plane would land and pick me up for the return. That would be the best way to get it hidden away and avoid using the ferry schedule."

Slingerland responded without hesitation. "Get a good, long enough strip mowed in the right wind direction and I'll fly the Swordfish myself, with young Lafessi aboard. The Swordfish can take off from a carrier deck, but I'll need a little longer runway since we won't have the carrier's speed into the wind to help us get up. Give me a half day's warning and I'll get a plane gassed up and ready to lead you where my spotter says. Just both of us keep away from those bloody rock fences up there." Slingerland walked away in one direction, and Rudy continued looking for Paul or his father, Vincent. Arrangements for mowing, and then hiding the Hawk up at the farm needed to get underway immediately.

Once Paul and Vincent heard the plan, the needed action, including what Paul had mentioned to Rudy the other day was immediately arranged by Paul's father, while Paul made sure the Hawk, still hidden in a Hal Far hangar, was ready to go. The next morning. Vincent Lafessi took the early ferry to Gozo, to be picked up at the ferry slip by his friends who were converting the big barn's entry doors and marking the main strip to be mowed that afternoon, along with two or three cross strips to confuse the longer strip's real purpose.

After Poland's invasion by what Germany was now calling a *blitzkrieg,* Captain Donalds, in Air Commodore Fairthorpe's absence, informed the others at the morning briefing that the Air Commodore had approved all of the decisions made by the Malta RAF group. Fairthorpe also reported that Poland had called on England and France to fulfill their treaty obligations, and that France had already responded positively. England, thus far, had not responded, but had ordered ten bomber squadrons to France. A Polish cavalry brigade of lancers had bravely attacked a German tank group and had been destroyed.

When his turn came to report, Rudy described the tasks begun yesterday at the semi-secret Gozo airstrip and the intent to fly the Hawk there using a guide plane, as soon as the mowed airstrip and barn-hangar were in place. No ready solution was offered by anyone addressing what steps might be possible to find a fighter-plane pilot apart from Rudy, and how to get the Hawk aloft from Gozo on a moment's notice of incoming enemy aircraft. Commander Bartell reported that their mysterious Captain Murrey had telephoned on the secure underwater cable that it might just be possible to arrange for Malta to receive an unofficial drop-off of crated Gladiators for later trans-shipment elsewhere by carrier. "More news on this later," Bartell said. All present expressed thanks that Italy had not yet cast her lot, thus giving Malta more time to prepare.

On Sunday, September 3, France and Britain demanded German soldiers withdraw immediately from Poland. When Germany refused, Britain, France, India, Australia, and New Zealand declared war on Germany. Canada waited days longer, until September 10th, the Malta group learned later, allowing US President Roosevelt time to push war materials across the US border into Canada, and not be in violation of the US neutrality laws barring aid to countries officially at war.

Captain Donalds also reported that the RAF had judged that the vastly outnumbered and outgunned Polish Air Force seemed unable to continue fighting as a unified, effective force. He hinted that his superior, Air Commodore Fairthorpe at RAF's London Headquarters, had thought that, "This might lead to something." Rudy reported that the Hawk's guided flight to a safe haven airstrip on Gozo likely would take place tomorrow, and hopefully without spectators of any type, especially Italian airline pilots on their almost daily Malta run. With Italy having not yet declared war on any country, Malta might well escape immediate attack by air or otherwise, but who could be sure that Italy would remain neutral from one day to the next?

Early the next morning, Rudy, in the fully fueled with 100 octane Hawk, armed with all the two fuselage machine guns and two wing cannon ammo it could carry, took off from Hal Far immediately following pilot Slingerland and guide Paul Lafessi in the larger, slower Swordfish biplane, headed on the short hop to Gozo. Rudy was happy to be "pilot-in-command" again, but highly concerned over his mowed strip landing quickly coming up. Over Gozo, he saw his lead plane bank in a tight 360 turn around a farm house and several barns, and there it was, clear as could be if you knew what you were looking at, a long, tightly mowed, absolutely clear, wide landing strip, complete with a light plume of smoke from the farmhouse chimney.

Already at 800 feet above runway level, Rudy set up for a long final against the wind, used his flaps, throttle, and rudder pedals effectively, and touched down, prop blowing cut vegetation over the Hawk and his head, with the canopy slid open. The strip was wide enough to turn the Hawk, and then s-turning, Rudy and the Hawk taxied back to the big barn with the extra wide rolling doors, followed by the Swordfish. There stood a small tractor with a long rod connected to it, fashioned by Vincent Lafessi to pull or push the nose wheel, thus moving the plane. With all switches off and guns confirmed on safety, Vincent and five or six other men, obviously his friends, had the Hawk in the barn and the rolling doors pushed shut in a very short time.

Rudy noticed that two of the men had shotguns hung over their backs on home made rope slings, while another had leaned a rifle against the barn wall. Vincent, seeing Rudy looking, said, "No matter, Mr. Worth. We take our own precautions up here, 'till everything gets settled. The plane is to help Malta, so Malta will help the plane. Paul will explain when you get back to the Shops. Just watch the prop on the Stringbag. Get up in the double rear cockpit with Paul, but always approach from the tail. Have a safe flight back. And with that, Slingerland gunned the engine to turn the biplane into the wind and Paul motioned for Rudy to get going. In just a few minutes they enjoyed a near perfect landing back at Hal Far, apparently sight unseen for the entire adventure.

After climbing down and thanking their expert pilot, Rudy began to question Paul about the Gozo arrangement, but was interrupted by Paul. "Rudy," Paul said as he pulled an envelope from his jacket pocket, "this is for you. Mr. Crayton knows all about the arrangements for the Hawk, and he'll tell you the whole business. I think my sister's letter to you will explain more. So just read the letter, and talk with Foster about the Hawk. I've got to get back to the Shop now, but I'll be there when you want me. The Hawk project you had me work on was fantastic, and I hope you'll assign me to help you on whatever is next. So I'll see you later or tomorrow, O.K.?"

His feet rooted to the ground, Rudy, his stomach already in knots, almost tore the envelope in half before he could pull out the single sheet neatly folded inside.

> *Dear Rudy, With these exciting times swirling around us you may not remember me, but we did motorcycle up to Gozo, in case you've forgotten I'm pleased to learn that your project is moving ahead, although my brother tells me almost nothing, and my father less. I write, first, on what I assume is of no matter to you. I've given notice at my job with the shipping company, and will soon be starting a new one at a place in Valletta I don't think you've heard of, but which should be of high interest to you, especially now, Lascaris. Second, and perhaps (although I hope not) more important information to you, is that your first guide to Gozo has returned, possibly to be followed shortly by Professor X. Robert probably has heard the same gossip. Narak iktar tard? Nina*

His first thought was exclaimed in a loud voice: "What the hell! How could I forget her? What's this Lascaris company?" Then to himself he thought, so Ana Boiano's in town, and with her big mistake! Or has she changed her mind? I pity her father. Anyway, was I supposed to call Nina already; I don't know how to call her without her number. Where did her brother go to, and what does this Narak thing mean at the end? I hate you, you jerk, or find me right now? And what did Paul mean about Foster telling me about the Hawk business? OK, Rudy, slow down and see if Paul will tell me where his sister is, and then see what Foster wants about the plane.

Paul was not far into the Shops before Rudy called to him and, pulling him aside from his co-workers, asked the best way to contact Nina. Paul gave a number for her still current shipping office, and Rudy asked where it was located. Rudy than asked the meaning of the last three words, although Paul had to listen carefully to understand his attempted pronunciation before he smiled and said, "See you later." Rudy smiled to himself, sensing that Nina's question mark after her closing words opened the door a little, as did a couple of double entendre in her lines. Or so he hoped.

Only later did Rudy realize that his first concern was reaching Nina, his second was getting to Foster about the plane, and at that point hadn't even given a second thought to Ana. Well, maybe Robert would pass-on the full gossip.

Next on the to-do list was catching Foster in his office. Rudy did so, but Foster had, he said, "Only a moment, and yes, some basic decisions have been made which affect the Hawk and arrangements for its use. There's some other partial news, also, exciting, and of high interest to you, Rudy. Let's meet tomorrow morning, first thing, and I'll fill you in on what I know, and we can discuss it in detail. You've got a really major role to play, in all likelihood, and assuredly if and when Italy gets into it!" Rudy agreed, and as he turned to leave Foster's outer office, Robert said, "Rudy, if you're free for dinner at a great little restaurant tonight in Valletta – one I don't think you know about – let's go. I can stop by the hotel at seven and we'll drive up. Is that OK?" Rudy instantly agreed, thinking a new restaurant sounded good, and Robert wants to tell me the latest news. This should be an interesting meal.

As it turned out, it was more than an interesting meal. Rudy was delighted to discover a small, family type place with a nice menu and what proved to be a great chef. Almost every table was occupied when the two walked in, but one of the two waiters greeted Robert by name and brought them to a corner table. Robert suggested a couple of choices, both ordered, and Rudy specified a bottle of local wine as his treat. Half a glass later, Robert, apparently forgetting his remorse after telling Rudy his earlier news about Ana and her tragic adventure at the Italian university, began to describe what he called 'some news around town'. Apparently, Ana had returned to Italy after spending the several recent years here in Malta assisting her father, reasons unknown, but was now back and admitting to more than one acquaintance that her former romance with the mysterious American professor had rekindled. He was, she had hinted, on his way to Malta just as soon as he finished some European business elsewhere.

Before Robert could go on with this amazing tale, Rudy called a halt. "It's all interesting, but has no meaning to me. Ana and I never did hit it off, as we say in the US. I wish her well, but have really forgotten all about my brief infatuation with her good looks. I haven't thought a second about her since she drove me up to Gozo and back. I just hope she knows what she's doing, since her last visit to Italy didn't work out so well, did it? Her poor father, a real gentleman, must be alarmed. But let's get on with this amazing meal while you tell me about what Foster's got up his sleeve for me. I've got a meeting with him first thing tomorrow."

Robert professed to know nothing about any Hawk news, but did tell Rudy about the horrible report concerning the first British offensive attack, a mission to bomb some German navel bases in the North Sea. The day after Britain's declaration of war, twenty-nine RAF bombers set out, with ten returning to base with bombs still aboard, unable to find their targets. One bombed a town miles away in a neutral country, three attacked British ships by mistake, and seven others were shot down by antiaircraft fire. However, eight found the target and three duds were dropped on a German battleship. A few bombs hit the German cruiser Emden, but the most damage to that enemy ship was caused by one of the bombers crashing onto its deck. Both of them expressed hope that things would improve rapidly for the RAF.

The meal finished and the bill shared, Robert and Rudy left the Restaurant after dark and walked toward the corner down a steep, very narrow sidewalk, Rudy in the lead and headed for Robert's parked car. Two men were coming up the sidewalk hill, and Rudy moved against the building's wall to let them pass. Two other men, walking just behind Robert, suddenly jumped forward, knocking Robert down and into Rudy. As Rudy began to fall forward, one struck at Rudy's head with a short piece of pipe. The two men coming toward Rudy caught him as he went down, only semi-conscious, and, grabbing his arms, began to drag him downhill on the toes of his shoes, while the other two kicked Robert as he lay. Suddenly there was a loud yelling from across the street: "Le,Le, Wagfa! No, No. Stop!" Running across the street directly toward them, his loud yells bringing some others to windows and out of several buildings onto the narrow street. "Sejjah Pulizja, Sejjah Tabi, get the police, get a doctor!" shouted another, all to the backs of the four attackers who by now were running away down the middle of the street, leaving Rudy and Robert on their backs, half off the narrow sidewalk.

When Rudy opened his eyes hours later, daylight was streaming through the window of a small white room, onto the bed he was in, and a beautiful blond angel, he thought, was saying something to him. He tried to focus on the angel's face, but another angel in a white dress took her place and said, in understandable English, "Well, looks like you're awake and focusing your eyes. That's good. Here's a sip of water and I'll go get the doctor. As that angel disappeared, the blond angel stepped into view again and said, "Rudy, thank God. It's Ana, but I can't stay. You'll soon be OK." She leaned over, kissed his cheek before he could utter a sound, much less a word, and disappeared.

She was replaced by a man who looked into Rudy's eyes, one at a time, with a small flashlight beam and then asked Rudy to focus both eyes on the light of his 'torch' while he moved it around in a circle. "Good," he said, "you'll live." Rudy began to understand where he was and realized the man spoke with a British accent and sounded like the doctor back in high school when football playing Rudy got a concussion from a hard hit. "You're lucky the thieves ran off. I understand the first person to go at them was the Kappillan, and his yelling brought out others who called the clinic ambulance and the police. By the way, your friend was roughed up and has some bruises, but aside from the soreness, he's OK and was discharged earlier this morning.

Your blond girlfriend was here for a short time until you woke up, but said she had to go to work. Your friend, I believe, is returning with your boss and probably a policeman who will have a few questions. Otherwise I'm keeping you here over tonight just to be sure about your concussion. Fortunately, the blow was more glancing than a direct hit, and you have a hard head. No internal bleeding, and that's good. Now, shut your eyes and get more rest, flat on your back."

CHAPTER 16

NEW ARRANGEMENTS

Thursday, September 7, 1939

IT was mid-afternoon when Foster appeared at Rudy's door, accompanied by a man Rudy did not recognize, and followed by a slowly shuffling Robert. "Hello, Rudy," Foster began, but his voice began to waiver as he stepped closer. As he reached Rudy's bedside he cried out, almost as though he had been injured himself. "Oh Lord, what have they done to you! I am so sorry; they must be crazy! What can we do? We'll get to the bottom of this, mark my words."

"Rudy, I am very, very sorry. What an awful night, but thank God you're not hurt worse. The doctor said just one more night here so you can rest. I hurt, but you really must hurt a lot more. I'll never go to that restaurant again!" All this poured forth from Robert, by then leaning against the side of Rudy's bed to hold himself from trembling.

"Robert, my friend," said Rudy softly, "I'm sorry we both got it, but how could anyone know? We were at the wrong place at the wrong time. Everything happened so fast I didn't have even a second to throw up my arm. Who the hell were they? Just street thugs, I guess, looking for money. Damn, I wish I could get them one at a time!" At that, the stranger pushed forward to get a first row view of the head bandaged Rudy, and introduced himself before anyone else could.

"Mr. Worth," the man with an athletic build wrapped in a civilian suit, and looking ten years older than either Rudy or Robert, said, "I'm Joseph Sanno, appointed by the British government as Passport Control Officer here in Malta. I've been wanting to meet you, but hardly in these circumstances. However, I'm especially interested in learning more about this apparently random encounter, and Robert here has filled me in with some details, as sketchy as they understandably are. But no conversation now. You must get rested today, and I could stop by Mr. Crayton's office tomorrow morning to spend a few minutes with you. Until then, get the most from this excellent clinic and have a good sleep tonight." With that, he turned from the bed and walked into the hall. This allowed Foster and Robert a few words with Rudy and to wish him a good night and a promised pick up upon his discharge in the morning as they headed, also, for the door.

As he trailed Foster , Robert caught the hand signal from Rudy to step back to his bedside. "Robert," said Rudy, "what in hell is going on? Unless I'm delirious, Ana Boiano was in this room when I woke up this morning from the concussion, having told the doctor, he said, that she was my girlfriend. When the nurse stepped out Ana kissed my cheek and said I'd be OK. Then she disappeared. I mean left the room, not *disappeared* like a ghost. How did she know where I was and what happened? Have you seen her? Something's crazy here!"

"Rudy, I have no idea about what you're saying! I haven't seen her in months. It can't be. Maybe that's what happens with a concussion, but I really don't know. All I can say is get some quiet sleep here and we'll try to get an explanation tomorrow. Foster and I have really not spread the word about what happened to us, or where you are, so you shouldn't be getting any more visitors. And I also have no idea why the Passport Officer wants to talk with you. Tomorrow!" And Robert then disappeared, himself, out the door.

Five minutes later the nurse came in with food on a tray, pulled a table next to the bed, and swung an arm from the table to over Rudy's chest. "Wiggle up a bit and I'll prop you with a pillow so you can get some dinner. Then I'll take your temp, pulse, and BP, and you can get some sleep. You're out of here tomorrow, and your good looking blondie girlfriend can take care of you. If you need anything before you go to sleep, or during the night, just pull this cord and the bell will let us know. I'm off duty shortly, but another nurse will be on duty.

"Anyway, I guess somebody from your work or someplace wants to be sure you have a quiet night. There's a man with some kind of official government card sitting up the hall a bit. Says he's here for the night. Not too often that happens; guess you must be important? OK, eat now, I'll be back in a couple for your vitals, and then get some sleep. And there's a bathroom for you just through that door, next to the closet." From all of that, Rudy especially heard, first, *blond girlfriend,* then followed by *government man, dinner, and bathroom.* Something really is going on, he thought, but as Robert had said, "Tomorrow!"

As promised, Rudy – who really had gotten a good night's sleep – was transported the next morning by Robert back to his hotel for a shower and change of clothing, and then on to Foster's office. His discharge from the clinic had required only a few words with the doctor, his signature on a form, and a quick, fruitless look for what he now thought of as his personal government babysitter, assuming the nurse was serious in her description last evening. With an awakening jolt, Rudy recognized the man standing near Foster as Mr. Sanno, the Passport Control Officer. The idea flashed through his mind that he was about to be ejected from Malta and returned in some kind of shame all the way to the Curtiss plant in Buffalo. A 'good-bye to his job' message flashed across his mind, but Foster's warm welcome and Mr. Sanno's smiled greeting set him at ease; very, very curious, but at ease. Mr. Sanno extended his hand, Rudy responded, and Mr. Sanno said, "Rudy, my car is just outside. Would you be willing to accompany me to my office down at the Port so we can talk, and allow Mr. Crayton to conduct business this morning here in his own office. I think I can organize some lunch for us, also, since it's getting close to that time. What do you say?" Even more at ease now, Rudy agreed, and off they went to Foster's, "Good-by and see you later, Rudy," parting.

Passport Control Officer Sanno had the most impressive office Rudy had seen since his visits to the executive floor at the Curtiss plant, back in Buffalo. That was so long ago, it seemed, that he had to pause and count up the months since last June to remember how long he'd been gone. Time really does fly, he thought, when you're having fun. Or getting beaten over the head with a lead pipe! Mr. Sanno ushered Rudy through a large office space occupied by several men and women working at desks, telephones, and what Rudy took to be a large two-way radio, into a smaller but nicely appointed inner office. With a short sweep of his hand he motioned Rudy into a padded armchair. "Well," his host smiled, "Welcome to my digs. I thought we'd be more comfortable here than up at the Shops, and also more private, since I think what I shall say to you will be more than just interesting. And we'll lunch right here shortly.

"Mr. Worth – Rudy, if you please – allow me to explain my work here in Malta and account for my strong interest in meeting and talking with you. Before I begin, however, I must ask you directly to keep all of what you learn from our discussion in absolute confidence. Even as an American, the British Secrets Act of 1911 has some applicability here in British Commonwealth territory. Forgive me for reciting that, however, since my Director, Mr. Stephenson, who heads the British-US Security Coordination unit of M16 across the pond in the United States, has been told about your key role in getting Malta ready for the worst. Although his office is in Rockefeller Center, he meets often, I'm told, with your Colonel Whittaker in Washington, near the White House.

"I'm told, also, that the Colonel sends his regards to you, and his insistence to us to keep you absolutely safe. Which I intend to do. British Passport Control Officers cover quite a broad expanse of tasks, as you perhaps have guessed, and the man in the clinic all last night was one of ours. We're stretched a bit thin here in Malta, but just for the moment. Britain's official entry into the war last week has me very concerned about the possibility of Fascist and Nazi activities here, so improvements are coming. But now I shift, first, to your unfortunate adventure with Robert two evenings ago.

"Although Robert does not, do you have any idea who the assailants were or how they knew your location? Please understand that their attack was well-planned beforehand, and not random chance! They were not thieves." Rudy had no idea, and was almost unbelieving. "Rudy, it may well amaze you to learn that the active, and still legal, German American Bund, a pro Nazi organization founded in 1933 in your country, has an agent here in Malta. We are quite certain that, among other mischief, he intends to neutralize the work you are engaged in. Even more, he has an interest in neutralizing – or worse – you.

"Just consider. You have been assigned by a very influential warplane company HRM Ltd., and also charged by your President Roosevelt in coordinating plans to keep this key Mediterranean location out of Fascist and Nazi control. True? Further, our friend may well have an aide who, innocently or not, provides him with information concerning your activities and plans."

"What?"exclaimed Rudy. "You can't be serious?"

" Oh, but I am, and that brings us to surprising news number two. Rudy, do you know a young woman named Ana Boiano?"

"Oh my God," exclaimed Rudy, "what are you saying? That can't be. She was in my room at the clinic when I came out of the concussion and..."

"She was in your room while you were unconscious? Are you sure? What happened? Did she say anything? Do anything?"

Rudy went on, hesitating at every other word, but describing the entire episode, including the physician's off-hand comment about her being his girlfriend. Mr. Sanno interjected a request for Rudy to relate his entire history with Ana, beginning at the beginning, and recounting what Rudy thought about the young woman's immediate interest in him following his arrival on the island. What prompted her to see Rudy privately in the clinic? Where did they go while on Gozo? Importantly, did Ana know *why* they went to Gozo? How did she track down Rudy immediately following the attack, and how might she have known about his dinner plans with Robert for that evening? Was anyone else in the clinic room while Ana was present? Rudy did his best to answer these unanswerable questions, all the while stating he did not see any reason why Ana would do this, or imagine that she was his "girlfriend", although he had been enthusiastic about that idea early on.

Mr. Sanno held up his hand to quell Rudy's bewilderment and said, "Rudy, I'm glad you're seated while hearing what I next tell you. I do repeat, however, that this must remain absolutely unknown to anyone else. Do you agree?" Rudy, eyes wide, nodded. Mr. Sanno, looking straight at Rudy, explained that Ana's instructor at the Italian University, the infamous American who had possibly seduced her, thus bringing great turmoil, was the very active member of the German American Bund. He was now operating again in Italy, plus Malta, on behalf of his organization and its purposes. All a shocked Rudy could manage in response was a loud gulp.

"By-the-way, we've already learned from your hotel reception desk that a phone call was received just after you left for the restaurant, asking for you. You had mentioned to the staff member at the entry door that you were headed for a different restaurant, saying the name. That information was innocently passed on to the caller. So those men were told where to wait by the American, I judge, who likely was watching the attack and saw the clinic's name on the ambulance. Draw your own conclusion about how Miss Boiano knew where to find you, and learn your condition. To confirm your clouded memory of awakening there, the doctor and the duty nurse both confirmed the presence of your blond girlfriend. Thus the armed man outside your room all night, perhaps preventing yet another attempt.

"Now, let's talk about what we, and you, do next. Do you come from an American city, Rudy, or from a more rural, country area? Are you a hunter, perhaps with some experience with guns? Now that we're officially at war with Germany, but not yet Italy, will you still be riding your motorcycle to the Shops each day? Are you frequently alone out walking? What will your relationship to Miss Boiano be should she contact you? What about her father, Anthony Boiano, a strong Malta patriot unhappy about England's withdrawal of defensive resources from his island? And last, a most important question: Will you cooperate with me concerning a plan I have to bring this troublesome business to an end?"

"Tell me the plan. If I can help I want to, but I wouldn't want to get into anything without knowing what you're thinking of. I really don't know much at all about Ana. Only what she told me on the Gozo trip, and that was pretty disturbing. I've put her out of my mind, that is until this talk with you and her mysterious visit at the clinic. By the way, I understand that the thugs were scared off by a man who ran at them while yelling for help, thank God. Who was he?"

"You just thanked the right person, Rudy, when you said 'Thank God'. The mysterious man was a Kappillan, and a popular one around the island. A priest, Rudy, Father Thomas you would say, but better known here as as Dun Thom. It's certainly possible that the "thugs", as you call them, knew who he was as he started yelling. Anyway, that's probably what saved you and Robert from even worse treatment. Now, listen to the little plan I've worked out, and tell me what you think about it, and the role I propose for you in it. Not an extensive role, certainly, but a key one..."

Rudy listened, asked a few questions, emphasized that he couldn't guarantee success, but said he would give it a try. He pointed out that someone at a higher level than he would have to agree, and Mr. Sanno assured him that had already been checked out and agreed to. The goal, as Rudy now understood, was to rid Malta of a clever and vicious enemy, with as little public awareness as possible. They talked more about details, while the lunch was brought to the room by a man introduced by Mr. Sanno as Rudy's night time room watcher at the clinic.

As they finished, Mr. Sanno once again asked if Rudy had been a hunter back home. Rudy described hunting for deer with his father, once a year during the hunting season, and wondered why that question. "Good," said Mr. Sanno, "then why not familiarize yourself with this and carry it in your pocket if you feel the need for an evening stroll. Until our little plan works out, I mean. It's loaded and the safety is on. Small and only six shots from a short barrel, but it's a noise-maker. I'll not insist, but I'd feel better. Just to make some noise, you understand, in case Dun Thom isn't across the street. Ha ha! Be careful with it, just as you were with that rifle while hunting, and let me know as soon as you initiate the plan.

"Here's a card with two telephone numbers. The first is this office, open during regular business hours. But the second is a private number which will get you myself or a duty agent, any time of the day or night, all night, every day of the week. We maintain a house on Malta, up in Sliema, and someone knowledgeable is always there on duty. You must let me know right away that our plan has been implemented. The easiest way is by phone, so don't hesitate, but I know you understand. By-the-way, should you ever want a really secure line back to HRM in London or Washington, we can arrange that from the house."

The same agent, as Rudy thought of him, drove Rudy back to the Shops, after being urged by his host to "keep safe." Immediately upon getting there, he found Foster and determined that, indeed, the Hawk was going to be moved a bit, not because England was now officially at war with Germany, but because it was anticipated that Mr. Sanno's plan would be initiated by Rudy within the next week. Obviously, he realized, Foster and Mr. Sanno had already talked.

As it turned out, initiation took less than a week, and all Rudy had to do was answer a phone call made through the hotel switchboard early on Sunday evening, three days later. The call was from his blondie girlfriend, as the clinic nurse had called her, and Rudy was certainly pleased to respond to her suggestion that they meet for dinner at a small restaurant just down the street from the hotel. Could he possibly make it this evening? He certainly could! And in a half hour he had to admit to himself that Ana was as beautiful as he remembered her, strolling down the beach in what seemed a lifetime ago. Yes, Nina crossed his mind, but only briefly, as they sat across a table toward the rear of the little place. What the hell, he thought. I'm only doing this because I have to!

Ana acted as though she had never spoken that revealing story to him on the Gozo ferry, although Rudy briefly considered, as he sat facing her, that her story may not have been factual at all. Ana continued, saying all the right things about his injuries and her visiting him at the clinic, and how concerned she was as soon as she heard about the incident "They just would not let me in to see you unless I was a family member, so I said we were engaged. That worked, and I hope you understand? Thank God you're alright now." Rudy's reaction was that either she was sincere about her caring for him, or she was an excellent actress. He softened more as she spoke earnestly, while looking directly at him, and he found himself leaning more toward the former judgment. Later he remembered she had not revealed just how she had learned so quickly of the attack and to where the ambulance had taken him.

Ana continued, now shifting to Rudy's "important work in helping Malta" and wondering if their trip to Gozo to find a little airstrip had been successful? Oh Boy, thought Rudy, quickly leaning in the other direction, here it comes. "Well, actually yes, right next to your friends' the Lafessi's farmhouse on that back road to Victoria. There's a very large barn right there by the house, and my Hawk plane is safely stored in that barn, all fueled and ready to be used if Malta does have to go to war. Now I'll have a different project here, or maybe I'll be called back to my Company. I'm not sure. At any rate, the Hawk is safely tucked away, far from the public's eyes. But how are *you*, Ana, and are you still working to assist your father? I have great respect for him, and I hope he's well?"

Their dinner arrived at the table, they ate and continued a very generalized, meaningless conversation. It seemed to Rudy that Ana was now aimed toward ending this silly date as quickly as he was, and he wanted to assist in reaching a timely ending as well. After all, he assumed, they each had an important phone call to make, unless hers would require a personal conference with her instructor? "Sure," he whispered to himself, "that certainly was a quick romance!" The dinner-date over, Ana told Rudy how much she appreciated and enjoyed their friendship, how she anticipated their meeting again soon, and that she would give his best regards to her father. Rudy answered in like manner, and they left the restaurant, Rudy having paid for the dinner. *Insult added to injury*, he seethed. He turned immediately to walk to his hotel, while Ana crossed the street and headed in a different direction from her arrival.

In just a couple of minutes Rudy marched through the hotel's entry, pulling Mr. Sanno's card from his wallet. He asked for the desk phone and an outside line, dialed the second number on the card, and when a voice answered in English he said, "Tell Mr. Sanno the plan is initiated." The voice said, "I'll let him know immediately, Mr. Worth."

Rudy turned in very early, anxious with anticipation of what he thought would happen next, bitter with anger about how Ana had used him - and with a smile on that lovely face - and mentally listing all of the questions he would fire at Foster in the morning.

CHAPTER 17

MORE NEW ARRANGEMENTS

Monday, September 11

WHEN Rudy awakened next morning, a Monday workday following his Sunday evening tête-a-tête with the now less mysterious Ana Boiano, he hurried through a coffee and hard roll breakfast in the small cafe next to his hotel, climbed on his motorcycle, and arrived early at Foster's office in the Kalafrana Shops. So early that even the famously early Robert was not yet at his typewriter, affording Rudy the opportunity to go to his own narrow mail and memo box on the far wall shelf and pull out several sheets and two envelopes, all addressed to him. Two of the single sheets, clipped together, were Robert's summary of the morning informational meetings called by Captain Donalds following the invasion of Poland, and missed by Rudy due to his misadventure.

The summaries reported the United States declaring its neutrality on September 5th, and Britain's first air raid warning on the 6th. The warning was false, but the RAF interceptors fired at each other in error, and Spitfires had shot down two Hurricanes. Germany's Göring declared Berlin would never be bombed, and British forces began moving into France, but not Poland, on September 10th. The third single sheet listed the work assignment schedules for the Shops for last week and next. While the war, although declared, was not yet upon them, Shop personnel were urged to keep ahead of schedule demands while remembering that a curfew had been announced for Malta, and public transportation was being curtailed. All must work together as a team, etc., etc. This last, while likely voiced by Foster, Rudy judged, sounded more like Robert's authorship.

The fourth sheet was brief in its reporting, but important to Rudy. It announced, first, that London's Air Ministry had decided that two experienced RAF fighter pilots would be transported to Malta from the ranks of some existing squadron (or squadrons) on the home island and assigned to the newly acquired Curtiss Hawk, if such pilots could be spared and safely transported. Second, all reasonable efforts would be made to locate some number of Gloster Gladiators or Sea Gladiators to be assigned to RAF Hal Far, Malta and sent there as soon as feasible, considering circumstances and War Ministry defined needs. The Ministry understood that more modern fighter aircraft would be better suited, but such were deemed impossible to spare at this time. Swallowing internal turmoil over his "ownership" of the Hawk and his strong desire to be its pilot, however completely inexperienced in war flying, Rudy could only think, rationally, to each of the British desires: *Lots Of Luck! Who do you think you're kidding?*

He continued by opening the two envelopes included in his mail. The first memo was signed by both Captain Donalds and the Squadron Leader, and requested that he continue in his HRM assignment at the Kalafrana Shops, focusing now on bringing improvements to any existing RAF planes remaining on Malta, and any aircraft brought to the Island by the RAF or other sources, to be used in Malta's defense. His expertise, skill, and devotion to this important task was not only deeply appreciated by all levels of British government, but necessary and vital to the Island's defense and very life when the coming war descends upon us. Wow, thought an almost impressed Rudy.

The second envelope's single sheet, signed by Captain Donalds, informed that Rudy's influence with Lieutenant General H. J. Garrison, decorated veteran of the Second Boer War and The Great War, very soon to be appointed as Acting Governor of Malta, brought about through Rudy's friendship with Major Gordon H.L. Astill, V.C. D.S.O. M.C., could now appropriately be applied. Captain Donalds would greatly appreciate Mr. Worth's agreement to meet with the Army, Navy, and RAF Commanders on Malta to discuss such a plan. Rudy thought, almost out loud, "Oh, good grief, I barely remember that business. Didn't Major Astill give me a card for the General, and an envelope? Where in hell do I have them? Do I still have them? I'll look tonight before I send a message to Captain Donalds. Cripe, what next? And did anything happen to the Hawk last night?"

As that last question raced through Rudy's mind, the office door opened to admit both Foster and Robert. "Rudy," Foster said, let's huddle immediately. I've much to discuss with you. Ah, I see you have your mail. Good, let's go into our little conference room as soon as I shed my jacket. Do you want coffee? Robert, could you organize some coffee for the three of us? And bring your notepad in with you, please. Rudy, have you at least scanned your mail? Yes? But bring it into our meeting as part of our discussion, and a pad for yourself. OK, let's get to work, if we're going to make Captain Donalds' 10:00 o'clock briefing meeting up at his office."

In they went, Robert delayed in search of coffee, but soon returning with a tray, coffee cups filled, and the necessaries on a small tray. "All right," Foster began, "Rudy, from your mail, at least, you can see that somehow the RAF intends to provide experienced pilots for the Hawk. But unless they'll come from the recent Spanish air fighting – and I don't know how – we'll just have to wait and see. So far, as you both know, the RAF is showing its inexperience in both shooting and bombing, but we'll quickly catch on, as we Brits always do. Also, we won't hold our breaths, but I do believe we'll soon have some Sea Gladiators to work on, Rudy, if that's how you Americans say it? I observe that your presence here is Americanizing our idioms! And I'll also wager that Jim Conners will be the man to thank for the planes. We do need to stay alert for the opportunity to abscond with any, be they in crates or already assembled. I intend to speak with George and a few others in the Shops who have good friends working in the port areas, so that we can take advantage of any crates left down there in transit. If the balloon goes up here in Malta, no one anywhere will need them more than we.

Rudy cut into Foster's oral planning with, "What does that balloon thing mean, anyway? I've heard it several times here and coming over on the boat, but I have no reference for it."

Foster responded quickly, cutting off Robert's attempt to get into the conversation. "That's because you never had an air raid across the Pond, my lad. The balloons were cable tethered barrage balloons – big blimpy things held at various altitudes with a bit of hope that enemy bombers would run into them, or their cables. But more likely, their presence would cause the bombers to head into areas where there were no balloons, thus setting them up for spotlight and antiaircraft pre-aimed fire. They were weapons of war, thus the term. When the balloons go up, we're going to get bombed." "If we do get into it now," added Robert, "we'll need balloons, since my friend in the anti-aircraft artillery unit tells me we're nowhere near the guns or spotlights recommended we have by the Imperial Defence Committee." *Wonderful*, thought Rudy.

Rudy now steered Foster into the topic of his work and research assignments, as spelled out in the memorandum signed by both Donalds and Bartell. Foster appeared well aware of the memorandum, and certainly in favor of it. "With the immediate and short term future projections just discussed," he said, "there is no question but that Rudy's knowledge and skill, as well as his familiarity with the responsibilities of the Kalafrana Shops, makes it imperative that he shift his attention to strengthening both the Shops capabilities and the fighting effectiveness of all aircraft here or sent here to defend the Island and keep it from the hands of enemies." All things considered, Rudy could hardly disagree, nor did he want to, unless his assignment from the HRM Aviation Company was changed. He was, though, fascinated that Foster had just spoken dramatically of Rudy in the third person, as though Rudy were not present to hear. Foster was getting to be quite a speech maker, praised Rudy to himself.

"That sounds fine to me," Rudy voiced, "assuming HRM doesn't summon me home or change my assignment." Foster countered with the suggestion that Rudy, using a secure line, report to HRM the status of the Hawk, the state of affairs in Malta, and the urging by the RAF that he now focus on applying his research and experience to upgrading all other available aircraft in preparation for war.

"Again, I agree, and I know where I can get a very secure phone line back to London and Washington. But shouldn't I wait until we hear from Mr. Sanno? I'm anxious to hear any news in detail before I tell them I need to get off the Hawk and get on with basic air protection." As Rudy finished, all three heard the phone on Foster's desk sound an outside call with the two closely spaced rings, then repeated twice more as Foster raced Robert out the doorway and into the office. Rudy heard Foster answer the call and after a moment say, "Good, he's right here and I'll give him your message immediately. I understand. Twenty minutes. Thank you." Foster then hung up and Rudy practically yelled, "What?"

"You'll be picked up by Mr. Sanno, right here, in twenty minutes. That's all the woman told me, so you let me know as soon as you can. In the meantime, I'm going to Donalds' meeting, and I'll explain about your absence. Call me with any news as soon as you can." Foster walked out the door and headed toward the Captain's office, while Rudy stood outside the office outer door, watching the road, shifting his weight from one foot to the other, and licking his dry lips.

As the car pulled up to the office door, Rudy was in the front passenger seat before the wheels had stopped rolling. "What's the news, what happened?" Mr. Sanno looked at him, put the car in gear again, and started out toward the main road. Where the road branched he turned north toward the Grand Harbour, Sliema, and the Gozo Ferry landing, still not answering Rudy. "Are we going up to Gozo? What happened?" Rudy twisted in his seat, leaning closer toward the driver.

"We don't need to go all the way to Gozo, just to our house in Sliema. Well, the fool tried it late last night. In the middle of the night, really. Hired a motorboat ride to Gozo from a boatman in a tavern last evening, after you had dinner with the young woman who, by-the-way, got right to him with the big news. He also hired two of the idiots who had a go at you and Robert the other night, telling them he was owed money and never paid by a Gozo farmer. Said he'd get even by burning down one of his barns. He was really too much in a hurry to plan his steps and pull it off properly. We had a minder on him, of course, and were kept abreast of his actions by radio. Even the suspicious boat owner got word to the police by phone as soon as he crossed back to the Malta island side. Of course, we knew their intent before they even left for the boat run up to Gozo, and that was going on twilight.

"He'd earlier left a car at the Gozo boat dock according to the boatman, and the three of them drove up to the Lafessi farm. That car they left at the Gozo dock shows they had a general idea of just where their dirty work was next needed, but not exactly where on Gozo. Our protection team was already there, of course, both inside and under cover outside. We had the advantage, all this week, of the fast RAF rescue launch to provide our transport back and forth to Gozo when ever we needed. I also had three squads of the second battalion, West Kent Regiment, well back and hidden, blocking the road and the foot trail through the wooded area. Same Regiment that's guarding your new radar station, so they knew what was wanted.

"But the one small group we didn't know about was the locals – nearby farmers, I'd say - quite determined to keep the plane safe from whomever looked suspicious. They knew the immediate area better than we did, and never showed themselves as we moved into place. At about the same time, the amateur arsonists got into their car at the Gozo dock for the short trip toward the farm. They had a petrol can and all, made the drive up to the farm, parked the car and sneaked around to the back of the barn. The doors were closed of course, so they didn't know that the plane had been towed to the other end of the mowed runway and covered with straw and branches all of several days before. We gather the locals lads knew that by observation, if not directly from a Lafessi, but they waited until our friend started to unscrew the petrol can's cap. At least one of them came up quickly toward him then. He must have sensed that and turned, starting to pull a pistol from his pocket, but the local was quicker on the trigger. Caught him right in the chest with a shotgun blast and just as quickly disappeared, like Bob's your uncle. All our group were running toward the action, and so all we could nab were the two hired thugs who were on the ground shaking with fear. Found his pistol half out of his pocket as we rolled him over. Looked just like the photo Washington had sent us.

"I'd like to learn who pulled the trigger, naturally, but I don't think the local police have the resources and the inclination to beat the bushes for very long finding that out. My task is to handle this in a sensitive way, letting our American counterparts know about the death of Mr. Arthur Horst Steffens of the Bund organization, and that his remains have already been photographed and properly handled. I believe Steffens was his name, although he used several others, including Professor Antony Stevens, which is what Ana Boiano knew him as, up in Italy, where he produced phony papers to get that temporary University position. Very clever and handsome he was, and a good actor. He'd been given instructions by his handler in Germany to get cozy with a useful student from Malta, Germany's future target. Didn't hurt that she was naive and pretty, I suppose, but, as we get closer to Sliema, let me tell you two additional factors in this escapade.

"First, and of no real consequence, the two local bullyboys who accompanied our friend are simply going to be charged with assault with a weapon and attempted robbery on two local businessmen, and will serve a bit of time, as we say. There'll be no mention by anyone, including those two, of the attempted arson and its consequences for the person who led them astray. They fully understand and accept those conditions. You and Robert will have to be content with that.

"Second, and much more important, is how to handle and what to do with the daughter of one of the most popular Malta patriots who is also a leading Maltese businessman. This is a young woman who naively fell in love with a lying, monstrous rogue who, once again, she'll learn from me, has disappeared after using her, and who, this time, will not return to trouble her. Or *us*, I might say, but only to you. She has no, and will not be provided with, any knowledge of what actually transpired last night. That assumes, as you can understand, that no communication concerning any of this will be revealed by you to her or anyone else. Would you agree to that?"

"Yes," replied Rudy after a long silent moment, strengthened with, "I do. In a way it makes sense to deal her out of it and hope that she heals this time and stops blaming herself for being stupid and trusting. But is she so pro-Fascist or so fond of Italy that she'll get herself into more trouble? I fully intend to steer clear of her."

Mr. Sanno added, "I know a close friend of her father, Anthony Boiano, and I hope to have my friend talk with Mr. Boiano at length, suggesting that, with war upon us, Ana's activities be closely monitored. I believe her father will get the message, since he undoubtedly has heard the earlier rumors concerning her problem at University, plus her recent taking up again with this so-called Antony Stevens. You know my friend also, the manager of your hotel. We'll keep a loose watch on her, at least for a couple of months. You, also, could keep us advised, should you become aware of her straying from the fold. We'll hope for the best, and today we want to set her on the right track, as it were.

"On a pretext, we brought her in. So I'm going to have a little talk with her, a bit hard, but more like a kindly uncle. Since I won't really know how to judge her, however, and since she has no close friends I could count on, I want you behind a one way mirror, seeing and hearing, so you can judge how she takes it all, and advise me. O.K.? I may even call a short break in my discussion with her, so I can check with you without her knowing you're even in the building."

Rudy reluctantly agreed, and shortly they pulled into the driveway of a nondescript house on a side street. Mr. Sanno instructed Rudy to remain in the small entryway while he talked to one of his staff in an inside room. The assistant then ushered Rudy into a small darkened room with only a chair and small table. She motioned Rudy to sit, while, with a finger to her lips, she indicated a one-way mirror and a tiny speaker mounted on the wall in back of the table. Rudy sat, looking at another darkened room, as his guide left and quietly closed the door. Rudy was startled when the next room came alive with a lamp, revealing a small table and two comfortable looking chairs. Almost immediately, Mr. Sanno ushered Ana Boiano into the room and invited her to be comfortable in one of the chairs. He sat in the other, the table between them, and asked if she would like a coffee? Ana declined, Rudy hearing every word softly over the small speaker.

The use of a one-way mirror, which Rudy had never before experienced, was unnerving. He found himself ducking down whenever Ana even glanced momentarily toward that wall mirror, perhaps looking at her beautiful self. Ana, appearing slightly nervous and certainly inquisitive, was sitting on the edge of the chair with hands tightly folded on the table top. Even so, Rudy thought, she really was a stunning blond, but immediately whipped his brain by calling himself an idiot, remembering that he'd never even tried to contact the just as beautiful Nina after receiving her teasing note, days ago. He needed, he considered, to pull himself together and get with it – whatever that implied – if he wanted to find romance on Malta! Rudy was snapped out of his momentary trance by the louder voice of Joseph Sanno coming through the speaker, and by his suddenly more dominant self in the one way window.

"Thank you, Miss Boiano, for agreeing to spend a few minutes helping me to clarify the two incidents occurring this week, the last as recent as early this morning. Your personal appearance in the first, that is your kind visit to Mr. Worth in the Malta Private Clinic a few evenings ago, has me wondering how you learned so quickly of the attack on him and his colleague and how you knew where to find him, unconscious and under medical treatment? Such quick action, however thoughtful, has me mystified."

"Don't be mystified Mr. Sanno, for the answer is a simple one. A woman friend was having dinner in that same restaurant, and knowing that Mr. Worth had been a short term suitor of mine, called me even before the excitement had ceased. She described the incident as reported by those who had rushed from the place upon the shouting, saying that he and his friend – whom she also recognized as a local young man - had been viciously attacked by robbers and injured. As she relayed this to me, the ambulance, marked with Malta Clinic signage, arrived and took them both away. While Mr. Worth – Rudy – had pressured me unsuccessfully to reciprocate his strong feelings, I did consider him a warmhearted acquaintance. After all, we had spent a tourist type day together shortly after he arrived here, so I decided to learn the extent of his injuries and drove myself to the Clinic. Since going into his clinic room was limited to family members, none of whom are in Malta, I said I was his fiancée. I sat in the room for a bit, said a few words when he awoke, kissed his cheek then, assuring him he'd be well, and left. If this was against the rules or unlawful, I do confess. But does that explain it?"

"It does'" said Mr. Sanno, "and I assume you wouldn't mind if I contacted the friend who was there and phoned you?"

"Oh dear," Ana replied, "that would present a problem for her, for I'm afraid she wasn't where she told another she was going that evening, nor was she with...well, I trust you understand? I really can't say more without exposing her, and I couldn't do that."

"Ah, well, I suppose that answers my first question. Now about my second mystery, I must ask if you know a Mr. Antony Stevens?"

"How strange you would ask that, for if you don't know the answer already you must be in the tiny percentage of the local population which ignores gossip. He was an instructor of mine at the University of Bologna, a visiting American, whose wife appeared unannounced one day, resulting in his dismissal by the Headmaster of my school and my returning home before graduating, and working as my father's assistant. I believe you might say that we had grown overly fond of each other, and that my dismissal caused me great unrest. However, my feelings for him had not diminished, and when he returned to Europe for business purposes, newly divorced, he contacted me here and we have communicated several times. He has serious feelings for me and is upset that other men here have shown their serious interest in me. He is doubly concerned that war might come to Malta from Italy, and is eager to forestall the great harm we would then have to endure. I don't know what business he represents, but he no longer teaches. I haven't seen him here for the past few weeks, but why do you ask about him? Your question has upset me! Please, tell me what this is all about."

"I ask only because I did know a little about your unfortunate situation at university, and as UK Passport Control Officer here in Malta I've recently come to learn that Mr. Stevens has represented some organizations which are not pro-British, nor are they pro-American, his own country. They may well be judged as pro-Nazi, and for that reason, some weeks ago, I declared his visa null and void, and I would be very, very surprised if you, or I for that matter, should hear from him again. We certainly won't be expecting him to return to Malta.

"I am stressed to know about the turmoil you've gone through because of him, and, I suppose, your fondness for him based on your earlier experience at Bologna. Britain, and thus Malta, as you certainly know, are at war with Germany – although it has not yet directly impacted us – and I fear that we may soon see Italy joining the Nazi group. Therefore, you must be cautious, as must we all, to keep in mind that we are first Maltese and not Italian, and second, part of the British Commonwealth. Anything less could be viewed as a serious error, or even a war-time crime. I beg you to keep that in your thoughts. Now, unless you want to continue, I'll thank you and ask my assistant to drive you home. I know it's not far, here in Sliema."

"I'll take the ride home, and I'll think carefully about what you've said. As you must realize, however, both fondness and loyalty require time to unfasten. And do give my regards to Mr. Worth, should you see him. I hope he's fully recovered from the attack, and from whatever he thought of me."

Two minutes after the car carrying Ana pulled away, Mr. Sanno was advising Rudy that Ana was far above average in her ability to fend off unwanted questions, and seemingly well able to manipulate most men as well as her former Professor had manipulated her. Thus Rudy should think long and hard...! Ana would require fairly frequent checking if war drew closer to Malta.

Rudy did not volunteer as an Ana checker.

CHAPTER 18

DOESN'T SEEM LIKE WAR

Mid-September

RUDY'S primary goal beginning the morning after Ana Boiano's interview by Mr. Sanno, the British whatever-he-was on Malta (Rudy was thinking 'secret agent'), had to do with finding Nina Lafessi and getting back in her good graces. He had reported for work, but his mind was racing with thoughts other than airplanes. It had been a week since her brother had handed her note to him, the message both sarcastic and promising, and listing a work phone number. But wait, Rudy thought, didn't she say she was leaving that job and going to work for a Mr. Lascaris? Who in hell is he? Great, now there's another one I've got to beat out. Alright, I'll try that phone number, but where did I put her note? This is ridiculous! I should have thought of this last night, since the note must be back in my room. Where's her brother? Maybe he's around the shops?

Paul Lafessi was, indeed, 'around the shops', and finding him produced again the phone number of Nina's office at the Port. Her brother reported that it would be at least another two weeks before she left that office manager's job at the international shipping firm and switched to her new one, "*The Operations Plotting Room*," Paul said, "and that's going to be interesting. I mean both the work and the fact that half the RAF officers there will want to meet her first day. Rudy, if you're seriously interested, you're going to have to move really soon. I'd say she's waiting to see what your intentions are. Believe me, I know her! And if you do talk with her, she doesn't know what happened up at the farm – about the Hawk and that guy the other night, and my father wants to keep it that way. But she's not dumb, and she knows there was trouble by the barn. So play it carefully with her, or the old man will let you know. No crap, she's his favorite!

153

"Look, I apologize for talking about your personal stuff. Obviously, what you do is your business, but I just want to give you the situation, since you said you intend to call her. Most important to me is wanting to continue my apprenticeship or assignment – whatever it is – working with you on your future projects. Oh, before I forget, Grandma's got a pretty good idea about the Hawk, but I think Foster will talk to you about it. All she knows about the other night is that some local screwball intended to damage the Hawk but got scared away. I think that's what set her off on this new idea. Anyway, please let me know what I can do to help with your new projects. I'd better run now, and I'll be working tomorrow right here."

The next challenge facing Rudy was finding a telephone with some privacy, since he was focused on getting to Nina right away, and doing it without an audience. When he returned to Robert's office it was empty of anyone, and a note hung on the side of Robert's desk: BACK AT 10:00. That would give Rudy 15 minutes of free time on Robert's desk phone, and so he carefully dialed the scribbled number Nina's brother had given him a few minutes before.

Amazingly, it was her voice that answered: *Starline Shipping, Valletta office.* Rudy's voice tightened as he quickly responded, "Nina, it's me, Rudy, I'm so sorry I couldn't get to you sooner. I'm up at the Shops now and," when she cut his apology off with a trembling cry.

"Oh, thank God! Rudy are you OK? I want to see you right away, this morning, if possible. Someplace where we can talk. Have you got your cycle there? Can you meet me at noon time at the main gate near the Port offices, by the big drydock cranes? I don't have a car today, my father dropped me off this morning. Can you? I've done little but worry about what happened to you and what's been going on! I want to talk with you. Can you?"

Rudy never hesitated, never gave anything else a thought. "Yes, I'll leave here in plenty of time. I'll find you, I'm OK, but I also need to see you. I'll be there at twelve."

It was two minutes after twelve when the motorcycle, Rudy without his helmet but with a most serious look on his face, slid to a stop at the main gate. She was waiting. Nina climbed to the seat behind him, holding tightly onto his arm to balance herself, and instructed him. "Turn around and head back toward Valletta. I'll give you directions. Thank heavens you're OK. I heard all kinds of stories about you and Robert ending up in hospital, and then the big mystery about trouble at the farm. But worst of all is the rumor that you had a romantic dinner rendezvous with that scheming bitch Ana Boiano. The second we get off this bike you had better be prepared to tell me what you want our relationship to be, if anything. Unless you feel the right way about that, for sure, we'll turn around and both go back to work and our separate ways for good. Do you understand what I'm trying to tell you? Do you?"

Rudy, hearing the concern, eagerness, and anger in her voice even over the sound of the bike's V-twin engine, answered with a vigorous nod. She said nothing else except, "Take the next left turning and then the first right, and then straight on and I'll tell you when to stop." After the turns and three blocks straight down another residential street, Nina squeezed his arms and said, "Turn into the drive entrance on the right. The three story building of flats, and roll this into the courtyard and lock it." Once stopped she continued, "We're going up to the first floor, to flat number six. One of the girls at the office has loaned it to me through lunch time. I've got the key, but before we go, and before you ask me the same question, tell me what you want for us, and don't say what seemed to be on your mind up at my Grandmother's barn. That's not on today's menu."

"I'm already overboard in my feelings for you, but I can't make a full confession about what kind of relationship I'm looking for here in this open courtyard. Can we go up to number six now? I promise I won't attack you, even though you're the most fascinating and beautiful woman I've ever met." With that, Nina surprised him by turning toward the stairs. She pulled a key from a pocket and started toward the entryway. Rudy followed, smiling to himself as he realized he was now in, what some might term, hot pursuit.

"As Nina turned the key and stepped inside the flat, Rudy followed, closed the door behind him, and said, "Nina, please turn around and listen to me. Then it's your turn. I want us to have a serious, long term relationship. I want us to really get to know each other. I want us to go out on dates and I want us to feel close to each other. I realize that we've barely spent a day together, but I'm half crazy about you. Back in the States I'd say I want us to go steady and see how it works out. You make me feel good! And I hope true romance will develop and then we'll know what we want to do next. I've never felt this way before and I never realized that there was such a thing as this happening so fast. I've really fallen for you. I've changed a lot since getting this assignment and coming to Malta, and I want to see what's beyond this feeling I have for you. And further, I did not, definitely not, have any kind of romantic dinner with the one *you* introduced me to. I've just had one heck of a time I can't talk about since I last saw you, and I don't know what else to say. I just hope you feel something special for me."

"That's the best speech I've heard in a long time.! This is insane. Other than for my family, I don't have the feelings for anyone I have for you. I think about you every day, and I miss you. I've never felt like this before, and I agree with what you said. I agree. In the States, what does 'going steady' mean?"

"It means you wear my class ring on a leather shoelace around your neck and we promise each other that neither will never even look at another person of the opposite sex, and we'll go out on dates every weekend night. It also means that we'll neck pretty often, and probably after a time do some petting. That's what high school kids do. In college things usually jump up a notch or two. If it all lasts, then talk turns to an engagement ring."

"In American talk, what do 'necking' and 'petting' mean?" Nina posed, possibly in all innocence, Rudy guessed, but probably not.

Why not, Rudy thought, so he explained, "If you want to know, necking means kissing, and possibly some touching above the waist, and petting could mean the same thing below the waist. At least that's what it meant before I left . But I realize that we've never even held hands, and we've both been to college already, so I guess we'll have to work out our own adult guidelines."

"It happens sometimes here in Malta also, but we have different words for it. So at least let's make up for never holding hands. Do they kiss in Buffalo the same way we do here?"

"Ha! I'm not falling for that question, since I've never kissed anybody in the ninety-some days I've been here. But can we find out now?"

In twenty minutes they were back on the motorcycle, having calmed down a little from 'finding out' in flat number six, and headed back toward the Port and Shops.

By early afternoon Rudy was meeting with Foster, who had invited Paul's father, Vincent Lafessi, to join the discussion. Rudy soon learned why. After indicating that they would be discussing something important concerning the Hawk, Foster asked Vincent to begin by describing a new and very clever idea advanced by his mother, Paul's grandmother, the person still in the key civilian role up in Gozo at the farm airstrip. Vincent began by explaining that the elderly woman knows only that an ineffective attempt was made recently to harm the Hawk airplane sent here by the American President to save Malta from her enemies, and she is extremely concerned. "My mother is strongly religious, and that is true of a very large percentage of us Maltese."

Rudy nodded his understanding, and Vincent continued. "You probably know, Mr. Worth, that great veneration is paid throughout Malta to the Apostle Saint Paul. He is the patron saint of Malta, and many churches have been built here in his honor. After all, history and the Gospels, including Saint Luke's, tell us that he was shipwrecked here about 60 A.D. and played a major role in causing us to become Catholics. If you have not already visited Saint Paul's Shipwreck Church in Valletta you should do so. But I will leave the Saint Paul story for another time. I mention it here only because my mother strongly believes that our Hawk aeroplane must be formally blessed to both keep it from harm and to honor the Apostle. To do this we must paint on the plane the iconic Camargue Cross, which represents Saint Paul's well known three cardinal virtues: Faith, Hope, and Charity. Below the horizontal cross piece is a heart, and at the bottom end of the vertical is a sea anchor. The cross itself represents Faith, the anchor Hope, and the heart Charity.

"Both the painted cross and the plane itself would be blessed by a Kappillan, one of our priests. I add only that the Camargue Cross comes from the south of France, the Camargue Delta salt pan area, from where our own Gozo salt pan gatherers came. All will recognize this cross, as does my mother. Mr. Worth, I believe that our Patron Saint would shield the Hawk and also give strength to our people when war comes to our island, as it surely will. Everyone on Malta knows and honors St. Paul and the three virtues of Faith, Hope, and Charity. Seeing the Cross in the sky will strengthen us!"

"Are you thinking the Camargue Cross would be painted on the fuselage?" asked Rudy.

"Exactly," responded Vincent "all in bright gold colour. We have an artist and the necessary aircraft paint right here in the Shops."

"Well, I certainly endorse the idea. The plane was originally to be shipped to the French, and the rudder is already in their colors, so the tie-in to Gozo you describe is a natural. But the plane, I guess, is now officially RAF. What would they say? Would you need official permission? But I like the idea, and I'm sure the citizens would love it."

Rudy glanced at Foster, who quickly said, "I've already presented the idea to Bartell and he to Captain Donalds. They both are positive. So, Vincent, sketch out what's wanted and get a painter to work right away. Would you do this?

"By-the-way, Captain Donalds pointed out that this ceremony, religious in nature, would be a sure draw to our newly appointed Governor and Commander in Chief, Lieutenant General H. J. Garrison, who replaces Governor Sir Bonham-Carter. The General is known to be strongly religious in every instance. And friend Rudy has a letter of introduction to General Garrison, written by a fellow officer and friend of our new leader. A splendid opportunity, Donalds believes, to make our plea for additional planes, Gladiators or anything else he could push our way and used as interceptor fighters. In fact, Captain Donalds, himself, is organizing the whole ceremony business to be held as soon as we can tell him the Hawk is painted up."

That seemed to end the meeting, except something occurred to Rudy. "I assume the guest list for the ceremony for the Hawk will be very limited? And shouldn't it take place down here rather than the Gozo farm, and have no publicity? And we should tell those few who are invited not to tell anyone else about our surprise weapon!" "Ah," said Foster, "I'd better caution the good Captain about that right now, before he has the invitations sent out and the *Times of Malta* photographer signed up! Give me a moment, Rudy, I need to talk with you about something else, and I'll just get word to the Captain and be right back here. Thank you, Vincent , and please let me know when the desired painting is completed on the Hawk. We want it ready to go within the next couple of days, this week certainly." With that, Rudy was left sitting alone for a few minutes, giving him time to calculate what should constitute his first official "going steady" date with Nina.

This particular planning was soon interrupted by Foster's return and his assurance that Captain Donalds was well aware of the need to limit severely the number of invitees as though it were his daughter's wedding, for which he would need to foot the bill. The ceremony was being planned for next Saturday, September 16.

Foster, looking somewhat embarrassed, then reseated himself directly in front of Rudy and explained that a firm decision had apparently been made by Air Ministry – all according to Captain Donalds' information from London this morning – regarding a pilot for the RAF's P-36 Hawk. Rudy visibly slumped in his chair, instantly assuming that one or two RAF pilots would be assigned to fly his precious plane, and would arrive on site within a week, if not sooner. Although he had anticipated this, it never-the-less hurt! He certainly intended to fly it down for the ceremony, and return it to Gozo, no matter when the RAF pilots appeared. If not for himself, he reasoned, Malta would have no Hawk, dammit.

He rose with a grimace, but was halted by Foster's raised hand. "That's not all of it. It's being assigned to a Polish fighter pilot who will be sent here as soon as they can get him out of Romania. Other Polish pilots, and their mechanics, according to the Air Ministry plan, will be sent to France and some to England to be retrained as bomber pilots for the RAF. Seems the Polish Air Force has had a bad time of it, as has their army, and England needs every pilot it can get. The Colonies, like Canada and South Africa and New Zealand will be sending pilots also. But the Poles are closer and eager to keep fighting any where they can get a plane. Rudy, my friend, when I learn more you'll be the first to know." Rudy remained seated, his mouth open in amazement. and all warm thoughts of Nina hanging in space.

"Foster, it's OK. Let's just see what happens when it happens. I've done about all that can be done to the Hawk, so let's get it painted up with this cross business and figure out how we're going to have it alerted and off the ground up in Gozo, climbing toward where the action is reported to be. Hopefully, it can get enough altitude to drop down on the enemy planes we assume, I guess, will be bombers, and shoot them up before they know what happened. Right now, I think the most important question is can Jim Conners line us up with any Gladiators, Hurricanes, or whatever he can beg, borrow, or steal that flies and has guns? Has Bartell or Donalds heard any news? I mean, really, the Hawk can't be all we've got besides the few slow Swordfish torpedo planes we've got hidden away in the old hangars. And I've heard what you have from the RAF pilots left on the Island: sorry predictions that the RAF is ill prepared for a modern airwar and that there are some scary types of planes the RAF has, such as biplanes older than the Gladiator, and a newer three crew multi-purpose fighter that can't cut it with the German 109. What do you think our chances are for planes?"

"Soon. Not many, but we'll make do. I believe the RAF's next challenge here on Malta, however, is to get the Lascaris Ops Center up and running, since no matter what we can get flying, we'll need to know what's coming our way, how many, how high, and on what heading. The Center will do more than that, including maintaining a radio communication link with our fighters – if we have any besides the Hawk. And that reminds me, we'll need a two-way wireless set in the Hawk, and there's a tech in the shops who can get that set up for you, if you haven't already. You should get up to the Center for a look-see. Techs are already up there working to get it going, and the new personnel training program will begin very soon. I know that a couple of our Swordfish will be used to give them practice in using the ground observer volunteers to report incoming information to the plotters and the communicators who will get our make-believe squadrons airborne and headed properly. Why don't you get an entry pass from Captain Donalds and go up there and familiarize yourself with the Lascaris Center? Take a day or two and learn all you can about it."

The two-track mind that now occupied much of Rudy's head, suddenly switched tracks at Foster's mention of *Nina's* Lascaris Center. Foster was delighted to see Rudy's enthusiastic response to that recommendation. Great, Foster thought, I really emphasized that Lascaris business to get his mind off the Hawk and the Polish pilot business. He seemed quite interested in the Operations Center, and until Jim Conners gets us those crated Gladiators he confidentially promised early this morning, I need to keep Rudy's mind positively occupied. Just a lucky thought on my part, but it worked! Clever me!

Foster would remember that self-congratulatory thought in a few days, when he discovered that the very brief list of recommended invitees to the Hawk's ceremony had included, at Rudy's suggestion, a quite stunning Lafessi daughter soon to begin her job as shift supervisor at the Ops Center. Ah, Foster thought, so much for my cleverness.

Painting the Camargue Cross on each side of the Hawk's fuselage, in place of the French roundel was completed in three days. During that same time, RAF wing roundels were added simply by overpainting the French roundel's red and blue circles for the UK's blue, white, and red sequence. Also painted over were the squadron and aircraft numbers on the rudder, which still bore the French rouge, blanc, and bleu vertical stripes.

What resulted, if the observer were familiar with typical warplane markings, appeared to be a camouflage painted fighter plane of non-European design belonging to either, or possibly both, the English and French air forces, and assigned to an unknown squadron unit using the insignia of St. Paul's Cross denoting faith, hope, and charity, painted in shining gold colour and outlined in white. Rudy thought the new markings and the Camargue Cross were spectacular, but couldn't help but judge that the weight of the additional aircraft paint likely equaled that of several of the 20mm cannon shells in the rotary ammunition drums he had stuffed into each wing's former machine gun slots to feed the new armament, also squeezed in them.

However, the ceremony, although brief, and with attendees numbering but sixteen, impressed Rudy, and apparently all the others. Captain Donalds, as host, had a very brief opening statement which included the serious request that all present not mention to any what was on hand, and notably did not reveal what most present already knew – that this lone fighter plane was not stationed here at the RAF's Hal Far Airstrip. Rudy supposed that the presence of five members of the Lafessi family might be a give away, as they would call it in Buffalo, but no one present even batted an eye, as they also might say back home.

Also there were Wing Commander Bartell, Foster Clayton, Robert, George from the Shop, as a reward for his extra work, Mr. Sanno, who obviously knew all about the Hawk, and as a complete surprise to Rudy, Mr. Anthony Boiano, Chair of the Malta Citizens Preparedness Committee. His presence caused Nina Lafessi to sidestep even closer to Rudy. This was much to Robert's and brother Paul's sly grins, Foster's surprise and realization, and the frowns of Paul's father, mother, and grandmother – she who was responsible for today's event. The priest who would conduct the brief ceremony, the Kappillan, was revealed later by Robert to be he who had saved both of them from worse harm from the thugs by running across the street and yelling so loudly.

Fortunately, Captain Donalds had forewarned Rudy that the new General might well honor his invitation to a semi-religious ceremony for a new Malta resource, and he, indeed, did arrive with an aide – his first visit to Hal Far and one of its more remote hangars into which the Hawk had been rolled after Rudy had flown it down. Rudy was impressed by the General's military bearing, his height and his deep, calm voice. Rudy was introduced by the Captain and made it a point to say that he had spent several days with a Major Astill and would like to bring the General two written messages the Major had entrusted him with, as well as responding to any questions the General might have about Rudy's research to enhance defense of the Island. The General certainly seemed interested in a meeting with Rudy, and turned to instruct his aide to so arrange it, and within the next two days.

That accomplished, and with a smile and nod from the Captain, Rudy moved back to Nina's side. There she whispered the translation of the blessing and prayer for the safety and well being of what the Kappillan termed "the Hawk of St. Paul", its pilots, and the safety and protection of Malta and its people, all implored from its patron Saint Paul. The Kappillan circled the plane, anointing it with drops of what Nina said was Blessed Water and then with the light smoke from a small brazier of burning incense which he slowly swung on a chain. Even though Rudy had to depend on Nina's softly spoken explanations of the priest's prayers, he told her later that what transpired caused the skin on his arms to tingle from the almost mystical effect of the ceremony.

As soon as all ended, and with Nina and Paul standing together and watching, Rudy signaled George to energize the engine and then pull the chocks. As the engine, still warm from his flight down, responded to the throttle, Rudy checked for a clear path and slowly urged the Hawk out of the large hangar. Then a short taxi, right by a trembling Nina waiving at him, and he was off on the short hop to the strip on Gozo, where Vincent's local team waited to hitch up the old tractor and get the Hawk bedded down in the barn. In a few flying minutes, Rudy, urged on by his knowledge that Nina would meet him at the Malta side of the Gozo Ferry terminal, fired up the motorcycle he had left at the farm and headed for the Gozo dock and ferry at Mgarr.

CHAPTER 19

A FRIEND FROM THE QUEEN MARY

September 20, 1939

THE Monday following Saturday's Hawk ceremony and Rudy's first real date with Nina, General Garrison's office phoned the Shop, politely asking if the meeting planned with Mr. Worth and the new Governor might be postponed a short time, until the 20th. Robert, who took the call, checked Rudy's schedule and without hesitation agreed to the two day delay. Upon being informed by a smirking Robert that the high and mighty General's office had been less than apologetic, with no reason for the delay even offered to the lowly American, Rudy ignored Robert's dig, shrugged his shoulders, and returned immediately to his recollection of Saturday evening's date with Nina. Whoever would think, he mused, that the back row of the Valletta cinema, showing an older American movie – *Anything Goes,* starring Bing Crosby and Ethel Merman - would happily resemble so closely its counterpart movie theatre last row in Buffalo. Early in the film, Nina had leaned close as Rudy whispered an explanation for an American idiomatic expression into her shapely ear, while at the same time sliding his arm over the back of her seat to get her even closer.

The reality of work, however, pulled Rudy back to the business of the Kalafrana Shops. With Foster's recent assurance that Gladiators would somehow begin to arrive, in large crates perhaps, or better yet flown from the flight deck of a British aircraft carrier, Rudy began to plan detailed steps for improving their fighting capability. Engine horsepower improvements and possibly augmented firepower topped his list, and he began to assemble the contents of the crated supplies shipped by Ian, together with additional parts and special tools from the Shop's supply room and central tool crib. His Wednesday meeting with General Garrison was almost forgotten in his renewed enthusiasm for implementing such things as the addition of water-methane injection systems for radial engines he had been designing. But, fortunately, Foster reminded him Tuesday afternoon to push Malta's new Governor/General at Wednesday morning's meeting for help in keeping the Shop's future supply chain open. The reminder prompted Rudy on Tuesday evening to dig out the two envelopes Major Astill had entrusted to him almost four months ago on the Queen Mary, and to search through his still limited wardrobe for appropriate business apparel for the next day.

Wednesday morning found him being escorted by a civilian aide, past two armed soldiers posted outside the main entrance to the Governor-General's residence, called *San Anton*, several long miles north of Hal Far, near the Takali airstrip. Thanks again to Foster, Rudy realized, who knowing Rudy's general ignorance of Malta's geography and winding roads, had arranged for a car and driver to pick him up, quite early, at the hotel. Dropped off at the palatial building's portico, Rudy now was both impressed and alerted to what might well be the nature of this meeting. It was not going to be, he feared, a friendly "drop by for a coffee and biscuit" type of visit! Indeed, as Rudy was ushered into a large, beautifully furnished office, the tall and striking looking General Garrison, the new civil and military leader of Malta, strode forward with outstretched hand, saying in a deep, sincere voice, "Mr. Worth, I'm so glad to see you and to have a discussion which I hope will be but the first of many during both our stays here on Malta. I apologize for postponing our meeting, but in a short time you'll appreciate the reason, I'm sure."

"Now, let's move over to the more comfortable corner of this opulent Palace office and have some coffee or tea, as you prefer, to begin our acquaintance. Very soon I'll be moving my official business down to more convenient space in the governmental building called, I'm told, *The Grand Master's Palace*, in Valletta. As you can imagine, with so many years in the military I'm hardly accustomed to such spectacular surroundings in which to labor for my Country. Should war come, as I fear, we both will likely find ourselves in much less splendid places, but be that as it may. And I do want to complement you and your colleagues on that remarkable and deeply stirring ceremony to christen your fighter plane. I was moved by what I saw, by the Kappillan's words, translated for me by my aide– and for you, I noticed, by that lovely young woman – and also by the special cross painted on the plane. Very moving, and most appreciated by all there. I was honored to be invited!

"As you know, I'm here as both civil and military head of this archipelago, so my work is cut out for me, without question. One can hardly succeed in such assignments without expert assistance – as you've been supplying the RAF here – nor without a master plan, and so I've asked you here to begin thinking about a bit more than your current HRM assignment calls for. I am well aware of the circumstances which brought you to Malta, and also the somewhat informal organization called *Friends of the RAF,* into which you have been initiated. I know also that you likely have in your pocket the two documents addressed to me, for delivery, I expect, at this meeting. Don't be surprised that I know this, because the person who gave them to you informed me concerning them. Now, allow me to surprise you once more and have my brand new adjutant step into this meeting." At this, the General rose, stepped to an adjoining door, opened it, and called out, "Colonel, would you come in, please."

As Rudy looked toward the doorway, a uniformed British officer, shorter than both the General and Rudy, husky in build, and noticeably older than Rudy, entered. He looked directly at Rudy and said, "Rudolph my friend, I am overjoyed to see you here on Malta and to know that we could be working together in common cause." Rudy was almost staggered by the totally unexpected sight of Major Gordon Astill, last seen at their final dinner aboard the Queen Mary liner. "Oh my gosh!" Rudy almost shouted. "Major Astill, I mean Colonel, yes, I'm so glad to see you again. Oh wow, this is really something. What's happening here? How is this going to work? What's the situation? And here are the two letters you wanted me to give to General Garrison." At this, Rudy reached into his breast pocket, pulled out the envelopes and handed them in the general direction of both the General and Colonel Astill.

The Governor-General, wearing a broad smile, said "let's the three of us sit down and take a look at Gordon's tasks as my second in planning and military command on these islands. And Rudy, what I would like to have from you, as a minimum, is your participation in our general planning for war, and your leadership in the focused strengthening of our sky defenses. I suspect I know what Gordon wrote in those letters, but I'll read them carefully later today. When Mr. Churchill pulled me from home and speculated likely assigning me here, I was able to get Gordon to agree to returning to active duty as my adjutant with the brevet rank of Lieutenant Colonel. That's pronounced *Lef-tenant* in our army, unlike your *Lewtenant*, but we'll just refer to him as Colonel Astill. Adjutant is the best military title I could come up with to describe my right-hand, at least with military matters. I'll certainly seek advice on civil matters as well, but I have to be out front to the residents there as Governor. Today needs to be a workday for the three of us, and I'll show you both what I've worked up as a preliminary organizational structure to cover both military defense plus basic civilian needs and well-being. Also, I'll have to identify a number of others, both military personnel and civilians, to fill in the empty group leader assignments – and in some cases, operational chiefs. Rudy, are you free for the entire day? If so, I'll have you driven back to your hotel when we're talked out. Agreed? Lunch here, of course.

"On a sad note, however, you two may not be aware of the bad news, since Gordon has been in transit getting here, and Rudy has been at work within the aircraft shops. On Sunday last, the 17th, Russia invaded Poland – from the east, naturally – joining the Nazi push from the west. Seems Mr. Stalin had a secret agreement with our friend Adolph to share the spoils of additional territory. Puts our War Ministry chaps in London in a bit of a quandary, I'd wager, although we've actually done little or nothing to help the Poles, even though we and France have had a mutual aid agreement with them. Too late now! Mr. Churchill must be even more angry at where our former cabinet placed our nation than he was when I met with him concerning my challenging assignment here. It's not difficult to see why Malta cannot be even near the top of the resource distribution list. Right now, France, the rest of western Europe, and our home Island need it all! And that, Rudy, clearly signals us on Malta to hold this British fortress in the middle of the Mediterranean until, most likely, America – your great nation – officially joins our alliance.

"If we can now move to that large work table, I'll show you the rough sheets I've worked up illustrating what might be an organizational structure chart for war preparation. I want your thinking concerning needed changes.

"First, the military side of things: above my level is London and the War Ministry plus all the various Ministers and Sea Lords and Air Marshals, and whatever else they're termed. Just below me are all of the Army, Royal Navy, and Royal Air Force commanders and what-have-yous, many of whom will simply believe that the directions given by Malta's Governor-General may safely be ignored, since each of them is part of another wartime hierarchy. I talked about this with Mr. Churchill, and he reminded me that he who pays the piper calls the tune. I shall, therefore, be watchful as I allocate our meager resources and approvals to proceed. So, Rudy, since if hell should make its appearance it most likely will be by air from Sicily, I want your planning and recommendations for enemy aircraft intercept plus reconnaissance flights and all the inventions, adjustments, and maintenance support services necessary. The RAF can handle our pilots, if any are to be found, and the Lascaris Operations Center. Ground to Air Defense will include ground to air artillery, blimps if any are to be found here, and the volunteer observer corps, all under an artillery officer.

"Invasion defense will plan for parachute and glider landings as well as naval shelling, torpedo boats coming into our harbors, subs, and landing boats at our shoreline carrying enemy troops. I want citizen hunters to form as volunteer anti-parachute and glider troop snipers, and I want shore anti-troop wire and tank barriers installed by our soldiers and civilian workers, as well as anti-glider posts spotted on prime landing fields. That includes Gozo. And we can't forget pre-aimed and locked in place mortars firing from defilade, if indeed we have any mortars. This all under Royal Army leadership augmented by a Royal Navy group setting plans and actual defenses should we be subject to ship bombardment as well as, or in place of, aircraft bombing. Both anti-aircraft artillery and rapid fire Orlikon cannon, plus emplaced machine guns and heavy artillery may be aimed at surface targets as well as aircraft – as my Adjutant well knows.

"Assuming our islands will be invaded by enemy troops following a softening up aerial bombing and heavy bombardment by naval ships possibly even coming into our harbor, our constabulary officers will function as infantry. This means extra orientation and training for them, and the issuing of infantry type weapons. I suspect that, following the British model, very few of them are currently armed, anyway. So, Colonel Astill, that adds yet another task to your fulsome list. Although on this peaceful island I doubt we have many police officers?

"I anticipate that the planning and the urging of continuing coordination and cooperation between these various fighting organizations of ours will call for a great amount of my time, patience, and talents, but that I am prepared to give. You, Gordon, just as you've worked with me on earlier assignments, know how to identify the detailed pushing needed by you to assure the best possible defense in the shortest time, so chart your own path here, but keep me apprised. Now, Rudy, your assignments require knowledge and experience that neither Gordon nor I have, so I shall expect you to do what you believe is needed and possible, but do lean on me to get you whatever resources are even remotely available. I would like a meeting of the three of us no less often than once a week, so each will know where we stand, and Gordon, will you schedule accordingly, please?

"Now I want to turn to my preliminary thinking on the civilian side of our war preparation organization. Rudy, I know that you are not here as a military officer, but rather as a civilian semi-volunteer aircraft expert, but you will give us a fresh, American view, and I truly value that. So I thank you, in advance as it were, for your willingness to continue as an aircraft engineer at our service and also as an objective American observer, neither Maltese nor English, but one exercising the analytical skills of a trained, experienced engineer. Now, before you two review the listing of civilian needs I foresee should – or perhaps I should use the word *when*, rather than *should* – we are attacked by Italian or German forces or both, I observe that there likely will be more challenges in meeting the needs of our Maltese residents and mostly English guests than in keeping our military organized and alive.

"Malta, unfortunately as you know, is not self sufficient. It is heavily dependent on continuing imports of foodstuffs, gasoline, fuel oil for generating electricity, cooking oils, medical supplies, and almost anything else you can imagine. Keeping a steady, continuing supply line of cargo vessels, including an occasional cargo submarine, flowing through the very active German submarine packs would require the air and sea resources we already lack. So, here are some thoughts of mine:

"Under the rubric of Civilian Protection Services I have listed: shelters; food and water; housing and temporary housing; medical services – normal and emergency, plus mass casualties; production raw materials availability; schools for children and training of many types for adults; enforcement of rules and laws; public alerts and warnings; religious services; local government activities and Council of Government functions; travel around the islands including bus and ferry service; newspaper publishing continuation; specialized library services; safe fishing; rescue services; demolition of severely damaged structures; maintenance of firefighting and ambulance services; air raid warden services; port and shipping services; general services; water taxi services; animal welfare services; public utility services including the running of the Redefussion Cable Service radio system; maintenance of public order; declaration of emergency; and additional categories you will advise me of plus those which will emerge as time passes.

"Gordon, you long ago reminded me of the old quip: 'If you want to make God laugh, show him your plans', and you need not recite it anew. I am well aware of the seeming futility of such comprehensive planning, except 'Hope for the best but plan for the worst' also may apply here as well. What do you both think? You first, Colonel Astill."

Rudy was happy to hear Gordon speak to the General's list at great length, not in the least because his head was swimming with the volume of input already provided by the General, and now added to by Gordon's experienced assessment. The General and his Adjutant went back and forth on several items, apparently sharpening the list but not shortening it. Rudy thought it wise to confine his observations to what the General had called air defense – or something like that – and held the first, and more detailed, part of his observations to the status of the Hawk and its possible pilots, and the expectation of some small number of Gladiators which would be upgraded by Rudy and piloted by several of the few remaining RAF members. Speaking, he said, as Governor rather than Military head, Governor Garrison observed that at the Hawk's ceremony he had enquired of Captain Donalds if the Hawk were an official RAF fighter plane and not to be piloted by the American civilian, Mr. Worth, in wartime. The RAF Captain had assured the General that the issue had already been clarified to the American. The Governor glanced at Rudy to be sure Rudy understood. Rudy nodded, and the Governor responded, "Good, your volunteering in our aerial defense is appreciated, but could not, for international reasons, be accepted. Besides, as you can now see, we have other expectations for you. "What," he then asked, "do you have to add to this list of civilian categories of concern?"

"I believe that the list covers everything I can think of at the moment, but just imagining the very tight concentration of Maltese living and working in Valletta and the the so-called three cities around the Grand Harbour and the area to the immediate northeast, such as Sliema, plus to the south around Marsxlokk Bay, such as Kalafrana, if bombers come, where would the air raid shelters be? I don't think anything has been built, has it? The former Governor didn't budget much in preparation for war, I don't believe. The other thing that occurs to me as I look at the long list of things needed and things to do is that the civilians appointed to the various categories are going to have to be experienced and already well-known to people, if they're going to be recognized as leaders. Is there a list of various citizens who could hit the ground running, as we say?" The remainder of the afternoon was spent in generating a list the units which would need a civilian head, or chairperson, or director, or commissioner, or supervisor, or what ever type of title seemed most appropriate for the nature of the work which would be required. Several, such as the Fire Service Chief and the Chief Ambulance Doctor, would simply get expanded job descriptions.

Those organizations which mostly called for a quasi-military approach might be led by a director or commissioner or chief, the three agreed. An example organization of that type, Rudy submitted, might be the controlling of food distribution and rationing. Assignment to designated air raid shelters depending on residence and workplace addresses, however, might call for a coordinating type of title instead. In several cases the answer was readily apparent, such as the local Bishop for religious functions and services, observed the Governor, and the existing Director of Education for the schools. Organizing the training of adults in new types of assignments, such as neighborhood air raid wardens, might become the responsibility of a carefully selected experienced teacher. As the meeting closed, it was evident that a local, active, experienced consultant or two would be useful in suggesting people for these various positions, and Rudy suggested both Mr. Farinacci and Mr. Boino as possibilities who could help with suggestions.

Rudy, climbing into the back seat of a provided car, while receiving the thanks for a good work session from the Governor-General and a cheerful good-bye and promise of a soon phone call from Colonel Astill, fell back into the seat. He told the driver his destination and began to relax for the first time this day. He felt charged with the excitement generated by the depth of a planning session he had never anticipated and he found himself looking forward to their promised weekly meetings. At the same time he realized that he had never even mentioned Foster's plea to put in a good word on behalf of keeping the supply chain for the Shops open, and for their work at Hal Far as well. Next week's meeting, he promised, and closed his eyes until the car pulled in front of the hotel. It was only then that he realized his hunger, for the Governor had never called for the promised lunch! He exited the car with his thanks for the ride, and headed for the hotel dining room, hoping it was still serving.

As he strode by the reception desk he was halted by hearing his name called out by the woman behind the desk. "Mr. Worth, You've been called by – she glanced at the message card in her hand – a Mr. Foster Crayton, twice this afternoon. He would like you to phone him at this number. He says it's urgent." Rudy reached for the card but did not recognize the number, although he sensed that the woman was sliding a desk phone over to him. Mumbling his thanks he accepted the phone and dialed the number. Foster's voice came over the line, repeating the number, and Rudy identified himself. "Ah, Rudy," Foster said. "Thank you for calling me back. I'm at home right now and hope you have nothing planned for tomorrow evening. I'll be home all day and won't see you until dinner time tomorrow. You and Robert are invited, and I'll have some news. If you agree, Robert will pick you up at 8:30 tomorrow morning for work, and will drive with you to my home for dinner. He'll drop you back at the hotel on his way home afterward, so don't ride your motorcycle to work. Is this OK with you? I hope you can make it."

Rudy instantly thought, Oh Boy! Somethings up. "Sure Foster, I can do it and I can't wait. Thank you. See you then...If there's nothing else, I'll work on our stuff tomorrow and see you then, with Robert. Good bye." On his short walk into the hotel's dining room he had one more thought: Somethings wrong, I can tell from his voice. This can't be good.

CHAPTER 20

IN WITH THE NEW

Autumn 1939

ONE night toward the end of September, not quite ready yet for sleep, Rudy began to marvel over the several new and exciting elements in his life. He began his list with the changes that were initiated during the dinner he and Robert had attended at Foster's home in Valletta that eventful evening, September 21. All the next day, following his first long work session with the Governor-General, Rudy and Robert had puzzled over Foster's cryptic invitation *"...and I'll have some news"*. In truth, it also occurred to Rudy that his changes had actually begun earlier than the dinner with Foster, really the day before, at the meeting with General Garrison. That was when the General's newly arrived Adjutant was revealed to be the "Friend of the RAF" Rudy had met and and learned a good deal from before he had even arrived in Malta: he of the Queen Mary's voyage, Major - and now Colonel - Gordon Astill, his new war planning colleague.

Around noon, when Rudy typically began to think of his bagged lunch in the office cooler, Robert came striding into what he typically referred to as *"Mad Rudolph's laboor-atree"* giving it the accent often used in British horror movies. "Well, my young friend from the American Colonies, I'm here to inform you of my analysis vis-a-vis tonight's dinner invitation: the good Madam Crayton has decided that you should have a home cooked meal, and has called upon me to transport you, since I have a real automobile, while you have only a junior motorcycle."

"Get off it, you lowly bus driver," was the response. "You're hoping to trade a meal for a quarter liter of gasoline in that excuse for a car you rattle around town in. Although I've never heard Foster mention a wife, I'll allow that there is one, but that's hardly the news he promised. Rather, I imagine

Captain Donalds' new boss, and ours, will soon be arriving on Malta from RAF London. And if that's so, then it's the end of the fun and games we've seen in this Phoney War, and double time, with daily inspections, for the Shops and for us."

Robert obviously had not thought of that, and he blurted out, "Stop that, please, you're scaring me! No, Arlene Crayton is a lovely British lady, kind and thoughtful, active with Mrs. Strickland, the pacemaker and trend setter of Malta's female British colony. If she has deemed it time to bring you into the fold, she either is feeling kindly toward you, an unpolished foreigner, or she has come up with a splendid and unmarried British woman of a certain age who would like to see your Statue of Liberty closeup, on the arm of her American husband, if you get my meaning."

"Now *you're* scaring *me*! I don't need a matchmaker, so I would much rather my guess than yours. Let's just stop guessing and wait to see. I'm ready for my sandwich. Let's go and eat."

"Did you know, Rudy, that the sandwiches you devour most days are named after our British Earl of Sandwich, who invented the meat between the bread fast meal you likely think was invented in – what is it called – Buffalo? But lead on to both our sandwiches." During their hurried lunch, both speculated what changes in their work lives, including Foster's, would be brought about by the arrival from RAF headquarters of the Air Commander, who would be everyone's new boss, including even friendly Captain Donalds and Wing Commander Bartell. Rudy, deliberately, spoke with apprehension, reinforcing his pure guess that this would be Foster's news at dinner, causing Robert to grew even more gloomy at the prospect.

As the two left the Shops late in the still sunny Malta afternoon, Rudy offered to purchase a bouquet of flowers for Mrs. Crayton since Robert was furnishing transportation. Robert instantly agreed, saying he know of a flower seller's shop on the way to the Crayton's flat which would not require the burning of extra gas. This prompted Rudy to ask just where they lived, since Foster had never talked about his personal life with him. Robert added that, in the several years he had worked as Foster's clerk, he had learned "scarce little" himself, although Arlene Crayton stopped by the Shop office each Christmas time to have a small glass of sherry, the bottle of which Foster had produced from his brief case.

Robert did know their address however, and how to get there through the streets of Valletta. Rather than Rudy's American idea of "a flat", the Fosters lived in what Rudy identified as a solid looking three story apartment building built, as was almost every building in Valletta, of whitish colored and thick looking stone. Robert's old Fiat sedan was parked quickly at one of several available open spaces at the British *kerb*, and clutching a colorful floral bouquet, Rudy followed Robert up one flight of stairs to the so-called first floor. Two apartment doors to the left of the stairs and two on the right, and Robert, with a quick look, went to the door marked number five and lifted a brass door knocker shaped as a two bladed propeller. Quickly opened, in the doorway stood a broadly smiling Foster glancing at his wristwatch while stepping back and saying, "I guessed you would leave work a bit early, thus getting here right about... now. I know. It's Arlene's fine cooking and not a desire to see me that brings this eagerness, but that's understandable, so get yourselves in here and, Rudy, meet my better half. She'll love the flowers. Mrs. Crayton, your guests have arrived, bearing a lovely gift."

Arlene Crayton, an attractive and well dressed woman Rudy would judge to be just about her husband's age, could not have been more welcoming, and she did admire the flowers as she lifted a vase from among the books on a shelf and took the flowers from Rudy's hand. He was careful to say they were from both guests, who very much appreciated the invitation. She commented that this was an overdue invitation to Foster's colleagues, as she stepped toward the kitchen to add water to the vase, and as she returned to the room she added that she would have failed in her long desire to have them to dinner had she not extended the invitation for this, her very last week before... obviously halted in mid-sentence by her husband's quick and loud *Harrumph*. "But that's for later conversation," she added. "Now, let's sit for a glass of sherry, and I'll then take just a few minutes to finish dinner preparations. I hope you both like roast beef? I thought a real English dinner for you might be a change. Foster, would you pour us all some of that sherry, please?" Foster poured, all sipped, and then their hostess went to put the final expert touches on an excellent joint of beef, which Robert later judged to have cost Foster a small fortune.

With the three now alone, Foster spoke. "Thank you both for coming on short notice; Arlene and I wanted to do this before she left for our daughter's home in Nottingham, and I thought she'd give away my little secret to you just now, before I had a chance. So, my daughter, her Royal Navy husband, and the two grandchildren back in Robin Hood land, coupled with the forthcoming real war against Malta – a place she and I both love – have pushed us to decide that she would go on the fast liner leaving for home next week, along with a number of spouses and children of Brits still living here. Some have already left, as you may be aware, but the feeling now is to leave while leaving is still possible. At least, Mrs. Strickland, who has decided to remain here with husband Roger, head of the local Council of Government, firmly judges that this special sailing is the safest thing to do. Leave while the leavings still good, I reckon!"

With their glasses of sherry topped-off by Foster, Rudy and Robert listened to him further describe his situation. "You can imagine all we have to do with this timetable. I'll start tomorrow, probably, to sell-off Arlene's little Morris Minor she drove to buzz around the Island, and than alert the building manager that I'll very likely not be entering the annual leasing agreement which starts each January first. Oh, I'll happily tell you two, if you won't spread it around, that as a recently retired RAF member, reemployed as a civilian in the same position I had as an officer, I'm seeking approval for lodging in the BOC, and I hope to be moving there the first of the year. That's the Bachelor Officer Quarters, Rudy, closer to the Shops so I can get there early and check up on both you rogues as well as everyone else, and less costly for me, of course. If my somewhat unusual request is approved by the higher-ups, and if the Officers' mess votes me in, I can take most of my meals in the Officers' Dining Room. The group is now reduced in population of course, with so many reassigned, but still functioning. The monthly meal fee is quite reasonable.

"The BOC digs aren't as spacious as here, naturally, and I must say this flat has suited us well. Good kitchen, this lounge room you Yanks call a living room, Rudy, a small dining room, and a nice bedroom with storage closets, plus a quite large bathroom with modern shower. I usually park out front at the kerb, with the Morris out in the rear under the building's carpark tin roof. Overall, a nice building, but the BOC will be advantageous for me, and I'm ready to move on.

"Who knows when the war will reach us, and in what form. We can only pray we're ready, so we continue to hope that the Hawk will soon have a few Sea Gladiators to help keep the nasties away. And speaking of prayer, remember, if you will, that we want Arlene's steamship to reach Liverpool safely. Now let's go in and enjoy our dinner, for I see Arlene beckoning us from the doorway. And, please, although I know you wouldn't, not a word of anything war related that could unsettle her."

Later, as Robert drove back toward Rudy's hotel, they discussed the evening. Robert thought that Foster's news was neither worrisome nor earth shattering. "The meal was fine and the beef truly was excellent One doesn't see a joint of beef as large and as tender as that one, at least not at my pay grade. And the rest of the meal was very, very nice as well. Even though Foster seems to accept Arlene's leaving for home, I know him to be a quiet person, dedicated to two things: keeping the Shops running effectively , and enjoying the life he and she have had here. Now he'll be alone. Of course, when the war begins, we'll have all the excitement we can handle, Foster's workload will skyrocket, and he'll hardly have time to think about his family in England, or anything else. But, while little that's basic will change for me – or at least not very much – I shouldn't speak for Foster. No one in my family is thinking of sailing away; we're Maltese and not leaving. Now you, my friend, are a different story. What do you think about what we learned tonight from Foster, and what differences in your life do you imagine if and when shooting starts? After all, you can go back home, if you want, or you may be instructed to return there by HRM Aviation, or whoever it is you really represent."

It took so long for Rudy to respond that Robert turned his head as he drove to ask: "Rudy?" Rudy had a very brief answer: "What I learned tonight may well change my entire life. A shooting war could complicate things, I suppose, but I can't think that far ahead right now!"

Robert waited for more, but in the mile or so left before they got to the hotel, Rudy said only five additional words, which were, "Thanks, Robert. See you tomorrow." And they were spoken only as he opened the car door to enter his hotel. The next morning, however, as soon as he could trap Foster alone in his office, he had more to say.

"We had a great time at your place last evening, Foster," Rudy began at 8:30 next morning. "The dinner was absolutely spectacular, and Arlene is more than spectacular herself. I'm sure you'll miss her, but I'd say you're making the right decision, considering what this island will have to undergo when the hot stuff really begins. The Governor-General certainly has no doubt that a real war is coming soon and that Malta will be right in the middle of it, and he didn't hesitate to say that at our planning session. I know Robert agrees with me that you and your wife were very kind to have us over, and I'm especially glad I had a chance to meet her – and sample her excellent cooking – before she leaves, her car gets sold, and you alert your building manager that you think you'll vacate your flat right after Christmas, if I heard you correctly last night.

"I've been thinking about all of that since you explained your time table, and while I don't want to speak prematurely, I'm very much in need of a car, especially as I have to meet with the planning group each week, so I want to say that I'd like to buy Arlene's car, if you would sell it to me. The motorcycle is fun, but hardly the type of vehicle I need right now. Finances are not a problem, and whatever price is fine with me."

Unsuccessfully hiding a slight grin, Foster replied. "Rudy, the way things are going, I think your idea makes sense. I would imagine that you do need a car. Would you keep the motorcycle, or put it up for sale? Not that I'm thinking of switching, the car I have is fine for my needs. I was just being curious, I guess. I'd be glad to see you get Arlene's Morris. It's not a big car, and it's not a fast car, but we've always kept it well maintained, and it's in pretty good shape. I can get the chaps at the garage to to tell me a fair selling price for a good friend, if that would suit you. I'll try to do that on my way home later today, or tomorrow at the latest. I'll drive it to work tomorrow, and you can look it over and take it for a spin, to be sure it will suit your needs. I'm happy to clear the Morris from my list of things to take care of. In a week or two I'll have to begin working out my leaving the place you saw last night and switching over to the BOC, assuming I get an approval to my request. So not having to advertise the car helps."

"Speaking of that, " Rudy mentioned in an off-hand way as he partly turned to leave Foster's office, "does England use a term that we do in the States: *Right of First Refusal?*"

"Oh I think so," Foster responded. "Are you thinking about the car?"

"No," Rudy said, "I'm just thinking about what Ian Standish advised me when we met and discussed a possible war. He suggested I move out of the hotel, farther from the Bay. Assuming our shooting and bombing war holds off until the new year, will you give me "Right of First Refusal" for the flat? Or at least don't tell the leasing agent just yet, until I can do some checking, and then tell him what a good tenant I'd be? Your current flat would be perfect for me. What do you think?"

"Do your checking, Rudy, and I'll slowly get some facts and figures together so you can see just what you'd be getting into. Up to a reasonable point in time – whatever that turns out to be as determined by the war situation – I'll give you first refusal rights on the flat announcement to the agent. OK?"

"Great, Foster, and many thanks. I'll check with you tomorrow so we can finish the car business. See you later!" And with that farewell, Rudy went directly to his assigned small mail and memo shelf box, mumbling a greeting of sorts to Robert who was preparing to leave with a handful of inter-office transfer envelopes for distribution. Repeatedly fumbling through the few documents on his shelf, Rudy moved quickly to the phone on Robert's desk as soon as Robert was out of sight, and dialed – this time from practice – the Starline Shipping office number.

"Nina, I bought a car today and I'll get it in a few days as soon as the owner leaves the island. But I'll tell you about it, and something else also, a kind of idea I've got that I want to try out with you. Can I see you tonight? We could have dinner some place, motorcycle I guess, unless you have your father's old car today. OK, great, what time's good for you? Meet at the little restaurant on St Pawl Street at quarter to six. Yes, I'll have the bike. Bye." I need that damn car, Rudy thought. How the hell can I impress her with no real transportation? This is ridiculous, nighttime with a gorgeous girl and a little motorcycle, and no place to be alone. Crap! Home with her mother and father, or the hotel with the desk clerk at the foot of the stairs, plus Mr. Farinacci, who knows both of us. No wonder I can't get anywhere with her! I've got to get this straightened out, and real soon. Or better yet, I've got to think through what would really make the most sense for Nina and me in the long run? Or is it too early to know? Lord, I'm confused.

At the restaurant, Nina began to speak as soon as they were seated and Rudy had enough sense not to interrupt her. Let her start, he calculated, since I've already told her I bought a car. Nina began by saying, "So you bought a car, you said on the phone? I imagine you can use it for getting around the island for work, and up to Gozo, as well as for your personal business. But I need to remind you of what I said on our motorcycle ride up to the farm. If you remember, I said if we're going to do this again we'd need goggles or a used car, or some words like that, because we were covered in dust and dirt when we got there. That was my reason for saying that, on what was not even a first date, and I was trying to distract you from the blond by acting cute.

"I know that we're now going steady, or whatever you called it when you described what fun it meant back in Buffalo, and that sitting on the Lafessi front steps twenty feet from my parents cramps your style. Oh, and getting up to your room at the hotel sight unseen is impossible, and so is your idea of this going steady business in the back seat of my father's old two-door, that one time I borrowed it. So I want you to know that we're not going to use the back seat - or even the front seat - of your new used car like, I guess, you might have in mind. Which is, if you remember, what you seemed to have in mind when you offered to show me the inside of my own grandmother's barn up in Gozo, on our motorcycle tour.

"To summarize that overly long speech, I would say that I'm in love with an exceedingly attractive, amazing American temporary visitor to my island home in the Mediterranean, in war time that likely will worsen soon, and that he can be called back to America at any time, and at a moments notice. So while I'm being *in love* with him now, I'm fighting myself every time I'm with him not *to love* him forever and ever, amen. Because, Rudy darling, love forever and ever can be spelled as pregnant and many years of happy togetherness, while being in love can mean goodbye, it's been absolutely great to know you, and we'll remember each other for at least a year. By-the-way, I too want to climb into the back seat with you, but not under our present circumstances. I hope you can understand what I'm trying to say, and I think I may cry, so forgive me. If you don't want to walk out of here right now, tell me about the car. And what was the idea you said you wanted to try out on me? Or have I spoiled the whole thing, and our going steady, and I hope not. I'm in love with you and I hope you feel that way about me, and I hope for whatever God will grant us – God and the war, I suppose. Now I'll shut up!"

Rudy sat absolutely still, amazed, speechless for a very long moment, as it came to him that she had just spelled out, had put her finger on, what made the best immediate sense. She was torn, as was he, by the prime question of what kind of future could there be for them? Did what they were doing make sense? Was it honest to continue without each knowing and agreeing what kind of future they wanted to share? So he gulped and answered.

"Nina, I understand completely what you've said, and I understand and agree that we must talk through whatever possibilities we each see for our relationship. Yes, I can see the difference between being in love during temporary and uncertain circumstances and loving the other person so that you want to be with them for the rest of your lives. My mother and father are that way, and I guess yours are, too. I'm certainly in love with you, and I see now that a temporary arrangement makes little sense and leads to frustration or stupid actions with very poor consequences.

"Lets use the going steady method to get us spending more time together. Mrs. Crayton's Morris car should help that, and I'll take out the back seat, if it has one. I won't see it until tomorrow. That's whom I'm buying it from, and I do need it for my expanded planning assignment. Why don't we see each other and do some things together as absolutely often as we can, find out all we need to know about each other, stay with the necking only part of going steady, and see what we're feeling in a couple of months. The idea I was thinking about can wait. Does that make sense? I repeat, not only am I crazy about you, but I know I'm at least in love with you, right now, more than ever."

At that point the waiter approached their table holding two menus out toward them. Nina took both menus, handed one to Rudy, looking directly in his eyes, and mouthed a kiss into the air, saying, "I think we can order now. What would you think of sharing a starter, first?"

CHAPTER 21

THE BRISTOL ENGINE

December 1939

FOR a couple of weeks after purchasing Arlene Crayton's 1936 low mileage Morris sedan, which the Brits termed a *Saloon* car, Rudy was carried away by what to him was new car ownership. Red with a black upper half, a small four cylinder engine, a four speed gear shift, and about 25 horsepower, Rudy had already driven it at top speed, almost 55 MPH, on one of the few straight stretches he could find. It sported a driver's outside rear view mirror, an electric windscreen wiper, and a narrow little arm called an indicator, which flipped up from an opening between the doors on either side to signal a turn. Best of all, Nina loved it. Wow, Rudy thought, very low mileage, great previous maintenance, 45 miles to an imperial gallon of gas, and Nina loved it, all for the 105 English pounds he had paid Foster. Best of all, he knew, was that *Red Rover,* as Nina had named it, provided just what had been lacking on his road to romantic happiness. Rudy's quick agreement to her rejection of his back seat imaginings, and his only hinted at idea of cohabitation, promoted, he judged, some tender front seat evening partings. These allowed him to rationalize his expenditure, so all was well on his personal front.

On the more global scene, however, the so-called Phoney War continued, with Malta being tasked by the Brits with assisting in the stoppage and inspection of neutral vessels which might be carrying cargo helpful to German war efforts. Ships discovered in the western Mediterranean were being led to Malta for inspection by patrolling British warships, and this new activity caused Nina's job as office manager at the international shipping firm in Valletta to be placed in a category labeled 'Active Emergency'. Many such cargo ships were escorted to Malta's port, with the number increasing each month. This delay in moving to her new job did not set well with her, but the RAF section of the Lascarus Operations Center had not yet been activated. Thus she remained for the time being, doing more and more of what she had been doing long before applying for her new and seemingly more exciting work as a Lascarus shift supervisor. That position would have Nina, already an experienced manager, functioning in a supervisory position, scheduling, assigning, and supervising a dozen or so other young women. These specially recruited Maltese civilian employees, slated for training as a coordinated team, will plot on a large flat map 'plotting board' the anticipated arrival of enemy aircraft over Malta, as advised by outside volunteer observers and radar operators. They then will dispatch RAF interceptor aircraft to attack the intruders, with continuing oversight by RAF observing officers. While Nina looked forward to switching over to the Lascarus Center job, Rudy avoided thinking about the fact that numerous dashing RAF officers would be working the same shifts at the Center, along with the beautiful young woman with whom he was 'going steady'. Wisely, he had so far kept this fear of unknown competition to himself, while commiserating the transfer delay with her.

His weekly planning meetings with the Governor-General and Colonel Astill did provide him with a good deal of current war information and speculation about Malta's future, but neither the news dispatches nor the speculation seldom gave any joy, as Colonel Astill would say. Britain was still slowly learning about war with an enemy which had invented modern war tactics and its own blitzkrieg style. From private dispatches learned at the planning meetings from an often upset General Garrison, Rudy heard, for example, that Luftwaffe planes were parachuting magnetic mines into the Thames Estuary, and that magnetic mines had already sunk 60,000 tons of Allied shipping off Britain's east coast in one week. Another terrible note was that on the first day of the German invasion of Poland, approximately one half of the Polish Air Force had been destroyed on the ground by German planes. To an infuriated Colonel Astill, private news revealed that the peacetime British design of a new antisubmarine bomb had been dropped accidentally by a British plane on a British submarine. The bomb hit the bottom of the conning tower but resulted in no damage to the submarine. Colonel Astill had learned that British coastal bombers then had to be switched to carrying regular old-fashioned destroyer depth charges. Occasional good news did cheer them up, as Rudy noted, when in early December British and New Zealand war ships sighted the infamous German *Graf Spee* marauding battleship half a world away, off Uruguay, which later caused its Captain to scuttle it in Montevideo Harbor and then commit suicide. So the Phoney War continued on during the winter: Russia, seeking military bases to the west, had invaded Finland, which was putting up a very good, but eventually losing fight; twenty-four British Wellington bombers had attacked a German naval target where twelve were shot down by German fighters; and, in their own war, China's strengthened air force sent 40 planes to defend Liuchow against 13 Japanese planes. That final score was14 to 0, with Japan winning the day.

"We allies are," as General Garrison remarked, "having our ups and downs, and in some places this Phoney War isn't so phoney."

At the current meeting, Rudy asked if the military resource report prepared last July by Mr. Simmons at the request of the former Governor-General had been passed on. It had been, according to Colonel Astill, and his review of it revealed that exceedingly few new resources had since been added, and some, such as trained soldiers and Maltese artillerymen, had been, and were still being transferred to British Egypt, as were shipments of anti-aircraft guns designated for Malta.

"Perhaps, if bombers do come," suggested Rudy, "they can be blinded by the searchlights. But may I ask, General, how are the civilian volunteer assignments coming? Are people volunteering in case we do get attacked? Also, are you able to increase the budget for civil defense, especially for bomb shelters?"

"Good people are volunteering for some positions, while others are being convinced by us that it's the patriotic thing to do. I've increased the official budget for civilian defense activities almost 30% over last year, and we're going hell-bent on the issue of bomb shelters and alternate living facilities. Fortunately, the island is composed of very soft stone, rather easily dug out – which we're doing – and also we have numerous tunnels and underground passageways – rather deep and large ones – some going back to ancient times, and they're being cleared out, cleaned up, and improved. Not enough, but a lot more than we had three months ago, when very few thought we might need them. But my big concern, gentlemen, is food, both cooking and fuel oils, gasoline for our generators and pumps, drinking water, grain storage, medical supplies, and the like. Our quarter million people couldn't go two months, I imagine, without such severe rationing of food that surrender would look sensible. That may be one reason causing our Government to hold back on sending us more resources. They wouldn't want guns and equipment just handed to an invading enemy as we disappeared." Oh, boy, Rudy gulped to himself, I never thought of that.

The Governor-General promised a completed organizational structure chart, with the names of the civilian volunteers, for the next week's meeting, and then mentioned Rudy's prime interest: fighter planes, how to get some, and how to improve them here on Malta. He nodded toward Colonel Astill and asked him to take over this next important subject. Gordon nodded back, turned to face Rudy directly, and said, "Rudolph, now my colleague in planning as well as my friend, I have some news for you, coming from certain 'Friends of the RAF' who have not forgotten you and your devoted efforts to help us. We know that you are patiently awaiting some Sea Gladiators, and we assure you they will arrive, but first we ask your assistance on another matter, quite in keeping with your assignment here.

"What I shall tell you next is not yet public information, but it presents the RAF with a bit of a quandary. During the past two weeks, in two separate instances, three Me 109 German aircraft have appeared far beyond what we know their range to be, yet in the first such sighting the plane appeared more than willing to engage in a time and fuel consuming attack on one of our reconnaissance light bombers. In the other instance the two German planes were seen at a long distance by a flight of Hurricanes, which never could get close enough to see more, if there were more to see. We know only that during the first instance, our bomber's copilot thinks the Me had a slightly modified profile, but beyond that he could not be helpful in his debriefing. I note that he is not long experienced, the sight of a Messerschmitt probably unnerved him, and our plane dove immediately for a nearby cloud bank.

"The resulting question of such long distance flying was raised officially by the RAF to the Air Ministry, which ignored it, and unofficially to one of our Friends at the Royal Aircraft Testing Establishment at Farnborough, who also was mystified. Thus, Rudolph, we are asking you to talk with the copilot and to consider, as our expert aircraft Friend, what this is all about and how we may extend our own fighter range as well, assuming our lad was not too frightened to see clearly. By-the-way, his pilot suspects he saw the same thing, but is too experienced in the military to say so on an official debriefing record form. Their commanding officer is eager to make both available to you. Will you do this for us?"

"Certainly I'll do it," Rudy nodded, "when will they arrive here?"

"Ah, Rudolph, that's the thing. You see, their commander can't release them, and – anyway – you may want to examine the one rather secret thing we *can* arrange for, and just between us, really, that's the Me109 flown to Britain by a Czech who claimed the reward. It's kept under guarded lock and key in a far out camouflaged hangar at RAF Biggen Hill, outside London. The plan is for you to fly to London and then to interview the copilot and pilot at their airfield, RAF Wyton, then examine the standard Me at Biggin Hill and meet with several RAF types there to talk over the greater range question, and then – if it can be arranged, and I'm sure it can – get you to really go over a Sea Gladiator in detail at RAF Tangmere. Then back here the same way you left, on a night courier flight. I'd guess less than a fortnight, all together. Maybe ten or twelve days, with an RAF air taxi Lysander from #16 at Old Sarum getting you around? Your principal HRM contact, American Colonel Whittaker, was off traveling somewhere, but Miss Townley, HRM's Finance Director, was consulted and agreeable to what I've described."

Nina! Rudy could only raise his head in silent thought while attempting to locate in his brain's vocabulary the chain of words he could use to explain the necessity for this unanticipated absence to her. He had to go; the issue was vital; the opportunity to learn was great; he had no choice; it would be of the highest value once Malta's Gladiators arrived; he would miss her terribly, he really did not want to go, and he would make it as short as he possibly could. Actually, in no more than two seconds he nodded again and said, "When would I be flying out, and who talks officially to Foster Crayton about my absence. Oh, and what can I tell people about my sudden departure from here?"

General Garrison responded himself by saying, "In no more than two days – or nights, really – we can have you on the evening fast courier, which typically is a modified Bristol Blenheim. Am I correct there, Gordon? Crayton's boss will inform him, the Wing Commander responsible for the Shops, as you call them. And you, Rudy, talk to as few people as you can manage, saying that HRM Aviation has called a winter meeting of their staff. What you tell that lovely translator I met at the Hawk ceremony is pretty much the same thing, but you could add – correctly – that this is an important professional opportunity for you, and a great aid for Malta, and that you are definitely returning ASAP. And Rudy, some advice: if necessary, Gordon will loan you a few quid to return with something nice for her from a known London shop. Don't forget that!"

"That sounds like good advice, Sir, and I won't forget. Just so long as I get an hour in London. I've never really been to the city, even on my way to Malta. At any rate, I'll pack a bag and my notepad and be ready to go tomorrow evening, if you can set it up. I'll just anticipate that Foster Crayton will be told I'm required at a London HRM staff meeting, and I won't dwell on that tomorrow. I'll talk to my 'translator' tonight, General, and think about a present. I won't need a loan, I hope, but I don't know London prices. You'll get me word of where and when for the plane ride?"

"I'll get word to you directly, tomorrow," Gordon answered, "and I'll be in our official car an hour before the plane leaves, at your hotel or wherever you tell me to get you. I'd suggest packing a jacket, shirt and tie, etc. in case you get invited to an officer's dinner or two. Otherwise, what you wear for meetings here at work. There's room on the courier plane for a bag, so don't stint. That plane is how I got here with my bag. Also, I will hand you an envelope with sufficient currency for your needs in England, a letter of introduction from the General, plus your itinerary. Bring some pounds if you wish, but you'll have plenty from me. Please keep track of expenditures for my records, and you can reimburse our official funds for that personal gift. Just don't make it a diamond ring! Har, Har..."

"Thank you, Gordon," said the Governor-General, "but you haven't yet seen this young lady!"

That evening, Rudy didn't know whether to be pleased at Nina's immediate assurance that, while he would be missed, she certainly understood he had to go, or concerned why she didn't break into tears at the announcement. He had anticipated the latter, and now was in mental turmoil, the turmoil increasing when she asked that he run by his hotel on the way to returning her home, so he could get the extra set of Red Rover keys for her. "It would be nice," she said, "to have the car while you're gone." The notion of her freedom of movement about the island somehow fed his anxiety, and he found himself biting his tongue to prevent speaking the questions of where, when, with whom, and - most importantly - why. She further tightened Rudy's stomach by observing that she was a very good driver, as he knew from her transporting him once to their favorite scenic belvedere in her father's old car, when he had only the small motorcycle and a strong desire to be alone with her. And, better yet, she would take good care of it each day when she drove it to work at the port, or the Lascarus RAF Operations Center, if her new position there commenced while he was gone. Rudy assuredly was learning about women, but he was unsure of the lesson's title! The best he could think of was, "I think there's plenty of gas in it, but watch the gauge."

The next morning at work, Foster greeted him with, "Good news, Rudy. They've just realized that there's a semi-crashed Bristol Type 1 up in the scrap hangar at Takali. It had a bad landing on the soft field, young pilot, with the usual Takali cross wind, and one of the two engines looks unscathed. If it's a Bristol Mercury VIII, it swung a three blade variable-pitch prop and most likely is what we'll find on the Sea Gladiators, if we ever get any. Anyway, I've sent young Lafessi up there with George to check it out. If it's what we could use as a test bed for your modifications, including the injection system, I'll see if we can truck the engine down here – along with everything that goes with it to make it run and operate, and get going with some horsepower related tests, after you play your stuff on it. We've got the heavy engine rolling hoist inside here and the engine test bed outside, so we should be able to get it bolted down, hooked up, and going. I hope!"

"Foster, that's great, and it would really give us a head start on the Gladiators. I learned late yesterday, though, that I've got to attend a staff meeting at HRM Aviation in London, unfortunately, and will be flown out of here – and returned ASAP– on the night courier flight. I'm to leave Malta either tonight or tomorrow. They'll let me know later today. Said I'll be gone a week or so, perhaps 10 days, if after the meetings they can arrange for me to get to a working Sea Gladiator and take a couple of days to really look it over and talk with their mechanics and pilots. That would make the trip worthwhile, even though it screws up my work schedule here. I got the news as I was leaving yesterday's planning meeting. I'll get back here as soon as possible, and I hope you can get that engine transported, hooked up, and running before I get back. Sorry, but they're my boss and I don't have a choice."

"Damn," came from a jolted Foster, "just when I think things are moving, they get sidetracked! I understand; that's who you work for, so you have to go. But if you can look over a Gladiator, that would really be helpful, since you never saw one in Buffalo, I'll bet. Don't mind me, Rudy. I'm still upset because no clearance yet, if you can believe it, for my getting into the BOC. Good Lord, it's been almost three months since I sent in the request I was told would go through in a matter of days. I'm glad you got the car when you did; at least that worked out. Right now I'm still living on the forbearance of the leasing agent, month to month, and you're still at the hotel instead of the flat you were thinking about. Oh well, it will work out eventually, I trust, as the dentist said about the stubborn tooth! But when, lad, when?"

The call from Colonel Astill came to Rudy early afternoon on Robert's office phone. "Go and pack now, if you haven't yet; the courier will depart a bit early, 1900 hours. Something about refueling at Gibraltar. I'll pick you up no later than six tonight, you and your bag, and I'll have the necessary clearance papers and your schedule, plus the packet we spoke of. I've jotted down several notes myself, aiming to be helpful to you, info about where you'll be going and the RAF chaps with whom you'll be meeting. Also a list of two or three shops in London, close by each other, which likely would have something appropriate for the translator, as our General calls her. One more thing: the name and rank of the very experienced Lysander pilot who will be your aerial taxi driver for the week. He'll know where and when you're to be, and will stay with you at the various meetings, and with the Gladiator inspection. I understand he's experienced with them, and he's cleared for all of the other topics you'll be addressing. Shall I be in front of your hotel at quarter to six, just to be sure you don't miss the train? Har, Har! Better bring a bite for supper with you from the hotel's dining room. Nothing on the plane."

"I'm leaving the shops right now and driving to the hotel. I'll be at the kerb with my steamer trunk from the Queen Mary – Har, Har – at five thirty, so don't be late! This is one train I don't want to miss, and I'll look over your notes on the ride to the station in case I have a question. Five thirty, OK?" This from an already excited Rudy to an always helpful, now humorous, Colonel Astill.

"Five thirty it shall be, my boy. I'll be sitting up with the driver, so you'll be going in great style. You'll depart from the middle tonight, just to keep people guessing, and head somewhere for a short bit before taking up whatever is proper. See you at half five. Cheerio."

Well, thought Rudy, leaving not from Hal Far but from the middle airport, Luqa, and starting on a non-direct route. They're just being careful, there *is* a war going on!

CHAPTER 22

ENGLAND BOUND

Mid-December

IT never occurred to Rudy until the night courier had taken off that if he didn't complete his special assignment quickly enough, he would be spending the coming holidays in England, while Nina would be enjoying her Christmas back on Malta. Definitely not good! He needed to give himself a head start in this assignment by thinking about possible explanations even before he arrived in England. Rudy immediately began mentally listing the ways that high powered fighter planes might extend their range. Better fuel management practices, boost pressure reduction, higher altitude cruising in less dense air, constant attention to such details as leaning the fuel mixture, readjusting the prop pitch or the fuel settings for a constant speed prop, and really trimming and re-trimming as fuel consumption changed the plane's weight and balance. All could help. So did total weight reduction, but none of these were ancient secrets known only to expert pilots. Flying instructors always hammered away at them and numerous other tricks-of-the-trade. Fliers knew that helpful tail and head wind direction varied with land contour, temperature fronts, and especially with altitude. Streamlining design tricks – even the reduction of protruding rivet heads or the addition of a prop spinner – could increase speed and thus ground covered in a given time.

However, conventional wisdom indicated that the greatest aid to long distance flying was more fuel, whether it was carried in larger wing tanks, bigger fuselage tanks, or five gallon Jerry cans stored between the seats. Stuffing the wings with Ping Pong balls so a plane might float sounded clever, but larger fuel tanks sounded safer. But wait, hadn't he read an article that mentioned extra fuel carried in small tanks hung beneath some planes early during the Spanish War, allowing increased range into remote regions? And didn't that war end only this past March? Could the eager Me109 pilot have already practiced in Spain both the use of an extended range tank hung under the fuselage, used up first and probably cast off when empty, and then the most deadly way to attack slower enemy bombers? Ah ha! We'll see if a drop tank wasn't the cause of – what did the co-pilot call it – the modified profile? If that's what it was the Brits had better get going in the drop tank business, if they aren't already, but forgotten to tell the RAF. Done right, you could fly Gladiators from a carrier off in the Med, all the way to Malta. I wonder if Curtiss is into drop tanks? I should find out. When I get to London maybe I can reach Jack at Curtiss Test Field and see. A few minutes of thought longer, and despite, or because of, the steady drone of the two engines of the bomber, now a carrier for no more than four passengers, Rudy fell asleep. He did so with a smile, thinking he had already solved the mystery of the Messerschmitts.

With fuel capacity enlarged a bit for some extra range, and a little less weight with a few passengers rather than a bomb load, the courier was refueling at Gibraltar by 1:00 am, and off the ground at 3:00. Rudy and his fellow passengers, each with a bag, deplaned a little before 9:00 am at the RAF field at Hendon, which one of them advised was no more than ten road miles north of London. Before he could even look around for a greeter, a uniformed RAF officer dressed in pilot gear approached, saying, "Mr. Worth, your air taxi is here. I'm your driver and guide, and glad to meet you. I'm Phillip Corbyn, Squadron Leader at Number 16, Old Sarum, and it's my pleasure to have an American engineer and pilot as our guest for a few days. Our taxi Lysander has plenty of room for your bag, and the Commanding Officer at RAF Wyton has BOQ digs all set up for you. You'll be able to get some rest after your flight here, and get a meal before you're put to work. Let me take your bag, and our Lysander is just over on the ramp, ready to go. Are you familiar with them? We've got a short flight this morning, about 80 miles, but I think you'll marvel at what it can do in getting us there. I thought you might enjoy a little stick time as we hop around from one RAF station to another, so I came with our trainer, which is fitted up with tandem controls. Lysanders taxi, fly, and land like no other plane. For example, wing slots and flaps operate entirely on their own, no handle or switch. And we take off three point. Never try to raise the tail on take off! And once you get set up looking good on final approach, don't change anything; and pray you won't have to go around! I'll get into all that as we fly around during the week."

As they walked toward the plane, Rudy was surprised to see that it was noticeable higher off the ground than even a Swordfish. Each streamlined landing gear leg ended in a large wheelspat, with a landing light and the stubnose of a machine gun protruding forward. Amazingly, sticking out from the side of each was a tiny horizontal wing with small bomb attachment points, now empty. This was designed as a multi-purposed airplane, was Rudy's first thought. His second was that with this size and weight it certainly needed the large radial engine enclosed in the sleek cowling with cooling flaps, looking suspiciously like the Hawk's front end. "If we can continue our togetherness as Philip and Rudy?," suggested the Squadron Leader, "we'll get you and your bag, Rudy, up in the rear seat area, both strapped in, where you can follow through lightly on the stick and rudder bar as I get us out of here. Use the ears and mic headset, and we can communicate. Our call sign is *Lysander 16 Co-op* this week, no matter where we go, and no matter that our side paint says KJ T. Rudy, as an American, you're pretty upper in the RAF hierarchy, and I'm glad to be along with you, learning the Me 109 mystery answer and seeing one up close. We'll have some fun when we get you to a Gladiator. I loved the many hours I enjoyed flying them, and so will you. We all just wish they could send Malta a few squadrons of them, complete with pilots. So up you go; look for the hand and toe holds and grab the struts, and I'll pass your bag up."

In a few minutes, taken up by Rudy and his bag getting squared away and by his new friend Philip getting the primer bowl and the Mercury's cylinders primed and the prop slowly turning, *Lysander 16 Co-Op* was cleared to taxi and roll. Rudy followed Philip's movements of the stick's spade hand grip and the old style rudder bar. He was pushed back in his bucket seat by the high take off and climb out angle. What a plane! Unlike any he's ever experienced before. And before he could fully enjoy the scenery passing below, they were letting down for RAF Wyton. At the ramp they were met by a vehicle, a driver and the Station Commander, who was quite formal in greeting Rudy, informal in greeting Philip – whom he obviously knew – and hopeful to 'Mr. Worth' that he would unravel the mystery which had, by now, spread a bit of anxious wonder among a number of RAF Stations. Rudy said the right things and soon found himself in a Bachelor Officer Quarters unit, "Ready for his wash-up and rest, with a knock on his door for a two o'clock lunch with the Commander, Squadron Leader Corbyn, and the Flying Officer who was the pilot of the bomber spotting the mysterious Messserschmitt," recited the Station Commander as they walked together into the bachelor officer abode. Rudy would interview the co-pilot later that afternoon, and enjoy supper in the Officers' Mess as the Station's guest. Departure would be tomorrow, whenever desired. At ten this evening, Rudy also was informed, he would have a phone call in the Commander's office from his HRM London headquarters.

All went as planned, and the interview of the RAF bomber pilot by him showed a skill in eliciting information that surprised even Rudy himself, although the others had assumed all along that 'Mr. Worth' had been sent to them because he had known expertise along those lines. Rudy wildly guessed later that his experiences with Ana Boiano had prepared him as a quiet, seemingly naive listener, and that encouraged the other person to talk openly. The bomber pilot did just that, saying that he had glimpsed an unusual side view of the German plane, certainly for a moment appearing not as a fighter but something else, possibly like a small bomber ready to drop its load. In an eye blink, however, the German plane slightly above them at a good distance, dipped its nose in a bank to head directly at them, without question a Messserschmitt 109 building speed to attack. Fortunately, our pilot went on to explain, looking alternately at his Station Commander and Mr. Worth, "I was able to get quickly into a cloud bank, and by some clever maneuvering and altitude changes, never see the 109 again. And, Sir, it definitely was a 109" A few minutes later, the pilot explained, while safely headed home by sliding from one large cloud to the next, his junior officer co-pilot described to him, in greater detail and with more certainty, quite what the pilot had just described to Rudy. With that final explanation, all three others around the table congratulated the pilot on his escape from an enemy fighter – certainly cannon equipped – and for his clear description of the incident. Rudy thanked him for his very helpful information, Squadron Leader Corbyn sagely nodded, and the Station Commander excused his pilot with thanks and almost a pat on the back for his good work.

As the pilot left, Rudy indicated he was ready to interview the co-pilot, and the Station Commander rose to have him summoned. Rudy held speaking until an attendant took away the sandwich plates, and then turned to Philip. "If the co-pilot's story is similar, I think we've got the mystery solved. Ah, here they come." The Station Commander ushered the young co-pilot into the room, introduced Rudy as Mr. Worth from RAF Headquarters and Philip as an unnamed Squadron Leader, "here as an observer." The young man – Rudy thought he looked barely out of his teens – spoke a trembling, "Yes Sir. Thank you Sir." Bending only his knees, he sat in the indicated chair, still at rigid attention. Rudy, as a now semi-experienced interviewer, spoke to put the young man at ease. "This is not an interrogation, just our getting together with you to get a fuller picture of your encounter with a mysterious German plane that appeared to be way off its regular patrol area. Your pilot has given us the general details, so we know that your plane escaped an attack by wisely using cloud cover. Since I'm especially interested in what you saw initially, I'd ask you to just sit back, at ease and relaxed – close your eyes if you want – and tell me how and what you saw of the German just when you first spotted him. Your after action report gives your precise location, but in which direction did you first see it? What did it look like? For how long could you see it" As if ordered, the man sat back in the chair, tilted his head slightly back, and closed his eyes.

Speaking slowly the co-pilot said, "I saw him, I'd guess farther off at first than I thought because I had his size off. Up higher than we were, not much higher though, moving from right to left on a steady line. I took him for a light bomber, like ours, thick fuselage but maybe a singe rudder. He must have been on a bomb run, because as soon as the bomb released, his bay doors closed, as ours would, and he banked right toward us. I mean a left bank to put him on an intercept line with us, and then his nose dropped. Single engine, no doubt, and more streamlined in the banked turn than he looked a second before. Came on, directly for us, full speed, but by then we were both yelling and going full throttles for the nearest cloud bank. We made it and went for the ground – which we couldn't see – but just as quickly jinxed a bit and got generally on our home heading, gaining a bit of height We lost him and made it back here OK. Saw him for just a few seconds, as I said in my report." With that, eyes now open, he looked at

Rudy as if he expected more questions. Rudy had only four. "Was there anything in that area worth bombing? And once he appeared more streamlined, is that when he made his turn toward you? Did he accelerate from his turn? When did you take him for an Me109 and not a bomber?"

Rudy nodded as the four answers were spoken: "Stupid place to bomb, maybe killed a cow, but not much besides farmland for a long way. Nothing ran but once a week on that spur rail line. Yes, after the bomb released it closed up, and with less drag he immediately banked left and seemed to really pour it on. Well, he hadn't opened up on us yet, but it was a 109 alright. I've studied all the models hanging in our ready room and that's all it could be as he got closer. Thank God for the clouds! Don't they have a nose cannon plus the MGs? First one I've seen, and hope it's the last while I'm in a Blenheim!" Rudy pushed back to signify he was out of questions, thanked the young man for his clarity in answering, and thus indicated the meeting was over.

The airman was released by the Station Commander, who, as soon as the three were alone, looked directly at Rudy and said, "What was that all about? Do you have an idea of what it was they saw, and how it got there?" "Yes." answered a smiling Rudy, "I believe so. What they saw was a Messerschmitt 109 fighter equipped with a drop fuel tank. As soon as the German saw your bomber he gave up hoping for a train on the old rail line in favor of a twin engine British bomber. The bomber was not quite as far from its home field as was the German, but the 109 had enough fuel remaining in its regular fuel tank for a fatal attack on a slower plane. Certainly worth dropping the empty tank, since the bomber was a prime target and the tank didn't cost that much. Of course, your bomber won that round, and the German had to explain the dropped tank. Drop tanks were used by the Luftwaffe in the Spanish war, and that was very recent. The pilot they encountered, I'll bet, was experienced with them in Spain. Tomorrow, when we get a look at that Messerschmitt the RAF has, I'll look to see if it has drop tank attachment points and provisions for getting the extra gasoline up to the engine." With all of that, Rudy went back to his borrowed BOC room, and Philip to his, each looking forward to tonight's invited session in the Officer's Mess. Rudy, of course was excited by the afternoon's problem solving, but in wonderment about tonight's HRM phone call.

Rudy realized he was being honored by the invitation to take a meal and a drink with a group of officers, and in their own Officer's Mess Dining Hall. He acknowledged the honor he felt and the warm welcome from the Station group. Since the Station Commander said nothing about the interviews, neither did Rudy, although there was some low conversation here and there in the room. Philip Corbyn, seemingly known by all in the room, sat next to Rudy, the Commander on the other, and quietly explained all of the historical hangings, icons, and mementos on the walls, all related to the long operational history of the many squadrons stationed there since 1916, and now the home of 139 Squadron. In the midst of this great and friendly group, unlike any in his experience, and following a splendid meal and a glass of wine, the Station Commander quietly reminded Rudy of the ten o'clock phone call coming into his office from HRM, London, and suggested they walk over in that direction. He assured Rudy he would return him to this very room and to Squadron Leader Corbyn as soon as the call was over. Rudy rose to follow, and soon was ensconced in the Wing Commanders private office, a clerk seated at a desk outside to switch the call over to Rudy, and the Commander promising to be outside, ready to return Rudy to the Officers Mess. No one had long to wait, since the call came promptly at one minute after ten. Switched to Rudy, he found Janice Townley at the other end. The call was brief and not revealing of anything, except Rudy was now scheduled to meet Ian Standish at RAF Station Biggen Hill whenever Rudy arrived there tomorrow for the inspection of the Messerschmitt. Ian would explain a slight change in Rudy's schedule, including an evening HRM meeting tomorrow night, and arrange for Rudy's taxi pilot to make an appropriate adjustment. "No problem." she said, "Just some business that you need to know about. You'll visit the Gladiator planes and get the courier back to Malta, as planned. Oh, and keep your travel bag with you, since you won't be at Biggen Hill overnight but elsewhere – all arranged for. See you at the meeting," she said, "and good night."

Rudy, returned to the gathering, whispered to Philip that there was a change in their schedule for tomorrow evening. His air taxi driver's response was, "Not a problem. Just let me know what's needed and we'll do it. I'm scheduled to get you around, no matter where or when." On their short walk back to their rooms, when Rudy said he'd be at the

HRM evening staff meeting and housed wherever that would be, Philip reassured him that his pilot would stay overnight at RAF Biggin Hill and meet Rudy wherever and whenever he was instructed to be. They would both learn the details tomorrow, he thought, at what Philip was now calling 'the Messerschmitt meeting'.

The Lysander touched down at RAF Biggin Hill next morning shortly before 11:00 am, and they were quickly driven to a remote hangar. A dozen or so uniformed men were standing in front of a wide closed door between two RAF guards. The group was milling about, and Rudy saw Ian Standish, in civilian dress, standing alone on the outskirts of the RAF officers, all apparently eager to see the captive plane and to hear Rudy's explanation for the long distance flying mystery. Rudy would never remember all of the names, ranks, and RAF Stations named in the brief introductions, but Philip later told him there were three Squadron Leaders, three Wing Commanders, a Group Captain, and an Air Commodore, plus a civilian and the two of them and the guards of the infamous plane – until Air Vice Marshal James Conners strode from the opening hangar doors to greet his special American Friend of the RAF, aircraft engineer and pilot, Mr. Rudolph Worth. That greeting by the highest ranking RAF officer present, cemented Rudy's position in the group. It was further justified by Rudy's brief, clear, and technically reasonable explanation of the extra fuel drop tank used by German planes in Spain and now, most likely, in this phase of this unusual-so-far war. Although Rudy was unable to find any provisions for a drop tank on this particular Messerschmitt, his explanation of the mystery was accepted by the group, with reassurances by Air Marshal Conners that a full exploration of this advancement would begin immediately by the design teams of both Hurricanes and Spitfires, as well as experts with the existing planes already assigned to the Stations. He would ask two or three of the assembled group to join the drop tank task force being instituted as soon as he returned to his office. "Nice leadership style," judged Philip to Rudy, with facial and body language from the back row. Rudy had to agree. The curious group went around, under, over, and into the German fighter, many entirely silent at the effectiveness of the design. Rudy spent his time, with engine and nose covers removed by the RAF

technicians standing by, looking for and examining in detail the boost system with supercharger, the water and X injection system (he guessed
methane), the armament, with cannon firing through the propeller shaft,
and, urged by Ian Standish, a type of gun-sight he had not seen before.
Happily, Ian told him there was a British made similar type packaged and
waiting for Rudy in his car. The only negative, in Rudy's judgment, was the
narrow span of the landing gear, which he thought would give the German
pilots fits, especially in unpaved airstrips, but that was their problem.

As the larger group clambered all around the fighter, James Conners
motioned Rudy and Ian aside, and an impromptu 'catch-up' meeting took
place on the tarmac ramp. As each thought of a topic it was voiced so that
all would know the current situation and near-future prediction. Questioned
about the Hawk, and prompted to install the new gun sight, described as
very helpful especially in deflection shooting at enemy planes flying off at
an angle, Rudy told that it was started and briefly run to warm up once a
week by Paul Lafessi or RAF pilot and engineer Slingerland, and had the
fuel, oil, and hydraulics plus the compressed air tanks checked. Over time,
having sufficient 100 octane fuel might be a problem. The question of
pilots for the Hawk was, Rudy thought, a huge problem. James speculated
that there was a solution, not yet agreed to, but the answer was close to
being announced, and Rudy would be among the first to know. James,
from his lofty RAF perch, also speculated that a small number of Sea
Gloster Gladiators, probably fewer than ten, would soon appear, awaiting
Rudy's improvements. After all this news, James shook their hands, patted
Rudy's shoulder, wished them both well, and turned back to the RAF
group. Rudy beckoned Philip over so Ian could tell them both that he was
now going to drive Rudy to the HRM meeting site, pick him up at the
hotel where a room had been reserved for him, and have him back here at
Biggin Hill no later than 11:00 am tomorrow morning for their flight to
RAF Tangmere, southwest of London for time with the Gladiators. Philip
saw that as a good schedule and asked Rudy, with his bag, to meet him in
the Operations Office by 11:00 tomorrow morning. He would alert
Tangmere of their approximate arrival time tomorrow and lodge here at
Biggin Hill tonight. He also would schedule Rudy for a confirmed seat on
the evening courier flight from RAF Hendon back to Malta four days
hence, giving Rudy the equivalent of three full days with Tangmere's

Gladiators. The courier leaves at 4:00 pm and arrives Malta early the next morning. Counting backwards, Rudy calculated he will have been gone from Malta, the Shops, and Nina six days and seven nights. Long enough, but seeing the Gladiators will make it well worth while.

CHAPTER 23

MANY HAPPY RETURNS

December 1939

"THIS is the same car I rode in when you picked me up at the Queen Mary's dock last June, isn't it?" asked Rudy, as Ian drove past the exit side of the gate house at Biggin Hill's RAF Station the next morning. "Of course." was Ian's response. "You're getting the big salary from HRM, not me. It still runs well, and the new models are priced like our war has already started, which it has. I'll likely be with this one until they stop turning out Hurricanes and Spitfires and switch back to Austins and the like, but don't hold your breath. The real war's around the corner for half the world, in case you Maltese don't know it yet. That's why HRM Aviation is in such high demand. We're very popular, especially since your President Roosevelt is putting out these great contracts for planes which are still in the design phase by aircraft companies that are just learning the difference between interceptors and bombers. The big change for HRM, my friend, is that our international Board of Directors – some of whom you'll meet tonight – have finally realized that HRM will not ever actually manufacture airplanes, as they initially planned, so what really is needed to save the world is HRM Aviation, as a consulting company focusing on air power, which is now the name of the game! In the eyes of Mr. Churchill, very likely our next Prime Minister, and his friend and backer, your own President FDR, you, dear Rudy Worth, are living evidence that the right person at the right time and place can do wonders – in case you don't realize that's what you're doing. Of course, your success is dependent on people like Foster Crayton and Gordon Astill and the expert workers in the Kalafrana Shops, and yours truly, who shipped the Hawk and all the goodies right under their noses. But that's what RAF Friends are for! God save the King and our Commonwealth.

"My boy, I'm neither clever enough nor paid enough to redesign HRM Aviation Ltd. on the fly, but I suspect that's what the primary topic of conversation will be at your meeting. I'd advise to keep the following in mind: Hitler is not going to slow down, and the strategy that worked for the European allies and the United States last war is never going to hold this time around. If France and England's current military leaders continue to depend on it, we're sunk before we leave the dock, or better said, while we're still digging the trenches deeper. Germany's blitzkrieg approach is dependent on *controlling* the air and rushing over the ground. France, and especially England, are thinking mostly bombers, and – God love them – the Poles just never imagined what would really be needed to stop them, and didn't have the resources, anyway. Nor do any of the other countries dotting the European landscape. Nor do we, at the moment. Mussolini, of course, will end up clobbering Malta, hardly stoppable by one Hawk and however many gallant biplanes you can beg, borrow or steal from the Royal Navy. We need all kinds of new planes, and in quantities not yet imagined, but right away we need modern, spectacular fighters. And HRM's task is to super-stimulate the design, testing, manufacture, and delivery of every type and number needed, from all available manufacturers here and in the US and Canada, with emphasis on great fighters that can clobber that Messerschmitt we saw today, and whatever else the Germans have up their sleeves. Forgive me Rudy, but you know how wound up I get over these things. I'll shut up, since you'll be hearing all this and more tonight, I expect. Besides, Philip told me you want to stop at some nice shop to pick up something, and we can do that on our way to the hotel you're meeting and staying at tonight in north London. I know just the swanky indoor cluster of shops on our way. Just watch the time, since you need to check in before six. I'm not at the meeting, but staying at the same hotel, so I'll see you at the hotel breakfast at 7:00 tomorrow morning, all packed and ready for the 11:00 o'clock Lysander flight with Philip to all those Gladiators." Rudy was able to squeeze into their conversation his heartfelt thanks to Ian for not only the Hawk, but the crates of absolutely great resources needed for Rudy's engine enhancement plans as well as Hawk improvements. Both knew that the mark of a great aircraft design is its ability to undergo continuing improvement, often out in the field rather than the factory.

They talked more as they drove, and eventually Ian asked if Rudy was looking to stop at a particular type of shop. This prompted Rudy, for the first time, to consider just what would be an appropriate gift for Nina, brought all the way from London, or at least somewhere near London. He realized he should not put its source exactly that way as he handed it to what he hoped would be a *very* grateful Nina, but with his inexperience in these things and her often unexpected responses, who could be sure? Running through this quandary took a minute, causing Ian to suggest, "Perhaps a nice little jewelry shop, or a stylish ladies clothing..."

"No, no, not clothing, and not a typical souvenir type shop. Maybe an inexpensive jewelry store?" was Rudy's delayed answer. He was a little dismayed to hear from Ian that, "In, or near London, there are no inexpensive jewelry stores, but a small globe containing a roughly cast metal replica of the Tower of London, or a genuine dyed cotton ladies scarf from India likely wouldn't do, either. Let's try a jewelry shop in the nice indoor shopping mall I have in mind, and you can see what they've got. Are you OK for British pounds, or can I loan..." Rudy assured him he had a few pounds and that he'd find something.

The mall sounded good, and thus in a few minutes, Ian waiting in the car, Rudy walked from a car park into a two story, quite large suburban mall. It housed, the welcoming sign said, a suitable variety of "London Style Shops". It wasn't far at all down the central corridor that a small jewelry shop with an attractive window display brought Rudy to a halt. He hesitated and then entered, and was warmly greeted, the only customer, by a stylish looking young woman clerk – as attractive as the window display, Rudy thought – who asked how she might help him. He literally stammered that he was looking for a small gift for a friend, not for a special occasion, but simply upon his return from a trip. The clerk understood immediately what Rudy wasn't saying, and asked immediately, "You must be from America? You sound exactly like those handsome men I see in the American movies that are so popular over here. Are you staying in this wonderful suburb of London? You can find anything you'd want right here without going all the way into that noisy city, you know. I live here myself."

Rudy answered, "No, I don't live here. I'm just on my way to a meeting in London, and tomorrow I'm off again toward home."

That declaration brought the clerk immediately to ask directly, "Does she have pierced ears?" "Why, I don't know," Rudy questioned, "maybe, but does that matter?" "Let me show you some nice bracelets," was the quick response. "Right over here in this case." In five minutes, Rudy was walking out of the jewelers clutching a small but attractively wrapped woman's bracelet of twisted very thin wire, each wire alternating with possibly some degree of real gold or silver coating, and with a safety type clasp. He was lighter in weight now, to the tune of 68 British pounds, but had the clerk's assurance that "She will truly love it!" Not now, but later, he would calculate the bracelet's exact cost in what he still considered "real money", American dollars. At least a hundred US, he estimated, and she was driving the car who knows where while he was gone. Also, wasn't that good looking clerk giving him a "come on" as they'd say in Buffalo? After all, she said anything you'd want, and she lived here.

In two more steps Rudy had silently talked himself into believing that Nina was going to..what? Owe him something? He couldn't put it that way exactly, but he was through fooling around! When he got back to Malta it was going to be different, by God, and, as he thought that, he almost walked into the wide staircase leading to the second floor shops, alongside the exit doors to the car park. A sign next to the stairs, with a printed arrow pointing straight up, listed a dozen shops, and at the top of the list was a Shores Pharmacy. Most likely directed by his sub-conscious desires, now inflamed by what he imagined was the good looking jewelry clerk's real intentions, coupled with his desire to see a most appreciative Nina tonight, not next week, directed him to climb quickly to the second floor and walk into what he would still call a drug store, the Shores chain pharmacy. He'd never had the nerve as a teenager back in little Watkins Glen to try this in the one drug store in the county, only getting enough nerve years later in urban Buffalo, and it would never even occur to him to try it back in Valletta, where he was well known. But, what the heck, for sure nobody knew him here, so as the elderly druggist looked up at him, Rudy questioned, "Do you sell condoms ?"

"Oh dear," the druggist answered, "Shores doesn't...a corporate policy, but your accent tells me you wouldn't have known that. Are you a visiting

American?" Rudy could only nod. The druggist, glancing around, continued with, "Perhaps I could look in the back to find a box of the Durex brand we once carried. Just between us, you know, and "for the weekend" as we used to say, you being a foreign visitor and all. Give me a moment, will you?" Rudy nodded again, and in a minute or two the man returned, carrying a paper bag. Now, are you finished shopping here in the mall and leaving? Good. There was this one box, a dozen packets of the latex type. I won't record the sale as that, but twenty five pounds should do it. Rudy nodded once again, dug in his pocket for his wallet, extracted a twenty plus a five pound note and, handing them over with a mumbled "Thank You", turned, clutching the bracelet bag as well, and walked out, down the stairs, and outside to Ian patiently waiting in the car. "Great," said Ian. "Did you get something nice?" "I hope so." Rudy softly answered. "I sure hope so."

The two continued on their way to the hotel and meeting site, Rudy voicing his thanks to Ian not only for the shopping stop, but for Ian's time, auto, and obvious knowledge of the highways and byways of England. "This part of England, the central and London area part only." answered Ian, with a chuckle. "If we were headed toward the Scottish border I'd be hopelessly lost. Now, if you want, I can fill you in – as you Americans would say – on just who might be at your meeting tonight, and why they might be there. I can say a word, too, about the new corporate role our finance lady, Miss Townley, has dropped into – or perhaps pushed herself into."

Without waiting for even an affirmative grunt, Ian launched into Rudy's orientation lesson to the new HRM Aviation Ltd. "First, the short term future for what we're already calling *The Allies* – Great Britain including the several Commonwealths, France, Poland, the several smaller nations in Europe not ever going to align with Germany, and, very hopefully very, very soon, the United States in an official, formal way – looks quite dismal. Germany is highly prepared, as you know, and will pull the usual suspects over to their side. Our fingers are crossed on many countries, some of which we'll see lost to Nazi armies anyway, and others which will officially stay neutral, but really not, probably such as Spain. Russia and Japan are suspect, to say the least. Italy is delaying, but nobody except the Duce knows for how long. Our boys in Parliament seem to have great faith in the French army, the now, to me, seemingly silly Maginot Line, and their navy and air force. I, personally, wouldn't bet on them. And Poland's come a cropper, as we say, except we're hoping to gain many of their pilots if the high mucky-mucks in the RAF can condescend to accept 'foreigners' in our, as yet, almost non-existent aircraft. In the mean time the Poles are fleeing to France and jumping into pilot's seats there, rather than here. We Brits have yet to develop the characteristics of openness and flexibility. As a matter of fact, we're just realizing that the real war to come after this Phoney War business will be won or lost in the air, if Adolph doesn't invade us first. Which is why we have a redesigned HRM.

"Just judging from the papers floating around our office in London, HRM's basic financial support is coming from Washington, the US aircraft manufacturers group, and from whatever Mr. Churchill can swing our way by leaning on his friends in Parliament. Soon after Winston gets the PM nod and takes over, Malta will begin to see some reinforcements, but right now, as you know, we're being helped greatly by all levels of the Friends of the RAF unofficial group, and by such military people as General Garrison and Gordon Astill in Malta. Right now, the HRM Board of Directors still has members from Poland, and of course, France. Poland will soon establish an exile government branch housed right in London, with General Sikorski leading. The President of Poland, in Paris just last month, dissolved the Republic of Poland's Parliament, so new provisions are just getting underway to take advantage of the escaped Polish pilots and mechanics and the new Polish Underground anti-Nazi activities. The Board members with the most power over HRM's new role are the British and American ones, and you'll see a few tonight. Colonel Whittaker is still the leader from America, but he won't be there tonight. Something about business in Washington, but I wonder if it's not a health problem? Instead, his chief assistant, a Major Carson, will be there tonight. Also the assistant's assistant, Captain Folino. Expect to see two or three or four from English aircraft manufacturers such as Bristol, Hawker, Supermarine, and Westland, and maybe somebody from De Havilland Canada. Every one is tooling up as fast as they can, since patriotism and getting contracts – not necessarily in that order – are great motivators. I don't know who will come over from France, you'll have one or two. They're moving their navy and planes pretty much as far east in the Med as they can, but tell us not to worry, they can cover Malta from there. We hope! Are you following me so far?"

"Yes, it all sounds logical. I understand that the HRM Board is mostly controlled by England and the US. But you mentioned Miss Townley and a new position? Where does she fit into this new, logical, change?" This all from Rudy.

"Ha," smiled Ian. "Remember, my friend, that if logic prevailed, men would ride side saddle! She is still the Finance Director, but her brand new additional title is Director of Strategic Planning and External Affairs, which puts that smart lady in charge of three vital HRM functions: finances, planning, and conducting business with all those important entities which are not operating members of HRM Aviation, Ltd. That list includes prospective consulting clients around the world plus the Allies' suppliers of warplanes and related materials. She's going to be running the show, my boy, mark my happy words. I say 'happy' because she knows the territory, understands the operating problems and challenges, and can push and pull others toward sensible decisions. How does that all sound to you?"

"Actually," Rudy responded, "it sounds OK to me, providing she really is on top of things and can keep the USA, my country, going along with this unified consulting operation, keep England, France, and whoever else happy getting good consulting results – including profitable contracts – and being a lady leader of a male dominated bunch of aircraft makers who are jealous of each other and not accustomed to getting directions from anybody else. Also, who are all the consultants going to be? Where are they coming from?"

"Exactly," Ian smiled again, "you have posed the key questions she hoped you would, and you now understand what's happening. She wanted me to brief you for tonight's session, and I have, and you're ready to assist her efforts at the meeting by assuring everyone of your support and assistance in recruiting and developing a strong consulting team."

"What," protested Rudy, "this was a planned lesson you just gave? She got you to prime me for tonight and to test my agreement with the changes? Amazing. You did it beautifully. Thank you, I think." "You are welcome, Rudy, as always." Once again, Rudy could only nod.

The hotel proved to be a fine choice for the meeting, with a splendid dinner served as the meeting progressed, and for a necessary stay-over, topped with a typical full English breakfast early next morning. Ian's listing of probable meeting participants was remarkably accurate, both as to number, origin, and voiced arguments during the long and involved discussion, and Rudy, upon spotting Ian in the 7:05 am breakfast crowd, promised to relate all he could understand and remember from the session during their morning ride. He did not even mention the late visit to his room for discussion of a special issue by Janice Townley and Major Louis Carson, Ed Whittaker's assistant. The surprising knock on his assigned room's door came only ten minutes after the HRM Board meeting ended and participants had left, some for their rooms and others for the hotel's lounge.

The purpose of their wanting to speak with Rudy, they explained, was to thank him for his supportive observations concerning the new organizational structure and for providing several excellent examples of aid provided by him to Malta. The Board members now realized the island was a key future Allied resource, located in a critical position, but at the moment very much in need of expert guidance, a fair amount of which was being provided, Rudy had detailed, through HRM. More important to Rudy was Janice's firm prediction that his Malta assignment would end, possibly in the near term, once the Hawk protection scheme was fully established with pilots, and additional fighter planes were located there and modified for improved performance through Rudy's work and protocol recommendations. As a leading HRM consultant, Rudy would then be transferred to his next assignment in Europe, possibly England, or even back to assist American aircraft designers, based on European flying needs and conditions as he had experienced them first hand. This prediction by her nearly floored Rudy, the first time it had truly occurred to him that his assignment there was, indeed, temporary, and that he could, and would, be transferred almost anywhere.

On a different tack completely, Major Carson first stated that what he was about to say was passed on to him by Colonel Ed Whittaker, who sends his best regards to Rudy for a hard job being very well done, and who wants Rudy to keep something in mind. That 'something', the Major said, was that if the United States entered the war officially, Rudy, as an experienced aeronautical engineer with Malta's experience already behind him, could be enrolled in the U.S. Army Air Corps, immediately commissioned as an officer in an essential professional field, and assigned to function as an internal consultant officer, serving his own country, rather than the HRM international firm; entry officer rank to be determined. Ed was voicing this possibility only to alert Rudy to one possible variation of his current role. Rudy, nodding his understanding, and head swimming with this possibility, began to thank both visitors for the information, but was interrupted by Janice Townley's sharply voiced, "Louis, don't you even suggest that! HRM convinced Curtiss to release him to us, and you're not going to steal him! Damn it!"

Major Carson's only response was, "Whatever. Blame Ed, not me. Let's let Mr. Worth get some sleep. Come on, I'll buy you a drink in the hotel's lounge." As they left, Janice Townley turned to Rudy, saying, "Rudy, forget what he said. I'll phone you next week in Malta."

As the hotel door shut, Rudy went to the edge of the bed and sat down. His brain was racing with the consequences of what he had been told tonight, each possibility bringing a mixture of excitement and fear. Excitement over the prospects of new work in new places, with new challenges and problems, and new people; fear mixed with sadness over thoughts of having to leave Malta, a place much more like home then now difficult-to-remember, Buffalo. But it dawned on him, as he sat there on the edge of the mattress, that leaving Nina was more than he could contemplate. He didn't think he could do it, but how to proceed with all this brand new business? Maybe back to Curtiss, but would he be drafted into what was described tonight? Sleep now, if he could, and meet Ian at the 7:00 breakfast, since he was still assigned to Malta and the Gladiators... and, apparently, his brain, or was it heart, to Nina.

CHAPTER 24

GLADIATORS ALL IN A ROW

RAF Tangmere
December 1939

THE morning after the HRM meeting in north London all went according to plan, thanks to Ian, who guided Rudy, a man still shaken from the
HRM news and the predictions offered by Janice Townley and Major
Carson concerning his up-and-coming assignments. Ian drove Rudy back
to RAF Biggin Hill airfield, to Squadron Leader Philip Corbyn and their
Lysander air taxi, and left him with best wishes and the promise to send
another shipment of useful resources to the port at Valletta, if that were
still possible. During the drive, neither Ian nor Rudy had raised the issue
of Rudy's likely reassignment from Malta to 'wherever', and that was good,
since Rudy was already depressed to the state of nausea from the unanticipated likelihood. Today's flight destination was Royal Air Force Station
Tangmere, located near the English coast southwest of London, not far
from the community of Gosport, and it was here that the Lysander headed.
The brief trip gave Rudy something to focus on, since Philip had his passenger take the dual training controls and experience piloting a quite
unusual aircraft. Indeed it was, but Rudy's anticipation of actually seeing
and examining Sea Gladiators overcame the thrill, even, of flying two 'lazy
eights' over the English country side.

Over many months earlier, in anticipation of the Phoney War shifting
to a more disastrous real war, Tangmere had been enlarged, with a number
of civilian buildings demolished and most families living near the site
moved. In place of the civilian community, Tangmere became a major
home to the RAF, with several types of planes including Gloster Sea
Gladiators and Hawker Hurricanes mounting a defense of London, and

later Lysanders for the taking and returning of special duty "agents" to France. (Only eight months after this visit by Rudy, German dive bombers and fighters would make a massive attack on Tangmere, killing 20 and causing extensive damage.)

As they approached Tangmere close enough to see the two runways, crossed in a large paved letter X, an impressive number of aircraft came into view, positioned around the hangars, ramps, and taxiways. Rudy, as they drew even closer, was astounded to see the largest number of Gladiators he had ever imagined, and was struck by the fact that Malta was hoping for a mere handful of them while here appeared dozens. No wonder he was sent here to actually examine one closeup, but how discouraging! Philip did his usual smooth landing, and a small group of airmen waiting on a hangar ramp to the left of the runway waved as one in welcome, or at least Rudy hoped it was a welcome, and indeed it turned out to be. The group's apparent leader, introducing himself as Wing Commander Barnaby, expressed their delight at having the opportunity to host a distinguished American Friend of the RAF and an aeronautical engineer to boot. Introducing him to the greatest biplane fighter ever made, and showing him both the design features and the engine advancements of their marvelous Gladiators would be an honor. As well, the Wing Commander said, the opportunity to prove to a Lysander pilot the significant advantages of Gladiators was something they all looked forward to. As he voiced this last, he smiled a friendly welcome to Philip, as all others in the group hurrahed. Rudy expressed his honor in being allowed here in "Gladiator Land", necessarily because Malta currently had none while they at Tangmere appeared to have a surplus, and he, too, smiled as he joked. Philip simply asked if they had any three winged fighters, perhaps an old Fokker Tri-plane or two from the last war, hidden away in case they came into style again? All laughed at that, and thus a friendly welcome was extended.

Adjoining to Wing Commander Barnaby's office, the visitors were assured that BOQ rooms were already assigned to them, as were meal chits for all meals in the Officers Mess, courtesy of Air Vice Marshal Conners. And it was the Air Vice Marshal, Commander Barnaby assured them, who had told the Tangmere group of Rudy's background and more recent history and challenges on Malta. Their itinerary was reviewed and amended as they discussed Rudy's needs, and a long general group session with the Gladiator mechanics and various technicians was scheduled in addition. Rudy was anticipating a necessity for quick turn-around of damaged planes, should fighting start and a Hal Far Fighter Flight ever be possible. At that point, good mechanics and technicians would be as necessary as good pilots. With the sessions involving Rudy and those assigned to those sessions by Commander Barnaby now in place, two of the local pilots were summoned to take Rudy for lunch and an initial discussion about Gladiators, while the Commander and Squadron Leader Corbyn discussed an item of common interest.

Philip, still seated in the Commander's office, looked up with interest as the ranking officer said, "While we're discussing the items I want to bring before you for your reaction, I would think we might not stand on formality and I invite you to call me what my close associates do, and that is 'John', and you are Philip, I believe.

"Philip it is, and happily, John, and I'm eager to learn the subject under our joint consideration."

With that beginning, Philip quickly learned that the Wing Commander had been doubly impressed with the degree of concern Air Vice Marshal Conners had displayed while recounting just how important it was for Tangmere Station to meet the engineering needs of the American guest. Listed had been the coming vast importance of Malta, the necessity to impress American President Roosevelt with the British intent to defend Malta, and the volume of assistance offered to Mr. Worth, who was sent to assist Malta's air defense by President Roosevelt at the urging of Mr. Churchill. All of these caused John to say that, should Mr. Worth not be satisfied at Tangmere, its Wing Commander, he himself, would be transferred to RAF Antarctica Station, if there is one. Philip laughed, but reassured John that the schedule set for Rudy should assure his satisfaction. "But not flying a Gladiator while here is a great lacking." John almost cried out, "As you may know, Philip, they are wonderful to fly, but demons when you taxi, take-off, dare to land, and attempt to taxi back to the ramp without going nose over teakettle. I would not dare to send Mr. Worth aloft in a Gladiator without having him here for a couple of weeks, at least, of preparatory training. That is not to be, I understand, but I do have a possible remedy, and I would value your judgment concerning it. May I tell you what I have in mind?"

Philip's nod was all the encouragement the Wing Commander needed to launch into a possible solution which immediately caught Philip's attention. A bit more than a year ago, John began, his chief pilot instructor, accompanied by the head of Tangmere's repair and maintenance shops, came to their Commander to reemphasize their concern over the seeming unending flow of minor and moderate repair jobs coming to the repair shop, the result of training flight accidents in Gloster Gladiators. Almost all were caused by pilots getting their beginning flight experiences in Gladiators, with only an occasional accident involving a more experienced Gladiator pilot, and those often in landing/taxiing, requiring great coordination and judgment in the use of the pneumatic brakes and rudder. Something additional was needed, they reasoned, between the primary biplane training provided at flight school locations using the older, slower, and much less complex Tiger Moths, and the Gladiator, recognized at least by England as the newest, fastest, and most advanced single seat biplane fighter in the world. What would provide the needed transition, they reasoned, was upgraded orientation in an advanced biplane trainer, including check-rides with an experienced advanced Gladiator instructor who would judge transition to Gladiator readiness. What advanced biplane trainer could there be, they inquired? Why the very biplane fighter which preceded the Gladiator they answered themselves, the Gloster Gauntlet, which was the leading biplane fighter in countless RAF Squadrons from 1935 to this very year, and numerous foreign ones as well. At its high in 1937, RAF Fighter Command had assigned it to more than a dozen squadrons. In appearance it closely resembled a Gladiator minus the closed cockpit and wing flaps, and in performance -while obviously not matching Gladiators – it was in a world beyond the Tiger Moths of flight school. But wasn't there a major problem, asked the Wing Commander, in that the Gauntlet was, like its replacement Gladiator, also a single seater? Would the instructor and check pilot ride on a wing? No, the two answered, with dual basic controls and in the jump seat they could fit just behind the pilots cockpit. And so they did, using the upgraded Gauntlet Mk II still in a Tangmere hangar, and they have been using it, quietly, as an unofficial and seldom mentioned advanced biplane trainer, saving significant injuries, costs, and repair work to the first line Gladiators of Tangmere and their young pilots.

Philip, smiling while nodding his appreciation, said, "Wonderful, but wasn't there a problem with the extra weight? And what about weight and balance? And fuselage strength, and splicing into the control cables? Did they fit an entire instrument panel, engine controls, and all the rest? Is it still flyable?"

"Yes to challenges, including some gun weight and a bit of the fuel tank. No to an entire additional cockpit. Yes to still in use. Now let's go and take a look at it on our way to lunch. Shall we?" A short walk had Philip climbing up into the small instructor's cockpit located immediately to the rear of the standard pilot's seat, but with a narrow metal separating strip supporting a streamlined windscreen. He saw a control stick, a rudder bar, engine controls, a few toggle and other switches, a very basic instrument panel, and an old style 'Gosport Tube' allowing voice and hearing communication between the two flyers. Taken together, he judged that the solution was simple yet effective, and safe, assuming flight characteristics were as originally designed by the Gloster Company. The two lunched at a side table at the Officers Mess, where all of the detailed questions by Philip were answered by the Wing Commander, who then asked Philip his thoughts about having Rudy go up with an advanced Tangmere pilot instructor, perhaps for an hour or so each day they were here, for a first hand experience with the next thing to a Gladiator? That question was followed by a second one before Philip could answer the first, which inquired about Rudy's ability in the air. Philip's advice to John listed Rudy's air racing experience, his flying at the Curtiss test field over almost ten years, and his several flights of the Hawk on Malta. "Oh, and his two lazy eights and basic air maneuvers on the way to Tangmere, in the Lysander." Philip's judgment was that Rudy, while a good pilot, could certainly benefit from a couple of dual hours in the Gauntlet fighter, and, just as important, enjoy it tremendously.

"Then done," said John, "and I'll organize those flights into his schedule. Now, Philip, I have another request of you. First, I'll tell you in confidence that, when the balloons go up, Tangmere will be in the thick of it defending our Sector II, especially the London area. However, in some hopeful anticipation of the initial defensive phase easing after time, it has been unofficially whispered to me that Tangmere is in an advantageous location to operate the Lysanders that, undoubtedly, will be used to ferry our special agents back and forth to France and elsewhere on the mainland, under the very noses of the Germans. Thus my inquiry of you. Would you be willing, while you are here, to provide two or three of my selected pilots in the intricacies of the mysterious plane you flew here, the Lysander? Without their knowing the reason, they will be naturally curious about such a different type plane. We would, anyway, be refueling it before you leave with our American Friend, so brief flights with your group would certainly be appreciated." To this request Philip instantly agreed, saying that a group of three experienced pilots should be fine, including some flying time and 'touch and go' short field landings. Fortunately, he had come in a dual control model, somewhat like the Gauntlet used here, so the take-offs and landings over very short distances should be of high interest. With those agreements made, their luncheon concluded, and both went off to check on Rudy's first orientation.

The first orientation to Gladiators consisted of three pilots from the Tangmere group, all experienced with the type plane, walking him around one and pointing out the important details. They quickly saw that he was hardly a novice around aircraft, although Rudy had already pointed out that he had never before seen a Gladiator. He was familiar with the big three place Fairey Swordfish torpedo bombers which came and went at Malta, he told them, one having led him in the Hawk to the Gozo airstrip and later returned him to Hal Far, but he was still impressed by the size of the single place fighter he was looking up at, sitting twelve feet high. In writing his daily log that night in his BOQ room, he underlined the following as items of special interest: flaps on both upper and lower wings; two fuselage mounted side guns, synchronized, each firing through rotary engine open spaces between cylinder heads, and a gun hung in a stream-lined pod under each lower wing, outboard past the prop radius; three bladed fixed pitch metal prop with spinner; unseen but reported upper wing gun fittings, same as below but not used; fixed main landing gear, swivel tail wheel; gyro adjusted optical gunsight; electric starter; surface oil cooler right side front fuselage; exterior fuselage access panels for battery, first aid kit, radio equipment, control cable access, compressed air containers; and quick access panels for engine work.

Once the walk-around tour finished, the guides brought Rudy over to the left side of the plane and, although there was a pilot in/out half door on both sides, they told him most pilots used the left side and showed him the hand and toe grips and steps, similar to the Lysander, and got him up and into the cockpit. Rudy's immediate impression was that both the design engineers and those who had worked later on improvements and upgrades had filled every possible flat or open space with gauges, handles, dials, switches, push-pull knobs, metal boxes, and indicators. In addition to a typical spade type control stick with buttons, a large flat compass rose from somewhere between the foot pedals, mounted on a very sturdy looking support rod. A rapid estimate indicated something like fifty 'things' to claim the pilots eyes and the possible attention of his hands at some point, not counting his feet on the pedals. There apparently was no real, solid floor either, simply unfilled spaces. Was this the way that an old style biplane had been modernized? Rudy wondered, did they add a sliding canopy and whatever else could be thought of, plus a lot more horsepower, and hope it would do the trick until hurricanes could be improved and many more Spitfires manufactured? But, he had just heard from his pilot guides that Gladiators were a joy to fly and splendid for aerobatics. Just hope an Me109 never found you up there. That would most likely not end well!

Wise enough not to question any of this out loud, Rudy did exclaim over the gyro driven optical gun sight firmly mounted between his eyes and the windscreen. Electrically powered, there were an on-off and cross-hairs dimmer controls located to its left, with provisions for distance aiming point adjustment on a kind of heads-up display projected in mid-air, or so his tour guides told him. It was as modern as the one Ian Standish had handed him for the Hawk just a couple of days ago. For any kind of shooting, including deflection shots, this little gem certainly was long ahead of the steel ring and bead post he had on the Hawk, but would soon replace. Hopefully, any Gladiators Malta received would have all of the upgrades already installed. One of the pilots suggested that he simply sit in the cockpit for a few minutes, identifying each of the many items he was looking at. He would understand the use of many since his Curtiss Hawk would undoubtedly have the same. Those which proved to be unidentifiable would be explained by one of his three guides, each of whom was crouched beside him, kneeling on one wing or the other. It took Rudy almost a quarter hour to know, guess, or learn from his new friends the what and why of each, knowing he would never remember the identity of each without more sitting and looking and touching...and reminding from a guide. Saying this prompted the pilots to promise him copies of every printed diagram and assembly and rigging manual they had at Tangmere before he left for Malta. That gift prompted profound thanks from him.

The remainder of the afternoon was spent by Rudy with the head engine technician, both on step-stools, and a Gladiator with all its engine access panels and the cowling removed on both sides, standing on a well lite hangar floor. Rudy spent the next morning with the same engine expert, the same Gladiator, and the same step-stool. Fortunately, he had mastered the use of a note pad and a pencil while standing, bending, asking questions, and scribbling, without loosing his balance, He was amazed at what on this engine and its accessories was brand new to him, and how lucky it was for him to be here before Malta received any Gladiators with the crowded engine compartments. His notes included information on the most effective props, and on their opposites, including the particular type two bladed wooden prop that vibrated shakily from over reving during a dive. Most time was spent on the Mercury VIII engine and its many necessary add-ons, from the spinner to the carburetor plus its air intake below and the single stage supercharger at the rear and the oil feed pipe to the prop RPM reduction gear in the front as only a few examples. He gulped when it was pointed out that, if a fuselage gun were not mounted exactly as designed, its off center firing through the cylinder head open spaces could result in a destroyed cylinder while in an aerial battle.

The afternoon session, to be conducted with two technicians, and covering design and construction features of the Gladiator extending from just behind the cockpit and sliding canopy to the tail surfaces, was delayed until mid afternoon because of a last minute adjustment in Rudy's schedule. Without more of an explanation than, "We have a nice surprise for you!", Rudy was escorted by one of the morning's tour guide pilots to a nearby ramp and introduced to the very recent predecessor of the Gladiator, the almost-as-modern Gloster Gauntlet, in which he and his pilot friend would now take an orientation ride. Rudy was so pleased and excited that he exclaimed, "Oh great!" three times before slipping on the helmet and goggles handed to him and being helped into a parachute harness. After a quick walk around pre-check, assisted by his now 'instructor', Rudy climbed aboard, followed directly by his flight companion, who helped him buckle in and settle into the seat, atop his parachute. No one had asked him if he were properly experienced with this 'cushion', so Rudy saw no need to respond. The instructor climbed into the small space just behind, buckled in, and tapped Rudy on the shoulder, instructing him to pick up and tryout the communication headset which connected them by tube. Not high tech, but it worked, so Rudy was given time to familiarize himself as he had in the Gladiator, conduct a proper engine prime and the starting procedure with throttle and mixture knobs, lean his head to one side and yell "clear-prop" – which he knew how to do – pull on both magneto switches, and push the starter button. From taxi to take off to landing and all in between, guided and assisted by the pilot in the rear jump seat, Rudy told Philip at dinner that it was an absolutely fabulous and very valuable experience, for which he was most grateful. Best of all, it was to be repeated tomorrow with rapid climbs and acrobatics. The plane, while not exactly a Gladiator, and not as high powered as the Hawk, was never-the-less a great biplane experience for him. Philip agreed, and never mentioned his own first day of the also semi-secret Lysander flight school. He did, however, get Rudy to express high satisfaction with the ground schooling he was receiving on the design and engineering aspects of Gladiators – the very reason they were at RAF Tangmere.

Rudy's ground school the next day proved to be, perhaps, the most useful to him. The long morning session was spent reviewing his ideas for Mercury engine enhancement in Gladiators with not only the shop head engineer, but three engine technicians with years of experience on, basically, not only the same engines that currently powered Gladiators, but the earlier Gauntlet and the still highly praised Bristol Blenheim bombers. The Malta challenge, as Rudy explained his task, would be to take whichever Gladiators would be made available, most likely Royal Navy

Sea Gladiators of random model years of manufacture, and do whatever was possible to upgrade their performance, especially in ability to climb quickly to whatever altitude Italian and/or German bombers and fighters would come in at over the Island, undoubtedly with limited warning time. And once they were met, the Gladiators would need enough top speed to catch the enemy and perform an effective attack. He listed what he hoped might be an addition to the four machine guns already installed, possibly either two more top wing guns using the already installed mounting points, or cannon, if they arrived in Malta on time and could be mounted somehow.

He mentioned his fear of running out of 100 octane fuel, and the possibility of using octane booster on whatever avgas was available, and the changing of wooden props to three bladed metal ones, if he had the right ones. He reported that during his time here he had abandoned his idea of substituting two stage superchargers he didn't have, for the single stage he hoped would be in place, but would want to try to install a water mist-methane injector system to create lower operating temperatures and thus longer use of the blower boost system which gave ten horsepower additional. While coming up with pilots for the Gladiators was the responsibility of the Hal Far Station Wing Commander – the officer currently without not only pilots, but also without planes, Rudy said he and the civilian shop manager saw their challenge to include keeping the not-yet-existing Gladiators flying through continuous air battles with very limited spare parts and fuel. One of the group added that a current rumor making RAF rounds was that the Malta Naval Commander actually commanded a navy without any sailors or ships. Rudy responded with a grim smile and the request that the group list what else he could do and what advice they would have for him about the brief list he had just mentioned. He was pleased that his idea of the injection system, which they knew was already installed on German fighters for extra power at higher altitudes, might well work as Rudy desired on Gladiators flying at lower levels. A very interesting and helpful discussion followed, looking at where the misting equipment, pump, and water-methane tanks could possibly be installed, what effect the added weight would have if a place were identified, and how might any positive results on Gladiator performance be measured.

Similar discussions went on, focusing on Rudy's ideas as well as more suggestions from the group, and Rudy judged it all excellent help.

The hour's flight in the early afternoon that day consisted first in climbing to given altitudes in the shortest possible time using varying climbing angles and engine RPM. The highlight of the hour, however, was the brief demonstration of mild aerobatics in this modified fighter. Rudy's instructor demonstrated high bank angle turns in a tight lazy eight, a chandelle turn which gained altitude and reversed direction in a gentle bank, a fast Immelmann turn which achieved the same thing but consisted of a half loop and a half roll out at the top, a hammerhead turn, and a wingover dive in order to keep fuel flowing into the carburetor when going from level flight into a steep dive. From his own flying, including pylon racing the 'little red' Mercury Aviation plane back home, Rudy knew about stalls and recovery from them, so-called graveyard spirals, and turns around a point. What he wanted to experience now was a complete loop, and he asked this over the Gosport Tube. In hesitant compliance, his pilot climbed to 5,000 feet, and well off from their field, did two tight clearing turns, a right and a left, told Rudy over the speaking tube that he was lining up with a straight road below, would build up speed a bit and then climb with full throttle and stick all the way back. As the Gauntlet reached the top of the climb, upside down, he would momentarily reverse the stick to flatten out the top of the loop, and then allow the nose to drop into the descending curve, throttle somewhat retarded and carb heat on until they leveled off, fuel still feeding the engine and carb still not frozen. Which they did, still lined up perfectly with that road, and the plane still in one piece, causing the pilot to pray his thanks and then hope no one below would report him for endangering the American, the unofficially modified plane, and himself, in that order. At least their visitor was happy, he reasoned, and he had flown his first loop in too many months.

Rudy returned to his afternoon session which had him completing his scrutiny of the Gladiator under the guidance of the shop's head engineer. This took him from the tail to the wings, and then to what he called the landing gear and the local expert called the undercarriage. Except for advice to remove the tail hook mechanism and the water dingy stored between the upper landing gear legs, if Malta got Sea Gladiators, that seemed to be 'it' for the plane itself. What remained now was a clear recommendation and detailed discussion for organizing a repair shop and work process for an active Station engaged in fighting a real war against a reported very strong enemy air force.

For this last session at Tangmere, Rudy and Phil had a half day tomorrow. Then it would be the flight back to Hendon RAF Station and the night courier flight back from there to Malta, first stopping for refueling at Gibraltar. That would be, of course, if Janice Townley and/or Ian Standish made sure that he had a seat on that flight. That doubting thought set Rudy's thoughts on another tack, one that intermixed the hope that his own Mercury engine from a wrecked bomber was waiting for him back at Clayton's Shop to try out the mist injection research, and the other, that a tearful, loving Nina would be waiting with open arms, at least, for his return. Oh Boy, he almost shivered out loud, but for which, or both?

CHAPTER 25

RETURNING

Malta
Winter, 1939-1940

THE last session for Rudy at Tangmere consisted of a dozen RAF Supervisors and civilian technicians, plus Section Heads and Maintenance Officers, and included Wing Commander Barnaby himself. Even Squadron Leader Corbyn was there, his impromptu Lysander flight school having finished the day before. The goal, as announced to the group by Commander Barnaby, was to provide an accurate description of work flow changes already planned for the Tangmere Shops once the status changes from the current 'Condition Yellow' to the expected wartime 'Condition Red'. "In other words," he asked, "as the number of daily Patrol Flights, Scrambles, and Tallyhos mounts to anticipated levels, how will our Shop keep all needed planes in daily service? How are we organized, and will we then mount 24/7 shifts? From where will we get the spare parts and other supplies? Since Malta's defenses are still in the preparation stage, how should Mr. Worth and his colleagues best proceed? We hope to provide a leg-up to our RAF comrades on Malta by describing the planning we've already done, so please don't hold back. Remember, their island is only fifteen minutes flying time from Italian bomber and fighter airstrips on Sicily."

The session, planned to last an hour or so, extended for two and a half, with Rudy busy the entire time filling pages in his notebook with what sounded like very workable ideas for possible transfer to Malta's operation. Judging from the volume of discussion and its fervor, this group certainly anticipated sustained and heavy air battles with the Luftwaffe as soon as the current Phoney War exploded. And, as one Division Head loudly said, "Very soon, Mr. Worth, you mark my words!"

The genuine 'Thank you' and 'Most helpful' and 'Very grateful' and 'Certainly the Air Vice Marshal shall receive my most positive description of what I learned here and your graciousness to me' were offered by Rudy to Wing Commander Barnaby at departure time. All remaining on the ramp near the Lysander either saluted or waved, or both, as Philip taxied to the runway and Rudy waved back, and shortly the visitors were a speck in the sky, headed for RAF Hendon and the courier flight. During the brief flight Rudy expressed his thanks to Philip for all he had done to make Rudy's adventure, as he called it, such a great success, and so enjoyable. As Rudy expressed it, "I don't want to sound maudlin, but you've given me much more than you know. I hope our paths cross again, and that you stay safe if what they were all predicting back there happens. Philip's response was, "Rudy, you don't need to thank me for doing my job, and also having an enjoyable time doing it. I hope we do get to meet again, and I want *you* to stay as safe as you can when the balloons go up. Malta's really going to catch hell. I know you love to fly, but in an old Gladiator or even that fine Hawk you've got, is nowhere you'll want to be when it starts. Anyway, by that time you may be transferred someplace else. I imagine you could move readily? You don't have a family here, do you? I'm somewhat glad now that my wife divorced me the second time I got transferred. No children yet, so that was the time to do it. I don't know how the families of married pilots are going to hold up when the real war starts. Without plenty of upgraded Spitfires we're going to get the short end of it against 109s; even a Mark II Hurrybox isn't going to look so great against 109s. Your country's not in it, at least yet, so don't get carried away with being the American pilot hero of Malta. Not my business, but I kind of like you, so think hard about the limits of your HRM assignment, won't you?"

After a few long moments, Philip heard, "I'm already thinking about my HRM assignment, and the rest of it. I'm thinking hard starting right now about what you said and a couple of other things. Thanks for pushing me; I guess I've been living in my own little world, up until this week. Now I'm more awake!" And think hard Rudy did, the entire courier flight back to Hal Far, Clayton and the Shops, Colonel Astill and the Governor-General, the Hawk and the lacking Gladiators, and – most of all – Nina and their future. Oh, and Rover, his car, borrowed in his absence by Nina. Otherwise, the first leg of the flight to Gibraltar, the refueling there, and the second leg to RAF Hal Far, Malta, were uneventful and pretty much on schedule.

Nina and Rover were standing close to Colonel Astill as Rudy deplaned, bag in hand, with his two purchases in the bag. The Colonel was the first to greet him, telling him he was due at their weekly meeting, tomorrow at 9:00, and that, "Miss Lafessi, here, with whom I've been chatting, will give you the Governor's new office address. I'm off now to a meeting, and I'll leave you two, and I look forward to meeting you again, Miss Lafessi. I'll see you tomorrow morning, Rudy." With that hurried and somewhat embarrassed farewell the Colonel almost jumped into the rear seat of his waiting car and his driver sped off toward Valletta. Nina clutched Rudy's arm and said, "That poor man had no idea who I was or how I got onto an RAF field, or why I was here. So I told him we were acquainted and I was here to give you a ride to your hotel. That seemed to throw him into a loop, and speaking of loops, how was your week's solo vacation, and I'm glad you're back. Did you miss me, or shouldn't I ask?"

Before he could answer, Nina said, "We're going to my house – nobody's home for hours, and I'm going to cook you a meal and hear all about it and what you've been thinking about, because I've been thinking about things myself. For the past few days the word around Malta is that Italy is going to go in with Germany, sooner rather than later, and Malta will probably be invaded and all the beautiful young girls taken to Rome and Berlin as bounty. My sister votes for Rome, but what does she know, she's just starting college. I haven't decided yet, so I want to hear what you think. And by-the-way, since I see you looking at Rover, it runs fine and I was very careful in racing the island buses around town. No scratches or dents. So pick up your bag and let's take advantage of a temporarily empty Lafessi house, handsome, shall we?"

By now, Rudy was totally ignoring the many complex scenarios that had run through his mind during the courier flight – his new thoughts of the future – and was in the middle of an old fashioned male sex alert bolstered by all the innuendos he was pretty sure Nina was throwing his way, her house with no one home serving as a prime example. Luckily he had bought the...well, you know, still in his bag. With those profound mascu-line thoughts forming his action plan, he mumbled something like, "Oh Honey, I've missed you so much." and strode directly to the driver's door of the car. Ignition key in her hand, Nina followed to the same car door, opened it, and told Rudy to "Shove over, I know the way." Pushing in, she started Rover and drove to the house in Sliema. Rudy, wisely this time, kept quiet during the quick trip.

They climbed the several front steps, she got the front door opened, yelled a loud Hello, and pulled him and the small suitcase into the entry-way. Rudy pushed the door shut with his foot and immediately pulled her into an embrace while pushing her back against the hallway's wall. As close together as they could be, she returned his kiss, but with less enthusiasm than he had remembered. As that realization hit him, Nina twisted her head away, got a hand free to push his arm, and said, "Rudy, back off! I didn't bring you here to get manhandled. Cool down, lover boy! We came here so we could talk in privacy, not over a restaurant table or on a car seat, or in the back row of the cinema with half the town there. At least that was my thinking. It's obvious that your thinking is just what it has been all along. Come on in the kitchen, sit down, and I'll get you some breakfast. I missed you, a lot, and I've been thinking that with a real war coming on, or so everybody says, you and I need to deal with the "what do we do next" question. Hopping into bed isn't a long term answer, and maybe there is no long term answer, but I don't want either of us to get into a situation that doesn't have any sensible future. Have you thought about that?" With that she began to prepare coffee and real food, not airplane biscuits. "Have you?"

Rudy pulled his thoughts together, did his best to cool down, pulled his bag over toward himself and, bending over while still seated, pulled the nicely wrapped bracelet out. "Yes, I've been doing a lot of thinking recently, and I still don't know what the best answer to your question about our future is. And during my trip I learned more from my bosses at HRM that adds to my uncertainty. I'm sorry that I have such a strong sexual need for you, but I don't think that's unusual. I'm only a few years older than you, and I'm not quite thirty. I haven't been running around Malta, or even Strait Street, looking for physical loving, only running after you, who seemed to give me a big come-on that day on the Gozo motorcycle ride and, I don't think you'll argue, a couple of times in the parked car. I can't take a cold shower every time I look at you, but I know how stupid it sounds for me to say I need you that way. I certainly know that, if that's all I need from you, this is a done deal. It's not the only way I need you at all, but what can we do? Should I become a citizen of Malta instead of the U.S. and try to get a good job here? Can you leave your family and Malta and come home with me to Buffalo, U.S.A. If we're going to do that, we'd better pack now while we can maybe still get there together. And shouldn't we be a married couple to make you an American citizen first? Should I refuse the transfer to some other country HRM is predicting for me and quit? Should we make believe there isn't going to be a really big, long war? How will we do it when Malta does face a Nazi invasion? What will happen to me and you if and when America enters the war and I'm ordered into the American Military? How in hell can we plan for ourselves with all those answers a mystery?" And, by-the-way, I do love you and, I think, also in the way my own father and mother still feel about each other after more than thirty years. I'm thinking of my parents and my sister whom I haven't seen in six months. And I got this for you in a little jewelry place in north London." Handing the package to her, he stopped. She began to cry, and he jumped and held her, near tears himself.

"Don't cry, we'll figure it out. We just need more information and a little time to see what's really going to happen. At least we've got some alternatives, and as we wait to see what the war business is going to do we can each think through what we see as the best option for us. In the meantime I'll just take more cold showers. It's more like an engineering problem that needs a little more time to percolate before the right answer appears." Nina's retort was, "Rudy, don't percolate too often. Our old coffee pot did that and finally burned out. O.K., I'm alright, we'll work it out and do the best thing, whatever that turns out to be. I was probably crying because you brought me a present from London, and I made a bet with myself that you'd forget." As she pulled at the wrapping and bow and then opened the box, Rudy heard a cry of joy. His immediate reward was more enthusiastic than what he experienced at the front door, and he wisely said, "I hoped you would like it," rather than reporting it was the young sales clerk's selection. As Nina warmly kissed him again he debated telling her, perhaps with a little chuckle, about the other purchase, still waiting beneath the clothing in his bag. But, fortunately, discretion proved he was growing wiser.

Still with Nina driving, they dropped his bag off at the hotel desk and then Nina at her office. With a promise to pick her up at 5:00, he drove himself to the Shops, eager to find out if they had gotten the wrecked bomber's engine transported to his engine "lab". Indeed they had, and there it rested, well secured to an engine stand anchored to the concrete floor and surrounded by various attachments, all still dangling wires, tubes, rods and bolts, spread on the floor and awaiting attachment, mechanical, hydraulic, or electrical, to what had once provided half the power to a now deceased Bristol Blenham bomber. "Wonderful," was Rudy's only thought, spoken aloud as Paul Lafessi strode into the shop-laboratory.

"Isn't it beautiful?" gushed his assistant. "I can attach all this stuff this afternoon, you can check it tomorrow morning, I'll fill the tank with whatever you want – 87 or 100 octane – and we're set to go!" Paul was disappointed when Rudy told him tomorrow, at least all morning, he would have to attend his weekly planning meeting, but that Paul should go ahead then and start hooking up all he could except for the small fuel tank. The first thing Rudy wanted to do when he returned to the lab was give Paul a type of practical test by having Paul explain, in detail, the parts and working of the Mercury engine and its supporting equipment, and respond to Rudy's technical questions. Rudy emphasized that he was seeking workable ways to increase the engine's output, and he wanted Paul to think about what modifications that would require.

"This afternoon," Rudy directed, "would be a good time for you to write down, in some detail, the ideas you can come up with to do that. Then tomorrow morning while I'm at the meeting, you can began to turn this engine and its sub-systems into a workable aero power plant. I've got a purpose in doing this, so take your time and do your usual excellent job. When we really get this one all tuned up and modified, we'll move it outside to the Shop's large engine test bed and see if we can measure how well we've done." With that, Rudy went off to find Foster Crayton and begin both his sanitized tale of the trip and what he had learned about RAF Tangmere's preparations for a real war and a much busier shop.

Early the next morning Rudy set off for his weekly meeting with the Governor-General and Colonel Astill, Nina having told him of the new offices for the Governor, the former Grand Master's Palace in Valletta, at the large square. He parked near Republic Street and was immediately awed by the Palace, both outside and especially inside, as he was escorted down long, elaborately beautiful corridors. In the Governor's inner office, the General and his Aide, Colonel Astill, heads close, were already in a discussion which ended abruptly as Rudy was ushered into the room by an armed soldier. Both greeted Rudy warmly and he was pointed toward a chair, joining the two high officials. He sat and was immediately invited by General Garrison to recount his trip to England and the RAF Stations. Was it useful? Interesting? Did he learn many new things? What was the rumor mill in England saying about the war? About Malta? Any hope for new resources? Was he treated well? Were they open in their discussions with him? Did he get to see Gladiator planes? Was his transportation satisfactory? The questions came too quickly to allow for individual answering, so Rudy held up his hand to stop more from flying at him, and said, simply, "I'll summarize the entire trip and in the process, answer these questions and any others I can. Shall I begin now? I'll need perhaps twenty minutes?" He was quickly signaled to begin, and within a half hour he had finished his oral report and had answered their few additional questions. "Rudy," said General Garrison, "it obviously was a most worthwhile trip, and I apologize for not offering you a coffee or cold drink before beginning. May I do so now, and tell you how pleased I am that you did so well and learned so much that will be useful to us, here on this fascinating, but remote, British colonial outpost. I know you returned just yesterday morning from the, shall I call it, 'reverse' courier flight from my home island, but, as you have seen, I...we, Astill and I, were very eager to hear your impressions. Thank you for that excellent report; your new information will help us quickly develop a plan for both of our purposes. Now to a different topic.

"Just before you arrived here this morning, we were discussing your charming young friend whom I met at the Hawk airplane ceremony, and with whom the Colonel chatted yesterday while awaiting your arrival. I will say that we are interested in learning more about Miss Lafessi from you, although I admit that we've already made an inquiry or two. Her ability to manage the logistics of the port's involvement in our Contraband Control Service, which, under War Orders, beginning last September has British cruisers herding suspect freighters here to Malta for searching, is marvelous. She's quite proficient, as I'm sure you know, not only in Malti and English, but in Italian and Spanish as well, with a degree in the maths and in geography to top it off. She, in her position at *Starline Shipping*, a company quite in line with our interests, has been serving us nicely since this unusual war began. We're impressed with her, and your friend Mr. Sanno is certainly satisfied with the brief look we asked him to take of her background. Oh, don't look so askance, Rudy. There's a war on, as they say, and these types of quiet steps are necessary at times. Since we may be approaching one of those times, I want you to be aware that we're impressed with her and may have a request coming up that could be of interest to you and her. Not immediately, and not yet for sure, but possibly. So I should ask, with apologies, Rudy, if you are seriously interested in Miss Lafessi, and she in you? Again, Rudy, with apologies for this seeming intrusion into your private life."

Rudy, thankfully seated through all of this jolting news rather than standing, had been tightly holding onto the arms of his probable antique chair. "Well, she certainly never said a word to me about this ship searching business, only that she has applied for a shift supervisor's job at the Lascarus Operations Center, if it ever opens, that is. Yes, I know she's smart as hell, pardon the expression, and she's often two thoughts ahead of me before I can finish the sentence. Am I serious? I want to be, but what kind of a future could we have with a real war coming and me transferred someplace else by HRM, or back to the U.S. if it gets into the war? She probably feels that way too, but I'm not really sure. We're not even engaged! I think, maybe, we're afraid to. She's got family here, you may know. Her brother and father work at the RAF Shops and her sister just started college here. The family farm up in Gozo is where the Hawk is hidden away in a barn, with a disguised grass strip. I don't know what else to tell you. It's complicated. I don't even know how soon HRM Aviation will tell me I'm transferred out of Malta."

"Rudy," said the Governor General, "in the trying, uncertain times of war, clear and certain decisions often seem impossible. Both Gordon and I are familiar with what you are experiencing, except, we realize, that you are here on Malta, and have been for a half year, in a very different type of country, without another American in sight much less your own friends and family, working wonderfully well in difficult circumstances for a company mostly unknown to you, in the first phase of what promises to be a world war, ready and wanting to enjoy the true love which you likely have found. Hardly a wonder, is it, that you are near wits end trying to select the right path? Therefore, I don't think it out of place for Gordon and I, acting in *loco parentis*, to speculate that your important concerns will work out to your ultimate satisfaction. The right answers will come to you and thus to Miss Lafessi. In fact, I'll start the process by saying that, under the authority vested in me as Governor of Malta and Commanding General of all military and related civilian forces currently on the archipelago, no individual persons previously assigned here may be removed except with my personal concurrence. Colonel Astill, as Adjutant, will you please file that General Order, effective thirty days ago? Thank you. Now, with that out-of-the-way, let us turn to the latest war information. Colonel Astill, please."

Colonel Astill opened his notebook of dispatches, underwater cablegrams, and decoded signals, looked at the Governor-General and Rudy, and began his report. "Every indication we are receiving matches what Rudy heard at RAF Station Tangmere: our so-called Phoney War, which does not yet involve Italy – so important to Malta's situation – will very soon grow to major, active fighting on land sea, and air, a real war far beyond the little activity we've thus far seen. Those most knowledgeable believe that superiority in the air will make the difference in winning. Next, on November 30 Russia invaded Finland on three fronts with 600,000 troops. Finland's 150,000 soldier army is still resisting, and Finland has requested concrete aid from the League of Nations, which has expelled Russia from membership. We've learned that in mid-December Hitler secretly ordered planning to begin for the invasion of Norway. This should be a special concern of the War Ministry, but apparently is not as yet. The Chino-Japanese war still rages. British conscription has been extended to all men between 19 and 41 years, then re-extended to age 60, and woman between 20 and 30 are required to join auxiliaries or take defense jobs. British food rationing is planned to begin in January. Approximate estimates of airpower, made by those believing it to become a vital factor in a large scale European war, have "guesstimated" for bombers 1,150 German, 530 British, and 180 French. For dive bombers 350 for Germany, and none for Britain and France. For Fighter planes 1,180 German, 605 British, and 549 France. One may readily see why no modern fighter planes are currently on their way to RAF Malta. So little in this report of which we were unaware, and none of it good. However, we are making progress on our civil defense preparations; not as slowly as earlier, but I remain anxious. Residents are still not quite believing that we are at war, and still wagering that Italy will remain friendly to Malta, no matter what. I hope to have our local defense volunteer recruitment and appointment statistics for you next week, with indications of what numbers would still be desired. I'm looking for voluntary recruits, of course, rather than appointees. Thus ends my report."

"Thank you, Gordon. I think that's it for today, and while I, also, am anxious about our future, I am buoyed up by Rudy's report of his RAF visits and also the firm intent of the HRM company to continue its work supported by the American President. So we are adjourned until next week. Thank you both," the Governor-General continued, "and Rudy, please, not a word of our inquires concerning Miss Lafessi to her, but I trust you returned with a suitable present? Good. Presents are always recommended. Do keep that in mind as a bit of wisdom from your Governor."

As Rudy left the meeting room he was more than puzzled, trying to reconstruct their discussion of Nina's ability, her work with this mysterious shipping business and her desire to change to the Operation Center. And what about this possible request to her. Most of all, why the inquiry about their possible relationship? What in hell is this all about, he asked himself, and why shouldn't I bring it up with her?

Still within the meeting room, Colonel Astill looked at his Commander for instructions and was told to wait one week and then summon both Mr. Sanno and Miss Lafessi to a meeting with the two of them "It will be most interesting to learn her reactions to what we shall propose and to see if she'll expand on the proposal, if she doesn't reject it out-of-hand."

"But what about young Rudy?" the Colonel questioned.

"AH," was the response, "that's the most interesting question of all."

CHAPTER 26

ANOTHER OLD FRIEND

Valletta and Points North
1940

BACK in his engine laboratory at the Shops following the planning meeting, Rudy is now convinced that the fun and games of his life are no longer appropriate in the face of war. The situation is serious, and all must be moved along quickly. He tests his assistant on the bomber's Mercury engine as though Paul were back in technical school. Paul, however, is well prepared, and explains the workings of the bomber's salvaged engine in sufficient detail to satisfy his mentor. He also responds well to Rudy's detailed questions, and then presents his ideas for increasing engine power. Rudy is pleased with Paul's technical knowledge concerning this same type engine used with the Gladiators they're anticipating, and happy with his creativity in describing possible improvements. He thinks all that's needed now are a few real Gladiators to upgrade.

Coming from her office at 5:00, Nina slips onto the Red Rover's passenger seat beside Rudy and they head for dinner. The meal they share in a favorite neighborhood restaurant is taken up with the exchange of news of the coming war, Nina's hope for a job transfer to the Lascarus Operations Center, and Rudy's off-hand probing about her work with the control of contraband shipping. Nina remains quite uninformative about that, which causes him to be even more wondering about what's going on and just what the Governor has in mind for her.

At work the next morning Rudy is asked to meet with Captain Donalds, Foster, and the Wing Commander. Very important news, he's told by the Captain, and it's better to be sitting down when he hears it. It's both important, and not entirely unanticipated: the Hawk is to be flown by two experienced former Polish Air Force pilots. They, a mechanic and an official from the defunct Polish PZL aircraft company, are being quietly led by a British agent to Malta from their enforced internment in Romania. Eventually the official, some type of aeronautical designer, will travel on to a British aircraft factory in Canada, de Havilland perhaps, or some other, while the pilots and mechanic will enter an RAF unit as part of a Polish squadron, if such a foreign unit could ever be imagined. Although vastly outnumbered, many Polish fighter pilots did well against the Luftwaffe, even if for a brief period during the invasion, and, now escaped, don't care whom they're fighting for as long as its against the Nazis.

Rudy, surprised at how well he takes this news, says that if he couldn't be the Hawk's pilot, this sounds like a workable plan. It's likely that the grass strip on Gozo will become a remote auxiliary field, the Captain explains, and those details are being worked out. Rudy understands he now has other tasks on which to focus.

Next morning Rudy hears more news from Foster. "Rudy," Foster greets him, "I have some good news. Hopefully I'll be letting you know soon what the time frame for renting my flat will be. If you're still interested, that is?" This jolts Rudy a bit, but never the less he responds that he's still interested and will think about the details. Somehow, he senses, the likely availability of the flat needs to be handled very carefully with Nina. He wants the possibility to be a positive and not a negative in his still unformulated plan to ... what? Convince her to share his lust? That didn't sound right, did it? So what *is* his goal, he puzzles? Oh Boy, it suddenly hits him as he ponders. There doesn't appear to be many options. Is it marriage? His knees weaken a trifle, in shock from this surprising thought.

On Friday afternoon there is a call to 'Mr. Worth' through Robert's phone, from the Governor's office, saying that the Planning Committee meeting scheduled for Monday next is postponed until Wednesday, two days following. On the same Friday afternoon, Nina receives a call from the Governor's office asking if she would attend a ten o'clock meeting on

Monday morning next with the Governor-General, at his Valletta office. She agrees, of course, thinking "What is this all about?" She is told, also, that a car would pick her up at her office at 9:30, and return her before 1:30. Added with emphasis to the message is a strong request directly from the Governor that she absolutely not communicate this invitation to anyone. All weekend Nina is greatly preoccupied with imagining answers to her self-posed question: "What the hell *is* this all about?" As it turns out, her imagined answers never came close.

With two of her co-workers sneaking looks out an office window, Nina is ushered into an official looking vehicle by a uniformed driver at exactly 9:30 am on Monday morning and driven to the imposing Palace housing the Governor-General's offices. At a few minutes before ten she is lead into the inner office, a magnificent palace room complete with antique furniture, and is immediately set at ease by the Governor's aide, whom she recognizes as the man she had chatted with while waiting for Rudy's return flight. "Miss Lafessi," he smiles at her, "we appreciate your coming this morning. You may remember our brief conversation while we awaited the courier plane? I'm Colonel Astill and this is Governor-General Garrison."

The Governor steps forward and holds out his hands to clasp Nina's. "Welcome, welcome my dear young lady. I have looked forward to seeing you again after that amazing test flight, and I'm grateful for your willingness to meet on short notice. Thank you, and allow me to introduce these gentlemen, Mr. Sanno, whom you possibly may recognize from his office at the port, and a visitor to our island, Mr. James Boyle. But let us move over to the table and chairs set for us, enjoy some coffee or tea, and I'll ask Mr. Sanno, as Malta's Passport Control Officer, to set the stage for this most interesting story brought to us by Mr. Boyle. But first I must thank you for the wonderful work you're doing with our Contraband Control Service. I appreciate your willingness to help so much with the logistics of international ships."

Once seated around the large table, Mr. Sanno begins, to Nina's astonishment, by telling her that all discussed today is covered by the British Secrets Act, etc.,etc., as he is sure she understands. Mr. Boyle, Nina learns, is a British officer working on some aspects of security and is here to ascertain the feasibility of a plan which, if successful, could ease the harm which Malta would undergo should the war extend through Italy's joining the

Axis powers, as anticipated. After that introduction of sorts, Mr. Sanno turns to Agent Boyle to continue.

"Miss Lafessi" the Agent begins, "would you remember a friend of yours who was an academy student here in Malta, in the same class as you, a young woman with whom you spent time during the teen years? You may well have considered her a close friend, one who shared confidences with you, and you with her? I doubt you have seen your former friend, however, since those school days."

Nina says,"If you mean Rose Salufa, she and Johnny Cardinale went up to Sicily right after we graduated. I think her younger brother followed them up there a year later. I tried to talk her out of it, wanted her to try college here with me, but she wouldn't have it. She was smart enough, but she was tied to Cardinale. He thought he was a real musician who could make it in a bigger place than Valletta. A decent young man, but quite unrealistic, I thought. I was sorry to see them leave. Is that who you mean?" Mr. Boyle nods and says, "I'll tell you the rest of Rose and Mr. Cardinale, and of her brother Francis. All three are still in Sicily, Catania, on the east coast, and when I talked with her two weeks ago, she spoke of how much your close friendship, understanding and kindness meant to her. Apparently her parents were furious when she left with her boyfriend. And then lured her brother there, or so her mother accused her."

Agent Boyle then pauses the tale and cautions Nina that to go further she will have to give her word that she understands and accepts the required absolute confidentiality, even secrecy, of what she would now hear. Nina voices her understanding and agreement, knowing she has to hear the rest. Who might she tell, anyway? What about her old school chum, Rose? What's happened to her?

"Actually," Agent Boyle continues, "John Cardinale has done a bit in the music world of eastern Sicily, but not as a musician or singer. Rather, he is a radio personality, with an early morning radio show playing records of popular music on what's called 'the Red Channel', where he is known as 'Johnny Red'. The radio station itself is housed in a commercial office building located just outside the large Catania Airport, which includes a large military portion. Rose works also, but she as a clerk in the operational headquarters office of the Regia Aeronautica, located also within the air-port. Rose and Johnny share an apartment in a nearby residential area.

"Until three months ago, her brother Francis lived with a young woman, not far from his sister. Unfortunately, some weeks ago he had a dispute with a member of a Fascist Blackshirt group. A dozen members of the group appeared as he left his workplace next day and a violent attack on Francis took place. Francis was beaten severely, near to death, and was blinded in one eye. He was hospitalized for several weeks and then taken to his sister's place, where he remains. Both Rose and John are terribly upset, greatly angered, and thinking of revenge.

"A neighborhood pub frequented in the past by Rose, Francis, and John had a small fund raising evening to aid Francis, and Rose spoke plainly there of her hatred for what happened to Francis, and what she sees as the larger, developing evil in Italy. She is very unhappy with Mussolini and his Fascist path, and greatly desires revenge for what his Blackshirt roughnecks did to her brother. A friend of Malta heard her speak at the pub function and my agency was informed. I since have met with her and John Cardinale. John suffers from the guilt of getting them all to leave their Malta homes for a musical career he thinks he'll never really achieve now in Sicily.

"Wouldn't it be nice, my agency Director imagined upon hearing all this, if somehow we could learn what Rose certainly will hear daily concerning Italian bomber missions to Malta, and beyond to crucial north Africa, once the war extends? Someone else in the Agency office suggested that perhaps the exact type of music first played over the airwaves by Johnny Red from his radio program early each morning, and his introductions to those particular popular songs, could be governed by a code we would provide that lets our listening station here know what, to where, and from which Sicilian airstrip the Italians were sending forth toward Malta and beyond that very day. This information would be determined by what Rose has learned the day before and described by her to Johnny at dinner time.

"And so we worked out the entire system of music and intros coded by type, to be broadcast openly, for a short time almost every morning. We coupled this with a monetary amount going to Rose to guarantee decent medical attention and surgical repairs to brother Francis. I carried the project's general idea to Catania for my meeting with Rose. As you might have guessed, Miss Lafessi, since the plan is to help Malta, Rose says she'll do business only with her oldest Malta friend, who would go up there to complete the agreement, and not a British agent such as myself from London. There you have it. And I believe the Governor now wants a word, Sir."

As the Governor begins to ask for Nina's reaction, she looks up at the faces of the four men seated with her around the table and, in a questioning voice asks, "If I were to walk alone down the busy High Street in an English city, would men notice me? "Well," responds the Governor instantly, "I believe on any street in most cities you would be looked at, certainly, as an attractive young woman. But what..." She cuts him off by asking, "Do any of you realize the difference in results between being noticed by men as an attractive young woman walking alone down a street in England and walking alone down a street in Italy? Really! How far do you think I'd get in Catania, Sicily before I had to physically fend off one or more over- appreciative Italian Romeos, or scream for the poliziotti?

What do you imagine the police response would be as I tried to explain my purpose in coming up from Malta to walk around in Catania objecting to, or perhaps enjoying, the amorous calls and possibly more? Come, come gentlemen. Consider the cultural and social differences. Your plan, while I appreciate its cleverness and value to the good of Malta, won't see me successfully getting to or from meetings with my old school friend. And imagine the questions officials will address to me concerning my visit, much less my local friend who works *where? Why only the Italian military headquarters!* Do you know the Italian word *puttana?* No, the plan as you've sketched it won't work. Just our poor luck that Rose wants me, and only me, as the contact person. I'm sorry!"

Mr. Boyle's plea to reconsider is cut short by the Governor's lifted hand. "Wait a moment," he says. "Miss Lafessi may be pointing us toward a more imaginative approach to the challenge. Miss Lafessi, if what's been outlined won't work, what would you suggest could do the trick?" The Governor appears willing to be imaginative, and both Mr. Boyle and his Malta resident counterpart, Mr. Sanno, are eager not to see the plan discarded entirely. Colonel Astill seems to still be considering Nina's stated cultural differences, and remains quietly thoughtful. Nina's silent thinking is now in high gear, and she decides to respond to the Governor's invitation to suggest a modification.

Nina looks up, saying, "As Colonel Astill knows, I am acquainted with the American, Rudy Worth. Or perhaps you all know? I believe that what the plan needs is an evident reason for the trip to Catania, and a party of two going, rather than solely Rose's Maltese old friend Nina. Suppose that Rudy Worth, with his American passport and his bride, Nina Lafessi Worth, with her new American Spousal Passport, provided quickly by Mr. Sanno, and all attested to by an official Maltese Civil Marriage Certificate dated a month ago, courtesy of our Governor, went on a brief honeymoon to Sicily? After all, if you've spent all your life thus far in Malta, as the newly wed bride has done, where would you travel to honeymoon on this tiny seventeen mile long island?

"Please understand that, while the Certification of Civil Marriage and the American Spousal Passport would look absolutely real, neither would be, in actuality. I assure you, I'm not plotting to use your plan or counterfeit documents in order to marry Mr. Worth ... at least not this season. If Rudy were to agree with this, I would handle the 'let's look like newly weds' business directly with him. Not your problem. And only we in this room and Rudy would know the plan's agreement, the arrangement concerning the documents, and the nature of the trip. And no mistaken announcement of the 'marriage' to be listed in the *Malta Times!* Meanwhile, the honeymoon couple would spend a couple of days in Catania, having flown there on a still regularly scheduled Italian Air flight from Valletta, visited with the Bride's old friend, and motorbiked, sightseeing along the scenic Sicilian southern coast, where the new airstrips you never mentioned but Malta gossip says are being built, Mr. Boyle, before catching an Italian flight back home. After all, Italy, like the United States, is a neutral country, and Malta is not involved in Germany's war, so why not a honeymoon trip to beautiful Sicily?"

Nina says no more, and for half a minute at least the group sits in silence. Colonel Astill tells the General later that one could almost hear the brains spinning round as realization dawned on the men that, if agreement could be reached on production of the false documents, she had just described the solution. Mr. Sanno comments first, saying that he probably

240

could come up with the type of passport Miss Lafessi referred to, but he would not want word to reach his American contacts. The Governor simply states that he assumes Colonel Astill could arrange for the civil document, and Mr. Boyle nods that, as far as he can judge, the augmented plan is now complete. Excepts, he wonders, would this Mr. Worth agree to his critical role. While Miss Lafessi remains with downcast eyes, looking demure, the remaining three men look disbelievingly at Mr. Boyle and nod "yes" in unison. Mr. Boyle later comments to Mr. Sanno that Miss Lafessi should be recruited immediately into 'the Service', and will hardly require the usual long training program.

The Governor-General has a confirming conversation with Nina, and comes away understanding that she first will get Rudy's agreement to secrecy, and then his understanding and agreement to the plan. She would take a few days vacation from the shipping office, and assumes Rudy could do as well. If the documents could be hurried and she be kept informed, the flight tickets would be purchased by Rudy as she directs. And, by-the-way, she assumes he would be reimbursed for all costs? "Of course," agreed the Governor, who by this time was fully realizing that Rudy really didn't stand a chance!

If the documents could be produced quickly, Nina judges, and if plane seats were available for the coming week, and if Mr. Boyle would prepare a very brief, innocuous, 'sanitized' page she could hand to Rose and John, and explain to Nina how the medical funds would reach Rose, she and Rudy might well go on their honeymoon next week. The Governor assures her he would deal with the requirements and assumes that Nina will have spoken to Rudy prior to the Planning Committee meeting Rudy will attend day after tomorrow. Both now satisfied with the process, the Governor hurries to catch the three men, while Nina is chauffeured back to the shipping office, which now seems to her a rather dull prospect.

The Governor returns to the three, smiles his congratulations to all, and says, "Well, we achieved Mr. Boyle's goal. She's going, and if the plan works as well as we hope, our people will be getting valuable information concerning our protection needs in North Africa, which is judged at least as important as Malta's. Isn't it interesting that we all, including Miss Lafessi, knew that all that was needed was someone to accompany her as part of some cover story, and provide a bit of camouflage. The documents we're going to quickly provide are part of the camouflage as well. And didn't she maneuver the discussion beautifully? She certainly is a highly intelligent and clever young woman! I wonder what this business with our friend Rudy is all about?"

"In other words," said Colonel Astill, "we were snookered."

CHAPTER 27

THE BALBO

Sicily
February 1940

AS the timetable for the trip to Sicily emerged, the make-believe newly weds were delayed for two weeks beyond Nina's anticipated departure. No matter in the long run, for the delay allowed more detailed preparations than had been anticipated. One was the proper preparation of the needed documents, including an innocent looking song and singer code list written in Malti. Not the least was a short, unintentional, but possibly useful education for the ersatz groom concerning a famous 1933 Regia Aeronautica adventure.

This education was triggered when Foster told Rudy he had been informed by Captain Donalds that Rudy was going to Sicily for a week, gathering general impressions of the Italian Air Force. No mention of Nina, but Foster was concerned over Rudy's lack of the Italian language. Of course, Foster admitted, English likely was spoken by many in Sicilian aviation, just as the RAF had picked up certain Italian words, *Balbo*, for example. "Wait," Rudy exclaimed, "*that* word rings a bell. *Balbo? Balbo?* I remember something from years ago when I first was working for Curtiss. Wait...I remember. I went on a long fifteen-hour car ride with some Curtiss engine guys from Buffalo to the Chicago World's Fair. A big group of Italian flying boats had just flown over from Italy and landed in the lake. Broke records. Flew over the Alps. Flew more than, what, 6000 miles, at way over 100 MPH. Leader was an Italian General. *Balbo*, that's it, *General Balbo*. All kinds of big deal officials, thousands of people, they said. Named a Chicago street after him. Big ceremony at the Italian Aviation building at the World's Fair. A university gave him an honorary degree, and I even think President Roosevelt later gave him the American Distinguished Flying Cross. We never saw any of that, or even their planes, but at the Fair we did go to the Italian building. Very interesting; all about aviation progress. But what does his name mean in the RAF?"

"What do you think?" Foster asked. "We use it to refer to an extra large formation of planes. We'd love to get enough Gladiators for the Hal Far Fighter Balbo. Ha, Ha! Even London HQ would know what that meant!"

The first step in implementing the trip to Sicily, however, required Nina to get Rudy's understanding of its unusual purpose and his agreement to accompany her under the travel arrangements she had imposed. This occurred the evening of the planning meeting, and agreement required less thought on Rudy's part than he would need next day with Foster to dredge from memory his 1933 trip to Chicago's International Exposition. Nina's explanation was simple. It was, she explained, part of the type of work she had been doing at the shipping office as a Maltese patriot, and an opportunity for them to spend some days together, almost -but not quite- "playing house" as a married couple. Such an opportunity, she believed, could illustrate the reality of the love they had recently been declaring to each other.

Wisely, Rudy thought, he would not question the exact meaning of her "not quite" phraseology. He calculated that, one way or another, her nighttime behavior would provide him with the understanding he needed to plan for his own future. Important, also, would be the possibility of his learning, first hand, something about the Regia Aeronautica's state of preparedness. This could be, he thought, a win-win arrangement. Or possibly a fiasco, but it was time to move things ahead, professionally and personally, or reverse course and move on to a new assignment elsewhere with a less confining life style.

It's fascinating, Nina thought, that both a counterfeit Maltese Civil Marriage Certificate and an authentic looking American passport in her name could be produced and handed to her. Rudy should carry the Certificate, she reasoned, and she must be sure he carried his own American passport as well. Buried in her luggage would be several sheets of paper, written in her hand, that would be appropriate for her to give to her friend Rose. These included names and Malta addresses of former classmates for correspondence, plus a list of the Italian songs and singers popular with Rose's old friends in Malta. Aldo Visconti's *Tornerai* is at the top of the list, Carlo Buti's *Viveri* second, and the Dino Olivieri Orchestra's *Senti l'Eco* next, followed by several others. Perhaps once-in-a-while Johnny could play some of them, since his radio broadcasts could sometimes be heard in Malta?

Nina was pleasantly surprised, also, by Rudy's ready agreement to accompany her. She had thought about the unspoken restriction on full sexual activity implied in her explanation of the trip, and Rudy's non-argument. He likely doesn't even realize that he's my long-term love, my intended husband, and the man I'm most likely to leave my family and Malta for, she judged. When packing for the plane ride she smiled as she rummaged through her brother Paul's dresser for the hidden package he never mentioned, but some evenings took from before going out. Finding it under some work shirts, she slid two out from the bottom of the cardboard box and stuffed them into her rolled up socks. At Paul's modest rate of usage it would be weeks before he wondered, and weeks after Rudy had finally realized the intensity of her affection. On second thought, she slid out two more.

Plane tickets were reserved both up and back for flights on the Italian air line, *Ala Littoria*, connecting Tripoli in Libya to Rome, with stops at Valletta, Syracuse, Catania, and Palermo on Sicily, then northward to Naples and Rome. The plane might be one of their big Savoia-Marchetti flying boats, but Rudy was hoping for one of the CNT Z.506 three engined, record breaking float planes the Shop technicians have been talking about. Records like 200 MPH, 25,000 altitude, and 4,500 pounds of payload and everyone knew there was already a military model. The other reservation made for them was at a small hotel, outside central Catania, closer to the area where Rose lived in a large apartment building, Johnny's radio station, and the big airport where she worked at the Regia Aeronautica's operational headquarters. Rose's apartment phone number had been given to Nina by Mr. Sanno, and Rose and she had talked, setting dates and getting the recommended albergo information. That hotel reservation, which caused both Nina and Rudy to tremble briefly, was made for Senor and Signora Rudolph Worth. At checking-in they found that Rose had called and requested *una camera speciale per una luna di miele*, a honeymoon suite.

Nina and Rudy received a final briefing where the Governor and Agent Boyle reviewed and answered last minute questions, made suggestions, and a little late Rudy thought, provided specific instructions on how to handle any legal or police issues that might arise there. Assurances were made concerning the quality of the documents furnished, the "musical list" as they referred to it, and the fact that the visiting couple carried only money for their honeymoon, some as American Express Travelers Checks. Italian funds for Rose to use for her brother's medical costs would be given to her by a person saying that he is representing friends from the local pub, which has sponsored a second evening in aid of her brother Francis. Monitoring of the early morning Johnny Redbird radio program should quickly follow any declaration of war involving Italy and Malta. A local Catania contact person, friendly to Malta and always referring to the name of the academy Rose and Nina attended as an identifier, would be communicating occasionally with Rose and John as the future evolved. Other than that information, Nina had nothing else to communicate or do on her 'honeymoon'.

Rudy was encouraged to keep his eyes and ears open for anything military relating to Malta and north Africa, and to tour around a bit for runway or related construction, especially along the coast. However he shouldn't be so curious as to raise any suspicion that this is more than a honeymoon vacation to visit a splendid scenic and historical area and see old friends.

"Keep it all very natural," was the advice given them by British Agent Boyle. For the first time, at that final meeting, both Nina and Rudy began to understand that their trip had the potential for serious problems should their luck turn bad or they not pay attention to details, prompting trouble.

Nina identified the first new possible problem as she read the pre-printed airline tickets made out to Rudy and Nina Worth, Signor and Signora, *Mr.* and *Mrs.* She thought a solution for the unmarried couple, now identified as newly weds to any one who might see them at the loading dock ticket taker, would be for them to board the plane very separately, acting quite unaware of the other's presence. Sneaking out of Valletta for a tryst, or why wasn't I invited to the wedding? That would be the reaction of any acquaintance seeing them, but so what, she thought. Thus, clutching her own ticket, she drifted up the line of boarding passengers, getting several people ahead of Rudy, who was engrossed in studying the CANT Z float plane roped to the seaplane dock. She boarded and found her assigned seat before he came down the short aisle, only seven seats on either side. They sat opposite each other, but each with a window occupying most of their time until the landing at Catania's shorefront.

A short and uneventful flight, and now Nina's Italian got them and their bags through the passport and customs officials and into a taxi. Nina sat close to Rudy in the taxi's backseat as she gave the driver the name and address of their hotel, speaking Italian, and also asked him the cost of the fare. She whispered to Rudy that Rose suggested she do that before the cab left the terminal. She called Rudy "darling" and squeezed his hand, saying in English that "Catania is such an interesting and beautiful city. I'm so happy you're taking me here!" In response, Rudy answered by attempting to slide his hand over her thigh, but she quickly pushed it back while mouthing the word "No." Rudy mouthed "Tonight," and she whispered back "In your dreams!" Rudy spent the remainder of the ride looking out at industrial and business neighborhoods plus several blocks of apartment buildings, silent, until they pulled up before a small hotel.

The driver was paid, and the two carried their bags into a pleasantly decorated reception area complete with an English speaking clerk who had difficulty addressing Mr. Worth, while not taking his eyes from Mrs. Worth. Rudy stiffened at that, but was more stressed when the clerk requested their passports, telling them that they could get them back tomorrow, after they were checked and recorded. That requirement, the clerk assured them, was required and common in all European countries. The documents were surrendered, and each was given a business card of the hotel, with its name, address, and telephone number, to carry whenever leaving the place. The room key would be left at the desk, and not carried off the premises. This, also, was a typical practice in European hotels, acknowledged by Nina from her earlier two trips to Milan on modeling assignments. They were not surprised to learn that this small hotel did not have a "honeymoon" suite, as someone had requested for them, but of course their room would be *en suite*, and, the clerk said, "Very nice".

And so it turned out to be, Rudy judged, for upon entering and shutting the door, Nina did not voice a protest to his immediate newly-wed approach. Rather, she slid from his amorous arms after a half minute, saying that this experience of togetherness needed to include the commonalities of living together, including such things as the brushing of teeth using the same bathroom, as the most simple example. "Perhaps there would be a time and place for other experiences of life together," she said, "but one must wait and see." Rudy, of course, wanted to view this last advisement from her as a promise that good things are worth waiting for, but was wise enough at this advanced stage of personal education to shut up and unpack his suitcase.

After both had unpacked and settled in, they discussed their schedule, knowing that tomorrow morning they had arranged to visit Rose for whatever time proved necessary for both visiting and describing arrangements. They then spent a few minutes looking through the few tourist brochures available from a rack in the reception foyer, and decided that they should reserve a Catania City tour for the day after Rose's visit, and then rent either a car, if that proved possible, or else a motorbike, and ride through the coast line south and west of Catania to provide Rudy a look at the countryside for evidence of new airstrips. They split the Italian Lira Nina had been given back in Malta to cover the trip's expenses, allowing Rudy to better play the part of a husband who makes most important decisions and handles the family finances. While reciting those reasons for her releasing Lira from her purse to her 'husband', Nina smiled as she said the words and counted out his half. When she finished, Rudy said, "Oh, by-the-way, what's your plan for sleeping arrangements? You made the reservation, and I see only one bed. Do I get the floor, or shall we destroy our cover story and ask that a cot be sent up?"

"Don't get nasty, sweetheart, or you might get the floor. No, our plan calls for a rolled-up blanket stretched down the middle of the bed, the great divide so to speak. But don't panic completely. I'll give you a clue. If you had been really attentive back when the plan was formed, you'd realize that we actually were fully prepared to depart Valletta a week before we did. Documents were ready to go and flights were available. I, however, booked a flight for today – this week – and asked Rose to reserve this room for us beginning today. Made up a 'can't leave the shipping office yet' type of story for Mr. Boyle, and here we are, this week not last week. Figure that one out, lover! It should make you happy. As I said earlier in this very room, the advantage of this time together is that we can experience all kinds of togetherness because we really are together on our own. OK? Now, let's go down and get a recommendation for a nearby restaurant we can walk to and then come back for some togetherness."

Back in their room, while Rudy hoped for a serving of special dessert as part of the "togetherness" menu, he was offered, instead, a serving of what Nina called "look but don't touch." He could only hope she understood that there were limits to his willingness to participate in her game, no matter how entrancing, and his limit was exceedingly close. This certainly is a weird arrangement! His immediate decision was to carry out this unusual portion of his assignment and to then head back to Malta, but perhaps, as he reconsidered, tomorrow would make a difference? And why was there an additional week of waiting that he should 'figure out'?" He thought about that as she signaled it now was his turn to go in and brush his teeth.

By arrangement with Rose, she picked them up at the hotel in her car, a Fiat as Rudy predicted. The time was 9:30 am, a happy, smiling Rose greeting them excitedly, and saying, "I hope you had a good night's sleep and time to get ready for a busy day today; we have a change in plan I hope is alright?" Rudy had ended up in the back seat so Nina and Rose could hug and talk, while he said silently to himself, "Yes, I've never had such a night's sleep before in my life, and I had time to fold up the great wall of Sicily blanket and put it back on the closet shelf. Wouldn't want the maid to wonder what that was all about. The things I put up with for Malta!"

At that point in his lamenting, Nina, seemingly concerned, turned from the front seat and said in a strained tone, "Rudy, sweetheart, Rose's boss, Colonel DiPalma, is very eager to meet you. She told him why she wanted a day off, and when she told him who would be visiting here he actually insisted that she drive you to their Operations Center later this morning, while she spends the rest of the day with me. Isn't that exciting? I mean he practically ordered her and said he wouldn't count today as a vacation day, but a special assignment for her. So we can see Rose's place right now and say hello to her brother Francis. Rose says we'll have supper tonight together so we can meet John. Should be very interesting for you, an American aviator, don't you think? Rose will pick you up at four o'clock at the Colonel's office. If all goes according to plan, I'll probably ride with her to get you. We'll talk tonight about renting a car tomorrow to see more of the area, assuming we're OK to do that? Sound sensible to you?"

This change in plan, apparently prompted by Rudy's presence in Catania, the seat of control for Sicily's Regia Aeronautica, sent a chilling tingle along his spine and a tightness in his response, as it had Nina's. Now Rose's boss knows he's an aeronautical something. How could their dual purposes here be known by the Fascists? No, it didn't make sense, but Rudy immediately imagined frightening possibilities, including hard questions and lying answers at the best, and a firing squad at the worst. Strange, but his immediate thought was actually hope for Nina's escape as a British agent. He knows he's stretching an unreasonable fear to the extreme, as well as her role, but he's worried. Back in Valletta he had been advised at their final meeting to emphasize his work for Curtiss Aviation, a neutral American firm, rather than the confusing HRM international group. Nina was his newly wed wife, he would point out, the romance having blossomed during his stay in Valletta while seeking leads concerning possible sales of older Curtiss models. He could add, of course, that he, with Signora Worth, would be returning soon to the clearly neutral United States. As an added safety factor, Nina had a Malta phone number which, when called and answered would prompt her to say the words *sorry, I mis-dialed*. This would result in a call from Malta to her hotel with a message summoning their immediate return to Valletta because of her seriously ill grandmother.

Thus, in a complex mood of unreasonable fear mixed with eagerness to finish their assignment, Nina and Rudy strain to keep calm. Rose continues to talk in the front seat about old times, and also Nina's entry to wedded life, with Rudy straining to hear responses to the wedded life business. He immediately likes Rose, an attractive, well-dressed young woman about Nina's age, not, he could see, with Nina's sharp intelligence and striking good looks, but with excellent English and a sense of what, in Buffalo, was termed 'street smarts'. Knowing Rose's planned war-time assignment, however, Rudy has to admire, also, her determination, her courage, and also her intent to even-the-score on her brother's behalf. This seemed more in place with what's happening in the present Sicilian environment than that of more isolated Malta, where the outlook of most residents remains unchanged and many deny even the possibility of war. But as Colonel Astill had once remarked at a planning meeting, the first dropped bomb could change minds and outlooks overnight.

In keeping with the new schedule imposed by Rose's boss Colonel DiPalma, Director of the Regia Aeronautica's administrative and operations center, Rose and her guests make a short stop at the apartment she shares with John Cardinale and her brother Francis. John, known on his morning radio broadcasts as Johnny Redbird, is at the radio station, Radio Amore Catania, and Rudy will meet him at this evening's supper. He's introduced to Rose's brother Francis as Nina's 'new husband', and seeing his condition fully understands Rose's willingness to carry out her truly dangerous assignment in order to get medical help for him, as well as strike back at the Fascisti Blackshirts who battered him. Nearing eleven o'clock, Rose and Nina make the short drive to the Catania airport and the Operations Center where Rose works in a civilian office clerical position. She is recognized by the military gate guards and hurries Rudy into the large, well constructed structure.

It appears Colonel DiPalma has been waiting for them near the entry-way, for he thanks Rose for her kindness before she can say a word of introduction, nods his dismissal, and takes Rudy's hand with both his. In perfect English he beams the warmest welcome Rudy can imagine, and continues to shake Rudy's hand while explaining his eagerness to meet him, an American aviator, here in Catania. "After all," he says, "we have something very important in common, and I very much have wanted to talk with you and show you how much the Regia Aeronautica has improved and grown, as soon as Rose explained that you are the husband of her school friend, now visiting, and aeronautical engineer and pilot. I thank you for your willingness to spend the day with me, hearing my personal tale of a wonderful, glorious trip to Chicago and New York City in America. In return I will illustrate how far we have improved military aeronautics here in Sicily – and all of Italy – so you can tell our friends in America how we are ready now to take our place among the great flying nations! Please, let us go into my private office and talk. Then, later, a little refreshment and a tour of several of our new planes, our Operations Center, and a look at how well we progress in aircraft design, in engine development, in organization and structure, and in providing suitable airports and satellite runways and airstrips for our *stormi*, our squadrons. This requires not a long trip, for I have a map room where all our Sicilian construction is indicated. You will readily see the tremendous effect of Il Duce's love for his 'Eagles' of the air and our impressive progress.

Colonel DiPalma's inner office is designed for a high volume of well-organized work production, and Rudy is impressed. He is invited to sit. The Colonel is so eager to speak that he remains pacing in excitement and immediately begins to explain what has mystified Rudy. "What," the officer says, "has prompted me to insist with Rose that we meet, you an American aviator and me an Italian Regia Aeronautica officer? It is because, in great part, that my position here was made possible by America, or I should say, by my wonderful trip to America six years ago." He pauses for emphasis, and proclaims, "I was an *Atlantici*, a pilota in one of the SM 55 planes, part of the great General Balbo's 1933 armada to fly from Italy to the International Exposition World's Fair in your city of Chicago and then to New York City before flying home. It was the greatest possible experience for me – for all us – pilots, navigators, mechanics, those on the weather station ships, everyone. About one hundred, you know, and all highly selected by General Balbo from more than a thousand who volunteered.

"I was one of the fortunate pilots selected by Balbo, and already a Capitano. At the end, back here after our triumphant march in our formal white uniforms under the Arch of Constantine, we were all promoted. General Balbo was made Air Marshal by Mussolini, and the rest of us raised one rank. So I became Major, a Maggiore, and last year when I was appointed to this position I was promoted to Tenente Colonnello, a Lieutenant Colonel. Now I'm not flying. How do you say it, I'm flying a desk? But I did a little in Spain before assigned here, but mostly administrative there, also. But the flight to Chicago and then New York City and back across the Atlantic I consider the high point of my career. I am still very grateful to General Balbo, and to the wonderful honors given us in America. That trip required 49 hours of flying time, over 6,000 miles, and due to our great 750 horsepower Isotto Fraschini engines, we averaged 124 miles per hour speed. This is why, my American friend and aviator, I insisted on meeting you and telling my experience. Next to my own country, America is the finest, most exciting in the world! I know this because I and my colleagues were honored there."

Rudy is stunned. Only a few days ago, courtesy of Foster, he had learned the meaning of the word *Balbo*, and now he is being welcomed to Italy by one of the armada's pilots. He speaks quickly in an amazed voice to the Colonel. "I was there! I was there in Chicago with co-workers from the Curtiss factory. We had driven to see the Italian Pavillion, designed to celebrate the record breaking flight of the 24 flying boats, And you were one of the pilots! I am amazed, and I'm honored to meet you. I can hardly believe it. We drove on our day off, a Saturday, over 650 miles, on the same day you landed on Lake Michigan, but you landed about six o'clock, I remember, and we didn't get there until two hours later. So we missed seeing you and General Balbo, but I certainly remember they had many big functions in honor of the General and his group over the next several days. I know that a street in Chicago is named Balbo Avenue, and that a University gave him an honorary degree. Our President Roosevelt even awarded him our Distinguished Flying Cross, one of the first to a non-citizen. General Balbo, the armada and all of you who flew that amazing round trip flight are honored still in my country. And those of us from Curtiss Aviation Company who made the drive were proud that some of the 43 American fighter planes that flew as an honor guard over your armada, in a formation spelling the word *Italy*, were Curtiss P-6E biplanes made in our plant. I repeat, I am honored to meet you, Colonel."

"No," exclaimed the Colonel, "it is I who am honored to have you as a guest today. How wonderful it is that ties us together this day, an amazing aeronautical adventure we shared six years ago in America. I remember well the American planes that were our honor guard to Chicago from our crossing of the Canadian border near the city of Montreal. And those planes were from your factory! Amazing. Come now while I show you the workings of our Catania Operations Center for all of Sicily. This next large room is meant to be the meeting place for those who would decide how many and what types of aircraft – bombers, fighters, observation, etc. – would be assigned to carry out missions elsewhere, such as north Africa for example, should war ever come again to Italy. Those tactical decisions would be carried to our communications section, housed in this large technical area, and transmitted by radio to the military flight sections of this Catania Airport, or to other fields here in Sicily I will show you on our construction maps, including the five being constructed nearby on what is called the plains of Catania, an ideal flat area. These instructions, of course, would give dates, take-off times, compass routes, altitudes, and all the other types of information bombers and fighter planes need to carry out their orders. I will say that Italy's experience in Spain during their recent war taught us important things and gave actual experience. I, and many others, have no desire to see Italy again in a war, and I dread the thought of our again becoming a junior partner to the Luftwaffe, as we experienced in Spain."

Highly interesting to Rudy is the realization that there apparently is no incoming enemy aircraft plotting room, nor does he see any other provisions directly and immediately applicable to air attacks from elsewhere aimed at Sicily. Everything so far appears focused on Regia Aeronautica planes carrying out missions southward. North Africa was deliberately mentioned by Colonel DiPalma, but never Malta. Reassurance, or a deliberate omission, knowing where his guest was housed? Well, others can figure that out. The next part of the tour is frightening. Large, wall mounted maps of Sicily are used to indicate three things: existing military airports and remote, satellite airstrips existing now; those under construction currently; and those planned for construction.

Rudy can hardly ask for a pad and pencil, so he attempts to come up with a mnemonic or other memory aid device so he can recall locations later with some accuracy. He'll learn how well he does once he gets back home and reports. As the two complete the lengthy, map tour of the existing and coming airstrips in Sicily, the Colonel and Rudy pause for refreshments which have been brought into the private office by someone, the only person Rudy realizes he has seen in the offices, and this one for only a moment. Obviously, the place has been cleared out for his tour. This gives an opportunity for the Colonel to ask Rudy if he is finding his time in Malta to be enjoyable and interesting. Rudy answers appropriately, saying that, after all, he has found a wonderful wife there, but he is cautious to say much more than general satisfaction in a small but interesting and scenic island.

"Ah," the Colonel says, but I can't imagine you'll be staying there much longer with no prospects of aircraft sales to a departing British military, or do I understand? I would think that you and your wife would be headed back to America and the great Curtiss Company very soon. Considering that we are now new friends, I would recommend that. I hate war, but so many are saying that it comes soon, but who can tell to where it will come? But please, finish your espresso and I will show you three of our new and interesting planes, all designed or modified based on our valuable Spanish experience.

The Colonel's tour now moves outside, just a short walk, to a large hangar, where inside are parked three planes. Outside the hangar are four armed soldiers, even though Colonel DiPalma has already mentioned to Rudy, in an off-hand way, that his entire headquarters staff, military and civilian, is not present today, attending a special training program he has ordered. Rudy's eyes open extra wide, for he's looking at three planes he's never seen before. The biplane in front, he's told, is the best biplane fighter in the world, a Fiat CR.42, highly maneuverable, with a 270 mph speed and a high rate of climb. It did very well in Spain. Rudy gulps at the speed and the streamlined design. The Colonel noted that Italian pilots seem to prefer open cockpits, as Rudy sees. The next is also a fighter, but a sleek low wing monoplane with a long, slim nose ahead of the enclosed cockpit, and a cannon protruding from each wing. The Macci 202, with a Daimler-Benz engine, has a top speed in excess of 350 mph and is a very quietly developing model based on the earlier model used in Spain. Production is to begin soon.

The third, the Colonel tells Rudy, is perhaps the world's best and fastest bomber to date. The Savoia-Marchetti SM.79, with three Alfa Romeo engines, has a top sped of 267 mph and can outrun many fighters. Armed with five machine guns, it can carry 2800 pounds of bombs internally, or two torpedoes. Plans are already underway to re-power, allowing a 276 mph speed, or so the Colonel boasts. Rudy understands that this is all meant to impress him, and so far it's worked. He says so, and the Colonel smiles.

As they walk back to the headquarters building he hears his 'new friend' say, "When you get back home to the United States, my aeronautical friend, you can now say you have seen first hand the progress our Italian friends have made in the Regia Aeronautica. And I hope also you and your wife will be safe all the way from Malta. Should you want, you must let me know soon that you would desire to fly from Malta and Sicily through other neutral countries back to America, and perhaps I can suggest a route. Ah, look around the corner of our building. I believe I just saw Rose's little Fiat with a passenger come to pick you up. If I may, I'll walk with you and meet the new Mrs. Worth? Excellent. There they are."

In the Fiat, driving the short trip to Rose's flat, both Nina and Rose are eager to hear how Rudy's day with Colonel DiPalma was spent. He exclaims how interesting and satisfying it was, but gives no details. Those he reserves for Nina once they're back in the hotel. To Rose he extols the Colonel's friendly and generous tour of where she works as well as the amazing coincidence of the Chicago trip he and the Colonel each made six years ago. It was a great day, and he is very glad Rose made it possible! Rose is happy, Nina is relaxed and smiling, and Rudy is looking forward to meeting Johnny and having what Rose tells him, "Will be a real Sicilian dinner, or supper, or whatever they're called in America."

Once at the apartment, Nina nods all is well with the plan, Rudy whispers he has a lot to tell her, John is fine with everything, and during the food and wine entertains them with tales of radio station life. A taxi will transport the two back to their hotel, Rose and Nina whisper together for a few minutes while waiting for the taxi, and soon Nina and Rudy are back in their room. Rudy is eager for two things: telling Nina what his day was all about, and learning just what arrangements Nina has for bed time. The first thing he says, however, is, "Tomorrow morning, first thing, make a phone call to Malta, that special number, and tell them you've mis-dialed, or whatever you're supposed to say, and then get us on a plane the day after tomorrow! We need an excuse for an early departure, but it needs to look right. I don't want my new friend, Colonel DiPalma, to wonder why I left town the next day after he gave me such a detailed education. Let's get a tour of Catania tomorrow, and our passports back first! Tomorrow night we're here at this hotel packing and arranging for a taxi to the airport or seaplane ramp for whatever time you can get for us on an early flight. Are you listening? Today was scary for me. Rose's boss, Colonel Di Palma, was so friendly and talkative I couldn't tell if he really just wanted an American pilot to tell his tale to, or if he was on to me and was feeding me a bunch of exaggerated stuff to carry back to the RAF on Malta. Or maybe have us arrested when we tried to leave Sicily. I couldn't take notes, but I heard a lot of info and I'm trying to keep it all straight and remember it. But I can't tell if it's accurate stuff about the Italian Air Force, or greatly exaggerated to scare us. It's for our secret agent friend, Mr. Boyle, to figure out, I guess. I just think we need to act pretty much as if we're on a real vacation, get our tour in tomorrow, and get out day after. Are you hearing me? Are you OK? Why are you...are you crying? What's wrong?"

CHAPTER 28

FROM THE FRYING PAN

Catania - Malta
February-March 1940

RUDY'S question was answered quickly. "Rudy, I've been scared ever since we dropped you off this morning. Rose told me her boss was furious when she said you might not have free time to visit the airport today. Said she'd better make sure or find a new job! What's going on? Yes, I'm crying and I've been worried sick about you all day. I don't care about our so called assignment, Take me home. No, come and hold me. I'll make the call early tomorrow. Come here. No more talking about this stupid business tonight, and no more rolled up blanket. As far as I'm concerned, this is our honeymoon and … wait a second… I brought some honeymoon clothes and I want you to see me in them before we go to bed. I'll change in the bath, and I've got something for you, too. This make believe honeymoon is about to change into a real one. Unless you've changed your mind about us, until we can get a real marriage certificate back home, this is the beginning of our life together. We've done what they wanted us to do here, so now its our turn. Let's do what both of us have been hoping for." And to Rudy's great joy and satisfaction, they did.

Nina's deliberately mis-dialed phone call next morning resulted in a call back to their hotel with a message for Signora Worth, taken by the receptionist. When the two returned in late-afternoon from their tour of Catania, the manager sadly reported that the message was that the Signora's ill grandmother had taken a turn for the worse and that they should take the earliest flight back to Valletta. The manager, himself, had arranged for Ala Littoria to hold two seats on the next morning's flight, and hoped that was helpful. Nina thanked him profusely and phoned the airline herself to confirm. They went immediately to their room to begin packing, they said, with the manager offering to order a taxi for the morning flight. Except for a brief supper at the family type restaurant just up the block, from which they hurried back to the hotel, they continued with what Nina had termed last night "what both of us have been hoping for". The manager told his desk clerk that, obviously, the Signora was greatly upset by her mother's illness, in need of quiet rest, and should not be disturbed.

The flight back to Malta next morning over Mount Etna was uneventful. They were met at its end by a car sent by Colonel Astill, who had checked with the airline's passenger list. Whisked off to the Governor's office for the earliest possible debriefing, Nina wryly observed that her grandmother must have recovered quickly. The waiting group at the Governor's office consisted of those who had finalized their assignment after Nina's negotiations, plus surprises. These were Captain Donalds and his finally arrived boss, the Air Officer Commanding Malta, Air Commodore Fairthorpe, and as a final surprise, Air Vice Marshal Conners. Introductions were made, since neither had met AOC Fairthorpe, and Nina knew neither Captain Donalds nor Rudy's "old friend" James Conners. The Air Marshal threw his arm over Rudy's shoulder and said, "I was the first RAF officer to discover Rudy Worth, who has since demonstrated his great personal value to the RAF, and I eagerly await his reporting today on the Italian strength in Sicily, for which we must prepare if we're to retain Malta and our territory in Africa. I only hope we may be allowed to keep Friend Rudy here on Malta a bit longer in our support! At that pronouncement, Rudy's face went from smiling to shock, noticed by none except Nina.

Without a preamble, the Governor-General called the group to order by asking them to move to the chairs which had been pushed into a corner of his office. He began by explaining that Nina had made the alerting call because of concern over the security of Rudy's special assignment, and that call brought them home today, earlier than planned. He then turned to the couple, and suggested they first hear from Nina regarding her meeting with Rose. Both Agent Boyle and Mr. Sanno gave rapt attention to Nina as she assured them that Rose was enthusiastic over the plan and the code. Boy-friend Johnny had understood his role and the danger his role opened to himself and Rose, but he pledged to support Rose's goals of revenge on the Fascists and receiving British financial support for her brother's medical treatments. Nina then described the reasons for her concern over Rudy's assignment to learn about any new Sicilian military airstrips, prompted by the high attention paid to his presence in Catania, and turned to Rudy.

Rudy pulled two sheets of paper from his bag, handing one to the Governor. He explained that the sheet, folded over several times, was slipped into his hand by Rose as they entered the taxi from her flat back to the hotel after their dinner. He stuffed it into his laundry later that night, and had not told Nina, wanting to keep her safely innocent of it should they be stopped by authorities. The sheet apparently contains a listing of all current military airstrips in Sicily, those now under construction, and those planned for ongoing expansion of the Regia Aeronautica's, or possible Luftwaffe's, operations. Next to each name is a three digit code identifier, as well as its approximate location. The group was speechless as he continued to explain that while he believed Rose was genuinely anti-Fascist and pro-Malta, he had no idea of the accuracy of the list or who had composed it, if not Rose herself.

The hours spent as a guest of Tenente Colonnello DiPalma were recounted by Rudy as accurately as he could, with some wonderment about the Colonel's sincerity. As Rudy attempted to explain, he said, "The Colonel either sees me as a fellow aviator and a genuine new friend from neutral America, or a not so clever spy for the RAF on Malta. He showed me their airstrip maps, their new Macci 202 fighter with a German in-line engine and 350 plus mph, and what he called the world's fastest bomber, the SM.79. I even got to see a really streamlined biplane, a Fiat 42 with 270 mph and a high rate of climb he boasted about. I know the Italians love fast planes. They broke world speed records with their thin winged seaplanes that required using long waterways for takeoffs. You Brits got into that as well, which I suppose is why your best fighter is called the Supermarine Spitfire, isn't it? But they've not really gotten into powerful in-line engines of their own however, only radials, nor heavy armament. They're still living mostly with two machine guns, and just getting started with canon. I'd guess they design great prototypes, but are weak at continuing high volume manufacturing? Not set up for efficient long run manufacturing, which is a Curtiss strong point."

When Rudy paused to take a breath, Jim Conners prompted him to keep going. "This is great info, Rudy. The RAF is highly interested in everything you can tell us. Don't stop!" Rudy readily continued by explaining that the various Italian air force units are assigned to operate in and from large areas. Sicily was being assigned to the 2nd *Aeria* which, if he remembered accurately, would be composed of approximately five bomber wings, one fighter wing and another large fighter group, one dive bomber group possibly to be equipped with foreign aircraft, whatever that meant, plus several reconnaissance units. And somewhere in there, he was told by the Colonel, the beginning of a specialized bomber unit was being considered, an *aerosiluranti* he badly pronounced, which Nina cut-in to say translated as 'air torpedoing'.

Rudy noted he was invited to visit by the Administrator of the Catania Operations Center, at a carefully specified day and time, which then was devoid of any other staff, as the Colonel had arranged. The facility was already operating as the nerve center for the Sicilian Area, and apparently would remain so. Rudy believed that his invitation and what he learned from the Colonel during his visit were intended to impact both American and RAF authorities through Rudy, and he admitted to being impressed himself by Colonel DiPalma's friendly demeanor and detailed presentation. Catania Aeroporto itself is large, busy, and seemingly dominated by the Regia Aeronautica's presence.

There are, however, several additional civilian-military airports in Sicily, and a number of dedicated military airports already operating. Many others are under construction or planned for construction as airstrips with basic support provisions. Consulting his copy of Rose's listing, Rudy noted Catania (#503) as the major east coast airport, and Comiso/Ragusa (#508) on the south coast. Two small island strips south of Sicily, Pantelleria (#515) and Lampedusa, were already built, as was the Sigonella Naval Air Station. Other seaplane bases were at Palermo (#507), Sirocusa (#510), and Marsala (#512). Landbased strips also were already at Trapani (#514) and Chinisia (#516), with others coming near eight or ten small villages ranging from Acate (#504) to Pachino (#517) and Sciacca (#501). Important to know about were the several additional airstrips planned for the flat area to the west of Catania. Especially to control the Mediterranean Sea sector within close flying distance from the south of Sicily, airfields such as Trapini-Milo (#514), Comiso (#508), Pantelleria (#515), and Ponte Olivo (#502) were constructed during the Fascist growth from 1936 to1939, undoubtedly with Italian lands in north Africa and very likely Malta in Mussolini's mind. Rudy admitted to no idea of how the numerical identifiers were assigned, obviously not by construction date.

Rudy ended his presentation by emphasizing that he had combined what he had been told and had actually seen with the written list of airfields Rose had pressed into his hand at parting. He could only judge Rose's list by comparing it with what he could remember from his visit to the Center's map room, and both indicated a very high number of airstrips in operation now or soon to be. A photoplane flyover on a clear day could provide accuracy, he offered, but who knows what else it likely would produce. Before Rudy could say more, Agent Boyle posed a question. "Nina, what do you think of Rose's list and the possibility that she was given instructions by her boss to help convince us that Italian air strength far exceeds ours? Is she still on our side?"

Nina answered, "My best thinking is that, even before we arrived, she judged there was more to our trip than just a honeymoon. Thinking that my aeronautical American, pro-RAF, new husband had another purpose when I proposed a rental car to explore the countryside, she put two and two together. I imagine she composed the list from her daily work as a file clerk at the Center, reacted negatively to the Colonel's nasty threat of firing if Rudy didn't show up, and that evening passed the sheet. I'm still convinced that she's pro-Malta and with us."

At that, both the Governor and Jim Conners voiced satisfaction with what the two had brought back from Sicily, Rose's and Johnny's agreement to carry out the code broadcasts if war with Italy were to be declared, and the names, likely locations, and identifying code numbers of Sicilian military airstrips to be used against Malta and British forces in north Africa. Commodore Fairthorpe observed that those locations would have to be bombing targets for the RAF, assuming Malta received suitable aircraft, crews, and bomb loads. That statement, of course, caused all in the room to turn questioningly to Jim Conners, the highest ranking RAF officer there. Where and when would planes arrive? Time to prepare even a few

Gladiators was drawing to a close, more modern Hawker Hurricanes were never even mentioned in current gossip, and the lone Curtiss Hawk hidden away on Gozo could hardly save Malta without help! "Air Marshal Conners," the Governor asked, "do you have any word on what we're all hoping for?"

"Without knowing what the situation with France and the Home Islands would be if Hitler scales up this so-called Phoney War, all I can give is a weak promise that several Sea Gladiators will be dropped off here for your magical upgrading. And that won't take place until RAF London learns more. In the mean time, I urge you all to court the Navy, for it's from them the Glads will have to come. Possibly depending on who is Prime Minister, I'd guess that Hurricanes and pilots will be assigned here from England once airspace over Great Britain is secured. But understand that if the Nazis invade Britain, or attempt to, all promised wagers are off. We need to strengthen our forces, with emphasis on the RAF, as fast as possible. If only Rudy's country could assist openly! At this point we can only hope."

On that negative but reasoned note, the Governor thanked all for attending, reminded them that everything said and learned at the meeting was covered by the Secrets Act, and the meeting was adjourned. Rudy, with Nina practically on his heels, moved to Jim Conners and asked for a word as the others moved out of the room. His friend spoke first, anticipating concern over Jim's earlier comment about Rudy's assignment, and realizing that Nina was holding onto Rudy's arm in mutual support. "I'm speaking now to both of you," Jim began, "since I'm guessing you two are planning a joint future?" The two nodded simultaneously, and Jim continued. "Rudy, I can't imagine the Gladiators – or the Hawk, for that matter – being made ready, upgraded and kept in flying condition without you here in the Shops when the air war begins. My estimation is very soon, and that we shall see a change in the Prime Minister's office and the War Council of Parliament once Hitler finally makes his move toward western Europe. Then we'll know more about Malta's role, as well as Italy's.

"However, considering the five organizers of the HRM group, for which you technically work, I suspect that only the United States, minus partners Poland-in-Exile, and possibly Norway, France, and Britain, will be in a position to keep HRM going financially. My informed hunch is that you will be recalled back to the United States and, most likely, given an officer's position in your Army Air Force. However, you would really be working as a technical consultant dispatched from the White House to help coordinate aircraft production among the growing number of American aircraft manufacturers. Please don't reveal that you heard that from me, else I'll be hearing from your old U.S. mentor, Colonel – now General – Whittaker. I would further wager that the shift I've described might well occur either later this year or early the next. In truth, following whatever happens here to Malta, that new assignment would do more to help Britain and all of allied Europe in the long run.

"May I suggest that you communicate with General Whittaker, who most certainly has been kept aware of your exploits here, ostensibly just to keep him informed of your great fortune in meeting Miss Lafessi and your personal plans, whatever they may be. And my apologies, Nina, for not mentioning earlier that Rudy's affection for you had not gone unnoticed here and mentioned favorably in occasional communications with our American colleagues. In fact, when told of your special negotiations prior to the Sicily trip, I didn't know whether to applaud or laugh. Thus your General, Rudy, should not be surprised if you describe at some point a need for joint return transportation to the States rather than for only one. And there you have it! Now, I believe you said you wanted a word with me before I left? Ah, all set, I judge? Excellent. So now I shall depart to hunt again for a few unattached Gloster Gladiators. I look forward to seeing both of you again, soon, and again, my thanks and congratulations on a successful mission to our flying friends in Sicily. Oh, one more thought. Air Officer Fairthorpe will pass on some vital information he's just received, Rudy, so please assist him all you can."

On the short drive from the meeting, neither Nina nor Rudy said more than ten words each, reflecting the obvious realization that they had a great deal of most important thinking to do, and in a hurry. Rudy asked the driver to drop them off at the seaplane departure dock where they had left the car, and from there they drove to Nina's home in Sliema. Parked in front of the house, still seated in the car, they each listed for the other the key decisions needed to get their individual and joint lives redirected and eventually stabilized. Nina began by seeking Rudy's confirmation that an official wedding should take place soon, and he readily agreed. This led to

Nina's strong desire to talk with her mother, sister, father, and brother – in that order – right away, explaining to them that the time had come for her to leave not only the family home as a new bride, but very possibly even Malta as the wife of an American who could be called home by his government at any time. Nina declared she was ready to do that, although the thought of leaving her family and Malta in war time seemed almost impossible. She imagined, she predicted to Rudy, that her parents would be overcome with dismay. But she was ready!

Rudy began, off the top of his head, by listing the need for them to arrange for their wedding and a suitable flat made ready. Foster's, he thought. Then he recalled to Nina his promise to officialdom that he intended to remain working in Malta, both in war planning and in his work as aeronautical engineer in the Shops. With careful attention to timing, he knew he would need to learn from Janice Townley HRM's plans for him, and General Whittaker's plan – if there is one – to haul him back to the States and assign him to another type of consulting position. One molded by wartime needs, obviously, but now, Rudy emphasized, with provisions for getting Mr. and Mrs. Worth to the United States, likely in wartime, and in a position enabling Rudy to support a wife. To Nina he included his desire to provide all the news to his parents back in Watkins Glenn, and to Mr. Juddson at Curtiss. He realized as well the need to inform his RAF and civilian friends as well as the Governor-General and Major Astill. Oh, and Mr. Farinacci and Mr. Sanno here in Malta, he thought, plus Mrs. Osborne back in Buffalo and Ian Standish in London.

Nina supplied the end of this emotional plan by saying, "The first thing that has to happen is for me to talk to my parents. We'll then get an official marriage ceremony set and a place of our own organized, and in the mean time you can figure out with whom you need to talk. If the damn war erupts before we get going to wherever we're to go, we'll have a time even getting off this island. So let's move fast. Agreed?" This was followed by, "No, we had our honeymoon before the wedding, remember? But maybe we do need that high school ring you once spoke of, or some ring, or don't you remember that either? I'd better eat dinner with the family tonight and start the explanation, but pick me up at the shipping office at 5:00 tomorrow for the latest news. I need to talk to at least my mother before you start your ball rolling, OK?"

As Rudy heads for the hotel and his unpacking, his thoughts turn immediately to Foster's flat. More than ever, it sounds like a good deal, and certainly is coming at the right time. Funny, Rudy thinks, how the trip to Sicily he wasn't really too excited about worked out so well. He couldn't have planned it better! But he can't jump the gun with Foster tomorrow, since Nina wants to get her family in agreement right away. That makes sense, he thinks, causing him to wonder how the folks in Watkins Glenn will take the news? Did he ever mention to Nina, he wonders, that the average winter temperature and snowfall in upstate New York, as well as life in general, are a bit different than Malta's? For a fleeting moment following that thought something like instinctive fear flashes across his brain. Happily, though, his mental swirl of love and lust for Nina causes his brain to pick itself up and hurry on as though nothing had happened.

At the hotel he is handed a written telephone message from Robert. It advises Rudy that he and the Shop hierarchy have been asked to attend a 1:30 pm meeting tomorrow with Air Commander Fairthorpe in Fairthorpe's conference room, to meet the several visitors from afar who will have arrived to assist the work of the Shop and the remaining RAF group. Three will eventually be assigned outside the Kalafrana area, while one could possibly be assigned to work with Rudy. A mysterious 'other topics as well' was added above Robert's name. Ah, reflected Rudy. Now the action starts!

In fact, the action started shortly after Rudy arrived for work at the Shops the next morning. Foster awaited him with the news that his long standing application for BOC housing had been approved, and that he now is able to move in 'at his convenience'. Would Rudy want to exercise his request for right of first refusal, or should Foster alert his rental agent that he would vacate the flat within two weeks and that it could be advertised? He explained that he had not signed a new lease agreement for the year, and had been living there on a week-by-week temporary arrangement. Rudy, unable to give a clear answer, asked if Foster could gather could gather the details as they had agreed earlier, and finalize tomorrow? "Of course," was Foster's instant response, and their conversation shifted quickly to the coming meeting called by the Air Commander.

Foster didn't hesitate to predict that the visitors would be fresh from the Polish Air Force and would be staying on Malta as provisional RAF flying staff for the Hawk, he reminded Rudy, who now showed a glum look, that this had been hinted at on several occasions, even before their new Air Commander had reported for duty. "Rudy," Foster offered, "you do remember that the Hawk is now an RAF plane and that you are not an RAF fighter pilot. This was agreed to several months ago, but I'll bet you'll have to check them out on the Hawk. I hope they've got some experience, or we've got a problem!"

"Yes, Foster. Thanks for reminding me, but checking someone out on a single seat fighter isn't going to give me any flying time. But now that I think about it, upgrading some Gladiators certainly will require me to test them out, and I actually have flown a Gloster Gauntlet, which is pretty similar, isn't it?"

On that happier note, Robert cut in and, addressing both, said, "This might be a good time for us to look at Rudy's workshop and think about fitting one of the newcomers in there, assuming one of them isn't a fighter pilot but somebody who worked with PZL, or whatever that Polish manufacturer was called. I'm saying this because, like you, Foster, I'm quite sure the Polish have arrived. And as more than tourist visitors, I'll wager." And so it proved to be, not two or three newcomers, but four, each introduced to all gathered by the Air Commander at his afternoon meeting.

Rudy's final surprise of the morning, before the meeting, came by a noon phone call from Nina. "My darling," she hurried," I just couldn't wait to tell you that last night I not only got to talk with my mother and father about our great news, but they told me of their news. It really helps us solve the challenges we listed last night, and I'll tell you all about it tonight when you pick me up at 5:00. I've got to run now. See you then, love." And that was it.

CHAPTER 29

INTO THE FIRE

Malta
Spring 1940

NOT much at all transpired with the Shops management staff prior to the early afternoon Air Commander's meeting, at least as far as Foster, Robert, and Rudy were concerned. With the Hawk's work completed for now, and no Gladiators waiting for assembly and/or upgrading, the issue of where to assign their anticipated newly arrived PZL aircraft designer easily was solved, as Robert had suggested, by shared space in Rudy's workshop. Rudy devoted little thinking space to that anyway, his main focus being on Nina's exuberant but hasty noontime call to him. He hoped he would share her enthusiasm tonight when she told him her parent's news. If it meant their wedding plans could go ahead full speed he would phone Watkins Glen tomorrow and tell them his news, at least as much of it as he could without talking to General Whittaker first, and then Janice Townley. The minutes dragged on, including a lunch made uneasy by their continued guessing of what would soon be made evident, or so they thought.

The trio entered the meeting room at 1:25, in anticipation of actually seeing the newcomers prior to the official starting time, but glanced around an empty room instead. "Good of you to come," said the Air Commodore, startling them, only a few steps behind. "I'm delighted to see you all, and arriving a few minutes early on your walk up from the Shops. I imagine you're as eager to greet our new staff additions as I was. Well, they'll be here shortly, but I want to tell you and the others a bit about them by way of a pre-introduction. Ah, and here are our colleagues, right on time. Come, come in. I believe you all know each other." Several RAF officers slid through the doorway and looked for seats, voicing greetings to Foster,

Rudy, and Robert, as they took chairs, all of which were facing the front of the meeting room. Rudy recognized several, including Captain Donalds and Squadron Leader Slingerland. Most, if not all were flying officers and would be interfacing with the Polish pilots, Rudy imagined, just as he would be working with whomever would be the aircraft engineer. Once again, Rudy resolved to be friendly and cooperative no matter who it might be. With their meeting's host now moving to the front, all greetings ceased and all eyes were on him.

"We shall be rather informal here, since my prime reason for calling you together is to introduce you to our new members, four men who, by choice, have elected to join with us here on Malta in anticipation of this so called Phoney War – what the Germans have termed the *sitzkrieg*– developing quite soon into what they, in their own country, have just experienced. That is, an outright and horrific war to the death of many and the destruction of much in Poland. Please understand that the Polish military, certainly without question including the Polish Air Force, put up a brave and magnificent series of battles against an overwhelming Nazi blitzkrieg. Our new comrades escaped to Romania after the Polish government surrendered and, encouraged and assisted by our own people, have made their way here to continue their fight against the hated Nazis. Many escaped Polish pilots, now with wartime flying hours of battle experience, including a number with downed German aircraft to their credit, are already flying for the French Air Force. Others are forming a Polish Squadron within the RAF on our home island. Our need here for two experienced fighter pilots for our P-36 Hawk, now an official RAF aircraft, was the magnet that pulled three experienced Poles to Malta, and I say three because an aircraft mechanic and armorer accompanied the pilots. Under the direction of Squadron Leader Slingerland they will be assigned to the Hawk, at least for now residing without notice at the remote strip quite north of Hal Far.

The two pilots are Andruz Machalski, who in English is called 'Andy', and Wozto Kaczmarek, who is called 'Wolf'. Their mechanic's name is Bogdan Ludoslaw, called Bogdan. I shall ask Robert to get the correct spelling of these names and see that you all get them. I know that you and all RAF personnel here on Malta will genuinely welcome our new flying officers and technician. However, last, but certainly not least, I am delighted to have with us a very senior aircraft designer and engineer from the well known PZL company of Poland. He was one of the key people on the canon equipped PZL model 25 design which we have being hearing about and which downed a number of ME 109s during the September invasion. He is Dr. Ludoslaw Mazur, and he will be working with Rudy Worth and Foster Crayton on the upgrading of the power and armament of our soon to arrive Gloster Gladiators. To renewed applause and shouts of 'Hear, Hear' he continued: "Yes, you heard me correctly; I'm told arrangements for their transport to Malta are being finalized as we speak. So, Foster and Rudy, you may be smiling and very busy quite soon. And now I'll ask Captain Donalds to step into my office where our new members are waiting, and you can welcome them here warmly I trust, and officially."

With mounting applause, all in the room were standing and applauding as the Captain ushered in the newcomers, Dr. Mazur nodding and giving thanks in excellent English. Andy and Wolf literally marched in behind him, wearing their military uniforms, smiling at the unexpected RAF welcome, and urging with small hand waves mechanic Bogdan to enter right along with them. Rudy's first impression of his new co-engineer brought relief and assurance that such a professional appearing man, coming all the way from Poland through Romania, and thanking a group of strangers so well in their own language, had to be OK. *The new arrangement will work out just fine!* As the RAF group, Rudy and Foster included, swarmed around the newcomers, shaking hands and patting shoulders in welcome, Rudy whispered to Foster how quickly and happily the RAF accepted the Poles. Foster glanced at him and mumbled something about the Commander's prefatory remarks concerning the group's expected enthusiasm to the introduction, which included rather obvious clues, and the RAF staff certainly knowing which side of the biscuit the jam is on! "Ah," sounded Rudy. "Of course. But I'm really glad all four are here and that some Gladiators are on the way."

Foster and Rudy spent much of the afternoon's remainder giving Dr. Mazur a grand tour of the Shops and equipment, including the special work space he and Rudy will use to direct engine and gun improvements on the Gladiators. The Doctor was impressed, he said, and pledged his best work to accomplish what could be done, saying he had some familiarity with Italian fighters and bombers and thought Rudy's ideas for the biplane engines would even the odds when the Regia Aeronautica made its appearance over Malta. He was just as excited, he remarked, about the Hawk, as were the two fighter pilots. Taken off by Captain Donalds to finish up administrative details, Dr. Mazur told them he was to be quartered in the BOQ and would be provided transportation to the Shops. He would begin his work with them tomorrow, he certainly hoped.

While Rudy was eager to not miss picking up Nina at 5:00, Foster was just as eager to tell Rudy about his facts and figures concerning the hopeful transfer of the flat. Certainly the news that the new engineer would also be quartered at the BOQ helped focus his interest in getting Rudy to decide.

"I've done the necessary checking, at least the initial part, until you decide whether you want it. I've jotted down the current monthly rental fee I'm paying for the flat, including whatever fees are added on for electricity, heating, telephone, and the re-diffusion radio cable. I imagine the rental agency would be happy to have you move in as soon as I move over to the BOC, and I'd be your local reference with them. It's a nice smallish flat, one bedroom only, but that's likely all you'd want. You'd use the rear car-park space for any guests, I'd think, and still be able to find a spot at the kerb for yourself. Oh, one more thought. The BOC spots are already set up complete with furnishings, so I was intending to have one of those used furnishing folks come over and give me a price for just about everything. If you want, I can get such a price and simply turn it all over to you for the same figure. That is, unless you want to furnish it yourself? It does come with what you Americans call a stove and fridge as part of the rental, and they work well. I'll have the numbers tomorrow or day after, if you decide you're going ahead with the plan. If you don't want a year's lease, we can see if the agency would agree to a shorter one, or, with the possibility of the war opening up, perhaps even a monthly arrangement. Should I pull the final numbers together and sound out the rental agent? I can do that by tomorrow or the day after, I would think."

"That would be fine." was Rudy's reply. "Let's talk tomorrow or next day. Anyway, I may have some news for you myself." Leaving Foster not sure if he had really been listening as the flat's details had been recited,

Rudy slid the Rover into an open parking spot at the shipping office a full quarter hour before 5:00, but only five minutes before Nina emerged, smiling and almost skipping as she hopped into the car and kissed Rudy in a smooth movement. "Rudy, I've always thought the brides-to-be I've known were carried away with silly, youthful, excitement, but now I know the feeling. I sat down last night with both my parents. I thought they'd be surprised, but they weren't. My father just kept on nodding and my mother must have said 'I knew it, I knew it' twenty times. They think you're a good man, they understand it probably means America, they agree Malta's soon going to be in a real war, and they know I love you. In fact, my father said that a person should get married not because the other one wants to marry you, but because you want to marry them. Which I do!

"I truly believe that applies to each of us, so we're cleared to go – at least from my parents – for both a civil ceremony and a church wedding as soon as we can arrange it. But wait, surprise, there's more. My sister is going to live with our Aunt Margaret in England and go to college there, and she's leaving right away, as soon as we can find a fast passenger boat headed to Gibraltar and a plane to England. I can do that through the shipping office, I hope. Aunt Margaret is my mother's younger sister. Married an English officer here in Malta years ago when he was stationed here and then moved to England. You've never met her, of course. She's got a daughter about Mila's age who also has started college, so Mila's excited to go. Margaret's husband has done really well as a civilian, and they're happy to have her live with them, far from the London area, during war. Mila and my parents have been quietly planning this for the last two weeks, as soon as my father became really convinced Malta was going to soon be in the middle of it. My mother intends to go up to the farm in Gozo quite soon, and stay with my grandmother. By-the-way, my father is guessing that the RAF will eventually bring the Hawk down to Hal Far where the fuel and ammo storage is, rather than try to coordinate its flights from Gozo with whatever few planes we get down here. My father and Paul will stay in the house in Sliema and continue working in the shops. They'll drive up to Gozo on weekends if they can get off from work and if they can get gas for the car or Paul's motorcycle. At least that's their plan." Out of breath, Nina paused for a moment, giving Rudy a chance to say, "But what about us? What's our situation?"

"Our plan," Nina said, "yours and mine, is for you to tell your family back in America, talk with General Whittaker and somebody from HRM, and find us a place to live – at least while we're still here. What else do you need to do about your work here, assuming you really are going to be called back to the US Air Force? And what do I do while we're here after we become Mr. and Mrs. Worth, and what happens to me in America? My mother and I will plan the wedding, tell you the date, and everything else is up to you."

Rudy at long last described the possible opportunity to take over the Crayton flat, hopefully on a month-to-month basis, if Nina were to look at the place and think it a good opportunity. He watched her nod in agreement and then said he would ask for a secure phone line at Mr. Sanno's office so he could talk to the General in Washington, Janice Townley at HRM, and his parents – in that order – tomorrow, considering time changes. She nodded again, and he promised to arrange for them both to visit Foster's flat tomorrow at lunch time. He'd phone her office as soon as he talked to Foster in the morning. "Let's agree to a possible date for the wedding," was his next idea, "or have you and your mother already settled that?" They had, but Nina didn't mention that immediately. Instead she began a monologue that illustrated some of the many details in addition to the actual date that needed consideration, some of which might possibly need Rudy's input before she and her mother made the final decisions. Once again, Rudy elected the choice of a sage nod, sans comment.

Next morning, after checking the availability of an overseas phone line with Mr. Sanno, Rudy succeeded in reaching General Whittaker, and after offering congratulations about his promotion to General, proceeded to hem and haw about what his professional future might appear to be in the General's crystal ball. Rudy added what sounded like an afterthought, and simply slid quickly through a sentence that described his meeting a young woman who...but was interrupted by the General, who said, "Yes, yes, of course, I've heard all about it including the phoney Sicilian honeymoon. I wish you both the best. I assume the wedding will take place soon. But in terms of your immediate future, you've already been told by that Captain who works with Townley at HRM that you'll be called back and drafted into the US Army Air Force to help coordinate the aircraft manufacturing circus race back here. So you won't return to Curtiss, at least not while there's a war involving us, but will work out of my office here in Washington as an Air Force officer. I could use your help and energy right now, but we're waiting for you to finish up with whatever in hell the Brits are finally going to get to your shop on Malta. Get those planes, do whatever can be done to upgrade, and we'll get word to FDR so he can advise his friend Mr. Churchill. He'll certainly be Prime Minister if the Brits want more of our help. Then we'll figure out how to get you and Mrs. Worth back here ASAP. I'll get things going here and I'll handle Townley, so you stay out of it. We still want to assist Malta in keeping out of Mussolini's hands, no matter what, but the good old USA is moving at last, so get yourselves ready to pack your bags and come back.

"By-the-way, I understand that the British have their eyes on your lady friend to work under her UK passport at some hush, hush office they're setting up in Washington since she's already cleared by their M something group. But don't mention this to her. It's still in the talking stage. I'll answer any questions when the time comes. Stay safe and I'll probably be seeing you sooner rather than later." Rudy's following call to his parents created happiness that he might return to the States fairly soon, and agreement that if he had met and really knew Miss Right, at his advanced age, no matter where he met her, they were looking forward to bringing her into the family. Or so both his mother and sister sounded like they said words to that effect during the very long distance call to his old home in Watkins Glen.

Although the back of his brain still realized that his Malta assignment continued to demand full time and professional attention, the personal side of Rudy's thoughts resulted in his meeting briefly with Foster as soon as he returned to the Shops from completing his two calls, and asking if he and Nina Lafessi – his fiancée– could have a brief tour of his flat. Foster, eager to get the matter settled, readily agreed to go with them in Rudy's car at noon. Upon looking briefly at each of the rooms, with an extra scan of the kitchen and a quicker review of the building's entryway, Nina voiced her approval, Rudy nodded to Foster, and Foster said he would talk to the rental agent and get the necessary papers to Rudy absolutely as soon as possible. *Ah*, thought Rudy, *if it all goes this quickly and easily, being married will be a snap!*

Foster, a long-ago married man, thought, *Ah, young love. An unusual honeymoon followed by a brief engagement and the rental of a furnished flat, and then – one wishes –followed very shortly by a wedding and a long, happy married life. At least I truly hope so!* With that he hurried off, heading for the sounds of Rudy, Dr. Mazur, Paul, and Robert talking up a storm in the Shop's now joint engine and armament laboratory. Their new aeronautical engineer was expressing his genuine pleasure at seeing the variety of tools, instruments, and work spaces now at his disposal, and his technical interest at the test engine, already hooked to the intake misting system and boost gauge. Robert was thanked by the Doctor, and again by Rudy, for arranging all of this months ago, and then, seeing Foster on the fringe of a now technical discussion, drifted off toward his office. Foster added comments about additional, and hopefully available enhancements, three bladed adjustable pitch propellers for example, and left the two engineers, aided by Paul, to plan their next steps.

Rudy, who had not wanted to discuss with Nina his calls back to America during their trip to Foster's flat, realized that she had no knowledge of his conversations with General Whittaker or his family. He saw now that he needed to consult with his bank in Malta as well as his bank in the US where his salary was, hopefully, being deposited, now that he would have a wife and additional living expenses. He needed a financial advisor, he reckoned, but who? It hit him in an instant, but would Mrs. Osborne, back in Buffalo at his former Curtiss employers, set him straight on his current financial standing and provide some friendly advice? Would HRM continue to cover as least his living expenses?

He had no idea of Nina's earnings, nor had he any idea of how joint finances should be arranged? Does he earn enough to really take on a wife? What will the flat's furnishings cost, and what's the monthly rent? Would Nina contribute? Ye gads, he realized, I haven't even thought about buying a ring much less funding a wedding and then a decent life on Malta for the two of us. And I haven't talked to Mr. Farinacci about my room at the hotel or Governor Garrison about my leaving, much less Foster. I'd better pull myself together, get some immediate financial information, and understand that I just can't send a brief good bye note to people here after we get back to America! Calm down Rudy, talk to Nina tonight, and come up with a plan. This is a case of the old saying that a workable plan today is better than a perfect plan whenever you can pull one together. OK. First, get to Nina tonight, get her thoughts on the financial things, and do a workable plan before I head back to the hotel tonight. Wait, isn't there a different old one that says if you want to make God laugh, show him your plans? Well OK. But at least a start-up plan tonight gets us started!

That evening, alone with Nina in the Fiat as usual, Rudy relayed the details of his brief call to General Whittaker describing the 'return to America with your wife' business, plus the warm welcome his family extended to their soon-to-be daughter-in-law during his call to New York. He followed that news with a promise to learn how much is now in his Buffalo bank account, and what the monthly rental of the flat will be, plus the cost if they were to buy Foster's furnishings. He believed it safe to assume that his HRM salary would not change, but he hoped that their hotel residence allocation could be applied to the flat's rental, and that his return to America, but not her tickets, would be covered. What did Nina project as costs for whatever type of wedding she and her parents were planning? With those reports and forecasts he stopped, shrugged, and looked at Nina for help. She responded with reassuring, concise answers, as expected.

"Rudy, the Lafessi family is not only planning the wedding, but traditionally covering all costs. You'll need to take care of getting our rings, selecting a best man, deciding what you'll wear, and working with me to get our civil license and whatever Dun Thom, the Kappillan who's going to marry us in a church wedding, requires. Remember him? He saved you and Robert and also blessed the Hawk. Plus, we should start my getting an American passport and American citizenship, as we had in Sicily, except for real. I think I should retain my British passport and have dual citizenship, at least for the time being, since I intend to live with you in your country while the rest of the Lafessi family intends to stay in Malta. Except for my sister, that is, who will be living in England for who knows how long. Sadly, Mila may have to leave for there before our big day, since the fast boat's schedule is still uncertain. I'm sure your salary is being saved in that bank back in Buffalo however, and that your Mrs. Osborne from Curtiss can tell you the amount and how you can withdraw and get sent here what ever we'll need. Maybe they can transfer that amount plus your monthly salary, once we're married, right to the

Bank of Malta. We won't need it tomorrow, since I've been saving money ever since our motorcycle ride to Gozo, just in case. Ha Ha! I'll keep working here, in one job or another, until we depart, and we'll save that money for whatever's needed to get us to wherever we're going. Why not check with Foster tomorrow so we can get the flat all set, and unless we're to leave right away, why don't we pay him for the furniture and kitchenware. We can always sell it when we go.

Oh, and by the way, the wedding is set for the Catholic parish church in Sliema I've always gone to, Stella Maris, Our Lady Star of the Sea, to be held on the last Sunday in April, next month, if war doesn't hit us sooner. The Kappillan says it's OK you're Anglican; He'll work it out. So get going on your end of things and we'll keep each other posted. OK? Oh, one more thing: let me know when you want us to go looking at rings. I do know a nice jewelry store with reasonable prices. I've already picked out the dress."

CHAPTER 30

THE KALAFRANA SHOPS

Malta

April 1940

WITH news that the biplane fighters were soon to arrive, the Shops seemed to come alive with focused action. The RAF officers, several of whom are pilots long confined to administrative posts for lack of planes, begin to jockey for positions on the active pilots list their Wing Commander, they assume, '*simply has to be compiling*'! Shop technicians,who have almost forgotten how to uncrate a Gladiator and reassemble it with adherence to specifications, now prod their brains and pray for muscle memory to see them through. Supervisors hunt their files for copies of the assembly manuals for Gladiators and Sea Gladiators, and both Wing Commander Bartell and Foster Crayton try to check on everything and everybody every day.

Rudy continues to be pleased with Dr. Mazur's evaluation and praise of the increased engine boost pressure and longer permitted boost time enabled by the methane-water mist injection system and resulting lower engine operating temperatures on Rudy and Paul's old Bristol engine. The Polish expert now is discussing advanced notions about aircraft armament placement, cannon and machine gun effectiveness, deflection shooting using powered optical gunsights, and importantly, the value of shorter range gun harmonization than that currently used by the RAF. All of this and more the PZL aircraft designer and armament expert relates to Rudy as the Polish pilots experienced it during their brief but intensive air war with the Nazis. Rudy knows that, aside from Germany, PZL, the Polish Government's aircraft design and construction organization, was farther ahead than most other nations in designing ultra-contemporary aircraft.

Unfortunately, only a very few saw even prototype models built and tested before the Nazi blitzkrieg invasion overwhelmed them.

The gun harmonization business is especially interesting to the engineering side of Rudy. It involves the selection, from a range of choices, at which distance ahead of the plane the bullets it is firing will converge. The tight convergence, especially of relatively light weight rifle size machine gun ammunition such as British 303, is necessary to deal the heaviest structural damage. Often 30 caliber machine gun fire, and even 50 caliber, will go in one side of the targeted plane and out the other without hitting a vital sub-area. One advantage of the less expensive fabric covering on Gladiators, Rudy laughs to himself, and one advantage of the cannon fire he wishes they did have. Even some parts of the British Hurricane, he knows, are fabric covered, as is most of the Gladiator. Not so, however, of the Italian bombers he's been learning about, adding to the difficulty he hopes may never come to Malta.

Dr. Mazur believes that, because of the zero war time, shooting at enemy planes, lack of experience that so many British pilots suffer from, their wing guns, most often only one or two per wing, deliberately are aimed using their lateral deflection adjustment screws for long range convergence. With broad bullet spread from longer range, inexperienced pilots firing too early and too far from an enemy plane typically may score just a few hits, only a bit better than none. Rudy learns that the higher scoring Polish pilots ordered wing gun angles reduced to a shorter convergence point, some as tight as 150 to 200 yards in front of their planes, producing more lethal effects through closer approach. Only nose mounted guns pointing straight ahead avoid convergence and approach issues and this point, made by Dr. Mazur, leads Rudy to an aircraft design revelation.

He now begins to think more broadly about the immediate future of fighter plane design, seeing the advantage of twin engine fighters and ground support planes such as the Bf 110C, used during the Polish invasion as the primary German fighter, with wing guns replaced by various type multiple nose guns aimed straight ahead. This avoids the need for elaborate mechanisms which enable fuselage mounted guns, such as on Gladiators, to fire synchronized through a spinning propeller without hitting the prop blades. Or, Rudy realizes, a Gladiator's cylinder head or engine cowl, as could happen if a side gun were misaligned.

As work in the engine and armament laboratory races ahead, prompted by thoughts of air attacks on Malta and Dr. Mazur's stimulating presence, Rudy often thinks of his impending transfer to an American Air Force position helping to coordinate the design and ultimate output of American warplane manufacturers. He realizes he will need to think along broader and more complex lines than required here during what he now sees as his HRM/RAF internship on Malta. His newly added co-engineer has been telling him about the German experiments, so far very promising, with a new rocket powered fighter identified only as an Me 160 and displaying unbelievable climbing ability of over 30,000 feet per minute, using an advanced chemical mixture including methyl alcohol and water, as does Rudy's 'booster'. Much more exciting and promising, says Dr. Mazur, only farther out in time, is the extreme interest of several nations in what he terms turbo type engines leading to 'jet engines'. "How soon?" Rudy questions.

"If this war comes to your country," says the Doctor, "and lasts even just a couple of years, young propulsion engineers like you will begin designing totally different type engines and the prototype planes for other young men to fly in quite different types of air battles, believe me. But Rudy, your next and biggest challenge, as you have explained your coming assignment to me, likely will not have you designing detailed engine improvements or locating additional wing machine gun positions. Rather, I think you will have to help identify the types of planes your air force and the allies will need in order to carry out the missions required for victory, calculate how to get these type aircraft and performance requirements designed, tested, manufactured and delivered in the necessary quantities over very tight time periods, and how to get the untold finances necessary to pay for them. Which are Britain's current problems, plus the training of more pilots. In addition you will have to judge the winner of each government contract, which is fraught with troublesome problems.

"And all of this involving, what? I'd think at least a dozen or more American aircraft companies, each very eager to get contract approval, whether deserved or not. Of course you will be one of several officials engaging in this vital work, but it will still be the most difficult and complicated you can imagine. My work at PZL and in the types of problems we encountered in trying to build a viable national air force for our little country may be of interest to you. Obviously there is no direct carryover; our countries share very little in common, but our sad recent history has already produced some interesting lessons learned. And like you, I will depart Malta once whatever can be accomplished by our little group has been accomplished. Perhaps we could have a meal and a glass of wine together some evening so I can share my story with you? I believe you would find it informative." Rudy, eager to learn quickly as much as he can, instantly responds, suggesting the next evening, his treat at a nice Valletta restaurant he knows.

But first, his watch indicates that a call to Mrs. Osborne in Buffalo still may be possible this afternoon because of the time zone difference. As well he can check to learn if Foster, right here in the Shops, has cost estimates for the flat's rental fee and the transfer of the Crayton's household furnishings. As it turns out, Rudy connects on both counts.

Foster provides the figures, which Rudy believes are more than reasonable, and the concurrence of the rental agent for a month-by-month lease due to an uncertain coming year for Malta. From his call to Curtiss in Buffalo he learns that dear Mrs. Osborne, even while rushed with administrative duties at the very busy Curtiss plant, still believes that Rudy will eventually return to a position at the plant as promised by the Curtiss Aircraft Division President a year ago, and thus maintains a running tally of Rudy's HRN monthly earnings, deposited automatically in his now sizable Buffalo bank account, He has only to tell her what sum he wants transferred, she says, large or small, to his account at the Bank of Malta.

He thinks of what he estimates is more than he'll need for the flat, the ring Nina reminded him of, his wedding and related expenses, plus living expenses for two over several more months, and he doubles that amount to include costs to cover the trip to the States. He has no idea as yet of his remaining time with HRM, nor of the future earnings for the position mentioned by General Whittaker. Nor did he burden Mrs. Osborne with the uncertainty of his near-term future, including even the certainty of his marital state and his probable return home, but not to Curtiss. That can wait until more news comes from General Whittaker, and until he can work up enough courage to tell her what he needs the money for. As well, he is now reminded that he has yet to speak of his future and to express his gratitude to Governor General Garrison, Colonel Astill, and Mr. Farinacci, who certainly eased Rudy's entry to Malta and its people. But first tonight, and a full report to Nina of all he's accomplished. Perhaps he'll suggest that necessary trip to the jewelry store on Saturday? That, he knows, would be a smart move!

Nina has to be pleased with what Rudy has accomplished, but obviously something is wrong. When Rudy gently questions her that evening he sees tears running down her face. The thought of leaving her family, he learns, has finally caught up with her, and it shows. Before he can even begin to comfort her, however, she begins to rationalize her leaving them and Malta, her home for more then twenty years. She recites out loud that her sister is also leaving, that it will be for stated periods, not forever, and she will return often to see her parents and hopefully they will visit her in the United States once this damn war is over – if it ever starts. Her mother and grandmother will live safely up in Gozo at the farm if war really does appear, and her father would never leave Malta and his beloved Shops, anyway. Paul will do a lot better staying here and moving up in the same Shops hierarchy. The farm will keep them in food, should things grow short, and all of the things they're buying for the flat will be moved up to the farm when she and Rudy leave for their new jobs. Her recitation seems to calm her, and this is added to when Rudy cleverly suggests they fund some additions to the farm's chicken, rabbit, and goat pens as well as leaving some funding for hired extra help should Nina's grandmother and mother need it if her father and brother can't get up to Gozo every weekend. Not a great idea, Rudy admits, but it does give an extra lift to Nina's morale. Besides, she says, everyone is busy for now focusing on their wedding, and yes, Saturday morning would be a good time to pick out the ring, or maybe rings, including one for Rudy to wear 'forever', Nina only half jokes. Rudy surprises himself by rather liking that idea, and he adds that according to his Buffalo Bank savings account, expenses are not going to be a big problem. Besides, both of them are still employed and planning to remain so. They have much, she says, to be thankful for, now that they've found each other on this crazy island. "Just think,'" she adds, "we certainly have an exciting trip ahead of us, going half way around the world to both amazing Washington and exotic Watkins Glen," causing Rudy to gulp.

The dinner conversation between the two aeronautical engineers, one Polish and the other American, is taking place the following evening in that same restaurant from which began Rudy and Robert's adventure with the four 'bully boys', as Mr. Sanno once described them. This time Rudy is getting an education in the politics of aircraft corporation management. To illustrate, Dr. Mazur recounts the case history of how a country can have produced a world-beating, award winning fighter plane, starting with the 1929 P.1, at a national design and production facility named PZL, the Polish 'State Aviation Factory', established only a year earlier. Due to highly successful international demonstrations, eleven countries expressed strong interest in purchasing. Improvements over the next ten years through several successful iterations, the last being the P. 24/III, produced sales of as many as 136 planes to other countries prior to World War II. Licensing other countries for the manufacturing of 75 additional planes occurred as well, and this PZL income to Poland was welcomed and encouraged by the government.

During those same years, France produced a very similar looking gull wing radial engine fighter design, as did Romania, Sweden, and Russia. Rudy interjects that, "This might be viewed as adding insult to injury," His colleague retorts, "Business is not always pleasant and fair." As it turned out, the Polish government delayed an internal contract to supply its own air force with replacement model P. 24s until it was too late for the Nazi invasion of Poland last September, and Dr. Mazur pauses in his informal lecture for emphasis. He then points out that, to be fair, by that time nothing could match the German Me 109 anyway, including the model 24 or the brand new PZL design of a low wing monoplane P.50 fighter that was still in the prototype stage. PZL was not a facility that could, like Curtiss in America, produce hundreds each of several different type planes annually, nor did it have financial backing from the Polish government or elsewhere to enable expansion, or even the ability to allow foreign buyers to stretch out payments or trade planes for raw materials rather than money.

Important to realize, also, neither PZL nor any other Polish facility had the ability to design and produce engines for their own planes. Polish aircraft production was entirely at the mercy of such foreign engine manufacturers as France, Germany, and England, and that was hardly a great situation. This lacking was one reason why the Polish Air Force, with highly trained, courageous, skillful pilots was caught early on the ground, vastly outnumbered and out-gunned by the Luftwaffe last September.

"So, Rudy," he is asked, "what lessons may we draw from my tale that could possibly be useful in your coming position?" Rudy hesitates a few seconds and lists the need for clearly stated and enforced goals which are within the realm of the possible. PZL, with limited production capability, could not function as a foreign sales cash cow for Poland and, at the same time, provide sufficient fighters for its own air force. Second, highly successful aircraft designs should not be provided to others through licensing agreements or otherwise except, possibly, long-time, proven allies who won't leave examples lying about after retreating, waiting to be examined by the enemy. Next, without a sound understanding of the various mission requirements wisely judged necessary to conduct the war, designing and producing the wrong type planes, or attempting to design and build multipurpose models unable to fill any single design purpose with satisfaction, is a waste of time and resources. Very few fighter-bombers, Rudy imagines, are outstanding in both modes, although economy over functionality seems always popular. Rudy wonders if the several aircraft manufacturers in Poland, in addition to PZL, competed or cooperated in design work and resource availability such as engines? As the two lingered over dinner and wine, the list of lessons learned extends, sometimes with very evident applicability to Rudy's still loosely defined, upcoming job and other times as simply a non-transferable oddity in the PZL story. At any rate, Rudy is well satisfied with his new colleague's case presentation, as is Dr. Mazur with Rudy's attentiveness, and both with an evening of thought provoking concepts and good food – plus excellent Malta wine.

The next day Rudy is called to a planning meeting at the Governor's office, where Colonel Astill recounts the numbers of civilian volunteers recruited in the various categories necessary for both defense and for the health and general well-being of the Maltese people in the likely event of war. He is, he remarks, satisfied but not overjoyed with the results, recognizing that so many still can not believe that Italy would ever turn on Malta and actually bomb its age-old neighbor. Good recruiting results have developed, however, in that excellent supervisors and directors are now in position over the newly formed civil defense organizations, and regularized training is taking place. The digging out and construction of bomb shelters also is underway, but largely because of the immense tunnels and assembly places already in existence, some for centuries, dug during historical periods in Malta's past by the Knights as defense against Turkish invasions. For example, the existing Lascaris Military Operations Center itself is located in such a tunnel. Also available as a bomb shelter is the old, unused Malta Railway tunnel which extends for perhaps a half mile. The Colonel cautions that these and other old excavations – while fortunately located in the more densely populated areas of Valletta and the nearby crowded areas around the Grand Harbour and Port – need extensive electrical lighting, ventilation shafts, bunks, sanitary provisions, and more if they are to be of real use to even a small portion of the quarter million population.

The Governor then observes that the work of the initial planning group appears to be coming to a close, and that a somewhat different group, heavy with official and volunteer leaders of the defense and related groups begins meeting next week with him and Colonel Astill. Looking at Rudy, the Governor goes on to reveal that he is aware of Rudy's current work needs – the Shops will soon be extremely busy upgrading Gladiators – and that, sadly, there will soon be a new assignment for Rudy far from here. Happily, though, the union of Rudy and his much admired Nina will soon be made official – not as they recently arranged, but now absolutely official – and that Nina's talents will continue to be at the service of the English, only elsewhere. "So, Rudy," the Governor says, with Colonel Astill – Rudy's first RAF 'Friend' – nodding in accord, "we'll save our goodbyes for when you actually fly off, or board an English submarine for all I know, but today we'll give you the most genuine Thank You and It's Been Absolutely Great to Know You and Work With You message. We wish you and Nina the very best and safest future, and we consider you not only one of those special RAF Friends, but *our* friend. Now go back to the Shops before I become maudlin, which as Astill here knows, I never am!" After Rudy leaves the room, the Governor turns to his Aide and asks "What do you think about our young friend and his prospects as an officer in his Air Force, with the challenge of coordinating all those aircraft companies? Myself, I've never seen anyone mature as rapidly. He came here, I remember you saying, as a young man awed by his new assignment, a very different country, and an impending world war. He leaves having aged in experience and awareness of what makes the world go 'round by what seems like ten years crammed into one. We've helped him, you and I, in reaching what we now see in him." Major Astill looks at his Governor-General, nods, and says, "The two of us and Miss Nina Lafessi I'd judge!"

A day later, at the weekly informational session called by Captain Donalds, which Rudy has been missing with regularity, he learns that on April fourth Parliament gave Winston Churchill all defense responsibility, but not the freedom to make all defense decisions. He is not Prime Minister! "Unfortunately," mouths Foster, sitting next to Rudy. But the big news is that Germany invaded Denmark and Norway a few days ago, with Denmark surrendering in a half-day. Air and sea battles are developing between German forces and the British. Both Britain and France have sent troops, and British planes and warships are engaging. The Phoney War is over, Rudy learns, but he wonders out-loud why Hitler wants Norway. "Heavy Water," supplies Captain Donalds in answer, "the stuff that German scientists want for some obscure reason." Rudy says, "Thank you," still mystified, but determined to ask Dr. Mazur why heavier than usual water is worth fighting over. Captain Donalds continues listing items which he knows, he says, are of high interest to his leadership group. They include the decision to move the Curtiss Hawk from the airstrip up on Gozo down to either Hal Far or Luqa immediately before Malta is attacked, but how that attack's date and time will be foreseen is yet to be determined. Apparently the two Polish pilots and their mechanic have experience in flying and maintaining the Netherlands built Koolhoven monoplane fighter, but very limited experience at that, so Rudy is asked to begin the next day with some kind of orientation to the Hawk beyond that which Paul Lafessi has been providing. All are aware that, while the Koolhoven looks like the Hawk, there are significant differences. Once it becomes operational during war, the Hawk's relocation to a main Malta airfield with fuel, ammunition, technicians, and instant communication with the Gladiators will be essential.

Just before the end of April, two events will occur which will alter Rudy's life, one having immediate but somewhat brief impact, the other, as he will learn, very long lasting impact. The latter, scheduled for Sunday, April 28, he had been alerted to by Nina some weeks before, and he will prove to be well prepared for his role. Some might judge that his preparation will have occurred simply by following the bride's instructions, but he had added several embellishments without consulting her, and this had earned him, as he later described it, several extra points. Weeks ago, when Nina had asked him to prepare a list of those friends he would like to invite to their church wedding and reception on what his friend Robert was calling 'the big day', he had instantly produced a list of twelve names, with Foster Crayton's already marked as 'Best Man'. He told her, also, that he had been measured twice for a custom tailored suit for the occasion that would serve also as his 'traveling suit' before eventually getting an American officers uniform. The rings, of course, had been selected, engraved with initials and the wedding date, and entrusted to Foster who would produce them during the ceremony.

Including Nina's friends, close family members and other relatives, friends of Nina's parents, and those on Rudy's invitation list, a hundred or so people attend the wedding at the family church and the reception following at a nearby hall. There is universal agreement that the Bride is a beautiful angel in a gorgeous gown and that the American Groom, while well dressed, hardly deserves such a prize. The Kappillan does a splendid ceremony in his own language, with nods and smiles to Rudy, He is, indeed, the same priest who had scared off the four thugs attacking Rudy and Robert, and who had later conducted the blessing ceremony of the Hawk.

It had not occurred to Rudy to inquire who had been selected for the "Maid of Honor", as it is called in the United States. Remembering that Nina's sister Mila was being sent to her aunt in England to attend college there, he assumed that Nina had selected one of her friends. He is astounded, therefore, to watch Mila, dressed in a gown and walking slowly down the church aisle as Maid of Honor, preceding the Bride. He didn't dare to question Nina about this mystery until after the ceremony when, reaching the reception hall, she answered before he even asked.

"Do you remember Colonel DiPalma, in Sicily, suggesting that he could advise Mr. and Mrs. Worth, the newlyweds, on the best route back to America through neutral countries such as Italy, Spain, and Portugal when they returned home to the United States? Well, Mila succeeded in missing her ship voyage date to London because she stubbornly refused to miss her only sister's wedding." To make a long story short, Nina tells her Groom that she phoned Rose in Catania and asked her to find out how Mila could fly to London the safest way through neutral countries. The excuse given was that Mila would visit her mother's sister in England, her Aunt Margaret, using her neutral Malta passport, After a few weeks she would return home the reverse way. The safe, neutral flights were promptly identified at the Catania Military Operations Center, courtesy of the Regia Aeronautica Colonel, and the tickets were purchased by the Lafessi family in Malta, but only one way. "Nina is leaving Malta for England tomorrow," says Nina to Rudy, "but please forget what I just told you. Naturally I had to tell Mr. Sanno because of the visa business and Mila leaving for the college in England. He guessed that the Colonel most likely figures that you and I are leaving Malta for America through neutral countries and going by neutral airlines, just as he recommended to you when we were in Catania. Let's hope the Colonel doesn't check passenger manifests, and continue to hope and pray that he never catches on to Rose. Now, lets visit the food and drinks at our reception, say thanks to people for attending our wedding, and act like we're newlyweds who never had a practice week in sunny Sicily! By the way, have you noticed that the Governor-General and his Aide are here? That's so nice of them to come, and our friends the Farinaccis also!"

Even though Rudy declined taking a few days off for a honeymoon, Foster insisted on at least a day or two so they could move into the flat and unpack, as he put it. Rudy actually did take the Monday off, but returns Tuesday morning because he is phoned the news very early: some number of crates of Gloster Sea Gladiators will be craned off the deck of a British aircraft carrier that afternoon and trucked, towed, or dragged if necessary, directly to the Kalafrana shops. "How many?" he asks. "We'll know when they get here!" he is told. There had been no prior notice of delivery, but no one complains. With a quick explanation to a still sleepy Nina, Rudy heads immediately for the Shops, knowing that much work will be needed over what may be too short a time frame. Now that the Phoney War is over, he, Dr. Mazur, and Paul are going to be swamped with Mercury engine work and the other upgrades.

CHAPTER 31

CAN WAR BE FAR BEHIND

Malta
Early May 1940

THE first problem Rudy encounters in his new role as husband occurs when he picks up the car keys for the Red Rover from their new official bowl on the entry table near the flat's door. He's half way out the door when Nina calls from their bedroom, "How am I to get to work if you take the car to the shops?" Ten minutes later Rudy has succeeded in the fifth try to get his old motorcycle started. He pulls out from the parking lot behind the apartments, hunched over, and heads for work.

Today the crated Gladiators would arrive, he was told, and he needs to get his engine laboratory ready to operate, and Paul and Dr. Mazur ready as well. Because he isn't responsible for the uncrating and assembly of the planes, he assumes Foster is already at work and planning where the actual putting together and wing rigging work will be carried out. As soon as the engines are bolted in place, Rudy will begin trying to get the injection systems and small tanks jammed into what he hopes will be sufficient space just behind the engines, a space already impossibly crowded with everything from a starter handle pickup just ahead of the bulkhead to the magnetos and the air intake casting plus the two oil cooler tubes. And much more, all essential. The Gladiator mechanics at RAF Station Tangmere had told him they thought it could be done, but all Rudy and Paul had to practice on was the Mercury engine from the wrecked Bristol, mounted on a Shop test stand surrounded by open space. Rudy remains optimistic, since the boost injection certainly improved the Mercury. He just has to hope for enough space and not too much extra weight.

At the Shops he sees that Dr. Mazur and Foster have come in together from their RAF housing, and Paul has arrived early with his father also, hours early, not wanting to be late for the exciting event. However, being loudly announced just then by Captain Donalds and Wing Commander Bartell hurrying into the Shops office, the HMS Eagle, a small and older aircraft carrier was right now, very early, preparing to tie up or anchor and have lifted off by crane six crated Gloster Gladiators destined for the Kalafrana Shops at the Kalafrana Seaplane Base. These to be signed for by the local Air Officer Commanding. Everyone runs outside and immediately into George, who is hurrying toward the office door. "George," shouts Foster, "where is the carrier with the planes?" George comes to an immediate halt and replies "It's crates it's got, so it's headed for the cranes. Where else would it go? The crates can't fly off the deck on their own. It's going to be time before we can haul the six of them up here into the Shops. Where do you want them put, Mr. Crayton, once we get them here? One at a time, I guess."

Foster, who is well accustomed to George's approach to heavy lifting tasks, says, "Yes George, we know they're crated. Just round up as many helpers as you'll need to get the crates. Line them up outside the entry doors for the two big side hangars. Each inside, and then drop the long side of the crate down to the floor so we can tally the contents and set the unpacking group to work. Then the assigned assembly team for each crate will take the unloading. I'll work out six assembly space areas, three for each of the hangars. Now that we know we're not getting fly-offs, which would have been nice, I might use just one really experienced wing assembly and rigging team for all six, and another for the engine and accessories, but I'll see how the RAF leaders and the tech supervisors judge it. Probably faster to have each team operate independently and just have the wing and engine supervisors check each one to be sure? A goodly number of our men have many years of experience doing this. Be faster if we didn't have to tow each one down that damn road to Hal Far and put the wings back on. There must be an easier way? And we'll want hangar space or camouflaged revetments for each." George having already dashed away, hopefully in the direction of the HMS Eagle's six crates, the others still clustered around Foster understand that he is really talking to himself as he fine tunes his plan to create six somewhat outdated biplane fighters from the contents of six large crates and get them up to the Hal Far so-called runway.

The important question on Rudy's mind has to do with the serial numbers of the six. The numbers could be possible indicators of the engine series, top wing universal attachment points for two additional machine guns, existing type of machine guns, type of propeller fitted, additional weight of Sea Gladiator special fittings, compressed air and oxygen tank locations, prop spinner, radio mast, downward light, and approximate age of at least the airframe.

Dr. Mazur has his own mental list in addition to Rudy's, and he's added the idea of armor plate just behind the pilot's seat, assuming some is available and the addition is possible. More added weight! Like Rudy, he certainly is interested in adding to the Gladiator's firepower, so he also hopes the planes they get have the upper wing gun mounts – or at least the possibility of adding something up there, someway, especially a cannon and a few rounds to surprise the bombers. The newer gunsights certainly would help. He'll check the horizontal harmonization of the wing guns, and is curious to see if the Gladiator has a streamlined rear view mirror for the pilot, as the Spitfires and a few Hurricanes do. Most important, though, is his strong interest in having his two Polish pilots talk with whomever the RAF selects as Gladiator pilots about joint tactics against the anticipated Italian bombers and fighters, each type reported as faster than the British biplanes. God forbid, he thinks, that the Germans loan a couple of Me109s to the Regia Aeronautica. That would likely be the end of Malta's beginning air arm. Only a little later will he and Rudy get to meet with the anti aircraft crew officers and learn the details of how the Hal Far fighters can force flights of bombers into the box barrages of AA exploding shells the Maltese gunners will set up, likely having better results in downed bombers than the Gladiators and Hawk combined!

In due time, of course, the six crates are muscled into the hangars and the front side of each crate is unbolted and lowered to the floor. It's a wonder that no one is injured by the process. At each crate eager spectators as well as the Shop technicians and mechanics accumulate, trying to help get the long, tall crate side unfastened and lowered out of the way and at the same time peer at the insides' carefully packed contents as the side is lowered, sometimes with a crash. Each does contain a dismantled, "un-erected"

Sea Gladiator complete with arresting hook for carrier landings and an emergency dinghy stored between the landing gear legs. A few pounds of weight to be removed to make way for some new additions, Rudy and Dr. Mazur hope. As Foster had planned, six teams are assigned, one to each Gladiator crate, but continuing checks by the engine and airframe RAF supervisors rotate among the erecting and assembling crews of technicians and mechanics – almost all experienced long term Maltese employees of the Kalafrana Shops.

After getting more than their share of peeks into the crates being unpacked, Rudy, Paul, and Doctor Mazur retreat to their engine workroom to lay out the misting equipment, anticipating that, if it can be installed in one engine compartment successfully, it can be fitted into all, assuming there are enough complete kits in the boxes sent by HRM's Ian Standish. As Paul points out, however, the real key to success after the initial test of each engine lies with the volume of methanol available – also sent by Standish – and the availability of 100 octane fuel. Before this could even be pondered by the three, Robert appears in the workroom's doorway and calls to Rudy. "There's a call come for you, Rudy, on Foster's line to London, so I guess you had better hustle over and take it."

Rudy looks up, nods, and hustles to a call from the highest ranking RAF officer he knows, Air Vice Marshal James Conners. "Rudy," the voice from London says, "Jim Conners here and I need a favor. A very quietly done favor for some information needed rather quickly here in RAF London, gathered outside of the formal communication channels and reports we undoubtedly will receive from RAF Malta at some later date. Don't misunderstand; this is not a spying request. We simply need to respond to a Royal Navy urgent question for information pertaining to some hazy number of Gloster Gladiators and Sea Gladiators which may be lost, strayed, stolen, misplaced, or otherwise not able to be located with certainty by the search dogs of our Royal Navy. Since you, an innocent neutral American assigned by HRM to assist the Governor-General of Malta with defense planning are available, I trust, to make a quick local inquiry about said Gladiators and any past or present relationship to Malta, I am requesting such an inquiry. I ask for a timely response telephoned directly, and only, to me. Rudy, is that hurried but long presentation from me understandable, and can you pull that information together quickly and phone it to me on a secure line?"

Rudy's answer is shorter than the question asked. "Yes, I think I understand what's needed in this instance, and I'll excuse myself today and tomorrow from working with some important supplies which arrived just yesterday and get a telephoned response to you on this inquiry before the end of business in London tomorrow. I'm glad to help and I'll speak with you ASAP. Is there anything else? If not, fine, and thank you for your support of our work here. Talk with you later. Goodbye."

Oh Lord, thinks Rudy, just what we need, an order to send them back. The hell we will! Let's see what I can come up with, and try to do it without going above the Kalafrana Wing Commander, if I can.

After instructing Paul to get word to him immediately the first plane is available for their work to insert the misting kit – this afternoon, this evening, or tomorrow – Rudy goes to his file of notes and Robert's minutes of the Wing Commander's meeting last July. He recalls this is the meeting where Bartell explained the confusion and rumors over the question of crated Gladiators being stored on Malta for transport to other locations or to assigned aircraft carriers. Both Rudy's jotted notes taken at the meeting, and Robert's later distributed minutes record Bartell's apologetic uncertainty concerning the number of planes crated, stored, and awaiting transport to elsewhere, and the reasons for uncertainty of count and assigned aircraft serial numbers, including the loss of one Gladiator to a crash at sea. Indeed, Bartell's oral report skirted entirely the serial number business, but included the mention of the HMS Glorious and the assembly of some planes for service on that ship as Squadron #802, flying off on 6 June 1939. Described as "to the best of my knowledge and confusing records", Bartell declared no crated Royal Navy aircraft on Malta as of that July 1939 meeting. As he perused his notes, Rudy realized that it was at that very meeting that he first met and reported his engine upgrade work to Captain Donalds, still now the Administrative Deputy to the RAF Air Officer Commanding.

Just minutes later, after finding the Wing Commander returning to his office from viewing the partial uncrating of a plane, Rudy asks for a moment of Bartell's time. Seated now in his office, Rudy says he's preparing a quick Gladiator report including newly arrived Gladiators. He remembers the Governor-General's July 1939 requested meeting and how the Wing Commander described Malta's uncertain history concerning its role in Gladiator storage. Rudy wonders, "how on earth the Commander figured it all out?" Bartell, not at all questioning the purpose of Rudy's report, says his task that July day did not require extensive research. He simply used what was provided to him when he inquired of Captain Donalds for historical records which could aid him in his task. Next day or two the Captain gave Bartell several older files provided unofficially, Bartell thinks, by someone of either the group at Naval Staff or possibly someone in stores records at Malta's Admiralty House. Bartell didn't inquire the source since they obviously looked official, and required only his copying aircraft identification numbers and dispositions. He still had the copied information in his meeting files, he was sure, and in a few minutes was handing it to Rudy. "Here, use this if it helps in some way with detailing what you need, and return them to my office whenever. Now, shouldn't you get back to doing your improvement business on my Hal Far Fighter flight, now finally arrived?"

With heartfelt thanks to Wing Commander Bartell and concealed wonderment at a form of aircraft accounting he'll want to beware of in his future assignment, Rudy hurries back to the Shops area. He is in search of an unused office where he can prepare a listing which is accurate, but which continues the confusion over what is now being unpacked just yards away. After all, the Hawk arrived in Malta in a similar way and is still here! Obfuscation, he thinks, may be a useful guide, since he highly suspects that Ian Standish was replaced by James Conners in this caper, as Ian's one Hawk now has six Gladiators to share the workload, and the Royal Navy may be seeking a culprit. By now Rudy has found an empty office and he begins by studying the aircraft and disposition lists.

Fortunately, Rudy realizes, he has been asked to telephone his findings, and not write out a report. In a sense he is to provide information orally plus suggestions for creating a bit of a tone of honest confusion over what has been Malta's complex role for decades in support of the air requirements of first the Royal Navy, plus some needs of the Royal Air Force. Malta's strategic position has long created a demand for its involvement in the Empire's business and defense. Complete understanding of Malta's role in the Royal Naval Air Service includes the long history of the airfield called Hal Far, but officially identified by the Royal Navy as HMS Falcon, as though it were a ship, heavily used in the late 1920s and 1930s.

It is both a land airfield for Fleet Air Arm planes, and actively flying carrier based planes as well. Despite the very heavy military usage of Hal Far and occasionally the two other airfields, prior to the outbreak of the war on September 1, 1939, little or no thought was given to the defense of Malta. The popular determination is still that Malta is indefensible due to its location so close to Sicily and so far from Alexandria to the east and Gibraltar to the west. The fear still exists on the island that Parliament could trade Malta, and more, to Hitler for continued peace.

Rudy drafts an outline of his coming phone call to Jim: several squadrons of Gladiators, Swordfish, Fairey, and other aircraft came on and off the Island numerous times over the years, and many replacement aircraft were dropped off in crates or flown in from carriers. These could be, and were, stored at Port facilities, at Hal Far, on or near the flying boat slipway, alongside the Kalafrana Shops or within if being erected, always being held until the assigned carriers or cargo ships could arrive as scheduled. However, scheduled arrivals did not always happen as scheduled, and carriers were redirected from time to time on other assignments. Records often needed to be amended.

Although exact records have proven difficult to identify, Rudy scribbles that apparently 24 Gladiators were sent to Malta on the HMS Glorious in 1939, six having been sourced from 801 Squadron and eighteen from 802. Of these 24, one was lost prior to 9/39; one crashed while training at sea, six were delivered to Alexandria, nine left on HMS Glorious when she sailed last month (April), and seven were remaining in crates on Malta, apparently scheduled, it is believed, for departure on HMS Eagle or another vessel. A shipment of six crated sea Gladiators arrived by vessel recently, destined for a very small Hal Far Fighter group to protect the Naval Air Station and Malta itself from anticipated Italian bombers, should war be declared on England by Italy. It may be that three planes will form an active patrol, with one held in active reserve. The two remaining will serve as spares and also as source for needed parts. The "N" numbers of the six are: 5519, 5520, 5523, 5524, 5529, and 5531.

Malta's Royal Governor-General has urgently requested and authorized this fighter flight, pilots to be drawn from the existing qualified RAF staff, some of whom are in administrative positions while waiting for the Governor-General's defensive group to made operational. The pilots will be directed by Air Controllers under Malta's Joint Royal Navy, Army, and Air Emergency Operations Center located within the Lascarus tunnel.

Rudy reads and rereads what he's composed, consults his watch, and sets out to try to get a secure phone line to the Air Vice Marshal, a day sooner than anticipated. Unless, he fears, more is requested. He hopes not, for there *is* no more without getting into some troublesome areas. Foster's secure line to London is available, Foster's office is still empty of Foster, and Rudy pulls his card with Jim's number still readable. The office door is closed, the call is placed, and Jim is asking only for a second as he reaches for a pad to jot down Rudy's very prompt findings and as Rudy advises, his thoughts about the value of confusing records in instances such as these. "After all, " Rudy says, "if the Fleet Air Arm had excellent records they wouldn't have asked the RAF in the first place." "Only'" Jim replies, "if they wanted to catch us up to save their own skins, do you think?"

Jim understands Rudy's point about honest obfuscation, but is hopeful that there will be no demand for the return of the six planes just now being assembled. He's also talked to the new Air Officer Commanding, Captain Donalds' boss, and asked him to line up the local Admiral on their side, should that be needed. The thinking, if push comes to shove, is that if the RAF can find pilots on Malta at this time, the Royal Navy can damn well provide a few old biplanes still in crates to defend the island! Rudy can hardly argue with that. But Rudy's carefully phrased insistence from the Governor-General that a fighter flight, even if small, be supplied and formed immediately is 'the way to go' should the wrong questions be asked in London. Further, Jim is highly pleased with the listing Rudy's read to him over the phone, no matter who supplied it. That those details were provided from Navy documents is even better. So Jim is hopeful and Rudy is pleased with the mild praise he's gotten for this quick response to a tricky issue.

Now, he hurries back to Paul and Dr. Mazur in the engine lab. They greet him with their concern that the limited supply of methane to be used for greater engine boost will never be enough for six flying Gladiators. Could they get some idea from the Wing Commander, for example, just how the planes will be used? Maybe not all six should get added boost... and Rudy interrupts, saying that he would like to see a three plane patrol or interceptor force established, with a fourth on standby reserve, ready to go. The two remaining would be hangared as the source of repair parts, unless they are absolutely needed as fighters. But in truth, with no actual experience and no relevant knowledge base except what he learned at Tangmere, he has no real idea. He suspects, he offers, that the local RAF hierarchy has not yet had time to decide how best to use these precious new resources, anyway. Rudy will consult with the RAF leaders no later than tomorrow morning.

For now, they decide, all attention will be paid to the first plane assembled, and thus the first eligible for their engine upgrade attempt. First will be the regular steps necessary for an engine run up, just to be sure everything done thus far is right, tight, and proper. This includes all mechanics' tools removed from the engine compartment, all necessary fluids added, pneumatic system and compressed air cylinders OK, with the battery fastened down. Once these and the many other checks are made, everything taking more time than Rudy anticipated, the engine is turned over and then started. Oil pressure is quickly noted, mags checked, and final inspections made and verified, the engine is shut down and the plane turned over to Rudy.

Paul's fine understanding of the how and why of a 50/50 water-methane injection system spliced into the carb airflow of an already supercharged engine makes Rudy proud and willing to let Paul play the lead in planning out where all the component parts will hopefully fit, including the additional fluid tank, hoses, pump, connectors, and injection nozzle. The added weight of the parts, but most especially the fluid tank containing the 50/50 mix may well be the deciding factor. Just the 50/50 mix weighs 7.5 pounds a gallon. Rudy's been told that British engineering evaluations of that secret Bf 109 the RAF has hidden away at RAF Biggin Hill, the one he saw, indicate that its MW-50 water methanol injection system seems to increase the engine horse power in that inverted V 12 from about 1,475 horsepower to about 1,800. "That's a bit more than 20%," he proclaims, "and to be exceedingly overly optimistic, that percentage increase would take the Gladiator's Mercury engine from about 830 horsepower to about 950. The factory manual boost override will take it now to just about 840 horses. It's worth a try, and if it runs cooler, a pilot should be able to get more boost time safely than now."

Several days and long evenings later, Nina gets to hear Rudy coming up the stairs to their flat, opening the door, and saying in a tired but happy voice, "We've finished three systems, thanks to your brother Paul's skill, and we're stopping while we're ahead. Only one's been up, and the pilot reports a significant improvement over one we didn't do that tried to catch him to compare. Climbs a lot faster, flies faster, and runs cool long enough for us to say it works. They're figuring the Hawk will already be waiting up on top, unseen, and the Gladiators can match the bomber's speed and then some if radar and the spotters do their thing. So the RAF fly boys are excited. Do you think Rose and Johnny will follow through? That would be something! Right now I'm tired, I'm hungry, and I'm...Ahhh, you gorgeous devil, you guessed."

The Shops are busy now, having decided that not every one of the six Sea Gladiators will get a full upgrade treatment, so three bladed metal props and spinners appear immediately on some but not all. Radios and proper antenna as well as 100 octane fuel, carefully measured out, are provided all, and happily the newer gunsights are already in place. Dr. Mazur is hard at experimenting with one plane, seeking to equip it with either two additional machine guns for a total of six, or installing two cannon underwing pods on the bottom wing in place of the two browning pods, for a 2/2 combination. All are getting a streamlined rear view mirror and he is talking with the Wing Commander about a steel backplate to the pilot's seat. The carrier arresting hooks and sea dinghies have already disappeared, but of course their weight is being quickly replaced.

At least as important are the scheduled orientation sessions for the RAF volunteer pilots, who as Robert said, "Are coming out of the woodwork to get on the favored list. A couple have been float plane and larger flying boat pilots, and a few have experience flying the old stringbag Swordfish. One had a brief experience with a Sea Gladiator on a carrier. Understandably, they are quite extremely light on fighter plane combat flying. For that reason, with Dr. Mazur as the interpreter, the RAF volunteer Sea Gladiator pilots and the more experienced Polish Hawk pilots are spending long sessions discussing combat tactics, joint tactics with the Hawk, gun harmonization and deflection shooting using the newer gunsights, economy of ammo use, gun and run, dog fights, jinxing, break right/left, use of the sun, thumbing the sun, use of the tail view mirror including when you're on an enemy's tail yourself, evasive tactics, use of boost, use of flaps, rapid climb, side slipping, crosswind take off and landing, emergency landing, use of parachute, communication with ground control, radio directed intercept, engine fire procedure, and with Gloster Gladiators the necessity to never relax your guard when taxiing, taking off, landing, or on roll out. They handle well in the air but are beasts on the ground! And never lessen attention while flying in formation, never fly victory rolls before landing lest your bullet-nicked control wire let go just then, turn your head and look around at least every ten seconds, and don't fly straight and level in enemy or questionable territory.

Tactics in cooperation with the searchlight controllers and with the high and medium altitude anti-aircraft gun officers are emphasized. The mystery of the deadly box barrage as an anti-aircraft tactic is discussed and practiced with Gladiators as the directional pushers, as are ground controlled intercepts. And in all of this, Italian aircraft identification from below, above, front, rear, and side, becomes almost a game. As well, the Hawk's various profiles are stressed to the RAF pilots. The favorite topics, of course, to both the RAF pilots and the Hawk pilots, are those practiced in the air, even while observing limited fuel restrictions.

In the midst of the flying and related excitement, and all of the group meetings, orientations, and classes, Foster Crayton, Squadron Leader Slingerland as the Command Engineer Officer, and Rudy as the planning consultant are agreeing to and executing the decisions which will put the entire Shops, and especially the aircraft maintenance and repair departments, on full war footing. Much of what they are implementing comes from information gathered by Rudy at RAF Tangmere. Just as Tangmere is exposed by proximity to the Luftwaffe airbases, the Kalafrana Shops, with their huge glassed-in walls and ceilings, are exposed to the nearby Regia Aeronautica bases. Moving the vulnerable aircraft and rescue launch maintenance and repair locations, parts supplies, and tool cribs of Kalafrana is of vital concern, but with no obvious quick and easy solution.

On Sunday May 5th, one week after the wedding and five days after the Gladiator delivery, at a quiet at-home anniversary dinner for two, Nina makes the mistake of asking Rudy what he thinks the next few months might bring them, her family in Sliema, and Malta, her homeland. Rudy answers, but taken up with the missing Gladiators, the challenges of really moving the Kalafrana aircraft repair shop, the local weak wagering odds on a real war where Italy attacks its old friend Malta, and the strong isolation-istic position of the United States Congress limiting the supportive action of President Roosevelt toward England, he voices the opinion that, as he jokes, the *status quo* will remain as is."Oh," he admits, "at work we're trying to plan ahead. The RAF types seem to think war's coming and the military here should be strengthened, but some say the military types are always too eager to get ready. The Governor-General's Planning Group, of which I was a very active member, has softened its tone, though, and the limited air raid shelter situation remains about the same. Until and if Hitler continues grabbing land in Europe, and until the Prime Minister stops talking about peace in our time, I suspect most of the remainder of this year will look like last year's. Remember, I haven't heard another word about our trip to Washington in quite a while. Besides, if something does come up and we have to leave here, all of our household stuff will be trucked to your par-ent's house in Sliema, and we'll leave them our car and extra money to tide them over, even if your mother decides to go live on the Gozo farm. Can you really picture Colonel DiPalma sending bombers to Gozo? I don't think so. Next year? Who knows? Roosevelt may convince Congress to really help England, and that would discourage Hitler, I would think. By then we both may have new jobs in America anyway. You know, Watkins Glen is eager to meet you, the very lucky Malta girl who captured my heart! Wait, stop, I'm kidding. Don't throw it! That dish was a wedding present!" A quiet one week anniversary spent at home.

But later that same week, on Friday May 10th in spite of Rudy's reassurances, his faulty crystal ball shatters. Germany under Hitler's command invades the so called low countries, Belgium, Netherlands, and Luxembourg, obviously on the way to France. The Phoney War has really ended and a World War begun. England's Prime Minister Neville Chamberlain resigns, and President Roosevelt's friend, Winston Churchill, becomes an entirely new type of Prime Minister. Malta will soon change dramatically as well, moving closer to its later unwanted title as *"The Most Bombed Place On Earth"*. And so will rapid change impact the immediate plans of the newlyweds.

It's no surprise that next day, Saturday, the administrative offices at the Shops are filled with staff, from high ranking officers to Foster, Robert, Rudy, and Dr. Mazur, the civilians. All have been talking for many weeks about what they would do if war came to Malta, and now it seems prudent to carry out those plans, even though nothing official has been declared as yet, and Italy is still as neutral as the United States. In a noticeable way, so is Malta. But how to begin is answered quickly by noontime, as the Air Officer Commanding directs Captain Donalds to place all RAF and related personnel at "Action Stations". Since no enemy is apparent as yet, this is generally interpreted as concluding final internal agreements concerning preparation for a possible attack.

Thus Rudy is not surprised to hear that the Hawk will be flown to Hal Far early on Sunday morning and quietly hangared far back from the earthen runways. Both its pilots and their mechanic will now be on standby here at Hal Far, as will be the four upgraded Sea Gladiators and the two designated as spares. The Hal Far Fighter Flight, staffed by the volunteer RAF pilots and Shops technicians, mechanics, armorers, and various other ground crew will begin shift assignments on Monday. By noon that day, all four duty planes shall be fueled and armed, but still hangared out of sight. Various old vehicles, large earth moving equipment, large waste containers, and similar hindrances shall be identified and made ready to block the runway strip from enemy planes landing. This and more is fed through Action Stations!

The AOC and selected others will meet on Sunday or Monday with anti-aircraft gun and searchlight officers as well as Air Control Officers from Lascarus to confirm final protocols and agreements. The Governor-

General will be briefed and consulted, and RAF London will be advised of local preparations and asked for orders and guidance. Adrenalin flows and nervous excitement reigns, whether you are RAF, civilian, or an American consultant. The Polish pilots and Dr. Mazur check and recheck, and the mechanic spends much time examining the gun belts and the rotating cannon shell containers. Tingling with excitement inside, Rudy takes all of this without any visible outward sign to others. This is until Robert, who has just ridden a bicycle back to the Shop office from the Hal Far strip, nervously tells Rudy he has just seen perhaps a hundred men circling the airbase, all in rough civilian clothing and all carrying hunting rifles. "What the hell for?" Rudy squeaks. Robert's answer, "To shoot the parachutists someone said!" causes Rudy to step back. He now remembers Colonel Astill describing that arrangement with some pride at a planning meeting. *Oh God*, he thinks. *This is war!*

CHAPTER 32

ACTION STATIONS

Malta, England, France, United States
May 1940

WHILE Monday is indeed a busy day at the Kalafrana Shops and at Hal Far, Takali, and Luqa airports on Malta, it is even a busier day in an area in northeast France, Sedan, where German Paratroops have landed and a General named Erwin Rommel, soon to become much better known, leads his 7th Panzer tank division into units of the French army. By the next day, Tuesday May 14th, Dutch military resistance stops and their government shifts to England rather than surrender. In an early attempt to halt or slow down German troop advances against the French, the RAF is called to action. In flights to aid the French on Friday the 10th, plus Saturday and Sunday, the RAF sends Fairey Battle "day bombers" on three missions, fighter escort if available.

Friday's mission sees 13 of 32 Battles lost and the remainder shot-up by ground fire. Seven of eight are shot down on Saturday's attempt, and on Sunday all five, flown by volunteer crews, are lost. By Wednesday the RAF likely lost approximately 100 Battles and Blenheim bombers, 50 of them in just a 72 hour period. The French military and government are pleading with Prime Minister Churchill to send not only more British troops, but many more RAF planes, else all is lost. Winston Churchill, fearing the British Isles will be attacked and invaded shortly, sees no way to send the requested aid. That nothing can be spared for Malta at this time is obvious to Malta's Governor-General, the RAF Mediterranean Officer Commanding, the Mediterranean Royal Navy Admiral who, a least for now, is an admiral without ships, and just about everyone else concerned over current war events on Malta and Gozo. Indeed, before another two weeks pass, the near utter disaster at Dunkirk will prove the pessimists right. For France, one might say that all *is* lost, at least for now.

Rudy has been resolved not to get trapped by his sharp thinking wife into offering any further predictions concerning the immediate future of their own micro situation in Malta or the macro situation of her country as part of the British empire. He is pushed into such a discussion one evening, however, when she offers that, in staff conversations in her Starline Shipping office, far less than half report not being surprised at all by Germany's hostile actions and expect Mussolini to align Italy with the Nazis and invade Malta soon. The others, more than half, were astounded that anyone could even imagine that peaceful Malta and its ages-old friend, dear Italy, would ever wage real war. But were not Malta's defense and safety being short-changed by the British? "Possibly," was answered, "but hasn't that always been true? Why should now be any different? All of this recruiting of volunteers from our neighborhoods is just show to keep us quiet. War is good for business and that's what counts on the negotiating table. Stop puzzling over it and stop worrying about it! Things will be worked out between Malta and our cousins in Italy as they always have."

Rudy just can't keep still with what he sees as nonsense, and he jumps in, saying "We'll be in a war this summer, and they'll see Mussolini and Hitler walking arm in arm over all the parts of Europe they can get by hook or crook. We're in a world war right now. All that's missing is the U.S. And I'll bet that will happen this year or next, especially if France and England can't hold Germany down. They're not thinking straight. The world has changed!"

Nina looks at him and says, "Does this mean you've reversed your thinking, Mr. Status Quo? Will all your old girl friends in Watkins Glen now get to see this extremely fortunate and lucky Malta girl who – what was it? – won your heart? You've changed your mind? Where do we stand with those fascinating jobs you thought we were getting? If I'm going to leave here we need to go before my anxiety changes my mind. As I'm sure you can see, dear husband, we're going to *your* family and country, and I hope you can understand that I'm having trouble thinking about leaving *mine*. Rudy, what's our situation now that the real war has started? Have you heard anything and not told me?" As she says all this her shoulders shake and her voice grows louder.

Fortunately, Rudy has learned how to respond when Nina starts to tremble, and he moves to her, puts his arms around her, and quietly says, "I've heard nothing new as yet, but with the fighting starting in earnest now, and France invaded, I'm sure I'll hear very soon just what the plan is for Mr. and Mrs. Worth. I'm not keeping anything from you, and I won't. Hold on and give it a couple more days. In the mean time, let's work out the details of turning over our stuff to your parents and whatever else you want to do to ease things for them if we think Malta will get impacted by the war. I know how I feel about leaving. Right now Malta is my home, my job, and where we fell in love, and I haven't been in the States in what feels like years. It's very difficult for me to think of leaving my second home if real trouble starts, believe me. So we'll just support each other through this uncertain time and make the best decisions we can. OK? If Malta and Gozo do get involved in the war, I certainly would feel terrible having to leave my co-workers and close friends and retreat back to the US, but we'll do what we have to. I love you and our being together is the most important thing by miles in my life, so together we'll do what's right for us, and we'll go wherever and do whatever together, no matter what, even a war! I know we won't be the only couple having to work it out. OK? And even a world war won't last forever! We'll be back here before you know it, and it will still be Malta!"

A few days later, on Friday Rudy is called to an unannounced meeting at the Governor's office. Colonel Astill and Mr. Sanno are both present, and surprise, so is Nina. The Governor is all smiles, both notice, and he apologizes for calling Nina and Rudy together, but jokingly blames it on Mr. Sanno. The Malta "visa , passport, and secret agent" as Nina sometimes refers to him, smiles, turns to Nina and presents her with an official United States of America Passport. "Here's a real one this time. I hope you like your photo; we used the same one as before. Now be sure to destroy the earlier one, as the ID numbers are different. Also, keep your British one and carry it with you when you leave for the States. I'm told by my London office that you'll be assigned to the Malta/Mediterranean group at our embassy, specializing in the Malta area and also shipping in the Med. You'll be happy, I imagine, that the work will keep you in contact with people and events here, including my Valletta office. With dual citizenship, we ask only that you limit your contacts with our American friends to non-classified and general information. Stay aware, as you have been, of the various provisions of the British Secrets Act and work through the designated head of your embassy group. Your work in Sicily for my Group has given you a head start over many ex-pat Brits working at our embassy in Washington, but no recounting any of that, if you will. Your salary will be paid from the embassy budget, but in American dollars commensurate with US wage levels. There may be some confusion over any incidental bills because Rudy, we are told, will be an officer member of the US Army Air Corps, with you listed as spouse and thus covered also. But those details are beyond my briefing material. You will receive initial contact information from our Washington Embassy before leaving for the States or immediately upon your arrival there. Now on a personal note, one hopes that whatever happens here will be short-lived and to our advantage, and so I expect to see you and Rudy again in the not too distant future. It has been my pleasure to know and to work with you both, and I shall leave you all now and get back to my daily tasks. Thank you, General Garrison and Colonel Astill, and my regards to all." With that, Mr. Sanno departs and the Governor turns to Rudy.

"Rudy. I think it fair to say that the Colonel and I have been privy to many of the remarkable events of your stay in support of Malta, and for those not involving us we have at least heard of the happenings. Not to that extent, but in many respects similarly, we are aware of Mrs. Worth's efforts on Malta and England's behalf. And well aware, also, of how you two have officially joined forces, as it were, and first suggested in this very room. Good Heavens, I don't mean to sound like the King making a speech, but I do want – joined by Colonel Astill here who met you first on the Queen Mary, before I had the pleasure – I do want to say a few words while we have the opportunity before you both depart, which I suspect may be fairly soon. I preface by saying to Nina that her excellent work on vessel search and control is recognized, applauded, and officially thanked by her transfer to our American Embassy staff.

Yours, Rudy, our dear Friend of the RAF, also is recognized, applauded, and thanked, but in what you might construe as a strange way. We have welcomed your many, many efforts and are now beginning to absolve you of what I know you consider your obligation, your duty perhaps, to reject and not leave for your new assignment, but to stay here and see it all through, whatever that might mean. As a much older and experienced soldier, though, I point out that what you will transition to will aid us here in your absence to an even greater extent than had you remained. Without America's military aid, I fear England and the free world cannot long survive the Nazi blitzgrieg assault. I would not even whisper this in a public statement, but I do know it is true. We desperately need you as Malta's and England's ally in America. We're keeping your Hawk here, but we're sending you back to America to fight for us there. Do you understand what I'm trying to say? We are extremely grateful you were sent here and genuinely thankful for what you accomplished, but it is time for you to take on much more. Go with our fondness for you both and our hope to see you both again in Malta." With at least two near to tears, all stood, shook hands all around, touched each other's shoulders as a final deep expression, and the meeting ended, Nina dismissing the official car waiting for her. Rudy and Nina say not a word as he drives her to the shipping office, but as Nina gets out there she turns to Rudy and says, "I pray to God we'll see them here when all of this is finished. Oh I do." With that she slides back onto the car seat, sobs several times, dries her eyes and slides out, headed for the office door. She never looks back, fortunately, as Rudy does his best to turn the car around and drive away toward the Shops.

Going through Robert's office domain once inside, Rudy is stopped by Foster's call. "Rudy, if you have a moment, I've some news for you. Good and Bad, I think, but the good news is really good." Once Foster's door is closed, both sit, the desk between, and Foster pulls several sheets from the usual tidy mess on his desk. "First the bad news from the wireless: German troops have breached the French Maginot Line in the northwest. I never thought it was impenetrable, but this quick is ridiculous! To worsen it, British troops are pulling back around Brussels before they get trapped. Doesn't look good, but we'll get going soon, I'm sure! Now, for the good news. Don't ask me how I got this, but I can tell you it came from the AOC's digs and I suppose they picked it off the cable, but who knows. Here, you can read it for yourself." He hands across the desk several smudged wrinkled sheets fastened together at an upper corner. Across the top of the first sheet is hand written: "FDR's Fifty Thousand Airplanes"

The heading reads: *President FDR's Address Before a Joint Session of Congress Asking For Additional Appropriations for National Defense, May 16, 1940.*

These are ominous days—days whose swift and shocking developments force every neutral nation to look to its defenses in the light of new factors...Combat conditions have changed even more rapidly in the air. With the amazing progress in the design of planes and engines, the airplane of today is out of date now. It is too slow; it is improperly protected; it is too weak in gun power...One belligerent power not only has many more planes than all its opponents combined, but also appears to have a weekly production capacity at the moment than is far greater than that of all its opponents...From the point of our own defense, therefore, great additional production capacity is our principal air requisite...Our immediate problem is to superimpose a greatly increased additional production capacity...the ability to turn out at least 50,000 planes a year... Furthermore, I believe this nation should plan at this time a program that would provide us with 50,000 military and naval planes...I ask for an immediate appropriation of $896,000,000...I ask for additional authorizations to make contract obligations of $200,000,000 to be used principally for the increase of production of airplanes and anti-aircraft guns, and the training of additional personnel for these weapons...

Rudy's quick reading of what obviously is only part of a much longer, continuous document brings an excited smile to his face. "This is great, assuming Congress comes across with all those millions, but it's going to take some time to get the first 50,000 planes in the air. I don't even think there are enough well thought out and designed prototypes, even with all the manufacturers there. Not even thinking about the production facilities, I would...Sorry, Foster, I'm cutting you off in my enthusiasm. What were you starting to say?"

"Rudy, in my excitement I forgot to tell you when you came in from your meeting that you're to phone on a secure line General Whittaker back in Washington. They said you have the number, and I've got to check something out on the work floor, so you can use my secure line right now, if you want. They said you should call anytime today or tonight, but as soon as you got back from the Governor's meeting. Sorry. Here, come around my desk and I'll pull out the secure phone. Go to it; I'll be out on the shop floor for at least a half hour."

The call reaches General Whittaker's office in Washington in just a few minutes, even though going through a secure line and complex system that Rudy can scarcely imagine. Used primarily for incoming calls of importance to the Shops, it is seldom put to use by Foster, hidden away in a lower desk drawer. While engaged in these random thoughts and listening to the wire's odd sounds, Rudy is jolted by General Whittaker's deep voice. Rudy acknowledges it is he on the line from Malta and is instructed by the General, who says he has only a minute or two before returning to a meeting, to listen carefully. In less than two minutes Rudy learns the following: excerpts from FDR's speech about more planes was sent to the Malta AOC office by the General, for Rudy's attention; Rudy is urgently needed to help start the General's new program to monitor and greatly increase American aircraft production; within 30 days Congress will approve the President's expenditures request, and the program must be launched no later than July 1st; Rudy must report in Washington by June 17 and will then terminate his HRM contract and simultaneously be appointed as a Major in the Army Air Corps assigned to the General's program; the "Townley woman" from HRM will contact Rudy next week with details concerning this switch of jobs and also transportation from Malta to Washington; and Mrs. Worth has been awarded dual citizenship and is assigned by London to staff an international position in the British Embassy in Washington.

With all of that information directly from his new American boss, Rudy hears the General end by saying, "So, Rudy, I suggest you and Mrs. Worth conclude all your Malta business within the next two weeks, pack your bags, and stand by to move over here by whatever means Townley comes up with. Call me only if there's an immense problem, and I'll see you in Washington no later than, or hopefully before, June 17. Thus ends the call that assures dramatic changes for Rudy and Nina. Other than the brief description of Nina's British Embassy job, all of this is new and very important news. It means, Rudy realizes, that they had better compose their "to do" lists tonight and begin their departure tasks tomorrow morning. They have only two weeks to close out their business in Malta. He hopes HRM's Miss Townley will phone him no later than tomorrow, as his new boss, the General, would put it!

That evening's dinner has both with note pads and pencils at the table, more important than knife and fork. As their list of tasks grows they assign each to one or another, usually an evident choice. Nina will take what needs to transpire with her mother and father and grandmother, plus all of the banking relating to her job and savings. She'll handle informing her boss at Starlight Shipping, although she suspects he may already know from Mr. Sanno. Rudy will handle his banking business and the transfer of his funds to his Buffalo Bank directly from Banco Malta. He'll talk with Foster, Robert, Dr. Mazur, Paul who is his new brother-in-law, and Nina's parents, Mr. Farinacci, and Mr. Boiano, plus the RAF officers. He will make arrangements to have their household things, just rearranged in the flat, moved for storage or use at the Lafessi home in Sliema, and he'll transfer ownership of Rover, their second-hand car, to Robert, along with his old motorbike. He'll do whatever he has to with the flat's rental agent, hopefully paying only one month's lease amount. Each of them will pack their own important documents, personal items, and whatever clothing can be jammed into a suitcase and a smaller carry bag. They assume they will travel by air, but don't know for sure. Each will carry some amount of English pounds plus passport, wallets and key travel items. It will be summer back home so the temperature shock should be minimal. Rudy will alert his family in "exotic" Watkins Glen about their return. With such a short time frame, it appears little other than the listed items, plus any emerging items not yet evident, will be accomplished. Rudy is less apprehensive about the upgrading needed for the Gladiators because some has already been accomplished, and because both Paul and Dr. Mazur are well-qualified to do whatever remains. Should the shooting start, Frasier and the Shops technicians and mechanics will be able to keep things going. And he wasn't going to be allowed to fly an RAF fighter plane, anyway. The Polish fighter pilots can fly the Hawk with the unusual painted crosses on it at least as well as the RAF pilots can fly the Gladiators, so why is he so anxious? He never mentions these concerns to Nina, but she has com-

311

mented that it took four weeks of preparation for her to go on a two-day clothes modeling job in Milan, but she's been given only two weeks to prepare and pack for a trip half way to China!

Janice Townley, who according to Ian Standish in London, runs HRM Aviation, Ltd., didn't call on Monday, but she did on Tuesday. "O.K. Rudy, here's the situation. Just listen till I tell you what's going to happen. I didn't want it to happen, but everything's changing so fast, and HRM is taking on what you're going to be doing in the States. So General Whittaker is stealing you back, but he'll make it up to HRM as we work with British, Canadian, and Australian aircraft manufacturers. You're going off our payroll and switching over to the US Army Air Corps budget as a Major – congratulations – around the middle of next month. HRM has the job of getting you and your lovely wife to Washington – by the way, I'm jealous, since I understand that "lovely" is a huge understatement – from Malta as quickly as possible. We'll handle her travel costs as well as yours since we can bill London for her as an embassy staff member being reassigned from Malta. Here's what Ian Standish, the British Foreign Service Department, and I have come up with, lucky you. In two weeks, hopefully less depending on seat availability, you two with a bag or so each, will leave Malta on a regular evening courier flight – as you've done before – to England, where Ian will meet you and transport you and yours with luggage to Southampton docks where you will – and you can thank me later – board a luxurious transatlantic Clipper run by BOAC, British Overseas Airways Corporation, hopping and skipping to someplace called...Oh, I can't remember. Anyway, you'll be met by a US official and driven to wherever Whittaker wants you. I hope you and the Mrs. can at least spend a day with your family and find an apartment in Washington before he puts you on the road. At least that's my thinking; you've been gone a year. By the way, BOAC knows you're a Friend of their RAF, so you may be listed as a "relief engineer" or something. They've already been told your wife is an M something agent, so they'll be cautious with her. Is she? Does she carry a gun? I was told you both took a special trip up to Italy or some place. Just an unbelievable story! So get rid of all your Malta stuff, pack, and wait for the call for the courier flight. Any questions, I hope not? Good bye for now. We'll talk again before you go."

Once again at dinner, Rudy told it all to Nina, and then reported on his task progress. By tomorrow night he would have every item on his list crossed out. Nina has already finished her shorter list, and has questions about her mother and fathers provisions for living on the Gozo farm if a real war begins, although her father is still refusing to stop his job at the Shops. That's where he would be needed, especially if fighting did start. Her mother is insisting otherwise, and Paul is just being Paul, as usual, and playing it by ear. By the way, Mila is ensconced at Aunt Margaret's home in the English countryside, getting along really well with cousin Francine, and excited to start at the local college. They agree to report to each other again tomorrow evening, to review their check lists and to add anything else necessary.

Rudy has been spending most of his time either talking with people at the Shops and at the RAF offices, or with people at the bank making fund transfer arrangements and, especially, Mr. Farinacci, who is deeply saddened but understanding. That session was difficult for Rudy, perhaps since he and the hotel manager had spent many conversations designed to help him understand what he needed to know in a foreign land. Rudy remembers well Mr. Farinacci's quiet cautions about Ana Boiano. *"Proceed carefully and slowly, I advise you. Learn all you can about her, consider carefully... tread slowly...I earnestly advise you."* That's what Mr Farinacci had told Rudy almost a year ago, and time had proven it very good advice!

All in all, leaving Malta is proving possible but cumbersome as far as business arrangements are concerned, but severing the personal relationships made over the past year by Rudy is proving emotionally quite difficult for him. In a small sense, Rudy understands that Nina is working hard to see their departure as the beginning of a new and more exciting life, while he senses a tearing apart of things he worked hard to understand and build.

CHAPTER 33

GOOD BYE FOR NOW

Valletta and Points West
Saturday, May 25 – Monday, May 27, 1940

WHEN the time for leaving arrived, Rudy and Nina were driven by Foster from their newly acquired flat, now minus almost everything except the stove and refrigerator, to the small office building close to the hard-packed runway at Hal Far. It was late afternoon on a Saturday, just nine days after Rudy had read President Roosevelt's speech calling for vastly increased warplane production in the United States. At the field, all Rudy could say was, "This is just where I landed in Malta a year ago. It seems like a lifetime." Foster exclaimed, "Rudy, I am so sad you're leaving. I know you'd rather stay, and I truly wish you could!" Nina watched as Foster half-hugged Rudy while Rudy patted Foster's back, mumbling something that sounded like "I'd much rather stay!"

"We'd both rather stay, but we can't." Nina called over the car's roof, "But thank you, Foster, for everything, and watch over my brother and father in the Shops when you can." With that, Nina pulled her carry bag out of the car, plus Rudy's, and started for the office door. Over her shoulder she yelled, "Rudy, I've got both our carry bags. Let's get through the check-out business in the office." And then more softly to herself, "Before I decide I'm not going," that thought producing a few tears.

Although Nina had met Rudy with their car when he returned on the courier flight from his England assignment, she had never imagined taking the same flight herself, and she had never been to Gibraltar or England, and certainly not to America. Her anxiety over leaving her family and Malta was eased, she realized, by the anticipation of going to such places and starting a new career with her American husband. She had prayed,

314

more than once, that this was the right decision, whatever that meant, but she had never faltered in her plan. Nor, she realized, had Rudy.

There was a surprise waiting for them inside. Mr. Sanno it was, who explained that he wanted to be sure there were no unforeseen questions asked of the two, or issues raised concerning official documents, especially Mrs. Worth's dual passports and exit visa. He wished them well, a safe trip, and success in their new assignments. He assured Nina that they would be in frequent communication as she carried out her Malta responsibilities in Washington, and he said that she could certainly get news to and from her family back on Malta through him. As they walked with him toward the office exit, he quietly told them that since Churchill had apparently decided not to pass control of Malta to Mussolini in return for "continuing Italian friendship", the possibility of Malta becoming involved in the war appeared more certain. "But who can tell," he remarked, "all is so uncertain these days. Malta may go on just as it has been, without war's impact." With that modest reassurance as he left the office, he wished them *Bon Voyage* and said, "Mrs. Worth, I imagine we'll be communicating soon, no matter what."

Nina's only comment to Rudy was that she will be overjoyed to remain in frequent contact with her family through Mr. Sanno's office, but otherwise he had revealed little or nothing about the possibility of war. "I'm not so sure," Rudy replied, "but we've done all we can here to get your family ready. We had everything we purchased from Foster for our flat trucked to your grandmother's big farmhouse up in Gozo. Lucky for us the leasing agent let us off with only one month's payment. I paid it, and I paid the moving men, including the Gozo ferry boat ticket price for the truck. And you said they agreed to expand their goats, chickens, rabbits, and vegetable gardens in anticipation of possible food shortages, using the cash you left. Right? And by-the-way, the Hawk's been moved down to Hal Far and hidden away with the Gladiators."

"Yes, gramma agreed, and I'll tell you some thing about the Hawk that I learned yesterday from my mother that I don't think you've heard." said Nina. "It's about what the men in the shops and the docks are saying, and the citizens who have looked up to see the Hawk and the Gladiators flying low over Valletta starting on their practice flights. People are really beginning to talk about it. They can see the white crosses painted on the Hawk's sides. Do you know what I'm talking about? The different cross with the heart in the middle and the anchor on the bottom that all the people here call St. Paul's cross, even though it's got another name. Do you remember?"

"Yes, of course I remember. It was your grandmother's idea. To raise the people's morale if trouble comes, because people would know that St. Paul came to Malta to keep it safe. Wasn't he your first Bishop? They were painted on just before we had the semi-private blessing ceremony, or whatever it was called. So the idea works? That's good, but I hope the RAF's not wasting fuel on these flights and tipping their hand the Island's got a few planes."

"Oh, better than that. You see, dear husband, that the Saint Paul cross stands for the three virtues of Faith, Hope, and Charity as written in the Bible by Saint Paul. There are three different parts to that cross, each signifying a different one of the three virtues that Saint Paul always preached to the people."

"Is there a point to this?" interjected Rudy.

"Yes, you dope, there is. When our tiny air force starts out on a practice flight, according to my brother who explained this part to me, the Hawk takes off and circles around low until the three patrol Gladiator interceptors, or whatever they're called, take off and follow the Hawk to get a heading, and then the Hawk zooms up and disappears. So the people figure that Faith, Hope, and Charity are following Saint Paul. Whatever number of Gladiators they see, one, two, or three, that's what they're called: Faith, Hope, Charity. The people know better, but they want to feel that Saint Paul is still protecting them."

"For Pete's sake – or should I say For Saint Paul's sake! Hey, if it raises morale I'm glad your grandmother thought of it and the RAF agreed, and the Shop painted them on. I like it! Faith, Hope, and Charity. And the Hawk!"

Once the courier was refueled it didn't take long to get airborne, and since Nina had not realized that the interior would be so sparse and the passenger seats so thin he began to provide some explanation. "It's really a converted Bristol Blenheim type 4 bomber, I believe, without so much armament and our luggage weight rather than bombs."

"Well that's really interesting, dear, but I'd rather hear about the giant and luxurious Clipper flying boat airliner we're going to take to America in. Miss Townley made it sound like a real treat. What's that plane like? Will we get to sleep in it going across the ocean?"

Fortunately for Rudy, who now frantically wanted his wife to see him as a true aviation expert, one of the left-over RAF flying boat pilots still on Malta awaiting an assignment elsewhere, and hearing about Rudy's transport arrangements to the USA told him some of the Clipper's brief history. Rudy recited this to Nina without bothering to explain how he knew it.

"It's built by Boeing, an American company, one of the biggest and heaviest planes made, and designed for luxury transoceanic flights. It's a flying boat design because there aren't very many world airports with thick, strong runways a mile long, needed for take-off, so it's designed for water take-off and landing, in big bays. I think they built six or eight of them and one of them – the one we're going on – has been sold or leased to British Overseas Airways. Our pilots, though, will be long time RAF heavy bomber officers transitioned over to Clippers for possible war use, I guess. There's supposed to be overnight cabins for sleeping, lounges, a dining room, and dressing rooms, just like on a first class train. Although we're headed in the other direction, it must be like the Orient Express, with ticket prices for the wealthy, or lucky ones like us. At almost 200 miles an hour, though, we'll really be moving along!"

"Sounds a lot more glamorous than that Italian seaplane we flew to Sicily. Now I'm really excited about it, but I think we'd better wait till we get on the Clipper before I express my thanks to you for getting your HRM Company to arrange this. Now I'm going to try to get some sleep on this bumpy rattletrap. Wake me up when we get to Gibraltar so I can at least say I've been there."

Nina did deplane while the courier was being refueled, so she added Gibraltar to her short list of international visits. All were soon back aboard the Courier and heading for RAF Hendon Station, a flight leg where all the passengers slept, or tried to. Rudy anticipated landing at Hendon about 9:00 am England time, having gained an hour from Malta, with Ian Standish waiting, representing HRM and ready to transport them to the Clipper. Rudy's status as a Friend of the RAF appeared to pay off, however, with a car and driver in RAF uniform waiting for them and their bags as they deplaned, and the statement that Mr. Standish's car was parked at the main gate. Bags loaded in the car and the young RAF driver holding the rear door open, they were on their way to Ian and the Clipper.

Ian was waiting at the main gate, and before even greeting his passengers felt the need to explain than the RAF wanted to accord the Worths every courtesy and had insisted that this RAF car and driver meet them right at the Courier. "Not like a year ago, Rudy, when my friend Foster Crayton couldn't greet you until the next day. But much has changed, even since I last saw you here a few months ago, including your marrying this lovely lady – whom I'm delighted to welcome to England. I'm Ian Standish, at your service, madam, and ready to transport you and your bags to the Clipper at Southampton docks." Rudy assisted Nina into the back seat of Ian's car, and climbed into the front seat, next to his friend.

Before launching into any other topic, Rudy profusely thanked Ian again for sending the Hawk to Malta, asking Nina to explain the latest news concerning the Hawk and the Gladiators now with names bestowed. As she finished repeating yesterday's story she leaned back into the rear seat, hearing Ian laughingly predict, "This will be the beginning of an aviation legend – Faith, Hope, and Charity – mark my words. I just hope the boys in the Shops can keep them in the air long enough to do some good when the shooting starts! The same for the Hawk. What I mean is, if the Germans loan the Italians any 109s, we've got a very large problem. Malta would than need Spitfires. And I don't mean Hurricanes, as good as they are!"

Ian turned his head toward Rudy for a moment. "Rudy, listen to me. I'm not a genius, but here in the home country I'm closer to what the hell's going on in the world than you were on Malta. Malta's in for it, and the boys there in the Shops and all the rest of the people on Malta and Gozo are going to do their best, and whether you're there or not won't make a real bit of difference one way or the other toward who comes out on top. Mussolini's not as determined as our new Prime Minister, so I'm thinking that first Hurriboxes, as the pilots are calling them, and then Spitfires a little later will arrive in Malta to hold the Axis off until we get the amount of supplies and planes we need from your country to go on the offensive. We'll most likely be fighting Messerschmitts and Stukas before we're through, and England doesn't have the production capability the United States does. We need everything your country can produce and we'll keep needing it for several years. Do you get what I'm trying to say? What you've been doing for Malta now has to be done for Malta, England, France, Poland, and the rest of the decent countries in the world including your own. HRM is one tiny resource; you're going Big Time, as they probably say back in Buffalo! Pardon me, Nina, for being so blunt with your husband and my friend."

Rudy sat quietly for half a minute and then, looking straight out the windscreen and almost talking to himself, said, "Yes, I know you're right. Of course. But I guess, with Nina and, you know, so many great people I met and worked with there, I kind of think of it as my second home. I know what my new job calls for. I know and I'm ready to take it on. Thanks for reminding me. HRM is going to stay alive working in Europe, then? You'll be OK? What happens to Miss Townley, and what about Major Carson, Whittaker's assistant?" As he was saying that, he turned to look in the back seat and saw that Nina was sound asleep. "My wife is catching up on her beauty sleep. Ha, ha. Like she needs it!" He turned again toward Ian and prompted him with, "HRM? Townley? Major Carson still around?"

"No, he's not," answered Ian. "Townley will always be OK in one organization or another. She's still running HRM from London and waiting to see if Prime Minister Churchill will appoint some big industrialist as head of national aircraft production, or whatever they end up calling it. If that happens, my money says she'll end up as that person's chief assistant. I'd hope to switch over also, or get picked up by one of our own manufacturers, like Hawker or Westland. Louis Carson is back in the States in the Army Air Corps, but I don't know in what position. Have they really, actually, pulled you into the air force?"

"Not quite yet, I guess as soon as I show up in Washington. I could refuse, but they probably could induct me anyway. I don't know anything about the details, but we're hoping that first we'll be able to see my folks in New York State and find an apartment, or something, in Washington. Nina's going to work in the British Embassy in Washington, so I hope that's my home base working for the General. I heard I'm going in as a Major, but who knows for sure? I was told, I think by Miss Townley, that somebody official will meet us when we deplane and tell us something.

Can you tell us anything about this trip and about the Clipper. If it's a Boeing, how did British Airways get it?"

"We, that is BOAC, have it on loan or lease or purchase – I don't know – from Boeing through the assistance of your President, and after negotiating so Pan Am could use our stop-offs on their Atlantic routes. Pan Am already had the big Martin 130 plane, but they wanted even longer range, so Boeing used the wing design of their experimental B-15 bomber, upped the four engines from 850 horses to 1500 each, put it on a small ocean liner and called it the Boeing 314. Near 80 daytime passenger seats which will convert, I understand, to 40 or so overnight bunks. Luxury all the way, Rudy, with lounges and dressing rooms, stewards, and gourmet food – and drinks.

"You two are in for a treat, like a second honeymoon, if you had the time on Malta to take one." Rudy silently thought *or a third!* Ian continued with, "Wingspan a bit more than 152 feet, fuselage – or whatever it's called on a flying boat – longer than 100 feet, and more than 40 American tons empty. Cruise at two thirds power, at over 180 mph. But even with its long range you're going to make some stops.

"By the way, act surprised when we get there or I'll be in trouble, but you two are boarding a bit early so you can have a special tour, courtesy of the RAF Friends, with Jim Conners passing the word. I should also let you know that your wife, identified as 'Nina M.' is getting special attention as a British Agent, on her way to our Embassy in Washington. Don't ask me who passed that word, I don't know, but Janice Townley told me she was a spy for us up in Italy and she carries a gun. Seriously, don't tell me anything else, I'd rather not know." Rudy smiled and thought, *If you really did know, Ha!*"

"The Southampton Docks are 70 miles or so from RAF Henley, south and a little west, right on the big bay," described Ian. "We've got a major road all the way down, so I'm thinking a two hour ride all told, depending on traffic. It won't be long, and it's not yet eleven. Departure time is 2:00 pm. I'd like to get you there before 1:00 so you and the bags can get through the formalities and board the Clipper for a tour before the others start loading."

On arriving at the docking area used by the Clipper, Ian pulled up to an official looking building used by BOAC as their Southampton facility, well within their calculated arrival time, and was immediately greeted by a welcoming wave from a uniformed young man. Through his rolled down window Ian told him his name and the names of his passengers, and the doors were opened, the boot emptied of the luggage, and Nina assisted from the rear seat by a second uniformed man who said, "Welcome to the British Airways Clipper, Mrs. Worth. We're honored to have you flying with us, and Mr. Worth as well. Your bags will be brought directly on board and placed in your compartment, and a steward will secure your carry bags and present them to you following a short private tour of our craft. As soon as you like, we'll escort you both to our guest area where you will be asked to present your passports, and where you can enjoy some refreshments. As soon as you're ready." Ian came immediately to the side of the car for a fond farewell from both, and from him to Rudy, whose hand he clasped with both of his, saying a quiet farewell and, "God speed and we'll meet again. Good bye." He glanced around to be sure all four bags were alongside the walkway, turned quickly, wiped his eyes, got into the car, and drove away.

The Worths, following the two attendants carrying their bags, entered the BOAC terminal and were warmly greeted by a third official. The formalities of departure were handled quickly without a question, and the two were then escorted into a nicely appointed lounge room, where a table laid out with attractive pastries and fruit plus several bottles of champagne set in as many iced silver tubs, were overseen by a young woman. Rudy was silently impressed to see it all, but Nina exclaimed in high satisfaction. Neither objected to the attendant's lifting of two wide, stemmed glasses and pointing with her eyes toward the nearest iced bucket. Rudy and Nina nibbled and sipped, relaxed, sipped again, and began to relax even more, helped along by early afternoon champagne. Ten minutes later the official who had handled their documents entered the room and announced, "Mr. and Mrs. Worth, Captain Ward of your Clipper says fueling is completed and he would enjoy having you board now and giving you a preliminary look at the craft."

Captain Ward reassuringly looked every inch the Captain of such a flying boat. He welcomed them, thanked them for the service they were doing for England in these trying times, and cautioned them to be careful as they walked down the short wharf and onto a hinged gangplank. This was secured to what appeared to be a floating dock leading to a partly submerged and very short lower wing. Technically, the Captain explained, this was a fuel holding sponson, which provided stability for the plane in the water, and for those walking over it to the small entry door, plus a wider smooth surface alongside the boat-like bottom of the plane to assist in lift during take off.

They eagerly followed him through the doorway and down a couple of steps to the floor of the entry room, straight walls, beautifully decorated, daylight entering through rectangular windows with blinds, everything style and colour coordinated including carpets and divans, concealed ceiling lights, and remarkably similar to a large entry foyer in a lovely home. Captain Ward explained that, with more than twenty feet of height, the Clipper had almost two stories of passenger lounges, dressing rooms, dining rooms, stowage spaces for luggage and cargo, crew berths providing for a rotation of personnel, and a large cockpit more than twenty feet long and nine feet wide.

Typically a Clipper carried eleven regular crew members including the Captain, a second flying officer, a navigator, a radio operator, a flight engineer, relief personnel, and two stewards. As they moved forward a steward joined them, and Captain Ward explained that this experienced steward would do a much better job than he of explaining the special passenger features of the Clipper to Mrs. Worth if they agreed that Mr. Worth could accompany him up to the cockpit, where the Captain's presence was necessary to check requirements for take off, while the flight engineer showed Mr. Worth that entire technical area. Of course they agreed that would be fine, and Captain Ward assured them they would be brought to their assigned compartment and reunited with their bags in plenty of time for take off. Neither noticed that the Captain smiled as he said *assigned compartment.*

Nina was astounded by the clever ways the Clipper's interior was designed to be completely functional yet totally attractive to passengers, most of them accustomed to deluxe, ultra-special, first class travel accommodations. From the passenger compartments which converted at night to individual sleeping bunks to the large lounge areas and dressing rooms, luxury and comfort surrounded her as the Steward led her from forward

Passenger Compartment number one, toward the tail end of the huge plane. They walked past, and sometimes through, lounges, passenger compartments, and service areas, eventually reaching what had to be the very tail end of the Clipper and its cargo space.

Here the steward said, "And this is where your luggage and carry bags are, as well as overnight accommodations for you and Mr. Worth. I hear the other passengers boarding now, so I'll leave you, and your husband will be here shortly, I'm sure. You can join other passengers for drinks and refreshments, if you desire, in the main Lounge up forward. BOAC thanks you both for your special services to England and we wish you a safe future in your work. I do hope your accommodations are satisfactory, and please let me know if anything is needed. Thank you." With that short speech he turned and left Nina, apparently to open the cargo compartment door herself. Surprised, she did, and when she turned the rather over-done, elaborate handle, the heavy door swung open smoothly and silently.

Nina stepped into a windowed and lighted room, immediately stunned by a hand lettered sign fastened to the wall reading: *Belated Welcome to the Clipper Bridal Suite, Rudy and Nina, From Your RAF FRIENDS. Happy Flying!* She, right away, began to cry and sat on the edge of a sizable bed, their bags on a luggage rack against the far wall next to the door to a small dressing room and loo. Nearer was a small table holding a filled, iced champagne bucket and two stemmed glasses. She was still happily brushing away tears when a knock on the door was followed by, "Nina, are you there? It's me, Rudy." She leaped from the bed, yanked open the door, pulled him in, shut the door, and threw her arms around him. He was stunned, completely surprised, as she broke her kiss and said, "Push the door lock and come here for the special thanks I promised you on the Courier plane. Oh my Lord, we're in a real bridal suite and we're going to use it. But pour us a little champers first, will you. We should toast the Friends!" They were trying out the bed as the plane's slight rocking increased, as did the four engines' sounds, and Rudy said, "I think we're going to begin our turn and take-off run..." to which Nina, he thought, voiced her agreement.

EPILOGUE

VALLETTA

Saturday June 26 – Friday July 2, 1965

STILL shaking his head over the emotional reaction to an incomplete Gladiator, Rudy keyed open their hotel room door to be greeted by, "Where have you been when we have to get dressed for the reception and dinner? Rudy, take a shower, get ready, and change into your formal getup. We're due at the reception at five o'clock and the fancy dinner and ceremony begin at six. Do you know with whom we're seated at the dinner? I haven't a clue. Get yourself in gear, darling, I want us to look just perfect tonight!"

Rudy, with almost 25 years of marriage and the training that goes with that, calmly answered, "Don't worry, I know what to wear. Won't make a difference anyway, they'll all be looking at the stunning older woman from Sliema who captured the heart of the handsome young American and flew away with Prince Charming years ago. You missed seeing part of a Gladiator at the museum this morning. A real disappointment! I should have asked your father last night, or Paul, why they don't have a complete one on exhibit, even if it were a total rebuild. I'll check that out when we get together with them and your mother later. I'm happy we're seeing your family, I really am, but I can sense your brother and father have something up their sleeves we don't know about. So stay alert."

"Paul always has some scheme he's thinking about. I'll ask my mother tomorrow morning when we're going to church. Now hurry up so we're not late. I want to see if there's a master seating chart for the dinner."

The sign on a tripod outside the reception area and main dining room announced:

Closed for Private Conference Reception and Dinner
MALTA 1965 AVIATION PLANNING GROUP

When they walked into the beautifully decorated reception room, both Nina and Rudy looked, as Nina had wanted, "just perfect". She dazzled in a gorgeous white gown, showing off the same figure that had captured Rudy's imagination years before on the Gozo ferry. Her black pearl earrings and necklace dazzled as well. He looked the part of a successful American businessman, well dressed and ready to make decisions, but definitely upstaged by the woman he was escorting. They entered only ten minutes after the cascading champagne fountain had been activated, but already the large room was seemingly filled with gowns and tuxedos. Nina leaned toward him and whispered that she was going to seek a dinner seating chart and scout the room for Paul's wife and anyone else she knew. "But first, get me a glass of champagne, will you? And start working the room."

With a glass in each hand, he turned from the fountain to be greeted by a loud voice, "Oh my lord, it's Rudy. I'm so glad to see you. It's Ian Standish, Colonel Worth." Rudy's instant response was , "Ian, and it's no longer Colonel. Hasn't been for a long time, and I'm glad you're here. I have a hundred questions to ask. Will you be at the meetings, so we can talk? I'm here with Nina and I'd better get this drink to her, but I'll see you tomorrow, or certainly at Monday's meeting for sure. Ian agreed, and as they parted he added, "Jim Conners from BOAC will be here starting Wednesday!" That, reflected Rudy, was good news.

And so the reception went, in some cases with only a friendly greeting or introduction , and with others a quick exchange of basic information and a promise for a detailed conversation during the conference. Some, he knew, he would not find, but still he wandered the room in vain looking for long-lost close friends such as Robert and Foster, and friendly old acquaintances like Mr. Sanno and Mr. Farinacci. At least he'd get to see the person who had extended him such a professional boost, James Conners.

With that happy thought, he saw Nina approaching, almost out of breath, with the news that they would be at a table in the first row, right in front of the podium, with brother Paul and Marcia, another couple from Australia named Corbyn something, and, "Get this!" she exclaimed, "Count and Contessa Dalossi, very wealthy and tremendously important to Malta's new, dual focus on aviation and finance." Nina obviously was impressed, and thinking Rudy should be as well. She was disappointed when Rudy's response was, "What was that name you said? I mean that couple from Australia?"

Back in their hotel room it was difficult to tell which of the Worths had the most surprises to recount to the other, having said their good-byes after midnight to all who remained at the party. Rudy readily admitted that seeing and talking with Phil Corbyn, who indeed it was, about their week together flying in the Westland Lysander from one RAF Station to another, was a great joy. Phil had emigrated to Australia, and was now a key player in strengthening *Trans Australia Airlines*. Neither had kept track of the other during the war, nor imagined they'd share a table at the conference. Rudy had been busy stimulating American aircraft manufacturers to the highest possible production of the right type warplanes, while Phil had spent much of the war flying British agents and weapons into and out of barely marked French fields on dark nights in slightly modified Westland Lysanders. Rudy told Nina that seeing Phil after all these years was a happy surprise.

"That's just super, dear husband, but was it as great a surprise as your learning – with the biggest open mouth I've ever seen – that you knew the blonde bombshell, Contessa Dalossi, 25 years ago? Come on, Rudy. I thought you were going to fall out your chair when I interrupted your chat with Philip to introduce you to the Count and his charming wife across the table. Were you blind or something when they finally got to our table late and sat down? Don't give me any crap, you were tongue tied when she smiled in your direction and said, 'Oh heavens, I remember Mr. Worth, the visitor from America wasn't he?'" Rudy remained tongue tied, unable to respond quickly. All he could say was, "You don't know anything about it, really, and I can't say any more because of the British Official Secrets Act." He knew before he finished those words that this was the wrong tack to take with Nina.

"Listen Rudy," Nina's *'don't screw with me'* voice proclaimed, "I know more about her and her German friend than you think I do, but I also know Paul's plans to help build a viable *Air Malta* are important to my native country, to my brother, and now to me. You may remember that I had a big surprise tonight myself. I was named to the *Daughters of Malta* list, a high honor for me, and also named a member of the Board of Directors of Air Malta. In fact, I'm the first woman to become a member of the board of *any* Malta Company. I like that, and I intend to fill my position very well! I also realize that while the Italian Count and his Maltese Contessa may complicate things, their financial and political support – I mean his financial backing and her agreeing with that – are essential for our airline and who knows how many other projects and "investment opportunities" our new government will come up with. Just don't mishandle our Contessa Ana Boiano Dalossi because of 25 years ago. OK? If what she may have done then doesn't upset *me* now, it shouldn't upset *you*. And by the way, she told me tonight that her father was killed during the German's first attack after the Luftwaffe took over for the Italian bombers, who weren't doing a terrible enough job of it. Let's go to bed now. Today has been a crazy day for me. A big surprise honor and also meeting my rival for you from years ago. I didn't like her then, but Malta needs her now. We'll work it out. Let's go to bed. We're going to church with my family at eleven tomorrow, and Paul said there's a surprise for us in the afternoon."

Rudy's conversation with Paul following services Sunday morning revealed answers to many of his unasked questions: Count Dalossi's interest and support were vital to Malta's current aspirations, thus his relationship needed ongoing encouragement; the Countess was not a fan of Germany, undoubtedly because of her father's untimely death by Luftwaffe bombs; the Kalafrana Shops had survived the bombings during the war and had continued their work in keeping one or two Gladiators and the Hawk in the air most of the early days, and the Hurricanes and Spitfires once they arrived. This was due, in the main, to Foster Crayton's strong leadership.

Foster did survive, retired a second time in 1945, and joined his wife in England. And yes, he's still alive and Paul has his address if Rudy wants it. Robert is still working, a manager with the expansion of Luga International Airport. Former Governor-General Garrison is honored now as retired Governor-General Garrison and living in England, and Mr. Farinacci, manager of Rudy's old hotel, passed on a couple of years ago. Rudy already knew about Mr. Boiano. His daughter Ana, now a Countess, had eventually gone up to Italy, but quite a time after the war; that's when the Count met her. Rudy's old hotel had not survived the intense bombing, but had served as an emergency family shelter before most people stayed each night in the infamous, long and effective bomb shelter, the old railway tunnel.

According to Nina's brother, a few RAF aircraft mechanics had salvaged the Gladiator fuselage of what may have been FAITH, restored what they had found, and the Brits had presented it to the citizens in a big public ceremony in 1943, according to Nina's brother. By then FAITH, HOPE, and CHARITY were already a legend in Malta and in the world's aviation history. The locals had all recognized the white crosses on the Hawk as St. Paul's cross, and so the three names of the Gladiators had originated with the resident's morale building beliefs, as Nina had said. Local politics entered into its current location, Paul believed. The plane had been moved from storage at least once, ending up where Rudy had viewed her. Most were hoping a Malta aviation museum, conceived as an elaborate educational and historical display, would become a great attraction at the proposed international airport, and home to displayed aircraft which had served Malta and the allies during WWII and after.

The average Malta citizen, by far, Paul estimated, was eager and happy to see Malta's relationship with England moving toward complete independence as a full republic, but desiring faster and more decisive movement. Rudy would see this uneasiness displayed tomorrow, where still frequent and unannounced RAF training flights to, from, and over Malta at low levels, were considered outrageous and would be protested. The role of a happy, subservient Crown Colony was not being accepted very favorably by many.

All this information was relayed by Paul as short news capsules and eagerly welcomed by Rudy. Paul's Sunday afternoon surprise alert, however, topped all these items. Paul said he and Marcia would meet them at the yacht basin's boarding pier at one o'clock, where they and other guests would be taken by tender to Count Dalossi's yacht for a buffet lunch and ocean tour around Malta, tiny Comino, and Gozo. He had looked from the yacht basin's walkway yesterday, from where the *Raffaella* appeared to be at least a luxurious 150 meters long, and attracting many viewers. Paul had been, he did not hesitate to say, very impressed by the yacht, named after the Count's mother.

A few minutes early due to Nina's prodding, the four met at the pier. There also were seven or eight other couples, probably Maltese officials and spouses, all dressed for the occasion. Everyone smiled and nodded at everyone else, and a news photographer kept busy. All were soon tendered to the yacht, where a boarding stairway with railing had been lowered alongside. Their host was first at the deck, warmly welcoming each and enjoying the amazed looks as each stepped up, level to the deck. Contessa Ana stood slightly apart, impressively sounding each person's name in English and air kissing each woman's cheek, including that of "*my very dear friend Nina*", but this spoken in Malti. Included in the view of those who looked toward the bow was a long, elaborately spread buffet and drinks table overseen by uniformed crew. Encouraged by the Count and Contessa, the visitors moved toward the buffet, where Ana slid smoothly into the role of hostess. It was here that Count Dalossi took Rudy's elbow and whispered a request for, "A few private words."

Rudy, smiling in Nina's direction and giving a reassuring nod, allowed the Count to lead him through a door, into a beautifully appointed salon area. Mystified, Rudy was invited to sit. The Count sat also directly facing Rudy, and said, "Colonel Worth, I know you have retired from your air force and are a very popular consultant. I address you, seeking your expertise and recommendations as I work to establish not just an international airline for Malta, which happily now has Mrs. Worth as a Board member, but for a similar airline to serve my own country, one which might become known as ROMA AIR or, I jest of course, Dalossi Air.

"I note Italy has been seeking airline development for decades, but with limited success. What I strive for faces the future with sound planning and more than sufficient financial backing. I must tell you I have been, for the past year and longer, communicating frequently with a fellow countryman who has a long history in aviation, and Italian aviation in particular. When I mentioned my notion of talking with you during this so interesting conference, he was overjoyed and had me pledge to give you his warmest greeting, since you have already met, he said, during your – what did he call it – *your special honeymoon*. His experience is very different from yours, and he has suggested to me that your much broader experience with civilian operating airlines would bring what we now need to continue advancing toward our goals. He is now, shall I say, more advanced in years than either of us, but he hopes you will remember meeting him once, years ago. I speak, of course, of my friend Colonnello DiPalma."

"Oh, good heavens, of course I remember him! How could I forget that day! Please give him my regards in return. I certainly do remember spending a most interesting day with him, at his headquarters in Sicily!"

"Colonel Worth," said the Count, "let us return to the guests and your wife, who must be wondering, as is mine, I'm sure. I do want you to see Malta from the ocean side and still avail yourself of our buffet, as will I. The Contessa and I shall remain here on the yacht till week's end, and, if you will think on our brief conversation, we'll hopefully complete a mutually agreeable arrangement before either of us leaves for home."

Back on the open deck and immediately seeking out a wondering Nina, his first words to her were, "Not here, but as soon as we're alone, and you're not going to believe it! My biggest surprise of all! Now, where are Paul and Marcia. I'm hungry and thirsty."

Despite their early misgivings about the afternoon's ocean tour of the Malta archipelago and the Dalossi's intentions, Nina and Rudy, back in the hotel, were telling each other how enjoyable and interesting the afternoon had been. Enjoyable more to Nina, and interesting mostly to Rudy, but only before he told her about Colonel DiPalma. That caused a shock, followed by her very high interest. "Did he imply he knew the reasons for our trip to see Catania," Nina questioned, "or only our fake honeymoon? Forget it, we'll never really know. But when Rose and Johnny get here on Thursday we'll have dinner together and we may learn a lot if they're willing to talk. By-the-way, I hope you're going to talk with me about Dalossi's offer before you even meet with him about details? Remember, we both agreed to back off business and not take on part time assignments. Although with my Board meetings back here every so often, I wonder if, maybe…OK, enough for now. Let's go down and meet Paul and Marcia and have a little supper after that huge buffet on that spectacular boat."

Rudy spent the next two days at large meetings of the conference attendees, and small sub-group discussions of topics specific to certain phases of airline development. Rudy, coming from the broader base of airline development in America, was interested in it all, and thinking about a series of articles he might write for a possible new airline association journal he had in mind to start. Being here had moved him from a domestic to an international frame of mind, and the thought of becoming a writer and publisher intrigued him. He'll have to plan carefully before broaching the idea to his wife.

He had an especially happy two hours with Ian Standish on Tuesday late afternoon, hearing about Malta's terrible time during the war. He worked in a query about the Gladiators and the Hawk, which evoked a quarter hour monologue by Ian, pretty well matching up with what he had already heard from Paul. Ian was thanked again for sending the Hawk, the total absence of which, without even mention in any report, obviously saddened Rudy but brought no sympathy from Ian. "It did what it and the Poles could do flying it, and certainly helped the people's morale in the frightening early days, so be grateful you never got a bill for the lost plane," counseled Ian, who moved on to other topics. Had Rudy heard, for example, that Janice Townley had served as chief aide to the famous British head of aircraft production during the war, met a well-placed widower with a title, went on to marry, and has been living happily ever after. "I told you never to worry about her, didn't I? And Jim Conners, who retired with high honors from the RAF immediately became associated with British Overseas Airways and helped bring about the merger with British South American Air in 1949. He's been on the BOAC Board for quite a few years and, although he's getting on in years himself, is still pushing BOAC into the future. I imagine he wants to see you about BOAC, but you'll learn that soon enough. We exchange news often. Friends for decades!"

Wednesday morning Rudy left a note at the desk for Jim Conners explaining that he had to be away from the conference during the day, but would check immediately upon returning to the hotel in hopes of having dinner together. The day would be taken up with Paul's organized trip up, as Paul had said, "To visit the family farm on Gozo." Paul and father Vince Lafessi, Nina, and Rudy were to make the trip in Paul's car, taking the morning Gozo Ferry. Rudy, while not especially eager to spend the day that way, knew better than to object, and left with the family of which, Nina pointed out, he was a member by marriage, and thus a partial inheritor of the farm. So he sat back and enjoyed the scenery, the ferry ride, and the winding Gozo ride up to the farm. At the sharp turn off , both riding in the back seat, Nina leaned over close to him and whispered, "Would you rather I were riding close in back of you and holding on tight so you could find every bump in the road and get that big thrill, like we did on the motorcycle 25 years ago? Or have you lost interest in anatomy in your old age?" He jumped and blurted what sounded like "Get your tongue out of my ear, and act *your* age lady!" This caused her father in the front seat to partially turn and loudly ask, in Maltese, "What the hell are you doing back there?"

Paul pulled up at the farm's entryway, invited them all to get out, and headed toward a heavy looking metal sign on a thick metal post just off the edge of the road in front of the car. Rudy, mystified, thought it might be a directional sign with raised metal letters he couldn't read, apparently in the Maltese language. As he moved a bit closer to the sign Paul told him, "This is one of the historical signs erected around Malta and Gozo to encourage tourism and knowledge about our country. Ana Boiano Dalossi sponsored them, convinced the Tourism Office, helped raise money for them and contributed the rest. She insisted on this particular one and approved the words. What do you think?"

Rudy, still baffled, said, "Sounds like a good idea. Common in the U.S., but how can tourists read it?" Nina simply walked around it and motioned to Rudy, who stood there, silent and becoming filled with an almost overwhelming emotion as Nina read the words printed on that side in English:

Near this signpost, in a barn, was hidden an American fighter plane, a
Curtiss P-36 Hawk, brought to Malta in a crate in 1939 by American

aeronautical engineer Rudolph Worth and assembled in the Kalafrana
Shops by Maltese technicians led by the American. "Rudy" Worth flew
the assembled airplane here to an improvised grass strip where it
remained safely hidden in case of need. It was officially given to the
RAF Hal Far Fighter Flight, and two war experienced Polish Air
Force fighter pilots seconded to the RAF were assigned to fly it. On it
was painted in white the Cross of Saint Paul, the Patron Saint of
Malta. Based at Hal Far airstrip as part of a small RAF Fighter group
of Sea Gladiator biplanes, the Hawk helped defend Malta against the
Regia Aeronautica beginning with the first bombing of Malta on the
morning of June 11, 1940, continuing until sufficient RAF Hurricane
fighter planes could reach Malta later that year.

Rudy, wet eyed, could hardly speak. His first words were, sadly, "If it had only survived."

"Rudy," Vince said, "a long time ago I told you that since the Hawk was here to take care of Malta, Malta would take care of the Hawk. Come, follow me." He then headed toward the barn, followed by all three, with Rudy in the lead. Vince unlocked a huge padlock, and aided by Paul, pushed a long door partly open to reveal in the dark interior a scattering of browned hay over a Curtiss P-36. It was jacked up on wooden stands but facing the barn-hangar door. Eerily, it seemed to be waiting to be rolled out, prop turning, radio on and listening for intercept instructions. Rudy staggered and sobbed once before Nina stepped alongside to bolster him, in perhaps the most traumatic event yet of his adult life. Paul and Vince, each filling-in the other's words, described when and how one of the Polish pilots returned it to the original hiding place. Vince and the neighboring farmers, for the last time, removed the ammo, pushed it back into the old hangar-barn, put the padlock on the door, and swore to never reveal where Gozo's guardian rested. "We'll get it to the Malta Aviation Museum, once we get one," promised Paul, and motioned them all back to the car.

On the trip back to Valletta, Rudy marveled at what the person he still thought of as Ana Boiano had done so many years ago, realizing all in the car were well aware of it, including, he assumed, his wife. Somewhere early in the conversation Nina commented that a father's death by German bombing and 25 years of thinking about it likely would redirect anyone's earlier fondness for a real bastard impostor. Rudy thought about that and the Hawk in the old barn all the way back to Valletta and the hotel.

Dinner with Jim Conners that evening was a happy affair, and Rudy learned that Dr. Mazur and his wife had remained in western Canada after the war, where he was now retired and enjoying a quiet life. It did not surprise Rudy that his old colleague, a master aircraft engineer, had led the design team of a British owned Canadian company that had resulted in one of the most popular workhorse type seaplanes ever produced. Nor did it surprise Rudy that the Board of BOAC would welcome Rudy's consulting advice about how best to expand into the American market. Rudy had laughed when Jim had used, as an example of a desirable new BOAC route, one from London to Miami and return. Jim had assumed Rudy's home in Hialeah, Florida must actually be in a Miami neighborhood. "No, Jim, it's a city unto itself, distinctly not Miami, and founded by an old hero of mine in his semi-retirement in Florida. Perhaps you've heard of him, Glen Curtiss? He did have something to do with airplanes, if I remember correctly."

"Har, har!" came from Jim. "I didn't know that, but you understand what I mean. You could do the research work at home, in that strange place, and we would fly you over for reports. Not full time, but well paid. Think it over, you and Nina, and we'll discuss details before we part. It would be a much more solid and satisfying experience than others you might be contemplating."

In addition to the conference events and the several business discussions Rudy and Nina scheduled, Rose and Johnny's trip to Malta to visit their relatives allowed for dinner with Nina and Rudy on Thursday evening, their packing to fly out the next day already done. On a couple of earlier trips to see her family, Nina had seen Rose and Johnny as well, but had never discussed the so-called honeymoon trip to Catania, only the war years and the allies' bombing and invasion of Sicily during July, 1943. Johnny now owned three radio stations, two in Sicily and one on the mainland, and Rose and her brother were involved in the business.

During the dinner discussion about the special honeymoon trip, Rose described Colonel DiPalma's fondness for America and dismay at Italy's war entry on the side of Hitler. The death of his former officer and personal hero, Italian Air Marshal Italo Balbo, because of supposedly mistaken anti-aircraft fire from his own unit just 18 days after Italy entered the war, was seen by the Colonel as an intended assassination ordered by a jealous Mussolini. The box of flowers and sympathetic note, dropped over Italian lines in Libya the day after Balbo's death by a British plane, called Balbo *"a leader and gallant aviator placed by fate on the wrong side"*. DiPalma loudly voiced his strong agreement, and from that point his favored position in the Regia Aeronautica quickly began to erode. Questions were raised by Rome headquarters about the tactics used for bombing Malta by Italian planes based under the Colonel in Sicily, and he was subsequently transferred to a lesser administrative position on the mainland. Fortunately, Rose's job as clerk at the Sicilian headquarters was untouched, as was Johnny's work and their joint effort at the Catania radio station. Anything further would be only a guess.

Back at the hotel, Nina and Rudy looked at each other and said pretty much the same thing at the same time: "That was some year in Malta we had, wouldn't you say, and some couple of days seeing it all played over again this week! This turned out to be SOME conference!" Rudy added, "I think we're all packed for tomorrow's flight", and Nina said, "Let's go to bed."